"Glenn Beck ... hailed Brad Th... radio host's de... became an insta... ...coast to coast.

Since then, Glenn Beck has kept America turning pages into the night with bestselling novels "ripped from today's headlines" (James Rollins)—including *The Overton Window*'s sequel, *The Eye of Moloch*; and his gripping vision of America under tyrannical rule, *Agenda 21*.

Praise for
AGENDA 21

"More frightening than anything Orwell could have envisioned. It is the ultimate thriller . . . a brilliantly written, exhilarating, pulse-pounding adventure. If this is what the future holds, I don't want to live to see it; I want to live to fight it!"

—Brad Thor, #1 *New York Times* bestselling author of *Hidden Order*

"Entertaining. . . . *Agenda 21* depicts not what is but rather what could be if the words and statements from Agenda 21's actual documents and U.N. promoters were to be carried out to their fullest meaning. . . ."

—*The New American*

Be sure to read
THE OVERTON WINDOW

Glenn Beck's stunning thriller seamlessly weaves together American history, frightening facts about our present condition, and a heart-stopping plot that educates, enlightens, and, most importantly, entertains with twists and revelations no one will see coming.

"Glenn Beck never fails to amaze. *The Overton Window*, a rip-roaring read of the first order, is as good a political thriller as you're going to find."

—Nelson DeMille, #1 *New York Times* bestselling author

"A novel destined to be as controversial as it is eye-opening. . . . No matter your politics, this Hitchcockian thriller will have you turning pages well into the night."

—James Rollins, *New York Times* bestselling author

"*The Overton Window* reminded me of Michael Crichton's speculative, fact-based thrillers. It's smart, provocative, and reads like the wind."

—Joseph Finder, *New York Times* bestselling author

"A visionary work of fiction."

—Vince Flynn, #1 *New York Times* bestselling author of *The Last Man*

"Like the best thriller writers out there, Glenn knows that the very best way to scare us is to show us what can really happen. You'll never look at history the same way again."

—Brad Meltzer, #1 *New York Times* bestselling author

"A top-drawer thriller of the first magnitude. The writing is blade sharp and taut as a high-tension wire."

—Ted Bell, *New York Times* bestselling author

"... I found myself thinking of *Atlas Shrugged* again and again.... A compelling main character, a political puzzle, and a fast-paced thriller, with forceful political discourse and debate along the way."

— Michael Graham, talk show host and bestselling author

"This story is not ripped from today's headlines; it foreshadows tomorrow's!"

—Dave Glover, FM News Talk 97.1, St. Louis, MO

"Compelling, provocative, and lightning-paced, *The Overton Window* is that rare thing: a page-turner about ideas that manages to inform and entertain in equal measures."

—Christopher Reich, *New York Times* bestselling author

ALSO BY GLENN BECK

THE
EYE
OF
MOLOCH

GLENN BECK

With

Jack Henderson

Special thanks to
Kevin Balfe, Hannah Beck, Emily Bestler,
and Kate Cetrulo

POCKET BOOKS—MERCURY RADIO ARTS

New York   London   Toronto   Sydney   New Delhi

The sale of this book without its cover is unauthorized. If you purchased this book without a cover, you should be aware that it was reported to the publisher as "unsold and destroyed." Neither the author nor the publisher has received payment for the sale of this "stripped book."

Pocket Books / Mercury Radio Arts
A Division of Simon & Schuster, Inc.
1230 Avenue of the Americas
New York, NY 10020

This book is a work of fiction. Any references to historical events, real people, or real places are used fictitiously. Other names, characters, places, and events are products of the author's imagination, and any resemblance to actual events or places or persons, living or dead, is entirely coincidental.

Copyright © 2013 by Mercury Radio Arts, Inc.

All rights reserved, including the right to reproduce this book or portions thereof in any form whatsoever. For information, address Threshold Editions Subsidiary Rights Department, 1230 Avenue of the Americas, New York, NY 10020.

First Pocket Books paperback edition January 2014

POCKET and colophon are trademarks of Simon & Schuster, Inc.

GLENN BECK is a trademark of Mercury Radio Arts, Inc.

For information about special discounts for bulk purchases, please contact Simon & Schuster Special Sales at 1-866-506-1949 or business@simonandschuster.com.

The Simon & Schuster Speakers Bureau can bring authors to your live event. For more information or to book an event, contact the Simon & Schuster Speakers Bureau at 1-866-248-3049 or visit our website at www.simonspeakers.com.

Manufactured in the United States of America

10   9   8   7   6   5   4   3   2   1

ISBN 978-1-4516-3584-3
ISBN 978-1-4516-3585-0 (ebook)

To those who have changed everything in their life,
including much of what they thought they knew.

To those who feel compelled to live their life in a way
that often makes them the object of ridicule and scorn.

To those who hide their fears and tears from
their tenderhearted spouse or children.

I dedicate this book to all of you who are living a life
you never hoped or asked for, but chose it anyway
because you know that freedom is worth standing for.

I admire you, love you, and pray that
history will remember your name.

In loving memory of Mercury's mom.

You taught us to work hard and never give up.

You gave us your love of books and reading.

Because you lived, Mercury came to life. Because of how you lived, we are all better people.

May you rest in peace knowing that those things, incredible as they are, were still just a very small part of *why* you lived.

Patricia Balfe
1944–2013

The liberties of our country, the freedoms of our civil Constitution are worth defending at all hazards; it is our duty to defend them against all attacks.

We have received them as a fair inheritance from our worthy ancestors. They purchased them for us with toil and danger and expense of treasure and blood.

It will bring a mark of everlasting infamy on the present generation—enlightened as it is—if we should suffer them to be wrested from us by violence without a struggle, or to be cheated out of them by the artifices of designing men.

—SAMUEL ADAMS

You are the salt of the earth; but if the salt has lost its taste, how shall its saltiness be restored? It is no longer good for anything except to be thrown out and trodden under foot by men.

You are the light of the world. A city set on a hill cannot be hid.

—MATTHEW 5:13–14

PROLOGUE

The Battle of Gannett Peak is not where this story started, but for those of us who lived to tell it that's as good a place as any to begin. A few brief remarks are in order, though, before we get well under way.

First, the great weakness of the enemy we face: there's no honor among thieves. And what they'd all forgotten—the globalist elites, the predator class, the puppet-masters, the kleptocrats, the red-carpet mafia, call them what you want—what they'd forgotten about pandemonium is that once you set it loose to rampage you can't as easily whistle it back into the box again.

It was to be their boldest move yet, the endgame of a hundred-year scheme to crash the old and usher in their new world order, once and for all. They would wield fear and chaos as weapons as they always had, and demonize those who opposed them so the uninformed majority would misplace their blame. Riots and food panics, incited uprisings and sponsored overthrows, blackouts, meltdowns, market crashes, hyperinflation, depression, currency and commodity wars every bit as deadly as the shooting kind—these contagious terrors were meant to drive the desperate people at the bottom to storm into the streets and cry out for the benevolent tyranny of a waiting savior from above.

These tactics had proved tried-and-true through thirty centuries of repeating history, but this time their mayhem spread too fast and got out of hand early on. Spawn too many devils all at once and they'll soon start to organize, and then those dangerous servants can forsake their masters and awaken to ambitions all their own.

Second, and you'll forgive me if, by your measure, I'm a trifle late to this simple understanding: there really is such a thing as Good, and likewise there is Evil. We each have a decision between the two that we're bound to make, and if the cynics among you should scoff at that need and decline to commit, that's a sure choice for the darker side. At times it's not at all clear who's with who; those who declare the loudest for one camp are often hard at work in the other. As Bob Dylan wrote it, sometimes Satan comes as a man of peace.

The last thing now, and I confess it was the hardest for me to finally believe: there is a God.

I won't pretend to know His nature or His plan, and put no trust in most who claim to. I don't know which faith is His chosen or what church He would have me attend, if any would abide me after all I've done. What I do know for certain is that this God of all creation would prefer us to be free. That means He must love this country, not so much for what we've allowed it to become, but deeply for what it was once meant to be. And if this great nation should fall, as we may well do, then in some distant age He'll move His children to try to refound it anew, with hopes that those future Americans are better, braver stewards of His brightest dreams for us all.

The Bible says the first thing God created was the light, but you'll notice that He also left the darkness.

Every dawn is a steadfast reminder that even the longest night can be overcome. Here on earth that overcoming is not the task of the Almighty; in His grace He's left that up to each of us. That choice to fight or to join the darkness is the first of the freedoms we mortals are born with, and like the others, it's ours until we prove ourselves unworthy and let it be taken away.

The sole thing tyranny fears is truth, and therein lies the simple, sworn mission of Molly Ross—to find and tell the truth to the good people of the United States, and through that revelation, to restore her country to the greatness it was founded to attain. That's why they feared her so much, why they came after her with everything they had, and also why this war will never cease. Because true Evil cannot be stopped, and the truly Good will not be moved. Hers was a battle that must be won or lost every day, by one side or the other, and no less than the fate of free mankind hangs in the balance.

Believe that and do your part, or don't, and sit by to let others lay down their lives on your behalf. But be assured of this one true thing, and I'm a witness: one more or one less can change the world.

I lived through what follows here, and in some small way through this account you may now do likewise. The outcome may still be in question, but I know where I stand. To those yet undecided, there's a place here beside me or out there against me when you're moved to make up your mind.

Humbly yours,

Thom Hollis

Thom Hollis
Founders' Keepers

PART ONE

CHAPTER 1

DHS-CDFO/USD19-47544-R60
Civilian/Conscript Field Deployment Order (US/Domestic)
Temporary Change of Station: -FOB- UN Joint Op. Iron Rain
Subj: Gardner Noah W
Desig: Embedded correspondent / combat support unit

Report to transport depot F23, bay 17—0530 tomorrow—
outfit for immed. transit to points west; duties TBD at
discretion of allied ground command.

** Intel determines surviving hostile forces to be pinned
down, poorly trained, and only lightly armed. Enemy
supply lines are cut, leadership is infiltrated, weakened,
and dispersed. Anticipate a rapid & decisive outcome,
requiring of coalition forces only a brief engagement; days,
not weeks. **

Four Months Post-Deployment: Gannett Peak, Wyoming

As it passes close by your head a hypervelocity bullet makes a little *snap* that's hard to describe until you've heard it for yourself. When you hear that *snap* with your boots on the ground in a shooting war it means that someone just wanted you dead but you're still alive, and the very next breath you draw brings a kind of thrill that doesn't fade with repetition.

Whoever was in command of this fiasco must have thought the day's job would be easy, because there didn't seem to be much strategy to the advance. Part of the reason for this lax approach might have been the language barrier; many of the men seemed to be fresh off the boat, as new to U.S. citizenry as Noah Gardner himself was to the field of battle. In any case, *FORWARD* was the only clear standing order—just keep moving in the most dangerous direction on the map until the enemy starts shooting and then concentrate your fire on their revealed position. With a big enough budget and plenty of expendable human resources, who could say? It might just work.

What had started months before as a simple manhunt had gradually escalated into a full-on, in-country paramilitary action. The target was Molly Ross and the Founders' Keepers. Though a national climate of fear was being carefully managed, so far the American people had been kept in the dark on the specifics—mostly because these supposedly dangerous fugitives were stubbornly refusing to shoot back. Until today, that is; today somebody out there was shooting back with a vengeance.

Something heavy whistled down from the sky and exploded thirty yards away and as the concussion hit, Noah felt himself pulled down into a muddy ditch for cover. Through the low morning haze and drifting smoke he saw a number of fallen men, heard the sharp clatter of returning gunfire and calls for a medic and shouts over the radio for the overdue air support.

Three combat helicopters thundered low overhead, moving out to flush the snipers and a mortar team thought to be hunkered down in the valley beyond. A pair of M1 tanks roared past at nearly highway speeds, not even slowed by the trenches the surprisingly resourceful rebels had dug out to confound the rolling artillery.

Noah clenched the rifle they'd given him in a white-knuckle grip across his chest; it was still an unfamiliar burden in his hands. The sounds around him swelled to a hollow scream; his eyes wouldn't focus; his brain was so overwhelmed with a hundred conflicting decisions that he couldn't make even one. He tried again to clear his head of the hell breaking loose all around him, his eyes shut tight, his back pressed to the cool sandy slope of the berm.

Someone shouted his name and smacked him on the shoulder, jolting Noah back to the earsplitting blur of his new reality.

Volleys of unguided Hydra rockets screamed from the stub-wings of the hovering Apaches downrange— *buh buh buh buh BOOM*—pounding a ragged tree line along the riverbank in the foothills of Gannett Peak. Though the virgin forest was taking a real beating, the true impact of all this firepower remained to be seen. Recon had placed the remaining enemy combatants in the general area ahead, but this was big, rough country with enough natural cover to hide almost anything.

Still, whatever their skills at evasion, there couldn't be more than a handful of them left out there. For weeks now it had seemed that these freedom fighters—or homegrown terrorists, depending on one's allegiances—

couldn't last much longer against such overwhelming odds. Maybe their persistence came from a shared devotion to some ideal, and that was a strength the forces on Noah's side certainly didn't possess. Nobody seemed to believe in anything, in fact, though the constant propaganda from the top assured these men that every skirmish could be a turning point in the most critical military effort in generations: the war on domestic terrorists.

He looked around again at the others as they assembled for a final rout of the surviving rebels. What this multisourced, multinational, mercenary peacekeeping unit might lack in patriotic zeal was more than balanced out by their advantages: sheer numbers, a license-to-kill bravado, and all the twenty-first-century military hardware they could carry.

The heavy artillery was apparently having its effect; the incoming enemy mortars soon ceased to fall. Likewise, the distant echoing reports from hidden sniper nests went gradually silent.

A few moments later from down the line came a barked order to move out and mop up.

Noah slung the rifle over his shoulder, then cautiously stood and took in the quieting, cratered landscape. The coast seemed clear enough, and after another moment he brought out his camera and notepad to record the morning's glorious campaign.

Though technically he was designated as a combat reporter with this unit, his ill-fitting, generic uniform lacked any indication that he wasn't as eligible to be shot as anyone else. The weapon they'd shoved into his hands was another clue that his true function might be only to serve as a slow-moving target, just an expendable cipher to walk point and take a bullet in the place of some more valuable guy—a man who could actually find the trigger, for example.

The nearby squad collected itself, huddled to confirm a hasty strategy, and fanned out for the forward march.

Noah pulled himself up over the lip of the trench and made his way to a slight elevation nearby. From this higher vantage point he dropped to a knee and snapped a series of pictures: the ranks of blue-helmeted ground forces, on foot and in light armored vehicles, advancing down into the wooded ravine for what would seem to be a low-risk search-and-destroy run; the Apaches moving in loose formation, scanning the terrain with superhuman sensors and unleashing an occasional salvo from their heavy guns at any suspect movement.

He began to walk in back of the descending troops, lagging farther and farther behind them each time he stopped to take a photograph, until he came to a fork in the path. One way dead-ended at a bare, shallow cliff, so there was no going there. The other branch wound on downward through a dense cluster of scraggly trees. That's the way the rest of the squad had taken and so he followed in the eerie morning quiet, watching his step, until a pair of eyes peering through the high foliage startled him to a halt.

Noah fumbled for his rifle but soon saw there wasn't any need. The danger had already passed through here and it had left a warning behind.

The face he'd seen belonged to a man he recognized. He was one of the veteran troopers of his unit, a swaggering retired SEAL washout who'd been far from the best of his breed before he retired from active service. In his second career as a consulting soldier he'd found the respect he'd always wanted and he abused his position to the hilt. In the weeks Noah had known him he'd never missed an opportunity to throw his weight around and let everyone know who was the man.

Eyes wide open, mouth agape in an expression of

abject horror and utter surprise, his head had now been separated from his body.

Shock numbed him in place before Noah could take a step or look away. More of these dead lined the narrow trail before him; much care had been taken to set this scene. The hacked-up corpses of the murdered men were scattered about on the side of the path, all showing signs that they'd suffered horribly before the savage end.

These were the remains of the morning's forward scouting party—contact with them had been abruptly lost earlier—and they'd been left here to deliver a primitive message in a language that all would understand.

This wasn't Molly's doing, Noah thought. *None of this was, it couldn't be, not in a million years.*

He fell to his hands and knees and vomited, his stomach heaving until nothing was left in his guts but the fear that had overcome him. When his pounding head began to clear he staggered to his feet and began to run. There was no going back the way he'd come, and if he tried to flee into the forest he knew he wouldn't last the day; long before the enemy or the elements could kill him he'd no doubt be found by his own side and shot for desertion.

By the time he reached the edge of the trees, the rest of his company was ahead of him by a quarter mile.

Down there, just in front of the men on foot, the tanks were slowing to navigate a narrowing path through the natural and man-made obstructions. They reached a choke point with the river on the left and then maneuvered into single file to begin to creep through the restricted pass.

But something wasn't right.

Through his zoomed-in viewfinder he searched the hilly terrain, finding nothing for long seconds but knowing it must be there, and then suddenly he saw a glint of reflected sunlight from above, on the steep face of the minor mountain to his right.

Noah took the camera from his eye and stood. The word formed in his mind but before he could shout it the fire had already begun to fly.

Ambush.

Dozens of gray-white streaks arced down from hidden emplacements in the high ground on either side of the valley. These rocket-propelled grenades were targeting the helicopters but the ones that missed fell with devastating effect among the boxed-in vehicles and the scattering foot soldiers. As the lumbering Abrams tanks swiveled and swung their turrets toward the threats, a flashing line of detonations shook the ground around them. The tanks and Humvees all stopped dead, pouring smoke, gutted by the explosively formed penetrators that had been buried along the bottleneck of the pass.

The last surviving Apache helicopter was maneuvering and returning fire, but the enemy commanders had saved an ace in the hole. Two guided missiles streaked into the air in the distance, shoulder-fired Stingers most likely. One missed wide as the chopper jinked and evaded, but the second tore through the blades into the heat of the turbines and the aircraft disappeared in a bright yellow ball of descending fire.

As the rebel forces coldly found their range and the mortars began to rain down again, in front, between, and behind, Noah Gardner had only a moment to turn and run before a final blinding, deafening *boom* carried him away.

The approach of his death seemed a lot like he'd always heard it might be. Calm, a warm, settling peace, almost no pain at all, darkness coming on, the scene before him softening around the edges, a blurring of the lines between the real and the remembered. As consciousness passed away, Noah's last thought shouldn't have surprised him, but it did.

Though her cause was lost, with all the world now joining forces against what remained of her fragile, fading American dream, he thought of Molly Ross, closed his eyes, and wished her luck.

CHAPTER 2

The last thing she'd ever seen clearly had been a nearby nuclear explosion, an instant of unimaginable brightness before the coming of the permanent dark. But Molly didn't need her eyes to know one thing for certain: as bad as the last few months had been, the gravest danger yet was right outside the door.

Though she was obviously a prisoner in this place, no one had been left to guard her, and no one was watching—even without vision she was assured of this somehow by the *atmosphere* of the space, the solitary feel of the strange, stuffy room around her.

After months on the run, she and her dwindling inner circle of Founders' Keepers had nearly been cornered by—what was an accurate term for them?—by the state-sponsored mercenaries who'd seemingly been granted federal police powers, a borderless jurisdiction, and the skeleton key to the national armory. The events of the weeks that followed had blurred into one long flight through the wilderness, broken only by stretches of tense, restless waiting in various safe houses and hiding places.

This day had started with an anonymous message that their pursuers were finally closing in for the kill with a massive force. After that urgent warning all she could remember was running, desperate and directionless. That, and the gradually building sounds of a moving battle, the fury of it echoing like rolling thunder and never far behind. Hollis, her friend and longtime body-guard, had split from the group at some point in hopes of drawing the enemy's attention and buying the rest of them some time.

And then, just as it seemed that she and her people had finally reached the hill they would die on, out of the blue they'd all been swept up and spirited away by a shockingly well-armed and -organized resistance. In the moment the help had seemed to be a gift from above. It was becoming clear now that these new allies had sprung up from another direction entirely.

Voices drifted through the rugged wall on the far side of the room. Their words were mostly sifted out by the dense old varnished logs and rosined mortar in between. Still, through only these muffled remnants the gist of the debate next door was unmistakable. These men who'd snatched her from the jaws of certain death had done so with an evil intent of their own. Now they were deciding what was to become of her, and their hasty mock tribunal seemed to be nearing its final verdict.

Her guide dog, Cody, was seated on the floor next to her chair, his chin resting on her knee, so attuned to her by then that he could hardly be counted as a sepa-rate being. Molly held the dog's harness, her free hand resting on his side. She could feel the tension in him, but, like his sworn companion, he was as calm as these circumstances would allow. Neither of them was at ease in the company of strangers, particularly men of the sort in the adjoining room.

A knot of fear had been twisting its way into her stomach, waiting there to cut free and flood her mind at the first invitation. Molly took a long moment to get a grip on what courage still remained, and resolved to think her way out of this place.

Blind is a tidy word coined by the able majority, a black-and-white term for what's been lost that overlooks all that might have been gained in the bargain. There were other, older forms of perception, much deeper than sight, that had been steadily reawakening in her over the past several months as she recovered. Only in the faintest hints at first, from out of the dark these neglected human senses had slowly knit together to restore a different kind of seeing. Lesser in some ways, greater in others, this subtle new vision was a sense she'd learned to believe in—to entrust with her life at times—and she would have to trust it now again.

Okay, then, she thought. *Now what do we need to know?*

A heavy door from the noisy meeting hall was behind and to her left, closed and key-locked from the outside. A pale yellow blur of flickering illumination shone high up and in front of her—an old cyclone lamp by the sooty coal-oil scent on the air. A different, cleaner light—the late afternoon sun through a tall, wide window—was there on the other side.

"Cody," she whispered, and Molly felt the dog stand ready beside her. She got to her feet as well, her right hand extended forward as though in preparation to explore unknown surroundings. "Let's have a look around, boy."

Cody took the cue and began to walk her carefully through the space, giving a polite head-nudge to her thigh or an outward tug on the harness to shift their path when an obstacle would have blocked her way. Step by step, she began to sketch the detail of the floor plan in her mind, measuring and memorizing along the tour.

Eight diagonal paces to the southeast corner and (thus far) the only door, sixteen more down a long credenza with wooden bookshelves up above—the books were bone-dry to the touch, old, leather-bound, and dusty, clearly on hand for show rather than any actual reading. What seating she encountered felt antique, handmade, almost formal, of carved wood and hammered metal with embroidered upholstery. A slick wall-mounted whiteboard and a rolltop secretary brought her to the corner.

Along the back wall her thumb was nicked by something smooth and sharp. With new care she felt around the protruding object: bared teeth in frozen jaws, stiff lacquered fur, wide glass-marble eyes. And there were more of these farther down, uneven rows and columns of them. It was like a taxidermist's front-room show-case—animal heads large and small, their last moments preserved as trophies on mounted plaques.

When she and Cody had come almost full circle her fingertips brushed against cool glass, an arm's length from a large varnished desk facing the chair where she'd been seated before. She walked the span of what must be a picture window, which in this direction would be looking out onto a vista of surrounding mountains to the west.

A workplace with perks like these would be reserved for the leader. That would account for the backwoods opulence of the furnishings, and for the garish wall of trophies as well.

After the walk-through she knew more than she had before, though there'd been little comfort to be found. Still, that they'd chosen to let her wait in here was the one piece of good news. They hadn't shoved her bound and gagged into a closet or a storeroom; that at least meant she retained some respect, and maybe just enough leverage to get out of this hornet's nest in one piece.

That tangle of fear in her gut worked loose for just an instant and a chill passed over her skin. Other things were lingering in this musty air, things quite beyond the physical. Cody must have felt them, too; by the end of the circuit he was pressed even closer by her side than he normally would be. There were ghosts of a wicked past within these walls, as present and real as any living person.

As they reached the gathered curtains she touched the bottom corner of the large windowpane. A small factory sticker was there; she couldn't be sure but in all likelihood it would certify this as tempered glass. No easy exit this way, then; grabbing that straight chair and swinging it against the window would serve only to bring her guard bursting in to investigate the noise.

Still facing the glass, Molly stepped to the center, where she was sure she could be seen from outside. She pointed back over her shoulder, toward that oil lamp burning high on the opposite wall. What had occurred to her didn't qualify as an actual plan of escape—more like the kind of last-resort improvisation reserved only for the soon-to-be far outnumbered and outgunned.

And then she held up a flat hand, palm near the glass.

These were signs meant for Thom Hollis, made with no reasonable expectation that he was even still alive to see them. Faith and friendship were all she had to count on, an unshakable belief that he would somehow be up there, watching.

Wait, her last gesture had said. *But don't wait too long.*

Stealth, endurance, navigation, marksmanship, survival off the land—any average rifleman who's worth his candle has mastered all those skills before the first day in combat. Deadliness, though, is the only meaningful measure of a sniper.

Hollis brought the long scope nearer to his eye. He took in a deep breath, held Molly's distant image centered in the hairline cross of the reticle, noted her measurement on the scale, and prepared to do the math to find the range.

There was no need to interrupt his view as he dialed in the distance; the Remington 700 in his hands had been with him since the early days of Desert Storm. After all that time together he could break it down to nuts and springs and rebuild it by feel.

At 791 yards this was far from the longest shot he'd ever taken, but the present prevailing conditions left much to be desired. A moderate variable breeze would demand moment-to-moment compensation. His position provided little cover; as long as he lay still he'd blend in well enough, but the first flash of gunpowder would stand him out against the bare terrain like a new copper penny. And the low sun at his back put a harsh migrant glare on the tinted picture window, obscuring the view inside that room right where he needed most to see.

He had watched as she walked the floor, no doubt searching out her options should the coming situation begin to slide farther southward. Hope for the best, but prepare for the worst; that was her watchword, and she'd stuck by it through these recent harsh months in which all hope should have long since dwindled away.

Hollis had seen only three sentries patrolling these foothills. Against instinct he'd only noted their patterns and positions, without taking further action. They were likely in radio contact, and if that communication was interrupted it could raise an alarm. But he'd also left them alive because he was under Molly's standing orders to avoid any violence unless absolutely necessary. His repeated objections to this policy had been overruled as usual, so if and when the fighting started on this hillside the hot lead would be arriving fast and loose from all four cardinal directions.

In the scope he saw her react to a sound behind her and hasten to the chair where she'd been seated before. A few moments later the door opened and a number of men began to file into the room. The short, skinny one in the lead he recognized, and if there'd been any remaining whim of a peaceful conclusion to this unholy summit, with this man's arrival that glimmer was gone.

For one side or the other, this waning day wasn't going to end well.

CHAPTER 3

L et us pray."

George Lincoln Rockwell Pierce, Molly thought. That voice identified the man beyond any doubt. As bad as this was, at least now she understood what she was facing.

Molly had long been aware of Pierce's fringe-banished clan, but even if you'd never heard of him within a handful of words his tone and manner would telegraph everything you needed to know. And he wanted it that way; his was a world divided down a clean bright line, with his brotherhood on one side and the hordes of wicked elitists and subhuman barbarians on the other, pounding at the gate. He pushed that separation into your face from the first contact; somehow even in the words "let us pray" he'd said it: *This is who I am, stranger. Now, just who in the hell are you?*

Around her chair the room felt packed to standing room only. While the air had been stale before, it was now thick with a humid funk of proudly unwashed humanity, an aggressive aroma somewhere between expired lunch meat and a neglected grease trap. Despite all these sweaty attendees the place was perfectly quiet except for the speaker's sanctimonious baritone.

Most prayers contain at least a smidgen of reverence or contrition, but not this one. It was glib and conversational, peer-to-peer, less a hosanna than a manager's to-do list organized for immediate heavenly intervention.

Molly let his words fade to a drone and returned in her mind to her own priorities.

Now she knew for sure: if the United Aryan Nations had a White House west of the Mississippi, she was seated in its godforsaken Oval Office. These outlaws were the source of the military aid she'd unknowingly accepted earlier in the day, and there would be a payment due for that brief alliance. George Pierce didn't have a reputation for taking on risk with no thought of his own reward.

To his lowlife friends and followers the man across the desk was known simply as George, in a thinly veiled reference to the father of our country. In his younger days, however, the full four names had often graced his mug shots on law enforcement bulletin boards in various jurisdictions. He'd been christened at birth in loving tribute to George Lincoln Rockwell, the mid-twentieth-century mastermind of the American Nazi Party. Legend had it that he was conceived at the moment of his namesake's friendly-fire assassination in 1967, though some of his faithful went so far as to claim he'd been secretly sired by the homeland Führer himself.

The Pierce tribe had grown large and dispersed over many generations, blown across the country like carnival trash on closing day. It's hard to put down roots when getting run out of town is the most celebrated tradition of your kin. Their ragbag family tree was hung with an assortment of thieves, thugs, grifters, Klansmen, and other such stellar representatives of the Übermensch.

From a home base in the row-house slums of East Baltimore, young George had accompanied his parents on caravan tours of tent shows and soapbox rallies. In town after town he'd watched and learned as they spouted a bizarre mélange of Bible-bending apocalyptic foolishness and race-baiting bull-roar. At age fifteen he was old enough to take up the pulpit himself, and this proved to be a turning point. Where Mom and Dad had enjoyed only limited appeal even with like-minded audiences, George showed an uncanny knack for drawing larger and larger crowds and filling the collection plates to overflowing.

He soon left home and took his own brand of revival show on the road, drumming up support, gathering disciples, and hawking self-published white-power pamphlets and paperbacks along the way. Back then the regional press gave him plenty of ink because most people really loved to hate him. But some, it seemed, just loved him; the more he was denounced and banned the more popular he became. His litany of run-ins with the law became a test case for the limits of the First Amendment, and with every arrest more anonymous money would pour in for his defense. He even ran for a seat in the state legislature at one point, and to the horror of the good people of Louisiana, he'd very nearly won.

It was only a decade later, though, with the explosion of the online social media revolution, that George Pierce graduated into a full-fledged underground phenomenon. In this new medium he enjoyed an advantage the old-school KKK leaders never had—no sheets or hoods were required for membership. His followers never even needed to step out of their homes to meet and plan and join in the crusade. Instead they hid behind members-only firewalls, closed forums, and scary nicknames, safe and secure in the anonymous darker corners of the Internet.

As Pierce's underground white-nationalist movement began to gather strength, the FBI added an alias to his criminal profile. In their internal alerts and briefings they called him the General, and by the look of things he'd now taken that rank to heart.

Grave times can bring out the best in good people, and open the door to all manner of evils for the rest. In the recent turbulent years Pierce had read the tea leaves and transformed himself, at least to the uninitiated, into a grassroots champion for the downtrodden majority. He'd retooled his public messages to be more appealing to a growing audience of hopeless and disillusioned Americans. He'd temporarily put aside his radical pose, in other words, for the sake of his radical ends. To the flocks of newcomers he presented himself as a simple man with plainspoken, commonsense answers to the troubles of a changing world.

All the pus and poison still festered at the core, though, waiting for its time. A day finally comes when the old hatreds begin to rise again and the enemy can be named, and in his twisted end-times gospel that day was dawning soon. George Lincoln Rockwell Pierce had a long list of enemies ready for indictment, trial, and punishment at his hands.

"Miss Ross?"

She'd heard the closing *amen* but hadn't spoken it herself. It was Pierce who'd addressed her with a subtle testiness, the headmaster calling out a promising student caught daydreaming in class.

"Yes?"

"I couldn't help but notice that you didn't make yourself a part of our prayer just now."

"That's right."

"And why is that?"

"I prayed earlier," Molly said.

"Ah."

In the ominous silence that followed she heard a match scrape and flare, then the distinctive sounds and scents of a third-rate cigar being lit and drawn upon.

"You rescued us today," Molly said, "and I was grateful for it." She turned her head and raised her voice slightly. "Thank you. I want to say that up front, to all of you here."

"And we all appreciate that expression of your gratitude," Pierce said, "tardy though it may be. I for one had begun to wonder—"

She turned back to the sound of his voice. "What I don't understand is why a man like you would stick his neck out for people like us."

"People like you?"

"Yes. People like us. People who've clearly and repeatedly condemned every single thing you stand for."

The room became somewhat restless, particularly toward the back, as her last words hung in the air. After a series of sharp raps on the desk—did he actually have a *gavel* over there?—the scattered muttering died down right away.

"Oh," Pierce said quietly, "surely you don't condemn everything we stand for, Molly. May I call you Molly?"

"Sure."

"Far from everything, Molly." A creaking of old wood and springs arose as he stood. By the sound she could tell that someone stationed behind him had slid his chair back, butler-style, to allow the great man adequate space for an anticipated oration. "All of us here have sworn to uphold the divinely inspired U.S. Constitution," Pierce said, "to the letter, as it was originally written and intended. We stand for American interests to be first and foremost in our foreign policies. We oppose globalism. We believe this country has the right and the obligation to secure its borders, its sacred heritage, and its values. We believe that American jobs, American ingenuity, and American resources must be protected and preserved for the good of the American people. We believe that the blame for our economic woes, past and present, lies with that incestuous den of thieves and shylocks in the revolving door between Washington, Wall Street, and the Federal Reserve. And we believe in a small and constrained federal government, with its inevitable corruption confined within the limited role set out for it by the Founding Fathers—"

"All due respect, Mr. Pierce," she said, "the few things we might happen to agree on are far outweighed by everything else. On which we don't."

"I met your late mother once, Molly, may God rest her soul. And I'm not surprised to learn that the apple didn't fall too far from the tree." This was obviously spoken for the benefit of the others in the room, and his crowd responded with tentative laughter.

Having grown up as a drifter Pierce never acquired a legitimate regional accent of his own. In his recorded speeches and videos, however, he had a way of mimicking the native dialect of his varied audiences. Hack politicians often engage in such faked familiarity in an attempt to ingratiate themselves to different ethnic or cultural groups while stumping on the campaign trail. Presumably on her behalf, he'd begun to shade his words with a generic cornpone twang that no true southerner, much less a real Tennessean, would ever mistake for authentic.

"I'd like to go now," she said.

"Hear me out, Molly—"

"Nothing you say will make a difference." She moved to stand but rough hands from either side gripped her shoulders and kept her seated. "I'm warning you—"

"Warning me," he said, with what was obviously meant to be a good-natured amusement in his voice. "It shouldn't come to this. We have a common enemy in this revolution. You shy away from the clarity of some of our beliefs, I understand that, but it's only a small step I'm asking you to take. We're both outlaws in the oppressors' eyes, after all. Have you seen what they've done to you, and your group, and to your mother's memory?" He paused. "You haven't, have you? You've been on the lam all these months, and you haven't seen, or your people have kept it from you. You've been spared from what the Jew-run blogs and the leftist underground media and their minions have made of you."

"What are you talking about?"

"You've officially become an enemy of the state, Miss Ross. You, and your insiders, and your dead friend Danny Bailey—by all accounts you're all homegrown terrorists, enemy combatants, the dreaded white al-Qaeda. You plotted with a turncoat FBI man to destroy a federal building and half of Las Vegas last fall, and you nearly succeeded. Your mother was so distraught over your treason that she committed suicide."

It took a physical effort, but Molly kept her voice steady. "All lies."

"If a hundred million people believe a lie and only one knows the truth, tell me, whose version do you think history will record?"

"More than one knows the truth."

Pierce sighed heavily and retook his chair. "Let's cut to the heart of it. On my orders we saved your life today, at a considerable cost of men and materials. Though some of my advisors disagreed with me on this course, the decision was mine. In my view what that means, at the minimum, is that you owe a great deal to me. In our discussion outside this door just now there were differing opinions on how that debt was to be paid.

"After much prayer and soul-searching I've determined there are two courses, and the one we take will be yours to choose. The first is an official and public alliance between us." The room was still as he waited for her to respond in some way. She didn't. "Do you understand?"

"I understand the word *alliance,* yes."

"With your eyesight as it is, can you see at all?"

"Only some light and shadow," she said.

"All right." There was a brief rustling of paper. Someone walked past her to the desk and then came back, took her wrist, and put a single sheet on a clipboard and a heavy marker into her hands. "Despite the best efforts of our enemies there are still likely hundreds of thousands of your mother's faithful who still may believe in you. These represent a valuable constituency to me. I've written a statement and you hold it there. We'll have someone read it to you so you can memorize it. I want you to sign it, and sign it big, John Hancock–style. We'll scan it then for a mass e-mail announcement, and when you're ready you will deliver it for the camera—"

"You don't have to read it to me. I'm sure I know the essence. It's addressed to your audience, and mine. It says that I've seen the error of my ways and decided to join forces with you. It says that everyone who believes in what my mother stood for, and that I still stand for, should all follow my lead and do the same."

". . . You'd rather speak it from the heart, then?"

"Actually," Molly said, "I'd much rather die."

Pierce crushed out his cigar with a good deal more force than would have been required to simply snuff it. "And there you've struck upon the second option, but you should know something before you choose it. Any noble stand you take will be for nothing. Out on the Internet a dead person can go on living for a long time, for years maybe. So through the magic of technology you'll sign and deliver that statement postmortem, and many others after that, and nobody will ever know that it wasn't really you.

"But I'd rather we didn't go that way. If you're to be a living ally you bring several advantages to me. If not, then you bring only one. My boys here haven't seen such a pretty young woman in a month of Sundays, at least one whose affections they didn't have to purchase. I expect they'll all want to enjoy you for a spell before we bury you alive."

Pierce said this with the inhuman detachment of a textbook sociopath, with no discernible anger or malice. Molly sat for a few seconds, thinking. The character of the waning light through that window had dimmed and grown warmer, but not yet quite enough. She would need just a little more time.

"I'm still listening," Molly said.

"That's better."

"What about the people who were with me?"

"What's left of the Founders' Keepers? They're out there under guard in the next room, sweating out your decision, and I'm afraid they're quite a bit worse for the wear. One's wounded and I'm told that we brought back another—a Mr. Church, if I recall—who'd sadly expired from the rigors of the day. But it's good you asked, because there's one of your number we can't account for. This big mulatto that rarely leaves your side, this Thom Hollis, I believe his name is. What is he to you, some kind of a Secret Service?"

"He's my friend."

"And he's a half-blood, is he? Or a quarter?"

"I wouldn't know. It's never come up."

"Well, despite the fact that he's a good fraction of a porch-monkey, I'm told that he's a rare breed. From what I hear he's not your typical black man; hell, I'd say the half that's Caucasian may be a better soldier than most of these whole white men right here. I hear he fought well for you. They also tell me he's articulate, and bright, and clean. He's light-skinned with no Negro dialect. I want you to know I need men like him, so don't you worry about that boy."

"What do you mean by that?"

"What I'm saying is, he'd have a place with us here if that's what's on your mind. You just think about how far we've come. A few years ago this guy would have been fetching us coffee, and here I'm pulling up a seat for him, right here next to me. And it would be a considerable load off my mind if you told me where he is right now."

"I wouldn't tell you that, even if I knew."

"Now, there's no need to be that way. Look, I've got three of my best trackers out there looking for him, and they'll bring him on in living or dead before too much longer. Three against one on enemy territory, them's tough odds to beat, I don't care how good he is. But, if I had an encouraging word from you about my proposal, well, then, I'd just radio my boys and it'd go much better for him. For both of you. The choice is yours, it's no skin off my nose either way."

His voice had taken on a new earnestness that only made the words that much uglier. "I think you've got me all wrong, Molly. I think one man is just as good as another so long as he's honest and decent and not a nigger or a Chinaman. My old mom told me, 'George, you can't go to heaven if you hate anybody.' We practice that. There are white niggers, I've seen a lot of white niggers in my time.

"See, I don't hate the kikes, or the spooks, or the beaners, or the rag-heads. I don't even hate the chinks anymore. I don't hate any of those unfortunate people. We should all just stay with our own, you see? I think even brother Farrakhan would join hands with me on that score.

"This is our time, Molly, and our God-given commission. It falls to this generation to cleanse this country, to take it back to the purity it once was. It's us or them. That's why I've got to know right now if you're going to be one of us. You've got a way with the common people I'll never have, but you've had no muscle behind you. These men here that fought for you today and thousands more like them across America, this is your army. We're ready to march. Now let's do what we have to do and take these sons of bitches out."

Since the accident that had nearly taken her life, she'd seen enough sunsets through her failing eyes to recognize the delicate transition to twilight. That moment when the last gleaming arc of the sun has passed just below the horizon had finally arrived.

"I have an answer for you." She pulled the cap from the marker and then, by feel, drew a thick diagonal line across the paper from the bottom right to the upper left corner and then down again, upper right to lower left from the other side. Still seated, with the large X complete she unclipped the sheet and held it up high and away, facing flat to the window, and said, "Nobody move."

For several endless seconds they all seemed dumbfounded; neither George Pierce nor any of his men behind her breathed a word.

And then there were three sounds at once, each distinct but simultaneous. A *clink* from the window, a solid *rap* on the wood of the bookshelf on the opposite wall, and a sharp flutter of the paper that she held high in her hand, as though someone had flicked it with a finger.

As she turned the sheet toward the man across the desk, just before the distant echoing sound of a rifle shot had arrived, she didn't need to see it to know what was there. A clean bullet hole, precisely through the cross of the X.

As she'd ordered them, nobody moved, and no one knew better than George Lincoln Rockwell Pierce who the next round would find if anyone acted against her.

"You'd asked about Hollis earlier," Molly said.

"Do you really expect to get out of here alive?" Pierce hissed. He'd denied hating anyone just before, but his voice now seemed to tell a different tale.

"Cody, *go!*" she shouted.

The instant her hand gripped his harness the dog rose and leaped toward the door with a snarl so fierce that men far braver than these would have jumped back and cleared his way. A crash of shattered glass and a bloom of bright yellow heat erupted high in the corner as Hollis's second shot blew the oil lamp there into an indoor wildfire, instantly out of control. Hands clutched at her as she flew from the room at a full run behind the dog, and she heard the sounds of her people overpowering their guard and then following her through a maze of stairs and hallways that seemed to go on forever.

But Cody knew the way. He burst through the last flimsy screen door with Molly and the others on his heels, and they were suddenly outside in the cool clean air, running and running toward the shelter of the forested hills, with gunshots soon sounding far ahead and from behind.

CHAPTER 4

A bullet *whumped* into the turf twenty-odd yards to Hollis's side, distant enough to tell the shooter hadn't yet drawn a solid bead on his position, but still far too close for comfort. A sensible man would've grabbed his gear and lit off for the high tree line, but self-preservation wasn't the first thing on his mind.

Through the scope he saw a knot of nine tiny figures stumble through the lower-level door of the lodge, coming on at a run, led by a familiar young woman and her loping guide dog. Two in the back were supporting a hobbled man between them, and their burdened gait would set the pace for all the others. To his unaided eye the considerable distance made their progress toward freedom look painfully slow.

A man with a raised handgun emerged from the same porch-lit exit, firing rapidly but wildly off into the dusk. With a quick, deliberate shift of his aim Hollis took him out cleanly, then worked the bolt and heeled it home to shoot again into the center mass of a second gunman, who'd appeared just behind the first.

He scanned the unfolding situation as he chambered the last round in the well. There would shortly be many more where those two came from. Without a

serious diversion this fight would soon take an unsur-
vivable turn.

The fire he'd started in the second story was only
dimly visible; the wide, clear window he'd shot through
before was hazed over like a shower door, no longer
transparent. *Safety glass.* Edge to edge the pane was a
brittle mosaic of a million cracks, but the shattered glaze
was still holding its fragile integrity.

He eased his crosshairs to the bottom corner of the
frame and took the shot. At impact a fist-sized ragged
hole punched through there, the weakened window
sagged, and then it buckled and collapsed in a sudden
waterfall of glassy pebbles.

A rush of coal-black smoke and bright curling flames
burst forth to meet the backdraft as the wind whipped in
to feed the combustion. In seconds the enlivened inferno
had spread to threaten the roof above and the unfinished
balcony beyond.

That should do it; vengeance may be sweet but a
four-alarm house fire in the wilderness trumps all other
urgencies. All hands would be recalled to give up the
chase and haul water to extinguish the spreading blaze.

All of them, that is, but three.

It was already half-past time to go. He stole a last
look at the progress of the escapees; they were well
on their way with no visible pursuit. As his thoughts
finally turned to saving his own skin an extended volley of automatic gunfire tore up the ground around
him on either side. He rolled and with a single sweep
of his arm threw off his camouflage of underbrush and
snagged his half-buried long duffel, then he crawled
into the clear and headed out for the cover uphill.
Crouched low, cutting right and left in no steady pattern, tracers hissing like hailstones through the canopy
of trees ahead—in the unlikely event that he made it,

these would surely be among the longest fifty yards he'd ever run.

A trio of sentries on their home field, presumably military-trained and well armed for their job, against a solitary man with a bolt-action deer rifle—on its face that scenario should grant unbeatable odds to the superior force. This is what they must have thought as they came for him, because they didn't do what they should have done. They didn't work their hunt as a unit, and with that rash oversight their tactical squad of three was diminished to one lone opponent at a time.

The moment he'd found a secluded spot to lay over, Hollis had traded out his Remington for weapons more suited to close work. A simple Springfield .45 was tucked into his belt in back. Slung over a shoulder was his old 12-bore semi-auto, loaded up with heavy rifled slugs. The rest of his gear was hidden in the brush for later retrieval, if such an opportunity should come.

The first one made it as easy as a kill can ever be.

With the sun fully set and no moonlight to speak of, the man hadn't paused to allow his eyes or his methods to adjust to the gathering night. He broached the woods at the last known position of his enemy and strode in fast and loud, sweeping the terrain with a barrel-mounted flashlight on his weapon, firing at anything that moved and many things that did not. Though his meandering search finally brought him just a stone's throw away, he never did see the man he came looking for. A single shot through the chest put him down, and then there were two.

The second was harder, and only a stroke of chance saved Thom Hollis from an early, shallow grave.

He'd taken up a cramped but hidden perch in the gnarled lower branches of a nearby cottonwood, on the premise that the earlier noise of combat might draw the others to the scene of their partner's demise. He was correct in predicting the response, but dead wrong on the approach.

From the only narrow angle of view where Hollis had no cover at all—that was the unlikely direction from which the second man had come. Quiet as doom he'd stolen up close, his target not yet sighted.

With a single glance upward the hunt would have ended differently. At less than twenty paces, though, a hiss from the two-way radio on his belt gave the hunter away.

Prey and predator then met eyes at the same instant, each frozen in momentary disbelief at this unexpected turn of events.

Hollis was pinned among the branches in his hiding place; there was no room to swing the long barrel of the shotgun around. The man on the ground backed away, calling out for the others and firing wildly at full auto as he retreated. Amid a storm of flying lead and splinters Hollis drew his pistol from the back and fired into the heart of the fray until the magazine was emptied.

At length the echoes faded and the deep woods grew quiet once again. He climbed down, reloaded, and set out to see if their fight was really done.

The other man had succumbed to his wounds by the time Hollis found him, but he hadn't died too quickly. He'd crawled to a sly lair in the heavy brush to lie in wait for the approach of his enemy. He'd lost consciousness just that way, still waiting, and bled out from the effects of a damned lucky shot in the dark.

And then, the third and last of them.

This last one was smart; he'd done his job right. Hollis had picked up the two-way handset from the second man's body and listened for a while, until it became clear that the enemy had wisely gone to radio silence. His two compatriots would be directly tracking the sniper, the last man had likely reasoned, so in the event that they failed he would choose instead to find his quarry's destination—his rendezvous point with the other, unarmed escapees—and then take them down all at once, by surprise.

The traces of a group bearing a wounded man were easy enough to follow, even at a prudent distance from their path. Still, the man hadn't lapsed into carelessness. He was wary and took cunning precautions against pursuit, though he had little reason to suspect he was followed. It took hours, in fact, not only to find him, but to catch him briefly unprepared for a hostile confrontation.

Near to his goal, less than a mile from the dim glow of a sheltered campfire up ahead, he'd stopped to rest and drink some water. That's when Thom Hollis stepped from the shadows behind him.

"I got you cold, son," he said.

The man had begun to turn toward the voice before stopping himself, his weapon still hanging at his side. A half-moon had risen as the night progressed, and by its pale filtered light it was the youth of this man that was most immediately apparent. His features were strong in profile but not quite fully mature, with that first sparse attempt at a beard that some adolescent rebels will try on at their first opportunity.

For seconds more he didn't move. Neither of them did; both knew well enough by then how this would end.

"I can't let you go," Hollis said quietly. "And I ain't taking prisoners."

CHAPTER 5

O nce Hollis had caught up to the others it took only a few minutes to take stock of their situation. Anyone inclined to count the blessings of this tattered band of fugitive patriots would find only this one: by all evidence their enemies had indeed elected to hold off until dawn before marching forth to wipe them off the face of the earth.

Scattered communications on the salvaged radio seemed to confirm this, although since the other side would know their frequencies might be monitored, this chatter could be part of a ruse. Despite that possibility Hollis believed what they said, and for one good reason: these men weren't quite as stupid as they looked. They had no need to risk rushing headlong into the dark. Their already decisive advantage would be even greater in the daylight. With such an overwhelming force behind them the next day's search-and-destroy operation would be a turkey shoot, and they knew it.

For the remainder of that night very little time was spared for rest and reflection. Wounds were tended to the crude extent possible in the absence of sterile supplies. Fresh water proved easy enough to find, though food was limited to what raw provisions of nature could be gathered in the depths of a bitter night in early spring. With those necessities tended to, Hollis took the watch and let the others try to sleep as best they could. As for himself, he couldn't remember even the last brief nap he'd had, or the last meal that had been more than a squirrel's portion. He'd never yet found the far limit of his endurance but he could feel complete exhaustion getting close.

In the morning, they took stock and prepared to press on.

The only shred of a map still in their possession was a worn pocket trifold that had been pocketed during that brief stay with the Pierce clan. It looked like a hunter's crib sheet, hand-traced from a legitimate chart and only crudely annotated with landmarks, spot-elevations, deer paths, and a mark for due north. Hollis spent a few minutes with this map to get his proper bearings, and for a welcome change what he discovered wasn't as bad as it could have been. They were days late and off course to be sure, but they also weren't so awfully far from where they'd planned to be before this latest trouble began. Whatever their chances, the best prospects lay ahead; they needed to get themselves under way immediately.

Before they left the campsite all visible evidence of the overnight stay was carefully erased, buried, or camouflaged. The path forward was simple enough: Molly and the others would start onward—seven walking and one dragged by two others on a makeshift stretcher—while Hollis took up the rear guard.

He'd given the handmade map and the only compass to the forward group. If they got too far beyond him he would find his way by the transit of the sun and the seat of his pants. There was little craft or subtlety to the travel scheme. They would head northeast, as the crow flies, toward a now-belated rendezvous with some regional allies of the organization. For the sake of speed it was a straight-line excursion, though along the way they would try to employ any natural features of the terrain to make themselves more difficult to overtake.

Despite the urgency to move, at the insistence of one of the more pious group members the ten of them elected to join hands and squander a few precious minutes in a prayer circle. Hollis declined to partake in this delay, choosing instead to devote his full attention to the threatening hush from the forest behind them.

That's why he was able to hear a sound that didn't belong, and how he recognized the dry mechanical whisper of its approach, faint and very distant though it was.

Helicopter.

Perhaps the others had heard it, too, because their circle was soon broken with a hasty benediction, and they were off.

As he followed, always watchful for signs of the inevitable pursuit, Hollis set about brushing out conspicuous tracks while periodically stepping off to fabricate decoy paths that might lead less experienced woodsmen astray. Naturally, if the enemy came with air reconnaissance, or even if they simply brought along dogs to aid in their hunt, most of these diversions would be for naught.

The hard fact was, in all likelihood they were fleeing down a one-way road to nowhere. The near strangers Molly had been hoping to meet would have little reason to risk waiting this long in the open, especially if they'd gotten word of how badly things had fallen apart for her out here. Even if those supposed allies were still waiting, with such primitive tools of navigation the odds of actually finding them were slim to none, much less of evading capture along such an obvious route. But there was no backup plan, and the group had all agreed that this path seemed to be their best hope among bleak options.

Of course, it could be worse, Hollis thought. *It could be raining.*

The downpour commenced about an hour after sunrise. What started as a gentle April shower rapidly angered and darkened into a legitimately violent thunderstorm. Before long the blowing sheets of frigid rain had reduced visibility to near zero, making hazardous business of even careful walking on the uneven, stony ground.

He pressed forward into the teeth of the gale, the drawstring hood of his jacket cinched down to a crumpled keyhole, every gained yard a struggle just to plant solid footing and hold his line. All the while he was imagining the assault of these same perils on those up ahead. In the midst of such a storm they could easily become separated and lose their way, walk into the rush of a sudden mudslide, or simply take one errant step and be lost over the verge of a ravine.

Concern for them was all that kept him going. The fatigue was getting worse; several times his legs simply failed him, his mind seemed determined to give up and wander off into a fog, and his arms felt barely capable of pushing him back to his feet when he'd fallen, time after time.

After an endless, treacherous downhill crawl that stretched on to late morning, at last the weather commenced to ease somewhat as the worst of it blew on southwesterly. Though the trailing rain continued, the sky gradually smoothed and lightened as the sun began to reassert itself beyond the thinning clouds.

Before too long Hollis caught sight of the rest of his party, taking refuge near a hillside beneath the overhang of a natural grotto. The storm had taken its toll on them but they all looked little worse for the wear. Despite his relief he didn't approach them right away. Instead he watched them for a time from a distance, from under the imperfect shelter of a tall evergreen.

They were huddled together against the cold, one obviously recounting some story from their deliverance with great animation, another catching a stream of rainwater with a length of curled birch bark and passing it to others for a sloppy drink, another tending the trail aches and injuries of those less able.

After a few minutes he came forward and joined them, accepted and returned their greetings, and took a seat on the ground near Molly's side. Hollis touched her shoulder and spoke a word to let her know he was near, but it seemed she knew already. She leaned to him and hugged him tight around the neck.

"Thank you," Molly said.

"For what? For getting you out of the frying pan, or back into the fire?"

"For everything." She sat back, smiling, fished something from the pocket of her jeans, and held it out for him. "For this, especially."

He took the damp, crumpled wad of stationery from her hand and carefully unfolded it: a half page of typewritten text, crossed out from corner to corner with a heavy black X, with a bullet hole near the middle.

He took a closer look at the condition of his target. While it had been a fair shot it was also far from the perfect bull's-eye he'd pictured as he pulled the trigger. Depending on whether she'd held the paper upright or inverted, his aim had been off either high and left or low and to the right. But well off it had certainly been.

"You're damn lucky you didn't lose a finger, or worse," Hollis said.

"There was never a doubt in my mind."

"I know." He took a long breath and then another moment to weigh the wisdom of broaching a subject too long avoided. This was neither the time nor the place, but it never was, and that's why some necessary things get left unspoken until it's too late to make a difference. The two were almost out of earshot of the others, and this seemed as good an opportunity as any. "We need to have a talk about that, I think, on the odd chance that we ever get to see another sunup."

"A talk about what?" Molly asked, and she turned her face to him.

Nearly all the scars from her injuries of that awful night were hidden inside; by outward appearances her gaze was as clear and bright as it had ever been. Though she could no longer see your eyes to look into them, she nevertheless had a way of looking *toward* you that somehow reached in deep to seize even more of a human connection.

"Doubts," Hollis said. "And how it might be healthy for us to entertain one or two of those right now."

She frowned a bit. It wasn't a hint of anger or hurt, but only empathy that showed on her face. "Go on."

"I don't want to have a fight about it, not here in the middle of all this." Now that he'd taken the platform he found he didn't know where to begin. "With all respect—"

"It's okay. Say what's on your mind."

"All right, then. We lost your mom, and then we lost Danny, we lost Ben Church yesterday, and now we've got the full force of the U.S. government after us—"

"Not the government. The people are the government."

"All right, then, not the government. Some freelance military-armed battalion of uniformed yahoos from the corrupted bowels of what the government's become.

Does it really matter? I stopped trying to keep track of all the jackboots when the Department of Education got their own SWAT team. The point is, we're marked as shoot-to-kill enemies and they're after us, with everything they can throw at us. And yesterday they chased us right into the only helping hands available, and those hands, I'm sure you noticed, were attached to some genuine homegrown, goose-stepping, brown-shirted, skinhead Wyoming Nazis. And now they're coming after us, too."

"Yes."

She was clearly still waiting for him to come to his point; just stating the obvious wasn't getting them anywhere.

"Molly, I need to ask you, now. You and I, and these few people—what is it exactly that we think we're trying to do?"

"That hasn't ever changed. We're going to show the American people the truth and keep on fighting for the future of our country."

"How are we going to do that? With what?" The others were beginning to notice this side discussion but he was fully committed now, and come to think of it, nothing was being said that they all shouldn't hear. "You know I'd walk straight into hell for you—"

"It's not just me. We have to make it about more than just me."

"But listen. You have to know that if we lose you, it's all over."

"But you're not going to lose me—"

"We almost lost you yesterday, and it's my job to protect you."

"You're not alone in that, Hollis. I'm already protected."

"Oh, are we gonna talk about God now? Because I

don't think I can take it if you're going to tell me that God got us out of that fix we were in back there."

"Okay—"

"And the next time you speak to God? I hope you'll ask Him for me, why in His infinite wisdom He reached down His all-knowing hand and got us into that fix in the first place."

"Okay, shh. Okay. I won't talk about God." She touched his arm, and her grip was firm and reassuring. "Just tell me what you're afraid of."

And there she'd seen to the heart of it, as she always seemed to do.

His voice was low when he finally spoke again. "I'm just about at the end of my rope, Molly. I'm not the man I used to be, and I'm afraid I'm not up to the task anymore."

"Oh," she said, nodding. "So it sounds like it's me that's about to lose you."

"No, of course you're not going to lose me." Hearing her say such a thing aloud had made him realize there was at least one truth he still knew for certain. "I'm with you. Whatever comes, I'm with you."

"Good. That's good."

The dog got to his feet, stretched, and shook off a magnificent spray of rainwater, and then sauntered over to sit himself down between them, as though far too much fond attention was being wasted upon others. Molly reached out to find him and stroked his unruly fur as he nuzzled closer to her.

Something arrived then on the tail end of a gentle breeze, and it was the dog who caught it first. He sat up straight, head cocked and hackles rising, sharp eyes intent and trained to the north—right along the path they'd been traveling.

Hollis motioned for the others to be still, and after a

few quiet seconds he heard it, too. The rain had all but ceased, so there was nothing but distance to obscure the sound. It was the deep, steady note of a heavy engine up ahead, maybe more than one, approaching from just beyond a narrowing valley of young pine trees and tall Wyoming sage.

CHAPTER 6

They'd been found.

There was nothing else this could mean. In the midst of this vast open land it was all but inconceivable that they could have crossed paths with someone by random chance alone.

And they were neatly cut off, as well. At this juncture the terrain itself would allow only two ill-advised avenues of flight—either back the punishing way they'd come, or forward to confront these new arrivals. It was out of the question to just sit tight and hope to lie low. That would only delay the inevitable and forfeit their last remaining initiative, exceedingly weak though it might be.

If this was to be a surrender—and short of a miracle that was the only realistic expectation—by any civilized code of conduct it would go better for the group if they gave themselves up without resistance, completely and visibly unarmed. But so far the ruthlessness of their enemies seemed unbound by any rules of engagement. They'd already made it clear that they would show no mercy.

With that in mind he gave his handgun and its last full magazine to the man he judged most prepared to do what might have to be done.

Hollis gathered them all close and made his instructions clear. He would walk out alone to face whoever had arrived in those vehicles they'd heard. In the far-fetched event that all was well, he would come back alone to tell them so. Any other development—for example, the distant sounds of a field execution by firing squad—was to be taken as a sure sign that something was badly wrong. He wouldn't allow himself to be used as a front for their deception. If the group didn't soon see him returning precisely that way—alone, unharmed, and unfettered—then he wouldn't be returning at all.

At that point they would need to quickly decide which of them, if any, wished to be taken alive. Even before their costly escape, George Pierce had made his designs quite clear: there was nothing but certain death waiting in his camp. As for their other adversaries, the government-sponsored men, indefinite detention without trial or charges appeared to be the prevailing standard of justice for those suspected of crimes against the homeland. But far worse fates had been reported at their hands, and in far better times than these.

Everyone seemed to understand the need for decision, and they took on the weight of it with courage. For his part, Hollis spoke a few private words with Molly, slung the shotgun over his shoulder, and then set off down the valley to meet whatever fate lay beyond it.

At the far edge of a thick brushwood the sapling timber thinned down toward a long grassy clearing, and he saw them, about a quarter of a mile away.

There were two massive pickup trucks, fully jacked up for all-terrain and both parked sideways to the tree line. A number of people were milling about, a pair of them wrangling three large black dogs by the leash. Four men stood in the long beds of the trucks with rifles in their hands.

These weren't official vehicles, at least they weren't marked as such, and the type of camouflaged clothing worn by those he could see suggested a civilian hunting party rather than an organized militia. Not that it mattered much what the look of them suggested; these days wolves in sheep's clothing were everywhere. Regardless, he would carry on as planned and see what he would see.

With his courage fully gathered he walked out into the open at a casual pace, shotgun stowed at his back in an American carry, as though he might be just another fellow sportsman strolling on toward hearth and home.

They seemed to spot him immediately, and the quiet passage of the next few seconds was revealing.

If these men had orders to shoot on sight they would have done so by then, but they didn't. They drew together somewhat, as if in wary conference, and then spread out and squared off to wait for him. Still at long distance, he raised a hand to acknowledge the contact. No one waved back. Some did adjust the readiness of their weapons slightly, though none had yet taken aim.

As Hollis nearly reached spitting distance a young man stepped up to the edge of the high truck bed where he stood and motioned for him to stop, which he did.

"Afternoon," the young man said. While outwardly a simple word of greeting, it was nevertheless spoken in a way that suggested the serious hazard of making any sudden moves.

Hollis glanced upward briefly, and took a moment to gauge the present elevation of the sun.

"So it is," he replied.

"Who are you?"

"My name's Thom Hollis. And who might you be?"

The young man exchanged an even look with those on either side of him before answering. "If you were Thom Hollis, then I figure you should know who I might be."

He'd thought he noticed something about this gathering as he walked up, and there had been time enough since to reinforce that first vague perception. He hadn't imagined it; there was a family resemblance among them. Prominent in some, in others barely there, an old, sturdy bloodline was clearly shared among these uncles, cousins, sons, and brothers.

This meant something, but far from everything. It was only reason enough to proceed as he'd been told. "If I was to happen upon a stranger out here," Hollis said, "and if I judged him to be a man of merit, I was advised I should ask for Silas Deane."

These words brought on an extended and thoughtful study of his face. Though probably only seconds in length, by the time it passed, the wait had felt much longer.

"That's a shame, friend," the young man replied at last. "Old Silas, he's gone on to greener pastures."

As this other half of the pass-phrase was spoken in response, though Hollis realized he should have felt something, he didn't. Having long since abandoned hope, he had no place in his mind to receive it. He knew what he'd heard, and he knew what it meant: *rescue*. But there was no rush of joy, nor any other such emotion; it seemed instead as though all the preceding sleepless, harrowing miles of toil and near starvation had caught up and come down upon his shoulders at once.

His vision went a little gray and sparkly at the edges; the horizon began to tilt and swing toward a drifting axis. He noted with a strange indifference that he was falling, but as his knees gave way strong arms on either side took on the weight he could no longer bear alone.

CHAPTER 7

The rotor blades were still spinning down as Warren Landers unbuckled his harness, removed and hung his headset on its hook, logged the time and coordinates, and then felt for the readiness of the submachine gun in its quick-release mount by his side.

As soon as the bird was officially shut down he stowed his charts and set himself up for a smooth restart later on. With that accomplished Landers sat back with his commuter mug of hot black coffee to take in the oncoming sunrise and await the arrival of the white-pride welcome wagon.

The Pierce compound had proved nearly impossible to find in the heart of this endless, rolling green sea of trees, mountains, and meadows. Even with the Terminator-vision of forward-looking infrared sensors he'd missed it in the predawn darkness and flown right past several times. The already minimal heat signature of the place seemed to be even further masked by cooling baffles, diffuser vents, buried outlet ducts, and other stealthy tricks usually employed only by first-class indoor marijuana farms.

Those precautions—in conjunction with the ingenious way the structure and its outbuildings were virtually buried in the surrounding forest—all made this remote hideout nearly invisible, even at close range. It certainly hadn't shown up in the few lo-res satellite images that had been available on short notice. Whatever their other failings of intellect and character, it was quite a feat for a rogue band of civilians to manage to hide so well in this surveillance age.

Even after he found them he'd had no success in trying to announce his proximity by radio, much less to negotiate clearance to land. Apparently these mongrels were interested only in talking among themselves; they maintained some kind of primitive analog scrambler on their ham signals and repeaters, and Landers hadn't brought along the specialized equipment required to crack such an old-school code.

Though they obviously valued their seclusion, once past any tense introductions he really didn't expect much hostility. The chopper's rear compartment had room for half a squad of hired soldiers and a mounted minigun if he'd ordered them, but the upcoming negotiation was one he'd elected to attend alone.

Not to imply that he was without protection—this Talion-owned MD600N was souped-up and loaded-out for twenty-first-century urban riot control. As such, the machine bristled with an arsenal of autonomous, hands-free antipersonnel weaponry as well as a raft of advanced targeting and spying gear. These made the helicopter, much like its veteran pilot, more than capable of both kicking ass and taking down names.

The control panel in front of him was dominated by a large multifunction touchscreen, which at the moment displayed a live picture of his surroundings in glowing 3-D wireframe. In its onscreen image the nearby multifloor log house was shown to contain the moving hot spots of more than fifty people clumped about in several locations. Many of them appeared to be armed and all had begun to converge toward the front of the place, apparently so they could observe their new arrival more clearly.

Since this was both a surprise visit and a first in-person encounter, it seemed wisest to let them come to him in their own time. When guys like these see a black helicopter land in their front yard, you need to give them a few minutes to calm down.

At length an exploratory party appeared from around the leeward side of the house. They came slowly, guns raised and ready as they advanced across the open ground. The aircraft recognized the danger and responded by initializing its active-denial electronics. A near-ultrasonic whine ascended behind him as the weapons charged and locked on, but Landers touched the onscreen button labeled HOLD, and only waited.

Despite some dark clouds that had begun to gather to the north, it was light enough by then to see the men clearly. As he sipped his coffee and followed their approach he was vaguely reminded of another scene, though it took a thoughtful moment to make the connection. It was an image from the opening minutes of *2001: A Space Odyssey*, when those early hominids had crept forth from their filthy caves one prehistoric morning to find an unexpected messenger. They gathered around it in wonder, awestruck, marveling at the dark obelisk that had arrived from somewhere beyond their understanding to nudge them toward an evolutionary rise.

He returned his mug to the cup-holder, reached into a side pouch of his satchel in the passenger seat, took a fistful from the many pounds of Krugerrands there, and then cracked open the door and tossed a small shower of gold coins out onto the nearby ground.

At first only one of the men outside broke ranks, and then another did, and another, until finally all but one of them had laid down their weapons and dropped to their knees to hunt for the shiny treasure he'd scattered in the rough-mown weeds.

The last armed man kept his discipline, and gave a specific, silent order with a motion from the muzzle of his gun. Landers eased the door open wide and smiled his most winning smile, his hands held high in mock surrender.

"Take me to your leader," he said.

CHAPTER 8

Inside the labyrinthine house the dank atmosphere was heavy with hanging smoke and the pungent stink of mold and close living. The halls were a trifle narrow, the rooms haphazardly placed, the doorways cut a little too low; refined architecture is something you so rarely notice until it isn't there.

He'd been thoroughly searched at three different stations, and Landers was still walking at gunpoint. Nevertheless, along the way he'd begun to sense that his escorts knew how to treat a superior being when they encountered one. They'd grown effusively polite as they directed his way through all the circuitous halls. Near the final flight of stairs one of them excused himself and ran on ahead, perhaps to alert the man in charge should he wish to groom himself before the arrival of a visiting dignitary.

After a final pat-down the guard detail left him on the shag-carpeted landing at the top of the steps.

Framed by the last open doorway, George Pierce was seated at the head of an austere conference table built up of sawhorses and wavy sheets of knotty plywood. A pair of shaved-headed, muscle-bound hooligans stood by, one on either side of his highness, each doing his level best to look as threatening as possible.

Pierce himself was a slighter wisp of a man than his notorious credentials might have suggested. Not that a bantamweight should lack authority simply because of his size, but in this one's self-conscious comportment, even while seated, he seemed determined to puff himself up in a way that only emphasized his below-average stature.

The monogrammed satchel from the helicopter's passenger seat was on the table at the far end, already fully ransacked, pockets splayed open, and contents stacked to the side. Landers's personal effects and identification had also been laid out for examination.

"That money is a greeting to you from my employer," Landers said. "It's about a half million in gold, and a few hundred thousand in laundered bills—"

"My men and I can count all right," George Pierce replied. He paused to glance again at the details of the open passport before him. "Mr. Warren Francis Landers, is it?"

"That's correct."

"What you brought there has bought you five minutes."

"Well, then. I suppose we'd best dispense with all pleasantries and get down to the brass tacks." Landers pulled a chair around and took a seat at his end of the table, flicked out his silver reading glasses and put them on, and then as an afterthought looked over the top of the half frames with a question. "May we speak freely in front of your associates?"

Pierce hesitated a little longer than he should have, and then he nodded.

"Fine." Landers caught the eye of one of the henchmen, pointed across the table to a pair of navy blue folders from his emptied bag, and said, "We'll need those."

When there was no immediate movement to comply,

he snapped his fingers and made a sharp come-hither gesture with his hand, as though summoning a tardy waiter for a neglected refill. With only this minor test of dominance-response the man seemed to instantly set aside his former attitude. He sprang into service like Pavlov's executive assistant, taking up the folders and placing one in front of each of the seated men.

"We'd like some cold water also," Landers said, and the man gave an earnest nod and left to fetch the refreshments with barely a glance back toward Pierce for his leave. "Now," Landers said as he opened his folder to its agenda page, "the first and most pressing order of business is this Ross woman—"

"Oh, I'm way out ahead of you on that score," Pierce said. "Thirty men left here not an hour ago, hot on the scent. She'll be dead and gone by sundown, and damn glad by then to be that way."

"No, she will not be," Landers said. "I want you to call back your men immediately. We're going to let her go."

"We?" Pierce laughed the word aloud and nearly triggered a fit of coughing in this blurt of his amusement. "Who is this 'we' you're talking about now? *We?* From where I sit, as of now I've got the better part of a million dollars and a brand-new helly-copter on my hands"—he checked his watch—"and you've got about four minutes left to breathe."

"You need to call back your men, immediately."

"Screw the four minutes." Pierce looked up at the remaining man beside him. "Do me a favor and put a hollow-point through the empty skull of this highfalutin son of a bitch."

The guard slipped his revolver from its holster and drew down and pulled back the hammer with his thumb, one slick motion and a steady, practiced ease with the prospect of killing an unarmed man.

Landers held up an index finger, as though to offer a polite suggestion for a wayward employee. "May I have a few last words, then?" he asked.

"This I've gotta hear."

He closed the folder, removed his glasses, and calmly began.

"We're already silent partners, Mr. Pierce, though you haven't realized it. Aside from one notable failure last year—again involving the troublesome Molly Ross—you've done good work for us in the past. The source of the funding and the guidance you've received remained in the shadows, but we're on the cusp of a great opportunity now, and the time is right to formalize our arrangement. You're free to decline, of course; at the moment it seems you're determined to do so. It's only fair that I tell you what it means if you do.

"Until this morning we didn't know precisely where to find you, nor had there been a particular need to do so. You enjoyed the safety of a hidden asset, but that's no longer to be the case. Since I landed, the sensors in that helicopter out there have been collecting, and recording, and relaying a torrent of information, all about you. It's listening to us right now. By now this headquarters of yours is pinpointed and mapped to the millimeter, and every man here has been identified and profiled with enough data to track him down wherever he might try to run. I'm sure you see how these new facts might weigh on your decision.

"Because I am at this moment overdue to check in with my employers," Landers continued, "about twenty minutes ago a small squadron of armed Predator drones and an A-10 Thunderbolt took off from the same private air base from which I departed earlier this morning. If you're not familiar with the primary weapon of the A-10, let me describe it for you. It's a Gatling gun that would span this room, loaded with depleted-uranium-tipped high-explosive shells the size of a Coke bottle, and it fires those at a rate of almost four thousand rounds per minute. The only way to improve on this gun as a killing machine, its designers once said, would be to make it fly. That's the A-10, and right now it's coming for you.

"Understand, this is not a rescue mission. Once they're convinced by my continued silence that I've failed to usher you into our service, they'll simply erase us all, myself included, and their plans will then proceed without pause, and without you and me. And one last thing you should know, if it's crossed your mind to try to coerce me into calling them off. It won't work, though you're free to waste our final minutes in the attempt."

He leaned forward to rest his elbows on the table. "You see," Landers said, "if I have to die, this is exactly how I want to do it. Looking into the eyes of a man who's about to see the wrath of hell rain down on him, and everything he's built be destroyed, all because he didn't have the good common sense to choose prosperity instead."

George Pierce sat quite speechless, and one got the distinct impression this was a state with which he was rather unaccustomed.

Landers had first seen this look in a man's eyes in the mid-1970s when he was only a fresh recruit. The circumstances of these standard introductory meetings differed, but this look never changed. It was dread mostly, gradually dawning, with the slightest whiff of desperate hope to color in the edges. To stare one's destiny in the face is a difficult thing—to reach that decision point when a tinhorn tyrant must choose between his own shortsighted ambitions and the many benefits of taking on a smaller role in the bigger picture.

His diplomatic efforts had always been confined to domestic players: party leaders, entrenched career politicians, union officials, rising icons of various social movements, media moguls, pundits and thought leaders, judges and legislators, masters of finance and industry, so-called community organizers of all shapes and sizes, even religious figures if they'd shown the proper appetites for corruption and control.

While Landers worked exclusively within North America, his colleagues had sat across similar tables all around the globe. They'd watched this same moment of truth dawn upon a hundred self-styled luminaries: Hussein, Qaddafi, Chávez, Kim, Duvalier, Mugabe, Karimov, Amin, Shwe, al-Bashir, al-Assad, Mubarak, Thein Sein, Afewerki, Biya, Zenawi, Ahmadinejad, Castro, Assad, Déby, Obiang, Museveni, Lukashenko—as the wheels of progress turned year by year the puppet list grew longer.

There'd been a real piece of work in Gambia who insisted on being addressed as *His Excellency Sheikh Professor Alhaji Dr. Yahya Abdul-Azziz Jemus Junkung Jammeh.* That hubris was short-lived indeed. Behind closed doors this one now answers simply to *Hadji,* and he's learned to accept this private mockery without objection. To such a man the reward for giving up his dignity was worth that small price paid. In return for doing as he was told he got to dress up like a real head of state, parade around in a long limousine, and indulge in his unique perversions with reckless abandon. And, if he continued to play his cards just right, he would also get to die in office of old age.

Obviously not everyone has the right stuff, both to get on board and then to ride to the end of the line. It remained to be seen on which side of the ledger the name of today's candidate would be written.

"Now then, George," Landers said, "what will it be? Death in obscurity, or an excellent chance to attain all your goals simply by playing a minor role in mine?"

Outside, that growing storm in the northern sky had nearly arrived and a low roll of thunder filled the silence as Pierce considered what his answer would be. To his credit, his deliberation didn't last very long.

"What is it that you want me to do?"

Landers smiled, replaced his glasses on his nose, and opened his folder once again. "First, you need to call back the men you've sent after Molly Ross. She's in our thoughts, believe me, but we're going to let her go for now."

After a seething moment George Pierce looked up at the guard beside him, who'd long since seen which way the wind was blowing and quietly reholstered his gun. Pierce gave a nod to pass along the order, and when the man had left he looked across the table again with something like respect in his eyes. Close enough for today, in any case.

"And what next?"

"What next?" Landers said. "Next, Mr. Pierce, we're going to spit upon our hands, hoist the black flag, and begin slitting throats."

CHAPTER 9

In a sudden swoon of vertigo Thom Hollis snapped wide awake with a start, heart pounding, drenched in a frigid sweat and clutching the quilted comforter like a slick lifeline. His throat was raw and his breathing labored, and though he felt all these physical things and knew that the warm, darkened room around him must be real, it still took the solemn march of several seconds before he could assure himself he was alive.

With the heavy curtains drawn there was just enough daylight seeping in to gauge the proportions of a large guest suite and trace the outlines of unfamiliar furniture. A silent figure stood backlit in the doorway with what appeared to be a basket in its hands.

"Who is that?"

"You called out just before," came the quiet answer. "You're safe now. Your friend Molly and all the others are okay, too."

Bedside lamps lit with the click of a wall switch and the woman who'd been standing there came into the room. The wicker basket she held was filled with pressed and folded clothes, and she placed it on a low dresser, pulled out a wide drawer, opened a closet, and began to put away the laundry.

"You'll have to pardon me, ma'am—but who are you, and where am I?"

She spoke to him as she worked. Her tone was genuinely pleasant, though hued with the good-natured patience of one who was explaining something very simple for the second time around.

"I'm Cathy Merrick. This is my dad's place. This is your room, and these are your clothes—the tatters you wore when you got here, along with some other things I figured might just fit you. The rest of the family met you for a few minutes yesterday night. In the state you all were in, I guess I'm not too surprised if you don't remember."

But he did remember, vaguely. The face reflected in the dresser mirror was handsome and mature, with clear brown eyes that seemed subtly amused by some unshared thought just behind them. These features were framed with dark brown hair that fell easily around her shoulders. A wisp of mid-thirties premature gray played here and there, along with the sort of highlights the sun would have left throughout a life lived in the great outdoors.

She looked more familiar, in fact, than his own more distant image alongside her in the glass. The man there looked quite thin and substantially younger than he felt, all due to the extra weight he'd gradually lost over their long winter on the run. He touched his cheek—the skin was clean-shaven for the first time in years.

"Oh, that reminds me." She came over to sit next to him, then took his chin to turn the far side of his face toward the nearest lamp. "You've got a cut here at the jawline that probably should have had a couple of stitches a few days ago." As he moved to feel the spot she stopped his hand with a gentle smack, as one might correct a greedy child about to take another cookie out of turn. "Just leave it be; we'll see how it heals. I had to shave that part to treat the laceration, and then you looked kind of funny that way, so I took off the rest."

She must have noticed he was fixating again on his transfigured face in the mirror across the room. "For heaven's sake, that bushy old beard'll grow back if you want it to. And you told me you didn't mind; you were talking to me all friendly just like you were downtown with the boys at the barbershop."

"I hope I didn't say anything I should be ashamed of."

"Oh no, you were quite the complimentary gentleman, even if you weren't strictly conscious. Exhaustion and running yourself half starved for weeks on end begins to play some havoc with the mind." She looked at him, with the slightest frown on her face. "You really can't recall?"

He shook his head, then pushed himself up through some sharp aches and pains to sit back against the headboard. "I don't even remember getting into this bed."

"Last night, while I was looking after some of the others, the men came to let me know you'd fallen asleep in the shower. So, we cleaned you up real good and dried you off and I found something for you to sleep in, and then we put you down for the night." She checked the clock on the wall. "That was about twenty hours ago."

He felt his face getting red. "You all got me dressed?"

She smiled at him, took his wrist, found the pulse, and turned her head aside again so she could watch the second hand as she counted the beats. "I was married for eleven years, I'm a rancher's only daughter in a family of nine, and I've been called upon to patch up farmhands and cowpokes since I was a teenager. Don't you worry, Mr. Hollis, you can rest assured I came across no undiscovered country."

"Try as I might, I'm finding little solace there."

"Do you have a headache at all?" Now she was running her hands over his unkempt hair, as though checking for signs of an unreported blow to the skull.

"No."

"The boys tell me that you fainted out there, when they found you."

"I wouldn't put it like that, exactly. Just let myself get stretched too thin, I guess, and the burden got the better of me."

"And they also said that even after that you insisted on walking back into the woods all alone to bring out your people."

Hollis nodded, though much of the memory was there only in bits and pieces.

"This loss of consciousness, has anything like that ever happened before?"

"I've had a . . ." He sought the proper words for a moment. "Since I got back from the war I've had a bad spell or two. Hadn't happened in years, though. They told me that stress could bring it on. And I guess I'm just not as young as I used to be."

She frowned a bit, and the transition from casual conversation to thinly disguised bedside exam was smooth and professional. As she continued he answered her questions and complied with each prompt and instruction, following her moving finger with his eyes, extending his arms and touching his nose, pressing against her outstretched palms with his own when so directed.

"Do you feel any nausea, or dizziness?"

"No, I don't."

A young lady arrived with a small wooden tray of fruit, bread, sliced cheese, and a tall glass of water. She handed the food to Cathy Merrick, the two exchanged some quiet words, and then the girl left again the way she'd come.

"Mom thought you'd be hungry," Cathy said, "but don't eat too much too fast." She rearranged some things, slid the tray onto the nightstand within his reach, and then walked over to the window. "You missed lunch already, so some of that can tide you over until dinnertime. Now, are you ready to see some sunshine?"

"I think I am."

She pulled the heavy outer drapes aside to the edges of a large bay window behind them, then drew the inner curtains by their braided cord. "There you go," Cathy said. "That's the best view we've got."

"Thank you."

"I'll send Tyler by to see you when you've had time to take care of your necessities." She retrieved her basket and started for the door. "He's my son, and he'll walk you around the place a bit, just so you can get your legs underneath you again."

Hollis was so absorbed in the magnificent view of the grounds beyond the window that he managed only a slow, inadequate nod in answer to her question. "Thank you," he heard himself repeat after a while longer, though when he glanced her way he found she'd already slipped out by then to leave him to his thoughts.

CHAPTER 10

Though his sleep had been troubled, it had served its purpose. After such a lengthy day of rest, in fact, Hollis felt he might never need another.

When the escort Cathy Merrick had offered failed to arrive in due time he decided to venture out on his own.

The hallway was spacious and meticulously rustic, all hardwoods and polish with native art hung here and there and simple Shaker furnishings. An old grandfather clock stood watch in a narrow alcove. Next to the clock was an oil painting of some stern pioneer who'd survived Red Cloud's War only to be reluctantly captured in canvas and hung up in a gilded frame.

At the far end of the hall the space opened out into a soaring log-framed atrium with several cozy sitting areas, well-stocked bookshelves, and a massive fieldstone fireplace that easily spanned twelve feet from end to end. This all engendered a homespun, welcoming atmosphere that nevertheless carried more the feel of a fine country hotel than a private residence.

He found Molly's suite near the corner. The door had been left half open; she was seated at a mirrored vanity near the far wall, facing away, wrapped in a woolly plaid dressing gown. Two older women attended to her, one fixing her hair in a braided ponytail while the other held her hands and finessed a long-neglected manicure. They didn't notice him as they fussed and smiled and spoke among themselves, and he didn't interrupt. For the moment he knew all he needed to; she was fine.

When Hollis looked to the atrium again he saw a young man of maybe sixteen years, sitting off alone in the corner of the large space. He was slumped down in a reclining posture, feet up on the burl-oak slab of a coffee table, completely absorbed in the content of an animated screen in his hands. On the assumption that this was the boy assigned to be his guide, he walked over and sat nearby.

"Are you Tyler?"

"Hold on."

The big-screen cell phone the boy was interacting with was more visible from this distance. He was playing a game, it appeared, dragging and tapping with a finger to slingshot cartoon birds toward a series of breakable structures.

Hollis watched and waited through another similar level or two, and then, seeing no intent in the boy to stop what he was doing, he got up to leave. "I don't mean to be a bother," he said. "I can show myself around."

"Jesus, just a second," the boy huffed. "I'll be right with you, okay?" He sighed and went through a quick procedure to save his progress and put the device into standby. "She told me to give you the tour, so I'd better give you the tour. I really don't need my mom any further up my ass today."

The impulse to apply a swift discipline to another person's offspring had rarely been stronger, but for a couple of weak reasons Hollis simply took a deep, cleansing breath and put it aside. Despite the boy's offhanded discourtesy to his absent mother, Hollis was reluctant to spoil his still-sunny mood by calling out the offense. Also, he was a guest, and it might test the bounds of hospitality to start a conversation that could easily end in a headlock. So he let it pass and only followed as the boy tucked away his phone and walked on ahead.

"If you're sure it's not too much trouble for you," Hollis said.

"Don't get too excited, bro," Tyler replied. "There's not that much to see."

The most expensive home in America is not in New York, or Honolulu, or Beverly Hills, but in Wyoming. This wasn't that home, Tyler was quick to note, but the once-humble Merrick ranch was regularly in and out of the top ten whenever such lists were compiled.

As they walked, through a series of one-word answers and bored descriptions from his guide Hollis was gradually able to glean a better understanding of the place and the people who lived there.

The boy's ancestors had made their substantial fortune in cattle, mineral rights, and various speculations. Since frontier times no part of the estate had ever left the family's hands. Today the spread was best known as an upscale dude ranch and a twelve-thousand-acre training facility for working horses and their riders. The roster of regular clients included people of all stripes, from reclusive billionaires and celebrities to national rodeo stars. There was also a long waiting list of normal-Joe vacationers who might save up for years in order to flee their teeming cities for a few precious weeks of a saner, simpler life.

These days the lion's share of any profits quietly went toward charitable endeavors. Throughout the summer the ranch played host to a number of youth retreats from service groups, and no child's request from the Make-A-Wish Foundation had ever been denied.

The guest annex where Hollis and the other new arrivals were staying was of relatively new construction.
On the private side of the atrium the original house
had been built around, added to, and augmented with
modern conveniences. Most of the growing lineage of
the Merrick family made their home in those quarters,
and they all made their living off the land. Tyler's great-
grandmother, in fact, still stayed in the rooms she'd
shared with her late husband back when this place was
still just a small, hand-built outpost in the heart of a lot
of rugged, untamed land.

The ranch was normally closed to guests during the
harsh winter season, and without much public explanation it had remained closed well beyond that time this
year.

This is where Tyler Merrick's understanding of the
recent goings-on became sketchy and incomplete. Whatever was currently happening, the details were being
guarded and shared on a need-to-know basis, and evidently there was a lot he didn't need to know. Still, he
seemed to have a sense that something slightly unlawful might be afoot this week. While that clearly didn't
trouble his morals he seemed very curious as to the
clandestine nature of these latest guests.

It turned out that Tyler was new to these surroundings himself. His parents had finally split up after a long
separation and sold their house in Albuquerque as the
assets were divided. His mother, Cathy, had left her life as
a successful graphic artist, moved back to her childhood
home, reclaimed her maiden name for them both, and
dragged her son along into this socially barren wilderness to start all over again.

While the boy had met these relatives over the years
he'd never imagined he'd one day be living with them.
Though he didn't say so, despite any warm welcomes it

would be hard for even a well-adjusted teenager in such a spot to feel like anything but an outsider.

The tour concluded at a small wooden pier on the lakefront, and they went to the end and sat down on its edge to rest. Having now walked a bit of the grounds, as far as Hollis could see it was all as picturesque as it had seemed through his window. But more striking than the view itself was how these surroundings made him feel. For the first time in months he found he could look at the horizon with no dread of what might soon be storming over it.

He heard a distracted, private laugh next to him, and Hollis glanced that way and leaned to read what was on the screen. He was so alarmed by what he saw that he nearly knocked the boy into the lake as he snatched the phone from his hands and canceled the entry before it could be sent.

Tyler's immediate verbal reaction went quiet in mid-profanity. Even if he didn't know what he'd almost done, it seemed by the look on his face that he knew he was in trouble.

"I'm sorry—"

"I'm afraid sorry's just not gonna cut it," Hollis said. "Your folks told you we were lying low here, didn't they? And you know what that means, don't you?"

"I said I was sorry. God, I didn't mean anything—"

"What you typed was *Showing some hilbilly around the farm. Somebody please shoot me.*" Hollis put the de-activated device into one of his pockets and its battery into another. "First off, you need to be careful what you wish for. Second, there are four *l*'s in *hillbilly*. And third, I imagine the reason your mother is up your backside so often, as you say, is because she damn well needs to be. Every year you get older, the mistakes you can make get bigger, and the consequences get harder to survive."

Before the boy could speak Hollis held up a hand to quiet him. "I don't need to hear a thing you've got to say right now, but you need to hear this. That phone's got a microphone and a camera, so it can see and hear whatever's around it. It can recognize a face, understand words, and match a voiceprint. It's got an accelerometer, so it knows when you sit, when you stand, and which way you're walking. It's got a GPS receiver that tracks where you are within a five-foot circle. And whether you know it or not, you've signed over your permission to strangers to monitor and make a record of all those things every minute of the day. Google's a quarter-of-a-trillion-dollar company but they give away almost every product they make for free. Don't you know what they're selling to make all that money? They're selling *you*.

"You wouldn't trust your best friend with what that phone knows about you, and yet you trust all those strangers lurking out there in the cloud, who've all said time and again that privacy is a relic of the past and a man's wish for it is a cause for suspicion. If you're dumb enough to believe that way, then go right on ahead. But you will not imperil me or mine with your foolishness."

The boy sat silent, and when he worked himself up to speak again his voice was timid. "Are you going to tell my mom?"

"No, I'm not. You're going to tell her, all about it, and then I'll be having a talk with both of you after dinner. Now get on back home."

Hollis turned away to look out across the water.

When the boy had left him alone Hollis stayed and thought and waited, but no trace of the serenity he'd felt just before would be returning. The unsullied vastness of this sovereign land shrank before his eyes, retreating to within its fragile, unprotected borders. This ranch was an island of peace and personal liberty, he'd allowed himself to think, a place of safety, and maybe even a glimmer of hope for a better future. But an island is another thing he'd failed until then to consider.

Surrounded.

CHAPTER 11

Upon his return to the main farmhouse Hollis stopped by to ask a favor of the fellow he'd been told was in charge of security and technological matters. Then, without identifying a specific offender, he made it clear that some strict remedial instruction should be given to all residents right away, particularly regarding the safe use of electronic communications during this sensitive time.

On his way to see Molly he took a shortcut through the kitchen. As the evening meal was being prepared the large bright room was a gauntlet of elbows, steaming pans, and jovial clatter, and few took much notice as he edged his way by. Near the swinging doors to the dining room, though, he did catch the eye of Cathy Merrick. By the carefree wink she gave him it seemed she hadn't yet heard the latest news from her wayward son.

Hollis arrived at Molly's room to find her alone, kneeling at the foot of her bed in prayer, hands clasped beneath her chin.

From his watchtower on an overstuffed easy chair in the corner, the dog *whuffed* to announce to his mistress that she had a visitor.

Molly breathed a few more earnest phrases and finished, then turned her head toward the door and got to her feet. "That's you, isn't it, Hollis?"

"It is." How exactly she'd known that, he didn't pause right then to wonder.

She took a small step and beckoned to him with open arms. There was a sweet, brittle smile on her face that seemed burdened underneath by some awful sadness. She caught her breath as though a flood of tears were on their way, and he went to her and hugged her close against his chest. There was nothing to be said or done for the moment; whatever grief it was that had overtaken her, he let her cry it out.

This was so unlike the old Molly Ross. In earlier times she'd kept her emotions well guarded and such displays of vulnerability were rare.

"I'm sorry," she whispered, after the worst of it had passed. "I know I need to be stronger."

"Don't trouble yourself now. I'd say you've been plenty strong enough."

They sat for a while, then, and caught up with one another. The Merrick family, he learned, were long-time friends of the Founders' Keepers—true dyed-in-the-wool libertarians and covert financial supporters of Molly's late mother and her cause. They'd volunteered their home as a shelter for the group more than a year before. Unlike some fair-weather patriots who scarcely dared to dip a toe into the shallows of the movement, these folks had stood by their offer to help even as the crisis in the country grew worse and worse. Until now, for their protection Molly had kept almost every detail of the family's involvement to herself.

Next she filled him in on the status of their companions, her brief time in the clutches of George Pierce, and some details of the past day that Hollis had nearly slept through. At length it seemed only a single topic remained to be raised. Throughout the conversation he could almost see her avoiding it; the answer would stay safely unreal if the question went unasked. But in the end she did ask about him.

"Have you heard anything about Noah Gardner?"

This was somewhat telling, the way she used his full name, as though to hold that rare, painful brush with intimacy at a more formal and comfortable distance.

In her role as her mother's civilian intelligence agent, Molly had worked her way into the lives of any number of gullible marks in the loftiest realms of the country's plutocracy. Most of them had been privileged young men of high position—political aides to corrupted candidates, media insiders, union apparatchiks, rising stars in nongovernmental organizations, sons of crony capitalists, Wall Street prodigies—all heirs to the unelected thrones of power bent on subverting the American way of life to their own selfish ends. Through one deception or another they'd each been charmed into revealing whatever small part of the enemy agenda had been entrusted to them. Once the prize was in hand and put to good use, she'd vanished and moved on to the next unsuspecting target without ever looking back.

Noah Gardner had once been just another of these brief, dispassionate assignments, but for a number of unexpected reasons her time with him had become a different story altogether.

"I haven't heard much of anything about anybody yet," Hollis said. "The last we knew for sure they were going to send him out with those so-called government peacekeepers that are hunting us now, I guess as some sort of a slap in the face to both of you." He hesitated to say more, but there seemed little use in pretending things were any better than they were. He couldn't lie to her, and only a lie would put her mind at ease. "I thought

I saw him through the scope, in fact, the other morning up at Gannett Peak."

"You saw him there?"

"It sure looked like him to me. They'd put a rifle into his hands and by the way he held it I doubt he'd ever touched a loaded gun before. They might as well have hung a bull's-eye on his back to go along with it."

"And what happened?"

"I sent a bullet past his ear to remind him to keep his head down at least, but I lost track of him once things lit off." He patted her knee, and she put her hand on his. "We know people that might be near to him, at least near enough to know. I'll try to find out later if he's—if he's all right, and where they've taken him next."

"Thank you."

"Now come on, let's eat. They've got enough glazed ham, and roast chicken, and salt potatoes in there to feed an army."

CHAPTER 12

The spread looked like four Thanksgivings, every homemade morsel of it mounded in steaming dishes around a long banquet table set with polished silver, cloth napkins, and company china. When everyone had taken their seats, the patriarch of the family stood at his place and spoke his welcome, introducing each of the guests by name and background as though he'd known them all his life.

Hollis had, in fact, known most of these ten people for as long as he could remember. Of late he'd known them chiefly as a disheveled band of tired, filthy, and cantankerous vagabonds who could neither run fast enough nor shoot straight enough to be of much use as legitimate fugitives. But looking around the table now as each one was called out in turn he began to see them differently again, through the admiring eyes of another.

As the name of their organization suggested, these ten had sworn an oath to be keepers of the words and thoughts of their nation's Founding Fathers. It was really as harmless as that, and not at all a political movement in its beginnings. They'd started out as nothing more than a quaint conservation society, a counterpoint to what they perceived as the subversive, progressive rewriting of mainstream U.S. history.

Each of the group's members had responsibility to preserve a single Founder's written wisdom. This wasn't a simple matter of rote memorization, though that's where each apprentice always started. Something odd would always happen then: after a few weeks of total immersion a peculiar transformation would begin to manifest in these people, as if the vital spirit captured on the page might be coming alive again to take up partial residence in a new incarnation.

He took a look around the table and paused a moment on each of his people as they sat interspersed among the Merricks. Day to day, to Hollis these ten were Doris, and Mae, and Paul, and Miles, and Grace, and Jeremiah; twin brothers Bill and Ronald; their father, Gene; and then Molly. Seeing them now, well dressed, upstanding, and largely recovered from their latest ordeal, he could also detect in them the faint but unmistakable presence of their alter egos: Hancock, Adams, Allen, Rush, Paine, Hamilton, Madison, and Jay. As Jefferson had proved to be too much for any single vessel to contain, his essence was divided evenly between the two brothers.

They'd never found a decent George Washington, and now with the death of Ben Church the group had lost their Benjamin Franklin as well. There had been others, too, who'd disappeared, defected, or otherwise fallen away in the past year as the going got tough. But as of tonight these core survivors were alive and well, and after a hot bath and a good day's rest they appeared to have once again begun to take on the distinguished mantle of their namesakes.

Hollis was seated next to Molly's place of honor at the foot of the table. When his time came he was briefly introduced, with only a few kind words to gild the lily, and thus his role in the group was left appropriately

vague. Then, with the opening toast complete, one of
the grandchildren was asked to step up and say grace.

As the child began to speak every head was bowed
to partake in her sweet, simple prayer, with only three
exceptions. Hollis himself was one of these outliers; he
generally used such ritual pauses to attend to his own private thoughts and observations. The second was young
Tyler Merrick, whose gaze seemed downcast mainly to
avoid eye contact with the big mean man on the end
who'd taken away his phone earlier in the day.

The last of these nonparticipants was seated at the
head of the table, down at the far end almost directly
opposite him. She was an old woman, very old it seemed,
who appeared to be composed of little more than ghost-
white hair, barbed wire, vinegar, and whit-leather. She
wasn't concerning herself with the prayer or the piety
of the other dinner guests; her attention was fixed on
only one person.

Old age can etch a sour expression onto a person's
face, but that alone couldn't account for the ire he saw
burning behind those sharp, watery eyes. As this frail,
withered woman stared across the table at Thom Hollis,
she looked for all the world as though she knew him,
and loathed him with every ancient fiber of her being.

He'd suddenly found his appetite wasn't what it should
have been, and just as soon as good manners allowed,
Hollis had quietly excused himself. He wandered to the
great room, perused the shelves, selected a Faulkner
novel he'd always hoped to tackle, and took a seat alone
to read by the light of the fire.

Later, when dinner was finished and the others began
to filter in to have their coffee, he closed his book and
retired to his suite. There he found the laptop computer
he'd requested earlier, opened on his desk and ready to

run. It had been several weeks since he'd had even brief online access so there was a great deal of catching up to be done.

The machine was configured for maximum stealth in its internet connection, bouncing all masked requests and responses through heavy firewalls, virtual private networks, and shadow servers scattered around the world. The performance was slow and spotty due to all this security, but the trade-offs were necessary and the setup would be more than adequate for his needs.

He'd just finished tapping into the group's many e-mail accounts to begin the long download of messages when Cathy Merrick and her son came to his door. She apologized profusely for the boy's confessed behavior, and this time when Tyler said he was sorry it was clear that he spoke from the heart. He'd obviously been read the riot act from multiple directions already, but Hollis felt the need to make the central point once again.

"There are lives on the line here, son," he said, "and my people and your folks believe there's a great deal more at stake than only that. Do you understand?"

The boy nodded.

"Good. Let's not speak of it again. Now, I'll be out in your uncle's workshop tomorrow morning at seven. I want you to come by then, seven sharp, and I'll give back what I took from you." Before the mother could raise an objection he continued on. "The people hunting us are looking for a trail to follow. There isn't much friendly shelter out here that we could have reached by this time, and one thing they'll be looking for is a place that's gone quiet, where something's changed in the past couple of days. We have to assume they're watching everyone and everything, and that means all of you here need to behave just like you did before, like nothing's any different. Okay?"

Tyler didn't respond until his mom gave a mild thump to the back of his head, and then he said, "Okay."

Hollis stood and walked over to them. "I regret I'll have to say good night to you both now. Ma'am, I hope you have a pleasant rest, and I thank you again for your kindness today. And Tyler, I'll see you tomorrow morning."

When they'd gone he closed the door and returned his attention to the scrolling computer screen. Though the massive influx of messages was far from complete he began to scan the subject lines and summaries to gauge their general tone.

From the old public boxes it was all-caps hate mail mostly, rife with the sort of empty threats, vulgar slurs, and general ugliness that anonymity promotes in the lowest class of mind. Already it was obvious that only a tiny fraction of what came in here would prove worthy to be passed along to the group for reading and response.

Next he opened a Web browser and clicked to one major news site after another to check the headlines.

He couldn't say what he'd expected to see being reported about Molly and her righteous struggle of good versus evil, but he had to sit for a while to fully comprehend what he actually found there.

Not a solitary word.

After these many grueling months and the sweat and toil they'd spent at the front lines of a battle for the very future of their country, according to the obedient, complicit mainstream media it had all apparently happened only in their fevered minds.

Instead the top-line "news" was filled with the vain antics of celebrities, breathless details of the scandal of the week, sports highlights, puff pieces, PR plants, and the opulent wedding plans of some royal offspring overseas. The rest was rounded out by name-calling and grandstanding from politicians and pundits embroiled in the upcoming national elections.

When any hint of the looming worldwide meltdown got a mention at all, it was there only to be spun toward someone's cynical agenda: the Fed chairman declaring that his next money-printing spree was all that could save us from ruin, the DHS head fear-mongering in her pitch for even more draconian search-and-seizure tactics to be aimed at ordinary Americans, and the incumbent President leading by deflection, still spouting vague and empty campaign promises while laying all blame at every doorstep but his own.

But the free press was still alive out there. Despite all attempts to tame the fourth estate, the Internet had spawned a million independent sources of real news, from amateurs and professionals alike. The best of them owed no allegiance to anything but the truth. They were doing their job as reporters, in other words. And as one might expect, their work was either being ridiculed by the old guard, attacked with blunt force, or marginalized, buried several levels deep under a never-ending flood of manufactured propaganda and infotainment.

As he gradually found and read these reliable sources he saw a chilling picture emerging—and it was all unfolding just as Molly's mother had predicted years before.

The lit fuse on $1.5 quadrillion in bogus financial derivatives had now burned down to within a hairsbreadth of the powder. Spain and Portugal were at the brink of fiscal and social catastrophe. Greece was already on fire, its economy destroyed and teetering like the first domino in a fragile line poised to tear across Europe and then on around the globe. And sure enough, sponsored revolutions igniting from North Africa to western Asia were revealing themselves to be only a foot in the door for the region-spanning rise of a virulent hard-line radical theocracy.

Domestically the stage was set for a plunge into total economic destruction with nobody's hands on the wheel. The price of oil was skyrocketing again. True inflation was well into double digits, dragging the middle class toward poverty and the poor into violence and desperation. True unemployment would soon blow through 25 percent, and all those Made-in-the-USA jobs weren't just temporarily lost, they were gone from these shores forever. Almost fifty million Americans, one in seven, were now hand-to-mouth dependent on monthly aid from their bloated and bankrupt federal government, with almost twelve thousand more joining them every day.

The United States had soldiers deployed to seven active fronts overseas, and inside sources revealed many more covert ops under way in hot zones from the Middle East to central and southern Asia and Africa. Old enemies were rising again; an axis of dark alliances seemed to be forming, testing their limits and preparing to surge forth and seize power amid the spreading global unrest. Meanwhile, the undeclared and unspoken war along our own southern border was advancing steadily northward, having already claimed almost fifty thousand lives in just a few short years.

There was more. While on the road he'd heard rumblings of this next bold stroke of fascistic audacity, but he hadn't really believed it. The latest National Defense Authorization Act had passed both the House and Senate before arriving at the Oval Office on New Year's Eve. This legislation finally made it official: anyone, anywhere, citizen or not, was now subject to arrest without charges and imprisonment without trial—and according to some, even outright assassination—based solely on being named as a suspect by the Chief Executive.

With typical bald-faced duplicity the President had protested the clause that applied to Americans at home, even as he'd signed this abomination into law. Assuming his objections were honest, of course, they were also meaningless. In recent years Americans had seen this very pattern play out with the Espionage Act, the PATRIOT Act, the Military Commissions Act, the Enemy Belligerent Act, and other such open-ended assaults. Once the NDAA was on the books neither his own nor any future administration would be bound by their election-year pledges of restraint.

The writ of habeas corpus had once ensured a fundamental civil right even older than the Magna Carta. Now it was reduced to a king's option, to be selectively granted or revoked as an increasingly grandiose and militarized bureaucracy saw fit.

A quiet rap on the door behind him nearly startled Hollis out of his chair.

"Come on in," he said, after he'd taken a long breath to reset his composure.

As the door creaked open the dog poked his head in first to get the lay of the land before leading Molly inside.

"Are you decent?" she asked.

"I'm fully clothed, if that passes."

Cody brought her over to a chair near the desk, and she sat.

"You left dinner early," Molly said.

"Yeah, about dinner. You know the old lady at the table?"

"Did you see her then? She came by and read me a Bible verse earlier, kind of as a gift. She said she had something for all of us, including you."

"I did see her, and she saw me, too. Mercy, she's got a scowl that would stop a Swiss watch. I haven't gotten such an evil eye since I backed over my aunt Ruby's coon hound."

"What does she look like?"

"With all candor, she looks like Death eatin' a Ritz cracker."

"Hollis."

"Well, you asked me and I told you. Not that it matters much, but you wouldn't have any idea what a person like that might have to hold against me, would you?"

"No, I said nothing but good things. And she hasn't come by to give you anything yet?"

"Nope."

"She's already visited everyone else."

"Well, if I'm to judge by her demeanor tonight the only gift she's cookin' up for me is a butcher's knife between the shoulder blades." The dog had jumped onto Hollis's bed, and after some pawing and a few rotations he settled down into a nest among the pillows. "Tell him not to get too comfortable, would you? I don't want to seem unwelcoming, but I'm in the middle of some business here."

"That's okay, I'll go. Before I forget, we're all going to have a planning meeting in the dining room, tomorrow morning before lunch. I just wanted to tell you that and say good night, and see if you'd gotten any news. They told me that you might be in here on the computer."

"I only just got started. There's no news to speak of yet." He studied her for a moment. "Molly, I need for you to do something for me."

"Anything."

"We're safe now, at least as safe as we could hope to be. And I need for you to give some serious thought to the idea of all of us staying on here, and lying low for a while."

"Okay." She frowned. "I thought that *was* the idea."

"No," Hollis said. "This is what we talked about before, out on the trail, remember? I mean staying here and staying quiet, for a long time. Maybe for the duration, if they'll have us."

She sat back. "Oh."

"I think after all we've been through that I know how you feel. It's not easy for me to come to you and ask you to give it all up, but I've got a real bad feeling. Lay it off on me if you want; I'm spent, Molly, and I'm worried I can't protect you anymore. Just promise me you'll give it some thought."

Her expression didn't change much but he could see the wheels turning. She made a subtle motion with her hand and the dog jumped down to her side as she stood to leave.

"I'll pray on it," Molly said.

"Well, amen to that."

When she'd gone he turned back to his research. Digging deeper now, way out in the far-left and far-right hinterlands of the Internet, he soon saw the beginnings of a rumor that was forming and making the rounds. It seemed to have started very recently and was the subject of much discussion among the basement-dwellers. With every repetition the unsupported facts gained strength and confirmation.

As he tried to swallow, Hollis found that his mouth had gone bone-dry.

The gist of the rumor was simple: like her blood brother Danny Bailey before her, Molly Ross and her Founders' Keepers had now joined forces with George Pierce and his neo-patriot army to wage open war against the U.S. government.

The battle lines were drawn, first blood had been spilled, and the legions of followers in this new alliance were being called to keep their weapons at hand and prepare in the coming days for a spectacular, devastating commencement of the second American Revolution.

CHAPTER 13

From the balcony outside George Pierce's burned-out office, Warren Landers watched as his latest domestic forward operating base took shape in the open field behind the compound. The work was proceeding apace; at last all the crates and pallets were beginning to disappear as the place transformed into something buttoned-down and functional.

Under the glare of tungsten work lights, tents and long supply shelters were going up and buried lines were being laid for power, data, water, and waste. In the distance a team of comm techs had raised a tall mast festooned along its length with gray parabolic dishes. Now that the support wires were ratcheted down to lock it precisely vertical, each antenna was being tuned and aligned to gather the many faint digital signals streaming down from the open sky.

To the east an HH-60 Pave Hawk settled through the ground effect to a rolling touchdown. A larger supply helicopter had landed an hour before sundown and was still being unloaded nearby. Even more men and material would be inbound through the night.

It had been a full day of logistics and coordination and still there was much to be done before his scheduled departure in the morning. Landers checked the scrolling time-and-events list on the touchscreen of his phone. While he was not without his concerns, and despite delays from the still-threatening weather, things had mostly gone according to plan.

A man from Pierce's crew named Olin Simmons stood by Landers's side on the balcony, sweating steroids and kissing ass like a champion. This was the same one who'd aimed a pistol at him when he first arrived—now he was acting as a self-appointed aide-de-camp and general teacher's pet to the new management. It was hard to miss the man's ambition, or his commitment to the rise of the master race; his manifesto was etched onto his skin in permanent ink. A dark, jagged "SS" dominated one side of his neck, and his right bicep bore the angular black-eagle crest of the Nazi coat of arms. The backs of his scarred fingers were tattooed with individual letters such that when he made fists side by side they spelled out "Y O U R   N E X T."

The obvious typographical error no doubt went unmentioned by his peers, at least by those who wished to keep their teeth off the tavern floor.

A bright flash lit up among the trees in the distance and after a beat the sharp sound and concussion arrived with a satisfying punch in the chest. By the character of the blast it was either a shoulder-fired LAW rocket test or a small IED. That would mean the ordnance and small-unit tactical training had gotten under way.

Earlier, George Pierce's men had been assessed individually and assigned an occupational specialty. Any competent gunmen and sharpshooters would be used as such. A few who'd shown the needed technical and language skills were already busy inciting verbal violence and stirring up trouble across the Web, social media, talk radio, and the ham bands. Those thugs with more brawn than brains would be agitators, pickets, and provocateurs for the coming street protests and other direct actions.

So far everyone but a stubborn few had taken the transition without resistance. It wouldn't seem such a difficult choice to make; their lives would go on essentially as before with the addition of new marching orders, financial support, and some much-needed adjustments in doctrine and leadership. Still, there were holdouts; depending on their value, the remaining dissenters would either be convinced through further inducements or dealt with in other, more permanent ways.

A man knocked politely at the balcony door and Landers motioned him through. The newcomer had a long, camouflaged duffel slung over his shoulder. The bag was caked with dirt and woodland debris, as though it had been buried for a time.

"We found this out back in the deep woods"—the man gestured off toward the general area—"and they sent me to bring it right on up to you."

Landers dragged the bag's rusty zipper across partway and looked inside; this might be a useful find indeed. "Has anyone opened this before me?" he asked.

"No, sir."

"Good." He refastened the bag and pulled the messenger nearer the railing. "Now listen. You take this immediately to that third tent out there; see it?" He pointed, and the man nodded. "Tell the technician in charge to run the prints first, and send the bag back to me with a full toolkit. You stay there and wait for the work to be done. Understand?"

"Yes, sir."

"Repeat it."

He did so, nearly verbatim, which was no small feat given the obvious mental vacancies behind his eyes.

"Good," Landers said. "Go get it done."

The man gave a sharp salute and set off to do as he was told.

How refreshing to find a soul so perfectly suited to his simple work. The backbone of any radical uprising is a legion of such loyal ciphers: oblivious, barely competent, and grateful for any subservient role in a grander scheme. They weren't all imbeciles, not in the literal sense. Some were professors emeriti, some were anchormen, some stood in the pulpit to shill every Sunday in service to the lesser gods. But from vagrant to vice president, beneath the skin these useful idiots were born from the same ankle-deep end of the gene pool. Give them a slogan and a promise, pin a chintzy tassel on their chest, and they would follow orders without a question or the burden of a moral core.

"Who's payin' for all this?" Olin Simmons asked. Throughout this break from the executive meeting he'd been salivating over the sights of the expanding base like a diabetic at a doughnut store.

"This?" Landers said. "For the men I report to, as spending goes this is a drop in the ocean. And the wealthy don't waste; compared to the fortunes to be had when this is over they're making a very small investment here."

"Tell you what, I never would have thought it was all about money."

"It's not—at least not in the way you and I think of money. They each already have more money than a million men could squander in a lifetime. Money, and land, and gold, and works of art—even whole governments— those are all just things to be collected and compared, like the notches on your bedpost. They're a simple way to keep score so they can prove who's won in the end."

The other man took a step closer and leaned against the railing. "Who are these people, the ones at the top, the ones you work for? You can't tell me, can you?"

"I'm sure you'd be disappointed."

"Try me."

"On paper, I work for a gentleman named Arthur Gardner."

"And he's in the New World Order, am I right? Or the Bilderbergers? Or the CFR?"

Landers smiled. "He's in public relations."

"Public relations?"

"He runs a multinational firm called Doyle & Merchant."

"Doyle & Merchant." Simmons pronounced the names as though they left an unmanly taste in his mouth. "Sounds like a couple of San Francisco rump-wranglers."

"Be that as it may. You can believe it or not, but as much as any single force in human history they've shaped the world you live in, and the world that's about to come."

"What with, words and pretty pictures?" He spat. "You're right. I don't believe it."

"Of course you don't," Landers said. "And they wouldn't have it any other way."

Another lackey came to the balcony and informed the two that Mr. Pierce was almost ready now for the conference to resume.

Olin Simmons let out a sigh, cracked his neck, and started for the door, but Landers stopped him.

"Tell me something," Landers said. "Are you ready for more?"

"Sure. I'm not much of a man for meetings, but this one's blowin' my mind—"

"No," Landers interrupted, and he made a subtle show of looking behind him and through the open door to ensure they were alone. "What I mean, Olin, is that a time may come soon when I need more from you. And I want to know if you'll be ready to step up and do what needs to be done when I ask you."

Simmons pocketed his tobacco pouch and considered that for a moment. "When you ask me what?" By the sly tone of this question it was already clear he had an inkling of its answer.

"I have to trust in the leadership I leave in charge here," Landers said. "I'm talking about Mr. Pierce, and his future with us. Just watch while we're in there, and you'll see what I'm seeing. Everyone must serve their purpose, and I need to decide how faithfully he's going to serve his. Be ready to give me your counsel before I leave."

Landers put out his right hand, and after a thoughtful moment Olin Simmons took it with a firm shake and all the gravity appropriate to the pledge of a new allegiance.

CHAPTER 14

Before the final session of their pre-deployment conference could resume, word arrived at the Pierce compound that the remains of two men had been found, identified, and recovered from the adjacent woods.

These had been a pair of the organization's best commandos, both sent out in pursuit of Molly Ross on the night of her recent escape. A third was still missing in action—the nineteen-year-old nephew of the little General himself—and considering the fate of the other two and the amount of time that had passed without contact, it was only realistic to presume this young man to be dead at the enemy's hands as well.

As Warren Landers returned to the meeting room the other attendees were still milling about on their break, grumbling about the dismal news from the field. George Pierce sat alone, deep in study at the head of the table, with unfolded maps and a ream of handwritten notes spread around him. A Bible lay open to its final pages nearby. He continued this way, seemingly engaged in his own intrigues even after the assembly was called back to order.

Throughout the night, Landers laid out the details of the nationwide tactical plan.

Their orders were simple enough for men of this class

to understand and carry out; no real comprehension of the broader design was required. Timing and orchestration would be the key to their role in this coup d'état, like the sequenced detonations of a controlled demolition. Without such an underlying scheme, in fact, if executed randomly and one by one these small assignments he gave might have little impact on a prepared and courageous public.

Fortunately, prepared and courageous was not the trending status of the modern American people.

Many thoughtful decades had been devoted to sinking deep faults into the foundation of what was once the home of the brave. Though a sad minority still clung stubbornly to their gold, God, and guns, it was fear, dependence, and submission that had finally replaced the rickety illusions of faith and freedom at the heart of the last great nation to fall.

The strategy was sound, and he knew it would work because it always had. The principles of leveraged terror—problem-reaction-solution—had proven themselves since the ancient reign of Diocletian. Three hundred organized men can easily bring 300 million simpering cowards to their knees. Still, timing and precision were required at every step and nothing could be left to chance. Terrorism done wrong can awaken strength and unity in a population under attack, and that could quickly undo even the best-laid plans.

At appropriate points he opened the floor for discussion. For the most part the men were concerned with *how, where,* and *when,* leaving the all-important *why* in the hands of their new leadership. During these interchanges George Pierce continued to offer nothing but the occasional terse comment and a conspicuous lack of engagement.

Near dawn, as things were winding down, two men

arrived at the conference room door. One carried the duffel bag that had been found earlier; the tags attached showed it had been forensically processed, as Landers had ordered. At a gesture from Landers the bag was brought over and slid onto the table near him.

The second man went directly to Pierce's side to whisper into his ear. From across the room Landers could see the color rising in his face and when the message had been fully delivered the little man brought his fist down onto the bare wood with enough force to overturn a dozen water glasses nearby.

The meeting had come to a full stop and no one uttered a sound until he spoke.

"They found my nephew Billy Clark," Pierce said softly. "And they found him dead."

A long moment of silence ensued, apparently out of group respect for the dear departed. For Landers himself it had always been a particular annoyance to try to summon a show of sympathy when he felt none whatsoever. He took the opportunity to glance over the stapled paperwork that accompanied the canvas bag and that passed a bit of the time. After what seemed an appropriate interval he let out a deep, vocal breath and checked his watch. There was, after all, a schedule to keep.

This obvious prompt did not escape the notice of George Pierce. "Have you got somewhere you need to be?" he hissed.

"As a matter of fact, yes."

"Then why don't you get on outta here? Go report back to your masters. We've got our pay, we've got our list of things to do"—he waved a scribbled page—"and we know how to get 'er done. Don't we, boys?"

The men were quiet; if there was going to be a confrontation no one seemed quite willing to commit themselves to one end of the table or the other.

"Before I leave I need to know we have an understanding," Landers said.

"Oh, you bet we do, we've got an understanding."

"If you have something to say you shouldn't dance around it, George; it's unbecoming. All night long it's seemed to me you've been keeping your thoughts from us. Is it the words you can't find, or the courage?"

"All right, then," Pierce said, and he stood to his full, inadequate height. "If you want to hear it I'll say what nobody else here will."

"I'm listening."

"You're a liar."

"And what have I lied about?"

"You've spent all this time talking about what we're supposed to do for you. I haven't heard one word about what you're gonna do for us. Not a word—and far as I can tell, you expect us to gear up and start working with our enemies now. Hell, you've got us rubbing elbows with the union bosses, and the hippies, and the lefties, and the towel-heads, and the socialists, and the commies—"

"That's exactly right."

"Am I the only one here that's got a problem with that?" Pierce looked briefly around the table but got no takers. "And how do we know, once we've put our shoulder to the wheel and made all this happen, that you're not just gonna pull all those other bastards together and turn against us?"

"I'll tell you all something, George, and I'm not lying now. You wonder if we'll turn against you in the end? You don't have to wonder; I *guarantee* we will. But between now and then you'll have plenty of time to get what you want—everything that's coming to you, all the allies you can muster, maybe even enough power to win a small kingdom for yourself when it's all over. We're playing the long game now, George. How can I get you to understand that?"

"You sure talk big, I'll give you that. But this ain't a game to me."

"Look at it this way," Landers said. "The Ku Klux Klan—they're yesterday's news but they used to talk big, too, back when they were a much larger mob than yours—the Klan's killed how many blacks in the last hundred years?"

"I don't know."

"I do. It's only a few thousand actual lynchings, and with the shootings and the church burnings and the beatings and other random acts, let's be conservative and round it up to four thousand total. In one hundred years. That's forty per year on average."

"So?"

"So more than that number have been shot in *one weekend* in present-day Chicago. There were one hundred and twenty blacks murdered in that one city in just the first quarter of last year. Eight thousand, nine thousand murders happen annually in their communities, over twice as many as the KKK has managed to commit in its entire history."

"That's just the damned jungle bunnies killing one another. What, now you're gonna stand there and take credit for the Vice Lords and the P-Stones and the Gangster Disciples?"

"I am." The question had been mocking but Landers's answer was delivered with such authority that they all seemed to see it must be true. "Since the start of the Great Society we've systematically destroyed their spirit and dismantled their families, all with their full cooperation. You're right, they're killing each other; it's easier for us that way. We saw Martin Luther King rising up to stop it, and we met him head-on, and we won.

Today the sanctimonious do-gooders you hate so much have rewritten King's words into nothing more than a shameless plea for handouts and reparations. We've made his people wards of the state and convinced the taxpayers it's the only compassionate thing to do for such a downtrodden and helpless inferior race.

"The loudest of their leaders—and we've handpicked them all—they'll march arm in arm in the streets to preserve the very chains we've used to enslave them. For every one that escapes the trap there are ten more for whom crime is the only career that seems wide open. In the inner cities we've herded them into a savage culture that glorifies the worst of their men, objectifies their women, and orphans their children. We've imprisoned whole generations and put them to work for us at twenty cents an hour. That's ethnic cleansing at its best, but that's only the beginning. You people believe abortion is murder, correct?"

Pierce blinked. "Yes, we do."

"In your own language, then, abortion on demand has murdered seventeen million blacks, and counting." He let that number sink in for a moment. "Do you get that? We've normalized the voluntary termination of their babies into just another form of birth control—and a sacred civil right of liberated, empowered women. That's the illusion we've created to make another genocidal weapon in the race war you say you've always wanted. Can you think it's an accident that this choice is made so much more often by the people you claim to hate? There are fifty percent fewer blacks in this country now than there otherwise would be, and we've pulled the wool over the eyes of the American people so completely that even you couldn't see that truth. But do you understand it now? The real war's been going on for quite a while, George. We're just inviting you to finally be a part of it."

"That may all be true," Pierce said. "But there's times when a man's got to pull the trigger himself to get his justice."

"Are we talking about Molly Ross again?"

"Yes, we are."

"You have to leave her to me."

"Why?"

"Because I'm not paying you to be subtle, and it's a delicate business to kill an idea," Landers said. "She'll be dealt with soon enough. She's just an insignificant person who's going to be used as a patsy, nothing more. If we can we're going to push her into some public act that we can call terrorism, and then we'll take her down. If she only continues to cower and hide, we'll stage a bombing or a mass shooting ourselves and pin it on her. See? All this violence you're about to commit is going to be blamed on Molly Ross and her ignorant followers, and once that's done, we're finished with her. Then I'll have her sent here and you can do whatever you want with her, but not until we've beaten the last breath of life out of this pathetic patriot movement she's stirred up."

"You'll never find her. They'll be long gone soon and hid underground, but I've got a man right now in the other room who can lead us right to her—"

"No need," Landers said. "We've already found her." He tapped a small square on the grid of the laptop screen in front of him, a small moving image ballooned wide, and he spun the display around so the room could see. The live video was an extreme telephoto view of a large house and its surroundings, drifting and correcting, streamed down from a surveillance drone orbiting its target at nearly twenty thousand feet. "In fact, we never lost sight of her."

"Where is that place?"

Pierce had started around the table but Landers

snapped the screen closed before he'd gotten near. "When it's time, and not before. For now, if you really want to hurt Molly Ross, you can use this." He unzipped the equipment bag next to him and took out the scoped rifle inside. "The report tells me this all belonged to a man named Thomas Hollis. He was a modestly decorated Army Ranger and I understand he's now her enforcer. If you've lost lives, he's the one that took them. But I'm sure you knew that already."

George Pierce nodded.

"Good," Landers said. "So this is how you'll start to take your justice. Who's your best marksman?" After a moment Olin Simmons raised his hand and Landers passed the weapon to him. "Gentlemen, this will be the last point on the agenda today. Mr. Thomas Hollis is about to go on a coast-to-coast killing spree." He briefly consulted the dossier again and turned to Simmons. "We only have an old description and one dim photograph of the man. You're tan enough to pass, you're about the right size, and with a wig and a beard from the costume shop you'll be a reasonable match for any eyewitnesses to report. It's a plus that Hollis is ex-military; good for the standard mythology. But he doesn't seem to have a middle name, and that's a pity."

"Why is that?" Simmons asked.

"It's better for the headlines." Landers smiled. "Every ruthless lone gunman should have a middle name."

CHAPTER 15

Alone in the conference room, from deep in his studies George Pierce became aware of a faraway sound outside. With a finger he held his place in the open Bible and listened; it was the shrill, swelling roar of a helicopter coming up to full power and lifting off. By the transit of its noise he could follow the craft as it slowly rose above the trees and made a single orbit low overhead, as if to complete a rude inspection, and then it faded steadily away on a heading toward the southeast.

Pierce smiled. With a final rattling of the shingles this smug interloper, Warren Landers, was gone, no doubt in full confidence that his mission here among the simpletons had been a success.

But a success for whom? Among other burning questions, that remained to be seen.

"Mr. Pierce?" A voice from the doorway interrupted his thoughts.

"Yes, what is it?"

"That prisoner we've got, he's come around now, and you said I should let you know."

"Bring him to me," Pierce said, but then another thought occurred. "Wait—where is Olin Simmons?"

"Him and some of the others walked out with the

gentleman you all was meetin' with before, I guess to see him off on his way home."

"Of course they did."

All will be tested, so the Good Book says, and all duly judged in the Lord's good time. But the darkest corners of perdition were reserved for those who once knew the ways of righteousness and then turned their backs on the sacred command.

"Don't just bring the prisoner," Pierce said. "Bring Mr. Simmons, as well. Bring them all."

When the men had been gathered, on his orders some cleared the central table to the side. Soon the guest of honor was brought into the middle of the room and roughly seated in a straight wooden chair. He was conscious, though so bloodied about the head it would be a genuine surprise if no permanent damage had been done to his brain. Whatever the case, he really wouldn't need to last much longer.

"My brothers," George Pierce began, "as you're all well aware we've been honored over the past few days with a visitation from the invisible empire. A messenger has descended to us, come down from Olympus and the awesome, faceless powers that be. I foresaw that it would happen at some point near to the end, and I've told you as much, and now it's come to pass. The great deceiver has sent forth his ambassador and finally shown his hand.

"But I am not taken in by his idolatries, I'm not deceived. We—will not be deceived. If you think we've lost our power with this new alliance, I tell you now, we've only gained. We will accept their money, we will use their weapons and resources, and to the degree that they coincide with our own ambitions we will execute their plans. We will help them collapse this broken American system, but it is we who will rebuild it, true to our vision. We will not lose ourselves. We will not lose this war."

The men responded enthusiastically, and amid the cheering and encouragements Pierce scanned each of their faces for any signs of duplicity or reserve. He committed what he saw to memory, and pressed on.

"Now I've got me a grudge to satisfy," he said, and the crowd hushed as one. "There's a wrong that cries out from the grave to be put right. Some of you may have heard that I've been forbidden from on high to act in this matter. That I've been warned by this Warren Landers against avenging the betrayal and the killing of my own nephew.

"And I don't know, some of you might even agree with that prohibition. You may have heard and seen what's been said and done here in the last two days, and you may be standing there believing that the only choice we've got is to kowtow to our new overlords, to worship at their pagan altar with our hats in our hands and hope to cuddle up and curry favor like gelded lapdogs. As for me, boys, that is not my way.

"Now, I'm not proud, and I'm not perfect. God's made no perfect men. But let me ask you, has it ever been said that George Lincoln Rockwell Pierce would ever shy from a fight? That I don't look out for my people?"

The long room erupted in a rowdy chorus of cheers, stomps, and loud applause.

"You!" Pierce shouted, as he pointed at the seated man. "What have you got to say?"

The prisoner raised his battered head to nearly level, and it seemed to take considerable effort to focus his good eye on the one who'd spoken to him. "I told them everything already—"

"You will *stand* when you address the company in this room."

It was all quiet as the shattered man strained and suffered to get to his feet. A would-be Good Samaritan took a step forward to help but at a stern gesture from George Pierce he stopped short and quickly resumed his place.

"For those here that may not know," Pierce said, "tell us all your name."

"My name is Ben Church." He was standing by then, but with an unsteady sway and crooked posture, clearly favoring something torn or broken inside.

"Mr. Church is a devotee of Molly Ross and the Founders' Keepers. He came to me with an olive branch just the other day, as a self-appointed peacemaker, without her knowledge or approval, as I later came to learn. When all of you were up to your necks in government lead and brimstone in that battle up at Gannett Peak, it was this man who'd come to solicit the help we provided her there. He knew his people were outmatched and he came begging for the kind of salvation that only we could offer. And now the lives we've lost since are on his hands, and no one else's. Isn't that right?"

Ben Church nodded, though he winced at a pain brought on by the movement.

"Once you brave men had done your duty I brought Molly Ross and her folks here in good faith. I kept Mr. Church's involvement a secret from her, I told her we'd found this man shot and killed by those government men so she could make her choice without feeling that one of her own had come to me, to set her up behind her back. I gave her every chance to make the right decision and join us. But it wasn't too long before she showed us her true colors, and we all saw the results."

Pierce turned again to the prisoner. "Three more of my men are dead, now, Mr. Church, and my own flesh is among them. Who'll answer for that?"

"It's my fault, I won't deny. I'm sorry for it. Coming here and asking for your help, it was the only thing I knew to do. I only wanted to save her life. I didn't know—"

"We're not here to receive your confession. We know what you did and why you did it. All you can do to help yourself now is to tell us where she is."

"But I don't know."

"Speak another lie," Pierce snapped, "and see what it gets you."

"She's no threat to you," Ben Church said. "She never was. Molly Ross is no leader; her mother was a leader, but she's not. She's young and weak, now she's blinded, and she's got no idea what to do next. It was all we could manage just trying to stay a step ahead of that army they'd sent after us. We were just trying to stay alive, that's what it got down to in the end. You don't need to kill her. She's no threat to you at all."

"I'll ask you once again," Pierce said, and he gave a nod to the men who'd been in charge of the prisoner before. "Where is Molly Ross?"

"I don't know." It was obvious that he could hear the heavy footsteps approaching but he kept on pleading as the men came for him. "She wouldn't tell any of us where we were going, none of us knew, not even the ones she trusted more than me—"

The words were cut off sharply by a bare-knuckled blow to his rib cage. His knees gave out and he would have fallen but a second man held him up from behind.

It went on that way for a time, the same question asked, the wrong answer given, and the punishment applied. This unappreciated art of controlled savagery can take years to properly refine. Considerable skill is involved in beating a man to the very edge of his endurance and yet keeping him conscious all the while so the pain can do its patient work.

"We were shown an image of the place she's run to," Pierce said. "A large house with many outbuildings, acreage fenced for livestock. It must be somewhere less than a day's drive from the nearest road they could have reached on foot. That much we know. Now, where is she?"

Ben Church's head lolled so loosely to the side it nearly came to rest on his shoulder. He was bleeding freely from the mouth and when he spoke next the words were largely drowned in fluid and slur. A sharp twist of his arm snapped him bolt upright and forced him alert enough to say it again, but clearly. "I don't know."

George Pierce approached the wretched man, whose handlers held him straight in the event that their leader might wish to strike him personally.

"Very well, then," Pierce said quietly. "We'll take you at your word."

Not much of Ben Church's face retained the capacity for expression, but still, he managed to look bewildered.

"The last we saw," Pierce continued, "she was headin' north up the foothills out there. If I was you I'd hurry up and take off that same way. Maybe you can catch up to them."

"I can go?" Church whispered.

"I've got no use here for a man like you. Go on, now, before I change my mind. A couple of you men"—he pointed them out—"you see Mr. Church safe out the door and get him walking off in the right direction."

When they'd left, with Ben Church half dragged between his escorts, Pierce walked over to the long canvas bag on the table, unzipped the length of it, and took out the long rifle that had been replaced there.

"Now if you fellows will accompany me to the portico, I want to show you something," Pierce said, as he opened the bolt, pulled a box of ammunition from the bag, and began pressing cartridges into the well. "That underhanded rat bastard Thom Hollis is about to claim the first of many innocent victims on his nationwide rampage."

The men filed behind him as he walked through his office and out onto the balcony beyond. His crew had worked around the clock and the damage from the fire was mostly erased already. Some valuables had been lost, but nothing irreplaceable.

On the other hand, as he'd told them, so much had been gained. From this high vantage point he could see the extent of the bounty of arms and supplies that his new alliance had already rendered. It had taken years to accumulate the few advanced weapons they'd expended in an hour at Gannett Peak, and many dealings with characters every bit as unsavory as Warren Landers.

But now arrayed there before him was an arsenal he wouldn't have dared to dream of holding only a week before. Stacks of crated Stinger missiles, factory-built RPGs, cases of advanced explosives and high-tech detonators, a truckload of untraceable guns and banned ammo—all that, and a free pass for under-the-radar transport to any target, any city, any time. Tomorrow, at long last, was when it all would begin. The possibilities might boggle the mind of a general less prepared for action.

But George Pierce had spent his life imagining such power at his command, dreaming of the glorious ends and only lacking the means to reach them. And here, from the midst of failure, those means had fallen right into his hands. The old saw was true: when God closes a door, somewhere else he opens up a window.

Down below, about fifty yards distant, the men had set him loose and Ben Church was stumbling and limping his way toward the far-off woods.

"Stop me if you've heard this story before, boys," Pierce said. "When I was a little kid, just knee-high to a duck, my daddy introduced me to the man who killed

John Kennedy. Now, a couple of people shot him, understand, I'm talking about the man who killed him. He was a Frenchie, his name was Lucien Sarti, they call him the badge-man in that one old picture of the grassy knoll.

"But let's consider, just for grins, that Lee Harvey Oswald had acted alone. In '79 even the dopes in the U.S. Congress had to admit that there had to be another shooter, but let's just say that he acted alone. Now, what's the best reason you know of that would cause you to disbelieve that?"

"Three good shots in seven seconds," a nearby man offered. "One man couldna' fired that fast and hit what he aimed for, not unless he was a whole lot better with a gun than Oswald ever was."

"That's what they say, isn't it?" Pierce asked. "All those damned conspiracy theorists. Well, sir, I'm here to tell you those skeptics are right about a lot, but they're wrong about that." Ben Church had picked up his pace somewhat, having adjusted his stride to accommodate his injuries. "The range is about right now, though he's moving a little slower than a top-down limousine. I've got me a better rifle here than Oswald had, but then I'm no Marine sharpshooter, either, so I'd say we're even enough. Let's give it a whirl."

Pierce worked the bolt twice to eject two cartridges and leave three, and to check the action—it was smooth as butter. "The first shot was a miss," he said. "Whoever's got a second hand on their watch, when you hear that shot that's when you start the time." He brought the stock to his shoulder and the scope near his eye. "Number two's what they call the magic bullet. I've gotta put it clean through his neck or it don't count. And the third, that's the money shot."

George Pierce took in a deep breath and held it, sighted down, and squeezed the trigger.

At the first loud report the fleeing man nearly fell as he reacted, though the bullet missed intentionally wide. He'd no sooner straightened up when the second shot struck him just below the base of his skull, and his hands clutched at his throat as though giving a sign that he was choking. He took a faltering step, and then another. Almost simultaneous with the crack of the final shot, the top of his skull exploded in a pink spray of blood and tissue, what remained of his head jerked back and to the left, and he folded like a rag doll to the ground.

The timekeeper called it at 6.5 seconds and with that the hoots and loud applause of the men nearly raised the rafters. Pierce let them go on for a while before quieting them with a raised hand, and then he motioned Olin Simmons to step forward, close to him, and passed him the empty rifle.

"Y'all leave me and Mr. Simmons alone now."

When they'd gone George Pierce let it stay quiet between the two of them, waiting until the other man spoke.

"That was a damn good shot."

"That was three damn good shots," Pierce replied.

"Yeah."

"Take a team out this afternoon and you dump that body by the highway, thirty miles or so down the road. We'll call it in next week if the dumb-ass cops take too long to find it. And then you're going to leave here tomorrow with that rifle, and go raise some hell, isn't that right? You're going to go out and terrorize the sheep, get 'em all so scared they'll be begging for the police state to come in and save them?"

"That's the plan."

Pierce nodded thoughtfully. "I noticed you were spending a lot of quality time with that snake-in-the-grass Warren Landers while he was here."

"Just keeping an eye on him for you."

"Uh huh." Pierce took a cigar from his breast pocket, bit a sliver from the cap, and then leaned slightly forward and spit over the rail. "It wouldn't be like you to forget where you came from, would it? And what you've sworn to me?"

"No, sir. I wouldn't forget."

"You know," Pierce said, "they spent a whole lotta energy over the years asking who killed JFK, with not near enough of them asking why. If they'd ever had the guts to get an answer to that one question—why?—then they would have known who it was a long time ago."

"So why'd they do it?" Simmons asked.

Pierce didn't answer right away. He lit up his stogie and let the pause stretch out until the other man turned his head and looked him in the eyes.

"Oldest reason in the world," Pierce said. "Those men in high places, the ones who made him what he was? They killed John Kennedy because he was disloyal."

CHAPTER 16

With a last ceremonial stroke of the sanding block, Thom Hollis pulled his work light nearer to examine the dovetail joint he'd just completed. The two maple boards mated flush at a perfect right angle.

He gathered and then dry-fit the sides, front, and floor with their fresh cedar liners and brass hardware. The drawer knit together so well it would almost seem an insult to smear it with glue and stain. There sat a work of art, if he did say so himself, sculpted as it was with only a fret saw and hand chisels.

As the old saying goes, you can judge a rich man by his shoes, a salesman by his necktie, and a tailor by his inside seams—but to size up a carpenter, you really need to look inside his drawers.

Some would see it as a waste of time, such obsessive attention paid to a humble household repair. Old and treasured things, though, deserve to be restored with all the care and patience shown by their creators, or so he'd been told by his teachers.

A strenuous yawn came from the direction of the doorway and he turned to see that the young man Tyler had arrived on time to retrieve his phone. They exchanged a polite good-morning and Hollis pointed out the reassembled gadget waiting on the far end of the bench. The boy came over and picked it up, but he only slipped it into his pocket without turning it on.

"Now you need to use that thing just like normal," Hollis said, "like we talked about."

"I know. Nobody would ever believe I actually got up this early, so I'll wait till later to sign on."

"That's good thinking," Hollis said. "Say, do you like spiders?"

The boy's sleepy eyes grew wide. "Don't say it. There's one on me, isn't there?"

"I'm just asking."

He shuddered a bit. "I hate spiders."

"That's bad news for you, Tyler, because they're everywhere. Throughout your whole life, city or country, every minute you're almost never more than six feet away from a spider. You don't see 'em most of the time, but they're seeing you, with all those shiny black eyes. They're thinking about you, too, if you can call what they do thinking. Mainly they're just wondering what sort of a web they'd need to spin to catch you."

Hollis turned back to the bench and set about cleaning the work surface with a hand brush and dustpan. "I'm not saying they're all bad. There's some deadly ones out there to be sure, but some can be very helpful little creatures. You shouldn't ever forget, though, they don't care what's good for you, not for a minute. They've always got their own best interests in mind."

"Okay, okay, jeez, I get it."

"I'm sorry, you get what?"

"You're saying Big Brother's watching, and even when he's not, the phone, the computer, and Facebook, and Google, and Skype, and Twitter, and Pinterest, and Instagram, and all the games and the apps, whatever, even if they say they're free, they're not really, and I need to be careful, yadda yadda yadda—"

Hollis frowned and pointed to the boy's shoulder. "No, I'm saying there's a gigantic spider on your shoulder."

The frantic clog-dance of swats, stomps, and curses that ensued got Hollis to laughing like he hadn't laughed in months. When he realized he'd been fooled the boy laughed, too, despite himself, though in the course of it he did refer to his elder by a few choice names that wouldn't bear repeating in polite company.

"Really, thanks a lot for freaking me out," Tyler said. "Very mature."

"Any time."

Hollis went on with his cleanup, replacing tools and storing unused stock. After a few minutes of this he noticed that the boy hadn't yet gone.

"This ain't a punishment detail," he said. "Go on, now. You're a free man."

"Yeah, I know." Still, he didn't move to leave. "Can I ask you something?"

"Sure."

"My cousin said you fainted the other day, when they found you guys out in the woods. Is that true?"

"Am I the only subject of loose conversation around here? Why do you want to know?"

"I don't know," Tyler said. "It's just that you're this big strong guy, and I guess I never heard of a grown man fainting before."

"If you must know, I've had a bit of a condition, and since I got back from the service it's been known to flare up on me from time to time. I hadn't slept or eaten much for a week or so, and I suppose it all must have built up and got the better of me."

"What, like post-traumatic stress whatever?"

"Yeah. Something like that, I guess. Maybe we should

put it up on the bulletin board to save the others the trouble of asking."

"And why's your voice sound that way? It's kind of, I don't know, kind of wheezy."

Hollis took an extended look at the worn edge of one of the chisels, then put it aside for later sharpening. "Bring me a Coke from the fridge over there, and I'll tell you."

The young man went to the corner and brought back the bottle as requested. "So?"

"So, I took a piece of shrapnel in the throat one time. I was out to cover an allied patrol, nothing special about the mission, just an afternoon milk run in year five of a sixty-day war. We got hit outside of Sangin, total surprise, by some local warlord who'd switched hats and took a better bribe than what we'd offered. I was lucky with what I got, compared to some." He touched the scars; they were easier to trace without his beard. "Like the other thing, it comes and goes. Believe me, I've sounded worse."

"Sangin. Where's that, like Vietnam?"

"It's in Afghanistan." Hollis hooked the bottle cap on the metal lip of the workbench, popped it smartly with the heel of his hand, and took a drink. "And you know something? I understand it's not top-of-mind for a lot of folks these days, but for all the people who're still dying in service to this country, whether or not you believe in the wisdom of these perpetual wars, I think it would be a pretty damn good thing if we all at least knew the names of the places where they're giving their lives."

The boy didn't speak for a while, and then he said, "I'm sorry."

Even as he'd said them Hollis knew his last words were too harsh, and he hadn't meant them to come out as they had. All in all, it seemed best to change the subject.

"Well, if you're going to hang around, would you give me a hand with something?"

"Why not? I guess there's nothing better to do at the crack of dawn," Tyler said.

The two carried the assembled drawer over to the bachelor's chest it had been made to repair. With some delicate maneuvering they worked it onto the slides and eased it home until it came to rest at the cushioned stops in back. Hollis ran his thumb over each junction to test the fit, and then stood and took a step back to receive the full effect. Once the finish was matched and perfectly weathered it would take a big-city appraiser to ever tell the new parts from the old.

"Looks like somebody's been slacking off," Tyler said.

"Hmm?"

"There's a ton of stuff to do here."

"Do you want to see what your folks have been dealing with, instead of doing this work and looking after their business?" Hollis leaned to the side, picked up a fat file from the nearby desk, and slid it over in front of the boy. "What's been taking up their time is right in there. I don't think they'd mind if you knew about it."

Tyler opened the folder and began to leaf through the many regulatory letters, writs, notices, citations, affidavits, audits, and notarized decrees inside. As Hollis worked the boy stopped occasionally to read various items more carefully.

"Dude, this is messed up," Tyler said.

"It sure is."

About a year before, an odd couple had visited the ranch for a week's stay. They seemed to be allergic to almost everything and kept to themselves most of the time, but they'd asked a lot of questions.

Shortly thereafter the first of many official registered letters had arrived.

Hundreds of supposed violations had been reported to an army of bureaucrats, boards, and commissions.

Fresh raw milk was being served to guests who requested it, along with ungraded butter and eggs. Wild horses and "feral" animals were alleged to be present, perhaps to be bred and raised on the property. Child labor laws were being flagrantly sidestepped. Dinner menus lacked the required nutritional data. The trumped-up charges and obscure technicalities went on and on.

As a result, multiple licenses and permits were under review or in the process of revocation. Retroactive taxes, fees, and fines were being assessed, and several cease-and-desist orders had been served. All these charges were baseless and most were trivial, but some were dead serious. One of the Merrick brothers traveled the gun-show circuit with hand-tuned and legally augmented high-end firearms; his inventory was actually being named in a preliminary injunction as an illegal cache of assault weapons.

"What does this one mean?" Tyler asked.

"They're accusing your aunt Mary of diverting storm water."

"Wait, what? You mean the stuff that falls from the sky?"

"Yeah. She's got a sixty-gallon rain barrel out by the vegetable garden."

"How can that be against the law?"

"Those paper-pushers made a mistake because it's not against the law yet here in Wyoming, but it is in more states than you'd think. Doesn't matter, though. It still takes time and lawyers to answer it all."

Tyler put the paper back with the others and closed the folder. "This is just, I don't know . . ."

"Harassment?"

"Yeah."

"It's un-American, is what it is," Hollis said. "Intimidation by regulation, and selective enforcement against a hit list of political enemies. Now don't get me wrong, government's not all bad. Once you let these corrupt control freaks get their hooks into office, though, they never stop. It just grows and grows. This is the kind of nonsense they thrive on."

The next few hours passed quickly as honest work gradually replaced the conversation. At the start what this boy knew about carpentry wouldn't pack a thimble, but he picked things up with ease and he seemed to like to learn. It was almost eleven when Tyler's mother dropped by to bring her son a ham-and-egg sandwich and to let Hollis know that Molly's meeting was about to begin.

"My mom's been talking about you," Tyler said, when she'd left.

"Is that a fact?"

"Yup. I think she's smitten, as grossed-out as I am to say it."

"There's a compliment in there somewhere," Hollis said, "and by George I'll take it."

"Can I ask you something else?"

"I guess there's no stopping you."

"It's not because anyone's including me in all the secret talk around here, but I've picked up a little in the past couple of days on what you and your friends are all about."

"Okay. What do you want to ask?"

"Now, don't take this the wrong way," Tyler said, "but you're sitting in here fixing old drawers and bitching and moaning about regulations and bureaucrats and stuff."

"So what?"

"So if you're all on this great mission, shouldn't you be out there saving the country instead of sitting here?"

From the mouths of babes, Hollis thought. He wasn't looking forward to it, but in a few minutes down the hall that very important question would be put to a final vote.

CHAPTER 17

Hollis wasn't anxious to get where he had to go, so he took the scenic route to the dining room.

When he could avoid his destination no longer he arrived at the meeting place with the sheaf of printouts he'd collected from the Web. He paced for a while, listening in, before finally opening the door to step inside. The program was going full steam by then, and the current speaker went right ahead without taking much notice as Hollis found a seat near Molly's side.

The spirit of '76 was running high in these people, and it sounded all too familiar. They were deep in their Founding Fathers' roles, talking on about various grassroots actions to ignite a reawakening in the American people.

Samuel Adams stressed the critical importance of the clergy as a sure route to reach a wider, sympathetic congregation—there were 180 million churchgoers across America who might be reached with this message through the pulpit. Alexander Hamilton put forth a more political agenda, with goals secured by throwing the group's support behind enlightened and right-minded candidates in future elections. Ethan Allen spoke of organized boycotts, protests, and other high-profile public acts of civil resistance meant to raise awareness of the unfolding crisis threatening to destroy the great country they loved.

Incredibly, they proposed these things as though they were actually possible, as though some vast and dormant constituency was out there just waiting to embrace the message, hit the streets, and take up the cause.

Hollis watched Molly through each of the impassioned speeches. With every untenable tactic put forth and debated, not a trace of uncertainty showed on her face. She looked as driven and determined as ever, ready to take any measure whatever the risk, as long as the action might move their campaign of liberty forward.

And when it was Molly's turn to speak, Hollis learned that she had an idea of her own that made the others seem mild by comparison.

In her past work as a white-collar spy and whistle-blower, Molly would infiltrate her target organizations and then, through contacts in the press, leak what she'd learned to the world at large. These escapades would sometimes yield a few days of below-the-fold headlines before fading into the general swamp of corruption and vice in the news. More often than not, though, the stories found no traction and simply disappeared. By and large the public seemed to have grown completely immune to outrage anymore.

The problem had been one of scale, she now said, not of substance. This time, rather than taking on these targets and exposing them piecemeal, Molly proposed an elaborate scheme to bring about a single, massive day of truth-telling far too big for her enemies to cover up.

Apparently she'd been thinking this through for a long while. When they'd been together in New York, Noah Gardner had inadvertently told Molly of the place where his father sent the most sensitive and damning information concerning his list of powerful clients. And it wasn't only Arthur Gardner, but all the scheming villains in every hidden seat of power—in government, in media, in activist corporations, in global finance, every one of them, right to the very top—they all stored the evidence of their dark designs in this one ultrasecure facility.

This near-mythological place was called Garrison Archives, and its heavily guarded doorway was Molly's new finish line. Her goal was to take a team and travel east to open up this vault of secrets to the sunlight, unmasking the enemy's agenda all at once in a scorched-earth exposé that finally couldn't be ignored.

No one present raised the slightest concern at the prospect of such a dangerous, one-way mission, and "one-way" described it perfectly. It was clever to a fault, right up until the all-important moment of the getaway. This group talked a lot about miracles and, at the end of such a fool's errand, they'd need one.

After all his warnings, after all they'd just been through, the sad truth of their situation still hadn't dawned on these people.

At last he'd heard enough. Before he could temper the impulse he brought the flat of his hand down onto the table, hard, and put the whole room quiet at the sound.

"No," Hollis said.

The others turned to him and stared.

Not being a bona fide member of the group, he had no official voice in these meetings. But in another area—when it came to Molly's safety—he would always hold the deciding vote.

"I've tried to tell you every way I know how"—Hollis stood as he continued—"but somehow it ain't sunk in. So let me put the hay down where the goats can get it. We've lost, people. The other side won.

"I guess you've all forgotten where we were a few days ago, so I'll remind you. We had no food or water or shelter and no money to buy any more. We'd been chased until we'd finally painted ourselves into a corner and had no place left to run. We were one inch away from being dead and gone forever, and you can thank God all you want but dumb luck and some damned neo-Nazis were the only things that pulled us through and got us here.

"And this house we're in? Far as I can tell this is the home of the last friends we've got. If you don't believe me, you read what I've been reading." As Hollis shoved his tall stack of Internet printouts the papers fanned across the polished table and some slid onto the floor.

"Go on and read it if you've got the stomach, but I'll summarize. After what happened last year to put us on the run, everybody else has turned tail and jumped ship. The things we believe in have been thoroughly smeared and demonized in the mainstream press, and they'd treat every one of you the same way if they'd bother to talk about you at all. You're just the butt of a vulgar joke to the majority of people who never took you serious in the first place. Outside of this house the only folks that still seem to want us are employed by the FBI.

"The most we can do now is try to survive. So I say it stops, right here. I say we disappear while that option's still available. The minute I see that it's safe we'll hightail it up north. We've got a place there that's all built for us, dug-in and ready, and we'll ride out the crash and make the best lives we can in what's left of this country in the aftermath.

"This time, what I say goes," Hollis continued. "That's the way it's going to be. You all fought the good fight, and everyone who matters still respects you for what you tried to do. But it's over now."

He waited for a rebuttal, having come fully armed to make his case, but none came forth.

They might have already known these things—how could they not?—and had managed to stay in a fragile state of denial, swept along one day to the next, borne on false hope, until finally faced here with the indisputable facts from one of their own.

A few had begun to read from the printed pages he'd brought, touching the words with their fingers, grim and baffled as if they'd come across their own obituaries in the Sunday morning gazette. The rest, it seemed, didn't really need the confirmation. As the silence persisted all of them appeared to be slowly deflating from the soul on outward. The heroes they'd each embodied were dissipating before his eyes, retreating from the needful present to resume their hallowed place in history.

Then, before he knew what was happening, Molly had taken up her guide dog's harness and run from the room.

By the time he caught up with her she'd already made it to her suite. He found her kneeling by the side of her bed, but this time she wasn't praying. She was weeping from some awful place deep inside. An admission of defeat this final was something she'd never had to face before.

Hollis sat next to her, near enough so she would know he was there, but he didn't try to comfort her. Coming from him, the things normally said at these times would all ring hollow because he knew them to be empty and untrue.

Everything will be all right.

Better days are coming.

This, too, shall pass.

And of course, *Have faith.*

Her breathing eased after a time, her hand found his, and she said only a single word, but it was enough.

"Okay."

"Good," Hollis said. "Now don't you trouble yourself; you stay and rest. I'll tell the others myself." He paused before deciding to leave her with the only bit of good news that he had. "I got word this morning that Noah Gardner made it through that battle up at Gannett Peak. He's hurt, but he's alive, Molly. And he'd want you to stay that way, too."

When he returned to the group they were still assembled and waiting. They took the news of their coming retreat better than he might have expected, and just like that, it was over.

Hollis stood at the window of the dining room after the others had left to return to their quarters. In the end they'd seemed relieved, more so than their still-tenuous situation should warrant. These days, to disappear completely was a difficult thing. Safety was within reach, but they weren't nearly there yet.

Then, across the enclosed interior garden he saw that ancient woman again, seated in a rocking chair, watching him from a second-story dormer in the rustic, original part of the Merrick house.

Just as he had at dinner, he tried at first to convince himself that she couldn't really be focused on him from such a distance. But no, she saw him all right, and that black scowl of hers was locked on like a geriatric heat-seeker.

It wasn't just the old lady that seemed to be haunting him. Outside the sky was as clear and blue as he'd ever seen it; the winds were unusually calm for that time of year. This peace and quiet was deceptive, though.

At high altitude a glitter of sunlight reflected off something that shouldn't be there. If that something overhead was one of those domestic government drones that were all over the news, up there searching and watching, it only confirmed his decision.

They were down to one choice, now: hunker down, keep watch, pack and prepare, and then at the first safe opportunity, sneak out and run for their lives into hiding.

CHAPTER 18

As sunrise touched the spires of the man-made paradise of Dubai City, Aaron Doyle awoke in his palatial bedroom among the clouds to a gentle pattering against the windows. It was the quiet, comforting sound of the desert rain he had summoned the night before.

He let sleep depart him slowly; morning was the worst time of day for the discomforts of his age. Over the years every organ, joint, and tissue that medical science could improve had been surgically repaired or replaced—some more than once—but wherever the decaying original parts were still in service the pain in them was constant and every movement scraped nerve against bone.

He wasn't quite ready to face the physical punishments of a new day; the dawn could wait. Instead, as his dreams of the preceding night were still lingering he would close his eyes and hang on to the memories for a little while longer. There in his mind he'd be young again, in a place where time itself had not yet turned against him.

In those olden days, youth was a near-terminal condition that only the strong survived. After fleeing to America to escape the Czar's persecutions, he settled into the tenements of New York's Lower East Side. From a family of ten he'd seen his younger brothers and sisters taken one by one by the pestilence that arose amid the squalor of the breeding poor—smallpox, dysentery, influenza, pneumonia, and scarlet fever.

He'd somehow cheated death by epidemic only to be rounded up in quarantine, locked far away from the privileged classes, fenced off with the untended sick and dying as cholera stalked the fetid slums. It was there that his parents had passed away, but again, he'd somehow lived on.

Where disease had failed, starvation and exposure nearly killed him. Barely an adolescent, he was all alone in the cold gray city, a scrawny urchin from a despised minority living on whatever he could beg or steal.

Between the cops and the hoodlums there was nowhere safe to hide. He ran errands and grifted and panhandled until one day a local boss took a shine to him and he was brought under the wing of the Eastman Gang. Those street boys could have schooled the modern Crips and Bloods about thug life, and they showed their new mascot the simple laws of survival in the depths of that cruel metropolis.

They changed his name to one less likely to invite harassment and discrimination—Ilya Reinier became Aaron Doyle. As he rose through their ranks and learned to live by his wits, he also taught himself to read and write and speak in English like an educated native son.

In a few years' time Aaron Doyle felt the limits of a life of petty larceny. Though he'd found his first taste of success as a thief and a confidence man, the triumph over his childhood trials had convinced him that he must have been chosen for something much higher.

Through the gang's connections with the Sons of St. Tammany he'd already seen that the true, gold-paved path to riches led down the very thin line between politics and organized crime. While his cohorts were mostly called upon for strong-arm tactics and intimidation at the polls, young Aaron spent his time in the smoke-filled rooms, forging friendships among those who greased the wheels of the corrupt New York machine.

In the course of his candlelight studies, as he sought to find his way to the next milestone of achievement, he'd discovered something fundamental. A moment before it had been invisible, but once perceived it was so obvious that he couldn't imagine how it had ever eluded his grasp. Through this single, sudden insight his true life's work began.

While guns and knives could strike fear and level threats, leaders rarely rose to greatness through violence alone. No, he'd already seen the most fearsome weapons ever conceived, and he'd seen them in his books. They'd been wielded throughout man's brutal history by despots and saviors alike. The ones who built and brought down nations, amassed fortunes, murdered millions, and founded dynasties, at the core their mighty war machines were built of nothing more than words.

When he was nineteen and the *New York Times* had just marked forty-six years in business, he left his gangland years behind, donned a suit and tie, and walked into the newspaper offices to seek an entry-level job. He had no credentials, no references, no experience, and no degree; all he brought to recommend him was a clever pitch and a masthead slogan he'd written, which they quickly purloined: *All the News That's Fit to Print.*

From copy boy to typesetter to cub reporter to columnist, his roles soon brought him into contact with the captains of thriving empires of their own invention: Ford, Woolworth, Carnegie, Bell, Hilton, Lehman, Warburg, Westinghouse, Rothschild, Rockefeller, Edison, and more. He wrote their stories when they would allow the exposure, elbowed his way into inner circles, and learned from everyone. Along the way he saw elections swung, wars ignited, genocides launched, great men created and destroyed, kings enthroned and deposed, all through the awesome, subtle persuasion of the printed and spoken word.

As his skills improved he grew to prominence in the most powerful medium of its day. Then quite by chance he happened to meet a grudging admirer named William Merchant. Their first fiery discussion had nearly been their last, but after much correspondence over the ensuing months a permanent bond had formed between them. Neither would ever call it a friendship; their differences were far too profound. From background to worldview, in fact, they had only one thing in common. For as long as they could remember, they'd both had a recurring vision that they would one day change the world.

Their ambitions were diametrically opposed: one dreamed to tame and rule mankind, the other to free it. While they never stopped battling over which had conceived the most fitting destiny for the species, they each had a keen understanding of the dark magic they would use to pursue their aims. They each knew they would need a vast fortune to fund their efforts, and they also knew that, despite their rivalry, they could amass that wealth far better together than alone.

And so, hand in hateful hand, Doyle & Merchant would build a business empire and found a secretive industry of public influence, media control, and mind manipulation. Their century-defining science wouldn't even have a name until it was later brought to unwelcome prominence by a brash young protégé named Edward Bernays.

In the late 1960s their company was left in the able

care of Arthur Gardner, a devoted colleague Doyle had come to love like the son he'd never had. But despite his announced retirement, the globe-spanning work of Aaron Doyle had continued without pause. His philosophical rivalry with William Merchant still raged to the present moment—such is the nature of a fight to the death—even though the two men had long since parted ways.

They'd last seen one another in the flesh in late November 1941, and it was the first time they had ever come to blows. This had been the culmination of their most vicious and personal contest so far, concerning the question of whether the United States would intervene against the Axis powers in World War II.

The incitement of the sneak attack on Pearl Harbor had been a brilliant move by his opponent to be sure, but the resulting reversal of fortunes created a rift between the partners from which their strange, contentious relationship would never again recover.

He remembered feeling much younger then, but on that day that would live in infamy, Aaron Doyle was sixty-three.

This coming November—the gods and doctors willing and barring anything unforeseen—three most significant things would come to pass: his plans to unite this miserable world under the iron fist of a new social order would finally come to their fruition; he would at last declare a decisive win against the libertarian delusions of his old nemesis, William Merchant; and he would become only the third man in recorded human history to turn 132 years old.

A bevy of nurses on constant call would aid him if required but he'd vowed to himself that he would stand and walk on his own through all but the most trying days.

After swallowing the line of pills and arcane tinctures arranged as always on his bedside table, he set his jaw, took up his cane, and readied himself to rise again. With some effort he sat upright, endured a wave of dizziness and let it pass on through, and then left his bed and stood upon the smooth, cool floor.

As was his custom, while still in pajamas he took his morning inventory of the most treasured things in his surroundings. All were priceless and quite irreplaceable, but more important, they were reminders.

The veined white marble beneath his feet was harvested from the towering halls once walked by the pharaohs of Egypt. For a period far longer than the upstart reign of Christendom their subjects believed these earthbound rulers to be divine, and they might as well have been; their unbroken dominion spanned forty centuries.

The Great Pyramid had been as old and mysterious to Cleopatra as her own time is to the present day; the very apex of its long-lost capstone, nearly half a ton of inlaid gold and alabaster, was now the cornerstone of his décor in the grand foyer.

An Irish temple nestled near a bend on the River Boyne was older still, older than Stonehenge by a millennium and once a place of pagan worship in the cult of Baal. Its stolen altar now graced his western balcony, where he often sat to reflect with his afternoon tea.

A heavy faceted orb of purest emerald, whose aspect suggested a great unblinking eye, was set above the granite hearth in his study. This priceless, cursed stone had been taken in the spoils of some ancient war, chipped from the face of a great graven image of Moloch once worshiped by the high priests of Sidon. It was a symbol now of an awesome power that technology was fast delivering into his waiting hands. The myriad human sacrifices this eye had overseen would be dwarfed by those in the terrible, cleansing carnage soon to come.

Even the wood in his walking stick spoke an encouraging whisper from the ages. It was turned from the trunk of a precious Norway spruce that had lived and grown on the side of a mountain in Sweden for nearly ten thousand years. When this oldest of trees was only a seedling, the polished stone ax was still the pinnacle of human invention.

In the presence of such things his own age seemed less daunting, his enemies less formidable, and the completion of his lifelong project somehow nearer at hand. These things helped him remember that on the long timeline of history, the United States of America had managed to survive for barely an instant. And its last days were numbered; that failing experiment was the only remaining barrier that stood between Aaron Doyle and the realization of his dream.

And then, in his private study he came to the centerpiece of his home. This, a twelfth-century chessboard with pieces carved from walrus ivory, was the arena where he had once spent many an hour matching wits with his philosophical rival, William Merchant. Those early bitter contests had often ended in a draw, but now the real-world game was finally about to be won.

Though the two men had been estranged for many years, once this was all over Doyle had always hoped they might meet again. To that end, two comfortable chairs were placed on either side and the old board was set up for a last match, should the day of their reunion ever come.

When he returned to the bedroom he dressed himself in simple clothes; years before he'd chosen comfort over style when there was no one left above him to impress.

A fetching young lady in a plain uniform appeared to do his zippers, clasps, and buttons. She left a tray of fresh juices for his breakfast, her pretty eyes averted all the while, and promptly vanished again.

With his morning pains eased somewhat after the walk, now dressed, fed, and medicated he felt ready for the day's agenda to begin.

His lingering storm would be causing havoc with the rush-hour commuters scuttling far below; it was still much easier for science to make it rain than to make it stop again. Despite the snarled traffic, however, he was pleased to see that his first appointment had already arrived and was waiting in the sunroom. He was standing by the windows, taking in his first view of the Persian Gulf from the dizzying heights of the Burj Khalifa.

His guest turned to face him as he walked up close beside. He seemed utterly tongue-tied at the sudden sight of his reclusive host, a man he'd no doubt heard described only in the folklore of his cutthroat profession. At length it fell to the elder man to break the reverent silence that hung between them.

"At last we meet in person," he said, extending his fragile hand. "Mr. Warren Landers, I'm Aaron Doyle."

Landers reported that the muscle was now in place for the upcoming structured chaos to be unleashed on American soil. The decaying European Union, the ever-volatile Middle East, the chaos pillaging Africa, the powder kegs of central and southern Asia—in those regions the downward spirals Aaron Doyle had also fostered were already building momentum past the point of no return. Soon, as their own nations fell toward ruin all eyes would turn to the United States, and they would see then that the mythic soul of this last citadel of hope and freedom was as empty and diseased as all the rest.

"You've done good work," Doyle said.

"Thank you, sir."

"But you must be wondering why I asked you to come here and discuss these matters with me. In the past I've always dealt only with Arthur Gardner, so it seems I've put you in an awkward position. You've now gone over the head of your employer, or behind his back as the case may be."

"I trust your judgment," Landers said, "and I do have a sense of why I'm here."

"He has changed, hasn't he, of late? Then it isn't my imagination. You know, I have an old adversary in this campaign, and in the past he's occasionally turned the hearts of my best generals to his side of the cause, and I've done the same to him. But with Arthur I believe it's different. He couldn't be bought with any offer of money or power, but he's been vulnerable in another way. After all I'd invested in him, I once nearly lost him to the love of a common woman. And now I fear I may be losing him to a late-blooming love for his only son."

Landers nodded, looking appropriately concerned. Despite the nearly authentic expression of solemn regret on his face, there was also an undercurrent there that could best be described as anticipation.

"Now then, before we enjoy our brunch," Aaron Doyle said, "let us discuss how we shall finally bring the brief and teetering empire of the United States of America to an unceremonious close. And on a related subject, tell me everything you know about this little troublemaker, Molly Ross, and the possibly useful bond she still maintains with our young man, Noah Gardner."

CHAPTER 19

You Can Lead a Horse to Slaughter,
but You Can't Make Him Think
or
How I Spent My 16th Birthday

by Noah W. Gardner
Period 7, Mrs. Schantz
3/21/1997
Honors English

Introduction

How are a modern slaughterhouse
and the field of public relations
alike?

Last year, when a group of inves-
tors set out to build a new kind of
meat-processing plant—far bigger and
more efficient than ever—they didn't
go to an architect, or a stockman,
or any general contractor experienced in the field. Instead they

hired the world's preeminent social
engineer. So on my 16th birthday
they came to 500 Fifth Avenue in New
York City, and they sat down with my
father, Arthur Gardner.

If it seems strange to you that
the principles of public relations might apply so directly to the
mechanics of a humane slaughterhouse, you're not alone. I didn't
get it either, not until that
Saturday morning when I watched this
client presentation unfold.

My father took the men through
his drawings and explained things as
he went. A great deal of information
was given, but the basic concepts
behind his compassionate killing
machine were as follows:

1. **The Overton Window.** There must
   be no straight lines-of-sight on
   that last mile leading to the
   long knives and electric saws.
   Gentle winding curves would obscure the forward view and break
   the distance down into an easy
   series of short and nonthreatening segments, each willingly
   taken, the animals nudged along
   to one point after the next.
   Safety and rest—not the butcher's blade—must always seem to be
   waiting just beyond the next corner up ahead.

2. **Divide and Conquer.** Pigs and
   cattle and sheep are natural sub-
   scribers to the two-party system. They will blindly follow a
   kindred leader, and will tend to
   walk in the opposite direction
   to that traveled by a thing they
   distrust. Either or both of these
   instincts can be employed to
   march them peacefully to a place
   they would never otherwise choose
   to go.

3. **Misdirection and Media Control.** Lest fear should spoil the
   meat, along the path toward the
   kill-chute everything the animals see and hear must be crafted
   to lull them into a state of calm
   submission. Any whiff of the truth
   could interrupt progress and
   alert them to the danger they're
   approaching.

4. **The Free Choice Illusion.** Throughout their final walk they should
   have just enough space around them
   to feel the comfort of false freedom. Even as the path constricts
   and their choices narrow, moving
   steadily onward must seem to be
   their own decision, right up until
   the moment when the hammer falls.

5. **The Rebel Gene.** A lone, independent agitator is the most
   dangerous animal in the herd.
   These rare individuals seem to

be born with a sense of what's
to come and will endure harsh
and repeated punishments as they
attempt to warn the others. Provision must be made to remove and
silence these unusual creatures
the instant they step out of
line.

For the men attending, this meeting was a huge success. By the
time it was over they'd gotten
everything they wanted and more.
For my part, I was left with the
troubling feeling that I had
glimpsed behind the wizard's curtain and learned things I'd rather
not have known, both about my
father, Arthur Gardner, and the industry he'd helped to pioneer.

There was a key difference, of
course, between the herding and han-
dling of that livestock and the crass
manipulation of the buying, voting,
and consuming public.

Once the animals were killed the
goal was to squeeze every last bit of
worth from the carcass: muscle, blood,
bone, sinew, skin, and entrails;
nothing should be left in the end.
In the case of the American people
the same sort of value extraction was
being plotted, only they were to be
systematically drained of all their
worth <u>before</u> they died, not after.

The youthful rebellion on display in this prep school essay was quickly put down without a fight. Noah's teacher valued her job and knew her place, so she reported to his father immediately and shredded all copies of the paper at the old man's request. She then quietly gave her student a grade of D-minus on the assignment and that was the end of it, in more ways than one.

His naïve exposé would turn out to be the high-water mark of Noah Gardner's adolescent protests against the establishment. He soon saw that it was a war he wouldn't win, so there was nothing to be gained in resistance and so many comforts to be lost.

Likewise, his stand as a conscientious vegetarian lasted less than half a year. His idealistic quest to become an establishment-battling lawyer barely survived one tough semester at New York University. Several devil-may-care and fun-filled years later, Noah found that he'd done what he'd once sworn to himself and his dying mother that he never, ever would.

There was no particular point when he could say he'd sold out and turned that final, gentle corner, but one day not long ago—the day he'd met Molly Ross, in fact—he woke up to fully realize he'd become his father's son.

Needless to say, that day didn't turn out so well.

As he dreamed, Noah wasn't reliving past days but only watching them file past in the dark, skipping parts he couldn't bear and dwelling in others that had gone by too quickly. In the midst of a particularly fond memory he felt an itch and a soreness by his ear. He tried to move his hand to ease the discomfort and felt the cinch of the strap, found his wrist restrained, and opened his eyes.

A wave of body panic shot through him, the really urgent kind the primitive brain reserves for those times when you absolutely, positively must escape from something nearby that would kill you if you tried to hold your ground.

The door banged open, the overhead lights blazed on, and a nurse and two muscular orderlies rushed into the room to keep him down.

A needle popped under the skin of his arm. He tried to cry out but there was no voice to it. And he never took his eyes from the mortal threat in the shape of Arthur Gardner sitting without emotion in the chair across the room, not until the drugs took hold, his surroundings began to swirl and recede, and he felt himself drifting away.

This time there'd been no dreams at all.

When he woke again he was looking into a winsome and familiar face at the bedside. If their aim had been to put him at ease with the presence of someone he trusted, they'd actually chosen pretty well. It was Ellen Davenport—now Dr. Ellen Davenport—his closest friend from their younger, country-clubbing years.

"Hi there," Ellen said, as if nothing whatsoever were wrong.

"What are you doing here?" Noah asked. His hands were no longer restrained though she was holding both of them in hers. "And where the hell are we?"

Her smile seemed forced and very professional, more a tool of patient management than a genuine expression. "We're at a clinic outside of Denver. You were injured and flown here by medevac, but that's been a little while ago now."

"How long?"

"Several days."

"Several *days*?"

"I just found out, and I dropped everything when

I got the call. That's all I know. And I'm here for you because your father called and said you needed me."

"My father."

"He wants to talk to you, Noah."

"Well, I don't want to talk to him."

She sighed, released his hands, and adjusted his covers. "Look, I know all about your issues with your dad—"

"Actually, I'd bet your debt to Johns Hopkins that you don't have any idea."

"Let me finish. He's changed, Noah. He told me that he had, and I've seen it. If you'd heard him when he called me—no, listen—if you'd heard him you'd know that whatever's gone on between you, letting him in here now is the right thing to do."

"He's why I'm here, Ellen. He did this, no one else. He's why all this has happened to me. When I came to you for help back then, remember? I'd gotten wrapped up with this girl named Molly Ross. She was just using me in the beginning, trying to expose what my father was doing, but in the end I really tried to help her. When he saw I'd turned against him he almost killed me for it, and then he had me locked up in some godforsaken government work camp, and—"

"Okay, okay, just relax." By her gentle tone and the look on her face Ellen was recalling her training on how to deal with a psychotic in the grip of a delusion. In any case, when she'd calmed him down that line of conversation was tabled for the moment. She stood, fussed a bit with the IV pump, lightly checked his bandages, and put a cool hand to his forehead as if to calm him as she gauged his temperature. "You've got some lacerations and some burns and a mild concussion. How do you feel?"

"Groggy."

"You must be. The chart says you've been in and out

since you got here, but mostly out. They've been overdoing the sedation for some reason. I've put a stop to that, and as long as you don't get physical with the staff again, my orders should stand."

He laid his head back, thinking. "Thank you."

She nodded. "Now, if I raise the bed a little so you can sit up and have a visitor, do you think you can handle that?"

"Sure. But not him."

"Look at it this way," she said. "He's here, and he won't leave until he sees you. I'm going to put my career and my normal relationships and my fine life in the big city on hold and stay here to take care of you. Whatever else he's done, he made that happen, too, Noah. And he's assured me that whatever's gone on since I last saw you in New York, everything will be different going forward."

"Different? Is that how he put it? Because it's like signing a pact with the devil when you're dealing with him; you've got to analyze every damned word."

"Better, then," Ellen said. "Everything will be better. He promised me, Gardner, and I promise you."

When she'd left, it seemed that whoever else was lurking outside the room felt it best to give him a few minutes alone. The quiet time didn't help anything. Every second that passed only dripped more acid tension into his gut. By the time the handle turned and the door began to open, his fists were clenched so hard he felt the nails biting into his palms.

And then his father came into the room.

Something had diminished about the man, there was no denying it. He'd always seemed younger than his age, buoyed up from within by some boundless hamster wheel of manic energy. Now he was seventy-five, and for the first time that Noah could remember, every single year of it showed.

Arthur Gardner turned to look up into the ceiling-mounted camera behind a smoky glass dome near the corner. He made a motion toward it with his hand as if to order a pause in the surveillance, and he waited to see it comply. That little red light just continued its steady glow. After a time he relented the effort and seemed to accept the fact that whatever he was going to say or do here, it would be watched.

There was a physical difference in his walk as he came on forward, maybe a weakness of one side that required a compensation.

"Stop right there," Noah said.

The old man halted so abruptly he had to brace himself with one hand on the footboard.

"Son," he began. But nothing more followed.

"Ellen told me you had something to say. Let's get on with it."

He nodded, and took a little while to begin. "When I last saw you—"

"When you last saw me?" Noah interrupted. "We're starting there? Because when you last saw me you were supervising my torture and interrogation. Then you put me into a white-collar prison job, and that went from white-collar to blue-collar to no-collar to an involuntary ride-along with a pack of mercenaries who were hunting people that I actually care about. That was your doing, and it almost put an end to me more than just this once. Hey, there were a lot of times that I actually could have used a fatherly visit in the last six months, but no, there wasn't a peep out of you then. Now, if I'm reading your signals properly, you actually came here to say you're sorry after all this time, and all you've put me through. Your apology is so unbelievably not accepted. If that's all you've got, you might as well shuffle out of here right now and piss off."

Arthur Gardner endured the onslaught of these words and again, quite out of character, he made no attempt to counter. He only took a small step closer before seeming to recall that he'd been told to stay right where he was.

"Son," he tried to begin again, "it may be very important—no—it is, very important, that you attempt to put the old feelings between us aside for now and do what I ask. Important for everyone, not only me. This concerns the young woman, Molly Ross."

Noah frowned. "What about Molly?"

"It's as simple as this." Arthur Gardner stole a glance toward that camera again. "If you'll do what I ask, she can live."

When listening to a man who's spent his career constructing deceptions so perfect as to shape entire cultures for his profit, it's a good idea to think hard before buying into his lines. Noah didn't speak, and the old man continued.

"More than that, son; you can have a future again. Back in New York, or in London, or Geneva, or Zurich, or the south of France. Anywhere, or nowhere if you'd prefer to disappear and put me and everything else you've ever known behind you forever. I'll arrange that myself, with Charlie Nelan. You'll trust Charlie; I can't blame you for doubting me but you must know he wouldn't let you down. He can set you up for life in a way that no one could ever undo it."

"Sounds just great," Noah said. "You know I had most of those options already, don't you? Before you took them away."

"Now you listen." And there it was, low and menacing, a venomous hiss from the real man had momentarily escaped containment. "The past is gone, son. There's a change coming, and soon. Our failure last year only delayed it, but the storm is gathering again. This offer I bring will cost me more than you'll ever know. But it will buy a life for you, a good life, and one for her, if that matters to you more than your own."

"It does," Noah said, and he was more than a little surprised to hear himself admit to that. As his mind raced to find the old man's hidden angle—because there was always at least one of those—he couldn't see how it could hurt to hear the proposal. "So what do you want from me?"

"I'd like to sit." He'd pulled a rumpled handkerchief from his pocket and was dabbing at his neck and his brow.

"Be my guest."

His father took a seat at the foot of the bed. He seemed unusually weary and short of breath when he spoke again.

"We'll bring someone in to meet with you," he said, "an investigator whose honor and integrity you'll know you can rely upon. She'll ask you what you know, and then she may require that you make contact with Ms. Ross and arrange a meeting, and you'll do that. Through this interaction she'll be brought into custody. She'll stand trial for a minor felony and spend as little time as we can bargain in a minimum-security federal penitentiary."

"And what about her people?"

"They don't matter at all without her. They'll scatter and soon be forgotten, and they'll be left alone."

It hurt to do it but Noah brought himself up to an elbow, a little closer to his father and on a more eye-to-eye level. "So that's it?"

"Yes."

"I mean, that's all? I just have to rat her out, and set her up, and then we all live happily ever after?"

His father didn't respond to this latest snide rejoinder because he must have known by then that he didn't have to. There comes a time in a sales transaction, right before the close, when the mark's been reeled in and both the salesman and his victim know the deed's already done. When it's over and everyone knows it, you stop the pitch, slide the contract across the table, and you wait.

It went without saying that Noah didn't believe a word of this, but he thought for a moment before he spoke again. Maybe there was something to be gained by playing along.

If he declined this deal he'd only be shut out while they continued to pursue her. They'd find her before too long and then they'd do whatever they wanted: kill her, humiliate her, publicly destroy her work, and erase any good she'd ever tried to do. Probably all of the above. As an afterthought they'd no doubt do the same to him.

But, if he said yes, he might retain some form of leverage and at least remain in the game. That way there was a chance that he could buy them both a little time.

"You know what?" Noah said. "Fine. You win, as usual. I'll do it."

CHAPTER 20

As the heavy door eased closed behind him, Arthur Gardner stopped at an interior window in the corridor and reviewed his reflection in the darkened glass. Gradually he straightened himself, adjusted his collar and perfected his cuffs, breathed in deeply, and shed the façade of physical weakness he'd worn for the benefit of his son.

Guilt was still an unfamiliar sensation; only lately had the capacity to feel it returned to him like a bad penny, or more correctly, like a debt that had finally come due. Still, the ache of his conscience wasn't as sharp as it might have been. There was some acquittal in the knowledge that almost half of what he'd said in there had been the unvarnished truth.

He bid a fond good night to Ellen Davenport and sent her off to her hotel with his thanks and all best wishes to her parents in East Hampton. She was innocent in all this and would remain that way, but she would still serve a role. His son would feel protective of his old friend, and with her close by he'd be far less likely to attempt any costly and unforeseen adventures as the finish line drew near.

That left just one more key player to be brought onto the stage.

Down the hall he saw his man arriving, apparently fresh from the airport with an overnight bag still slung over a shoulder.

"Where have you been lately?" Gardner asked when he'd come near. "I've needed you."

"I'm sorry, sir," Warren Landers said. "That George Pierce—what a piece of work. Those guys were more than a handful and it took longer than we'd hoped to get them into line out there."

"And what's the outcome?"

"Pierce and all his men are good to go. He's got a following you wouldn't believe, cells all across the country. We're deploying them now; if you've been watching the news you've seen the beginnings." Landers ticked his head toward Noah's room. "How are things here?"

"Good, I think." Despite the weight of the situation, he smiled. "And he's changed, Warren. I don't know how to say it exactly. There's something more to him now."

"More?" Landers asked. "In what way?"

"Balls, I think, is the term I'm seeking. We knew when we left him last year with the consequences of his acts that the experience would either kill him or make him stronger. At that time I had the considerable advantage of not really caring which one it did. And I'm not ashamed to tell you now that I'm glad he managed to survive." He paused and looked the other man over. "Just flew in, did you?"

"Yes, sir."

"From where? Not from Cheyenne."

"No." Landers seemed briefly to be searching his mind for a handhold. "Cheyenne's just a shuttle hop from here. No, after Pierce I had some business for you in Philly and Chicago, and there was weather, and some other delays I couldn't avoid. I'm sorry, again, I know I should have gotten word to you."

"Well." Arthur Gardner nodded and let a bit of thoughtful silence linger on. "I wasn't aware. Be sure to leave me a briefing about it all."

"Of course."

"Now then, I'll be returning to New York tomorrow morning, and you're off to Arizona by the afternoon." He took a small pad and pen from his pocket and wrote out a name and location as he spoke. "You'll meet with a woman there, an operations officer; her name is Virginia Ward. She's former CIA and now I suppose she could best be called a freelancer. I've worked it out with her higher-ups; she'll be expecting you, and she'll be central to our pursuits from here on, so please conduct yourself accordingly."

"Former CIA? Is she one of ours?"

"Oh, good heavens, no. You'll see when you meet her; she belongs to no one. She's a real straight arrow and a card-carrying, dyed-in-the-wool American hero."

Landers took the sheet and looked it over. "Isn't it quite a risk to take, someone like that in the middle of all this, running off the leash?"

"It's necessary. We'll need an advocate whose credentials are unimpeachable in order to bring the real force in behind us. We need someone who can go before Congress and testify as to the terrorist nature of this Molly Ross and her movement. Think of Colin Powell making that case for war with Iraq before the UN Security Council in 2002. We must weave a believable body of evidence from a tissue of lies and then have it served to the American people by a very attractive waitress. With someone like Virginia Ward on our side they'll swallow whatever we say, hook, line, and sinker."

" 'On our side' being the key phrase," Landers said. "The way you're describing her, how can you be sure she'll stay on our side?"

"That will depend in good part on the quality of your dirty work with Mr. Pierce, which I'm certain will be nothing short of exemplary. Do you feel he's ready and able to terrorize?"

"Oh, he's ready."

"Good. And this is far from the first time you've helped frame a perfectly innocent victim for the greater good. Surely you're not doubting that you're capable."

"No, sir, it's just—"

"Fine, then. We'll proceed as I've directed. I'm sure it's what Mr. Doyle would want." He gave Warren Landers a pat on the shoulder. "But you must be tired after your long trip. We'll wrap up tomorrow and then you'll do what needs to be done to line up Ms. Ward, yes?"

"Yes, sir."

"Good man. We both have a big day ahead, Warren. Go and rest."

As Gardner watched the other man leave he considered some revealing details of the encounter.

There's a visible difference between a man who's just come off a harrowing series of domestic connections and one who's spent those same fourteen hours enthroned in the splendors of nonstop international first class. His spindly cover story notwithstanding, by his vigorous and unwrinkled condition Mr. Landers had obviously arrived fresh from a sojourn in the lap of luxury.

That he'd lied about his whereabouts was obvious and not terribly unusual. But why he'd lied this time was the key question to be answered.

All things considered, it was more than likely that Mr. Landers had been invited overseas for a covert meeting with the Man Upstairs. Such a major break in the chain of command, especially under current circumstances, could foretell only one thing.

A forced retirement would be an inauspicious end to Arthur Gardner's long career. Still, after the previous year's failure someone had to take the blame—*such momentous plans upset by a band of patriotic amateurs, and with the assistance of his own son!* Indeed, his time had come, though when all was said and done his departure wouldn't be due to any reason that old Aaron Doyle might guess. That is, if he was allowed to depart voluntarily at all.

Long ago, when he was younger than his own son was today, the boss had laid down the cardinal rule of his world-changing enterprise. Great power and wealth were among the many rewards he offered, but the penalty for insubordination would be swift and permanent.

Once you're in, you're in, Aaron Doyle had said. *And once you're out, you're dead.*

CHAPTER 21

Though the day was done, there was something Arthur Gardner felt he needed to do before he left for the hotel.

As quietly as he could he eased open the door to Noah's room for a last look inside. He found the boy already sleeping and was thankful for that. There was a nagging feeling that this could be their final parting; it would have been a shame to have it end in another angry tirade.

As he stood watching, it also occurred to him that there must have been thousands of other nights when he'd neglected to make this sort of simple fatherly gesture. So many moments, now long lost, when the normal things expected of a parent had been the very lowest of his daily priorities—why, after all these years, were such feelings arising to haunt him now?

There was a ready answer to that question, of course. This and other equally unsettling emotions had suddenly begun to rear their ugly heads in the wake of a recent meeting. This wasn't a business conference, but a follow-up visit to a routine, company-mandated medical checkup.

The grim specialist had come in and clipped a single

X-ray transparency to a glowing panel on the wall. He then sat down uncomfortably close and delivered the prognosis without any adornment. *Stage 4 pancreatic cancer,* he'd said, with the sort of doctorly gravity that assured there was nothing to be done beyond getting one's affairs in order.

Death awaits us all and Gardner always would have said he didn't fear it. To see the certain schedule of its approach, though, to be told when it would come almost to the day, that knowledge had opened his eyes and altered him—it was still working on him now.

He'd told no one of his terminal condition and it would stay that way. He would neither wallow in regret nor beg repentance; it was worse than useless to bemoan the past. He'd brought about many terrible things in the course of his life's work, that was true, and he owned those things. Still, there was no denying that these new and unfamiliar feelings had led him, step by step, to the sort of turning point that he'd experienced only one other time in his entire life.

Arthur Gardner had experienced a change of heart.

At first he'd fought it tooth and nail. Doubt was only a symptom of weakness, his mentor had always told him. *Our way is hard but the rewards are unlimited. Good and evil, left and right, right and wrong, light and darkness—these are only childish illusions we create and maintain to confuse and control the feeble masses.* There was only one fundamental conflict—no less than the struggle to decide man's ultimate destiny—and throughout his career that battle had been embodied in the philosophical tug-of-war between the two senior partners of Doyle & Merchant.

One side envisioned a paradise of true liberty, divinely gifted. Blessed self-determination, the opportunity for each hearty soul to set forth and pursue his happiness upon the choppy and hazardous seas of commerce. Throughout all time this free-market fantasy had only once been realized in a society, and that one hadn't survived for very long. The fatal weakness of the United States was a doomed reliance on goodness and faith and charity in the black hearts of the common people.

The other side would end the human condition in utopian slavery to the almighty State. The built-in advantage of this solution was that it played to the lowest instincts of the corrupt and cynical leaders, their legion of obedient cronies, and their ever-more-dependent subjects. Vulnerability to the lures of wickedness, willful submission to sloth and avarice—without a guiding light from above these were the only reliable tendencies in every culture of human design. History had proved it over and over, worldwide; only an all-powerful government could ever hope to control a populace with no moral core.

Arthur Gardner had toiled for more than fifty years in service to the side he'd always assumed to be most likely to succeed. The one-world alternative might not end suffering—nothing ever could—but at least it would preserve the old fortunes and dynasties while spreading the inevitable misery evenly across the planet. Social justice indeed; the only righteous thing Aaron Doyle's coming regime would ensure was a permanent, unbreakable wall between the elites and the great unwashed. All the wealth and power would be kept safe at the very top, with the masses scrabbling for their metered rations on a perfectly level playing field at the bottom. Far from ideal, it nevertheless seemed to be the best available answer to an age-old global problem.

But something had happened to him very late one night as he struggled to quiet the thoughts of his own mortality. He'd sought refuge in his work, poring over

the dusty writings of his enemies as he tried to understand how his son, Noah, could have gone so far and so
suddenly astray. After many hours, near his wit's end,
he remembered something that could hold an answer—
something he'd long ago pushed safely to the back of
his mind.

Before her own untimely death twenty years ago, his
dear wife had written him a farewell note and asked him
to promise to read it only after she was gone. He hadn't
broken that promise; he'd kept his word in his own way.
In fear that it might only prolong his grief, he'd never
read the note at all.

That night he went to find it, still sealed at the bottom of a small box of keepsakes in the dresser drawer.
After more than an hour of sitting with it unopened, he'd
mustered his courage, cut the envelope across the flap,
unfolded the paper within, and read.

My darling Arthur,

*We'll have said our goodbyes before now, so
that isn't my purpose here. Though you haven't
shared my faith, I haven't any doubt that we'll
see each other again one day. When that time
comes, I'll be hoping that you'll have taken what
I write here to heart, and so there will be no
place for anything but joy at our reunion.*

*When we met, you and I could not have
been more different. I knew you were sent to try
to change me. You must know, too, that in those
first days together I also saw you as a project,
nothing more. Even as we fell in love each of us
still thought we could win over the other. Then
for the sake of keeping the peace, you finally gave
it up. But I confess, I never lost my hope for you.*

If only I'd had enough time, I know you would have come around. Not because I'm so stubborn, Arthur, but because you're so wise. With a little more time you would have seen my truth, and so I'm urging you now to continue to seek it after I'm gone.

This terrible man you've worked for has done everything he could to destroy our last, best chance at liberty. I won't ask you again to join the fight against him; that's the only thing we ever really argued about, and I don't want to leave you that way.

I only ask this: just for a while, do nothing. Stop building his machine, stand away from the barriers, leave the door open, and give the good people of the United States their one true chance.

Do that, then witness the miracle I dreamed I'd live to see; watch freedom succeed where mere mankind has always failed to create a better world for us all.

It was a strange marriage we had, I know you'd smile and agree, but I wouldn't have traded it; I have no regrets. Take care of yourself, Arthur, and take good care of our son. Don't let Noah waste himself in that world that had nearly consumed you by the time we met. Like you, my love, he was born for greater things.

> *Until you come home to me again,*
> *Jaime*

When he looked up from those words, through the tears in his eyes it was as though everything had been transformed. The old documents he'd been studying, his hands, his face reflected in the window glass, the very room around him was suddenly painted in a different light. He took in a deep breath, and just for a moment he'd allowed himself to consider the impossible.

Perhaps he'd been mistaken.

That burning question—whether it was safer to wager the world's destiny on the potential anarchy of human freedom, or to trust instead the steady, merciless hand of tyranny—perhaps it had already been answered.

Perhaps men even more astute than he had once wrestled with that same fundamental puzzle. They wrote and ratified their astounding solution in four simple pages—those pages were on the table in front of him— then they'd risked everything to establish a place—one single haven—where good people could come and prosper and live their lives free from the ceaseless meddling of the ruling class.

They hadn't presumed that they could save the whole world, and they'd never intended to conquer it. But if this brash experiment could manage to banish the tyrants and succeed on its own shores, and if the wider world was then saved through its example, all the better.

Such thinking was backward, simpleminded, a laughably naïve concept completely unfit for modern governance—that's what Arthur Gardner had always believed. These were only more lies of a different flavor than the ones he created, aimed to be embraced mainly by flag-waving, gun-toting, Bible-thumping misfits.

But his earlier thought arose again, and it persisted: perhaps he'd been wrong.

And so, in accordance with his late wife's final wishes, a few days ago he'd come to a decision. While he was far from a convert, as a social scientist he'd discovered an error in his method. There was an important hypothesis that had been neglected in his work, and that must be corrected. He would do nothing more in aid of either side, then, until the matter had been put to the test.

For this trial he would bring in a fair and impartial judge—a clear-eyed and apparently incorruptible pillar of virtue named Virginia Ward. If Jaime had been right, if these self-styled patriots truly had a cause worth fighting for, this woman would see it. And when she'd rendered her decision perhaps even Arthur Gardner might finally reconsider which side he should be on.

PART TWO

CHAPTER 22

Virginia Ward eased her Wrangler to a crawl, leaned right, and took her eyes off the rocky, pitted road just long enough for one last check of her face in the rearview mirror. Her features were lit warm in the last light of the day and she saw what she needed to see. There wasn't a speck of vanity in the gesture; this was a field inspection, nothing more. Surviving the night was the main thing on her mind.

During the three-hour inbound flight she'd put herself together to make a mission-critical first impression, and yes, the woman in the mirror would deliver the needed effect. Dollar Store makeup with a hard working day's wear; a sun-dried, honey-blond, no-nonsense hairdo, now mostly tucked up under a weathered bent-brim Lady Stetson—she wore no wedding jewelry, and her Los Diablos sweatshirt was authentically faded from the decade or so since a woman of her age might have led the pep squad at Arizona State, back in her glory days. To the ruthless men she would soon be facing she'd look like a nonthreatening nobody, maybe the only neighbor willing and able to help her friends in need, the harmless and somewhat attractive single rancher-mom from the next spread up the interstate.

In a word, she looked disarming, and that should do.

The command post soon appeared ahead at the bleak descending end of a desert trail just barely fit for a rugged four-wheel drive. The post itself wasn't much, and none of it had been there yesterday. A dark barracks-length tent, a hasty perimeter, and a couple of uniformed guards walking the line—still, it was the only trace of law and order in all these empty miles.

She saw that there was a diesel generator off to the side of the tent but it was still strapped to its trailer, untouched. Apparently these geniuses had decided to let the sun go down before anyone thought to get their power going. Such a lack of foresight didn't bode too well for the brilliance of the rest of their plan, if they had a plan at all.

One of a pair of young sentries straightened him-self up and began motioning toward a parking spot, sporting his best hard-guy face in preparation to challenge and screen the new arrival. But the wiser of the two, his weapon ready, wouldn't peel his eyes from the long, hostile flats stretching south toward the horizon, down toward the border where the real danger lay.

Virginia made the turn and pulled to a stop as she was directed, just to the side of a freshly planted government-issued warning sign. She scanned what it said as she unbuckled her seat belt and got her ID and her sidearm in order, and then she paused to read over the sign once again, but slowly. After seven years attached to the Special Activities Division of the CIA she'd made a lot of vivid memories, but if she happened to make it back to the motel alive tonight, this sign would get its own four-star WTF page in her personal journal.

**DANGER—PUBLIC
WARNING
TRAVEL NOT RECOMMENDED**

- Active Drug and Human Smuggling Area
- Visitors May Encounter Armed Criminals and Smuggling Vehicles Traveling at High Rates of Speed
- Stay Away from Trash, Clothing, Backpacks, and Abandoned Vehicles
- If You See Suspicious Activity, Do Not Confront! Move Away and Call 911

Then, as though to normalize the unreal content that preceded it, the last bullet included a friendly, official travel tip from the U.S. Bureau of Land Management:

- The Bureau of Land Management Encourages Visitors to Use Public Lands North of Interstate 8

In other words, my fellow Americans, despite those bold lines on the map that you can see with your own eyes, your fretful government strongly recommends a hasty retreat toward the distant lights of Tucson. Turn and run if you know what's good for you, because past this point it's every man for himself. Whatever this place is, it isn't Arizona anymore; you're no longer standing on the land of the free.

Well, then, she thought. *I guess we'll have to see about that.*

Virginia pulled her satchel and her cane from behind the passenger seat and pressed a switch on the dashboard to activate an all-band communications jammer in the rear compartment. Then she pocketed the keys, left her hat on the seat, flicked off the headlights, opened her door, and stepped out, good leg first.

In the course of a long and painful rehabilitation she'd come to think of her left leg in that way, as her good one, though of the two it wasn't the limb she was born with. On the positive side it could be whatever she needed it to be, with nearly all the utility but none of the frailties of mere flesh and bone. Synthetic from mid-thigh to the ground, it was interchangeable with a number of purpose-designed replacements hung in her walk-in closet at home. Most were best suited for any one application, be it running, rock climbing, biking, or barhopping. The model she'd chosen for that night was on loan from MIT, and it was special—smooth Barbie leg on the outside, bleeding-edge mechanics on the inside.

Not that all its high-tech and titanium imparted any superhuman abilities, but while this leg looked just like a standard, stiff cosmetic prosthesis, it also restored about three-quarters of the practical function she'd had before she lost the original. And as Virginia Ward had proved to all those skeptics behind her at the last Hawaii Ironman, three-quarters of normal is about a thousand percent more than most might expect from a unilateral amputee.

She didn't mind being underestimated by strangers at first, not at all. In about an hour, in fact, a number of innocent lives—plus her own—would depend upon it.

The nearby sentry was facing her as she approached. The dusk was fully descended by then and with maybe ten feet still between them he held out a flat hand and addressed her by the book, the blue-white glare from his flashlight in her face.

"Halt!" he shouted. "Identify yourself, and let me see your hands!"

In only these few words he'd told her more than he probably imagined. English was not this soldier's native tongue; his accent indicated a gutter strain of Spanish, Español Mexicano, with the faint but distinctive peculiarities heard in those proud to have been born and raised in the rougher parts of the Distrito Federal.

"Virginia Ward," she said. "I'm expected. I'm here to see—"

"Advance to be recognized."

With her patience fading fast she took a moment to bring out her ID and then came forward, the small black leather folder held open at eye level for his review. The large man briefly flicked his bright beam down to the turf in front of him, indicating without further courtesy where she should stop and await his full inspection.

In the spillover light Virginia had spied some details of his uniform. Where a badge or an indication of rank should be, there was only a nameplate and a sewn-on yellow crest. This chintzy embroidery identified him as an employee of Talion, a mercenary services company she'd been seeing more and more of in her deployments.

This wasn't a military man, not a law enforcement officer, maybe not even a U.S. citizen. He was nothing more than a dressed-up, spit-shined, testosterone-swollen gun for hire.

"Ma'am," he said sternly as she continued to approach, "put down your bag for me, extend your arms out to either side—"

The guy stopped talking then, and snapped to stiff attention. Evidently he'd finally caught sight of the three bold letters on the face of her ID folder, the ones that translated to *shut up and stand down* in every allied covert-ops phrase book around the world.

Virginia didn't bother to pause as she walked past the man, though she did make a mental note of the look in his eyes. He'd just seen a ghost, so it seemed, and that was as close an approach to the truth as someone like him should ever be allowed.

First things first: she began by sending a lieutenant outside so he could direct his men in firing up the electricity. She dismissed another soldier with orders to manage the clueless mercs and, more important, to receive the skilled reinforcements who would be arriving close behind her. Not that these new ground troops and heavy weapons would be of any help to her own solo mission, but if she should fail, this place might rapidly find itself on the southern front of a new war zone and they'd need to be ready for anything.

With those priorities addressed, by the light of battery-powered lanterns she began the mission briefing with the other senior officers in attendance.

What they already knew was this: A week earlier a truckload of heavy automatic rifles and cop-killer ammo had been prepared for passage out of the United States across the Arizona–Mexico border. This shipment was a small part of an ongoing and idiotic ATF gun-walking operation that for whatever reason was designed to put weapons into the hands of criminal gangs. Meanwhile, a completely separate Drug Enforcement Administration sting was in the process of spiriting five tons of primo Purple Haze and nearly a hundred kilos of nearly pure cocaine toward a distribution center in the same general area. Finally, the FBI (in cooperation with the Joint Terrorism Task Force and an armed subdivision of the Internal Revenue Service) had initiated a crafty setup that involved the delivery of several million dollars in unmarked cash to the nearby hub of a Sinaloa money-laundering enterprise.

All the while none of these agencies had been apprised of the converging actions of the others—but through its network of moles, informants, and double agents, the Los Zetas cartel was totally on top of all three.

As it turned out, a key target of these operations—a fearsome man known in his circles as the Executioner—was running a little sting of his own from his stronghold in Mexico. His planning was impeccable, his intel was frightfully detailed, and his men—an elite band of MS-13 foot soldiers and Sureños defectors, led by an underboss of the Texas Syndicate—proved to be far more organized and prepared than the U.S. attorney general and all the king's horses at the Justice Department.

The outcome had been a devastating surprise attack. When it was over, three federal agents were dead, six more were missing, and two Border Patrol officers had also lost their lives as the Los Zetas gangsters simultaneously hijacked the southbound trifecta of drugs, money, and guns.

After lying low for a few days at a stateside hole-in-the-wall they'd switched vehicles, consolidated their swag, and then set off toward the safety of their home base in Nuevo Laredo.

Barely sixty miles into the trip their single overloaded truck full of stolen treasures had broken down with a flat tire on the southern acres of some land owned by an Arizona rancher named Harland Dell. As the hoods were changing their tire Mr. Dell got the drop on them, apparently thinking they were just another pack of everyday smugglers or coyotes. He held the trespassers at gunpoint and called in the authorities.

The resulting bust didn't sit well at all with the Mexican kingpin, and it was more than just the loss of this unusually valuable shipment that enraged him. The precedent this might set for other brave U.S. citizens couldn't be allowed to stand, and so the head man announced a vendetta: an example was to be made of this American.

In a sudden move of unprecedented brass the Los Zetas outlaws surged across the border in force and commandeered the Dell property. They were now holding the family hostage, and the ransom they demanded was the release of their men and the return of their truck with all the spoils it contained. That's where the situation stood at the present moment.

Virginia checked her watch and addressed the post's young commander. "Do you know how many of them we're up against?"

"About a dozen that we could see, and probably more by now. We commissioned a flyover yesterday by a Cessna 206 from the Highway Patrol. They got a fairly good view before they started taking small-arms fire and had to back off. Then this morning we got as close as we could and put up a blimp with a camera system, and the Kestrel got some even more detailed images before the bastards shot it down."

"I'm sorry, what?"

"They shot it down with a SAM, probably a Stinger."

"They shot down a recon blimp with a guided missile."

"A U.S.-made guided missile. Overkill, I know. I guess they really didn't want to get their pictures taken." He slid across a small stack of photographs. "Have a look at what we got while the bird was up."

Though the photos were chilling they didn't tell her much she hadn't already suspected. The place was obviously fully occupied and well guarded. Corpses were strewn all about, probably left where they'd fallen after what must have been a short and futile defense of the property against a merciless, overwhelming invasion.

"You've cut the power and the landlines to the place."

"Right."

"Has anyone spoken to them?"

"We've harvested some cell numbers that they're using"—he passed her a sheet with the information—"but listen, these guys aren't negotiating. The last they told us was, midnight tonight they start kicking more bodies out the front door."

No surprise there, either. Virginia Ward was a fixer, not a negotiator. By the time she was called into service the opportunity for bargaining had always long passed.

"Okay," she said, as she stood. "Now I need to make a call, and I'll need some privacy for that."

"I'm sorry, our comms are down here right now. It's inexcusable, I know, it must be sunspots or something—"

"Your comms are down because I took them down." She stowed her pistol and her ID and then removed a special-purpose satellite phone from her satchel. "This one should punch through just fine, though. The next thing you're going to do is collect all the radios and phones from your men, and make your orders very clear. I've got people coming in specifically to enforce the communications blackout. If anyone's seen trying to get a message out of here to anyone, I don't care if they're telling their grandchildren good night, they won't get a warning, they're going to get shot. Not a word gets in or out except my own traffic and any calls coming from the perpetrators. You'll know I'm coming back when you see me."

The man nodded, and then he said, "Don't tell me you're going down there all alone."

"That's right."

"Unarmed?"

"Whatever weapons I bring they'll just take away. Don't worry, there won't be any shortage of guns available in that place, I'm sure."

"Can you at least tell me what you think you're going to do when you get there?"

"Sure," Virginia replied. "If anyone in that family is still alive, I'm going to bring them out. And if I can I'm going to kill every last one of the savages that took them hostage."

While she was outside making her call she heard the generator roaring to life and saw scattered lights fade on. During the briefing more equipment and a company of soldiers had arrived. Her own men were among them, and these exchanged a discreet acknowledgment with her as they started their work. Others began the task of positioning and raising four heavily armed mobile VIPR watchtowers along the base perimeter.

Off in the distance another vehicle approached; this would be her ride to the besieged home of Harland Dell and his wife and kids. In this midsized mover's truck was loaded all the loot and the bound prisoners that the kidnappers had demanded be returned to them immediately, or else.

And returned to them it would be.

By the time she'd driven to the final stretch of her route, the highway had become completely deserted. The roadblocks that accomplished this were disguised as drunk-driving checkpoints, and undercover teams posing as night-shift pavement crews rounded out the travel barricades. This layer of secrecy was mostly to aid in controlling the story, and as such it was probably a wasted effort. For whatever reason the American press had long since proven their bias to ignore the ever-widening, bloody war being fought along these southern borderlands.

Virginia made the turn onto private property and drove slowly down the long gravel drive. The entrance to the ranch was a hand-hewn wooden arch with the family cattle brand displayed at its central apex. Soon after she passed it, from the pitch dark of the moonless desert night the first visible signs of the Dell ranch emerged in the distance.

The place and its grounds were lit only by firelight, but it wasn't an inviting radiance of the hearth or a peaceful evening glow in the windows that she saw.

There was a crude line of smoky blazing torches lashed to random fence posts along the driveway and around the residence. A massive bonfire burned high in what used to be the front yard, fed by what looked like sticks of furniture and other belongings, and encircled by men with rifles and belts of ammo slung across their backs.

By the light of the torches, off to her left she saw a man crucified among the lower branches of a eucalyptus tree. Another was nailed up in the same way, but higher at the crossbeam of a utility pole. To the right three bodies still hung where they'd been lynched, two in the trees beyond the steep, rocky shoulder and the last one nearer to the inbound road. That accounted for the ranch hands, and one more. The last battered corpse swung from a hasty gallows by a noose suspended from the highest crossbar of a children's swing set.

Above this hanging body was affixed a makeshift wooden sign, and Virginia was able to read it by the ugly light of the bonfire. It was lettered in dripping black paint and a primitive scrawl as though it had been made by someone unaccustomed to expression in any written language.

HARLAND DELL, the sign read.

CHAPTER 23

As her headlights swept across the gathering of armed men by the fire, Virginia Ward scanned the scene and noticed one thing right away. There were quite a few more bad guys here than she'd been told to expect.

Her arrival had captured their full attention and soon a group of them put their heads together and then started walking up the driveway toward the approaching truck. They kept on coming and as she slowed they began shouting and gesturing her onward, some with their weapons raised.

Despite these threatening signals Virginia pulled to an abrupt stop, turned off the ignition, lowered the driver's-side window, and extended her hand outside, waving the white hand-towel she'd brought along to serve as a flag of truce.

The men had nearly reached her as she thumbed a button on the key-chain remote. A signal module under the dash blipped twice in response; she'd activated a one-way kill-switch that the Agency mechanics had installed. To anyone trying to restart it the engine would sound like it was on the verge of firing up, but this well-hidden device would ensure that it would never come to life again. She'd stopped a good distance from the house and that was where the truck would remain.

Now a timer was running and a slow-motion self-destruct procedure had begun. With this action the mission was fully committed and she set a counter ticking in the back of her mind.

The man in the lead grabbed the handle outside, jerked the door open, and shoved his pistol toward her face. Her hand was shaking as she handed him the keys, and then in response to a shouted order, with careful motions she took up her cane and made her way down to the turf from the high cab.

The one who'd opened the door cocked his arm and delivered a backhanded slap across her jaw that nearly put her on the ground. They weren't happy that she'd stopped where she had and they obviously weren't shy of violence against a defenseless woman, but that's where the punishment ended for the moment. It had been a calculated risk—they might have shot her immediately—but she had wagered on their standards as professional murderers. You can penalize disobedience as harshly as you want, but a pro doesn't kill a newly arrived hostage over nothing.

Two of the other men had climbed into the truck's cab and were attempting to get it going again. As they pumped the accelerator and worked the key she could already smell the fumes of excess gasoline filling the air. The starter ground away and popped occasionally but the engine wouldn't fire.

"*Ten cuidado,*" Virginia said, and she made it seem as though she struggled with the Spanish, "*To . . . to inicio, es difícil, muy difícil,*" she continued, pantomiming the turning of an ignition key. "It's something with the fuel pump. Tell him to be careful not to flood it, because it's very hard to start."

The lead man pushed her against the fender and twisted her around, playing rough. He searched her with his hands, groping and lingering here and there, and in the course of it he found her pepper spray, her counterfeit ID, her penknife, and the separate ring of keys to the padlocked rear compartment.

When he reached her left leg he flinched back and called the others nearer so they could see. One lifted her skirt and bent to feel the prosthesis, seemingly fascinated, starting at the ankle and continuing upward until he found bare skin. Others joined in and she endured all the pawing until the hooting, leering men were finally called back to order.

They left a couple of their mob to free their unconscious compatriots in the back and to check over the shrink-wrapped cargo. Two more were assigned to lift the hood and get the truck started, refueled, and ready to depart for the border. The rest led her back to the house. The pace was slowed due to her exaggerated limp but despite a few pokes in the back and some mockery they didn't seem too awfully hurried. As far as they knew, time was still on their side.

From the snippets of conversation she caught it was clear they were now faced with a conundrum. They'd obviously planned to immediately head south for home with their loot while delaying the authorities in fake negotiations for a turnover of the hostages, who by that time would already be dead. With the truck temporarily out of commission those plans might have to change.

Inside, the house was filthy and thoroughly defiled from its brief time under siege. Through an archway she saw the remainder of the Dell family clinging together on the floor of the dining room. The mother and the girls had obviously been brutalized; they were clutching their torn and bloodied clothes against their skin, pale faces looking shell-shocked and lifeless as the tomb.

The son, all of maybe twelve or thirteen, had somehow been permitted to live. He made eye contact with Virginia, and as he did she could see his initial confusion pass away and become an understanding.

These men had demanded that their truck be delivered by a civilian known to the family. The photo matched on the ID she'd brought and the name was verifiable to the extent that they might be able to check it. But the boy was already thinking and he was with her all the way; to cement her identification he got to his feet and ran to her and hugged her close.

Virginia Ward had whispered a question in his ear before they were pulled apart and the boy was shoved back toward his place. When he was near to his mother and sisters again he found her eyes, and nodded.

Are you ready to help me? was what she'd asked.

While she still held his gaze she glanced up toward the mantel, where a rack of family rifles were displayed. Under two showpieces hung an off-the-shelf Winchester 94 lever-action, something a father might give to his son on the occasion of his coming of age. She looked back to the boy, and though his expression was dark he nodded once again.

The boss man walked over. The phone in his hand was ringing, and upon double-checking the caller ID he held the device out toward her.

"This will be the authorities," he said in English. "You will tell them you're here and that this family is safe and sound, every one of them. Say any more and I'll have to cut your throat. Do you understand me?"

"Yes." With that she took the phone, thumbed the talk button, and brought the speaker to her ear.

Meanwhile, right on schedule, a commotion had begun outside.

With all their ham-fisted attempts to restart the truck they'd managed to ignite a small fire at the fuel pump under the hood. In truth, of course, their efforts weren't really to blame; an automated sequence of electronics and incendiaries was controlling every step of the un-folding diversion.

Amid a lot of yelling and mounting confusion among the *pandilleros* she heard the creak of a garden faucet turning and the hose being dragged from its reel, but it wouldn't be nearly long enough to reach. The exasper-ated ringleader left her with the phone and herded nearly every one of his crew outside to try to bring the now-urgent situation with the truck under control.

Virginia heard one of her own men on the other end of the call and she repeated the words as she'd been told, loud enough so all nearby could hear them. The caller asked a coded question. She took one last look around the room, and responded: "Yes."

Before her earlier departure she'd made a satellite call to the base commander of the 162nd Fighter Wing, stationed near Tucson International Airport. The con-firmation she'd just given hadn't really been necessary, she knew; the cavalry was coming regardless, and no one had been certain she'd make it this far. The subtle infrared signature of the truck afire, visible from satellite reconnaissance, had been their agreed-upon go-signal. A trio of F-16s were no doubt already orbiting the area and would have carried out their orders whether or not she and the hostages were still alive.

But just as she'd planned, all hostile attention was focused outside; no one there was expecting any trouble from a timid, crippled woman and a terrorized young boy.

As she'd spoken on the phone Virginia had also made an inventory of the firepower left in the room. Two holstered handguns, a jacked-up AR-15, a ridiculously converted Glock pistol—complete with shoulder stock and a double-canister magazine slung underneath—and then there was first prize: an Atchisson assault shotgun carried by the swaggering leader of the pack.

And that man was still at the open door watching as the truck's engine fire continued to bloom. The flames suddenly snaked down to a generous puddle of fuel that had dripped to the ground beneath the chassis. He began shouting orders to abandon the failing effort to extinguish the spreading blaze and to unload their valuable cargo while there was still time enough to save it.

"Hey, mister," Virginia said. She leaned heavily on her cane as she hobbled toward the head man, holding out the phone to him. "They want to talk to you."

From a great distance in the cloudless night a rumble from the sky arrived, just barely sufficient to rattle the standing china in a hallway cabinet. Unlike any variety of natural thunder this deep roll didn't recede as these final critical seconds crept by; it only grew.

She stopped a few feet away as the leader of the gang turned from the door. She could see his mind working as he stepped toward her, and he'd just begun to reach for the cell phone she offered when he froze, looked her directly in the eyes, and he knew.

Virginia Ward dropped the phone and let her cane fall aside as the man fumbled to ready the shotgun slung over his shoulder. In one practiced motion she moved into him, caught the barrel and pushed it down and away as it discharged, lashed an elbow into his neck as she grabbed the stock, and wrenched it up and under to bring the muzzle beneath his chin. His finger had snapped as it broke from the backward twist but the sting of the fracture would never reach his brain. She pulled the trigger with her thumb and blew his head through the ceiling.

She crouched behind cover just as a wild reaction shot rang out from the corner. With her weapon now free she flicked the selector to full-auto, stood quickly, and emptied the 20-round 12-gauge magazine in a four-second semicircular volley of solid buckshot and destruction that ripped through the remaining three inside-men and sent them all cut to pieces to the floor.

"Come on, kid!" she yelled, and Virginia leaped to the fireplace, snatched the racked Winchester from the mantel, and tossed it upright to the boy, who was already running toward her. He caught the rifle, worked the action, and fired through the door to take out a man running toward it, and he continued firing from the hip into the others as fast as he could shift his aim and squeeze the trigger.

Virginia pulled the boy down to relative safety be-hind her, dropped her empty shotgun, and picked up the AR-15 from the arm of one of the fallen thugs. She'd been hit but couldn't pause to determine how seriously; the next minute or so would tell.

With the butt of the rifle she broke out a window and then laid down a metered pattern of suppressing fire. The closest men outside had been caught unawares and now they turned and ran away from the house, shoot-ing backward and sideways without effect as they fled toward their cohorts and the nearest cover available: the burning truck about fifty yards away.

When their initial panic subsided they would no doubt hope to regroup out there and try to draw her attention from safety, then wait and watch until she and the boy had run out of ammunition, before moving back in for the easy kill.

Just as she'd glimpsed a tight line of formation lights moving among the stars to the northwest, an incoming round splintered the window frame and sprayed them both with razor shards of glass. She told the boy to stay low and then returned fire to cover him as she urged him away from danger with a gentle push toward his mother and sisters in the adjoining room.

The gunmen outside were getting bolder all the while. Their wild shooting had ceased, replaced by more accurate tries from more widely positioned hiding places. It was all she could do to mask and shift her location while keeping them mostly contained behind the truck.

Having had time to think and reestablish their pecking order, they must have been weighing the overwhelming strength of their numbers against the vulnerabilities of the single armed opponent they now faced. Their only real question would be how and when they would choose to make the final advance.

Whatever they might have been scheming, however, their designs were interrupted a split second later by the awesome and on-time arrival of the Arizona Air National Guard.

Virginia Ward had just expended her last round as the first of the Falcons tore through below treetop level at full afterburner, trailing the scream of an avenging angel. All the front windows shattered and blew violently inward as the clap of the pressure wave slammed against the house. Without firing a shot, in its supersonic wake the lead F-16 had flattened the men outside who'd still been standing.

As the first jet peeled off the second followed on, flying slow on a guns-only strafing run. In a flash of heavy-metal demolition its Vulcan cannon plowed a relentless, rooster-tailing furrow across the driveway and cut through the heart of the clustered enemies. The truck's fuel tanks burst and exploded and the fire roared heavenward, and as the dust swirled and settled, by the light of the gangsters' burning treasure she could see no human movement amid the devastation.

There would be a last stroke coming. She picked up a pistol from a dead man's hand as she hurried away from the window and back to Harland Dell's huddled family. She held them close, shielding them with her body as the shriek of a Maverick missile sheared the air overhead. A final concussion shook the house to its foundation as the explosion cratered whatever remained of the threat from the men outside.

As the echoes of the strike were still fading away she continued speaking softly to the four survivors. Her voice was reassuring and calm as she listened and watched with her pistol held cocked and rock-steady and trained upon the open door. The sounds of a helicopter approaching with the rescue party barely eased her mind at all; she knew from long experience that the last moment before salvation can be as deadly as any other.

And Virginia Ward also knew something else: the nightmare was far from over for this widowed woman and her children. In fact, it never fully would be; they'd have to learn to live with scars even deeper than her own.

But they would live through this, just as their brave father would have wanted. For tonight, that was the very best that she could do.

CHAPTER 24

When the rescue helicopter had arrived at the burned-out ranch, one of the physicians had insisted that Virginia be flown to a secure medical facility in Colorado for observation. She'd agreed, in part so she could accompany the Dell family to that same hospital and oversee the beginnings of their care.

Once she'd settled into her recovery room she had to admit that the rest would be welcome. She'd taken a legitimate beating and after two rough flights and an endless debriefing she was left feeling every blow this latest mission had dealt her. Despite multiple cuts and bruises and two grazing bullet wounds, she'd chosen to forgo most of the painkillers when they were offered. She needed to preserve all of her mental faculties for a supposedly urgent meeting set to take place later on.

At least there had been a good hot shower in the bargain, and there would be no more traveling for the moment, not even a walk down the hall. Her next appointment was coming directly to her hospital room; she wouldn't even need to change out of her bathrobe to meet with him.

With the bedside remote she adjusted herself to a more upright position. She was still too wired for a nap and too tired to pace the floor, but there was no shortage of reading to be done.

A stack of materials in various media had been brought and left alongside her dinner tray by someone's assistant. The encrypted touchscreen tablet placed on top would contain all things sensitive and classified, including issue-specific position papers from various intelligence services and an up-to-the-minute recap of the President's Daily Briefing. A generous bundle of domestic and international newspapers and magazines rounded out the pile, and that's where she began.

Not that she believed much of the sponsored propaganda that was parroted by the press in these times. No, Virginia kept up with the papers and periodicals purely to see what the general public was being told. Through study of the covert trends and agendas between the lines she could sometimes assemble a better forecast of where and when the next crisis might arise.

The truth was predictably scarce in all those spoon-fed pages. But as someone who spent her days immersed in the undisguised reality of a global house of cards on the brink of total catastrophe, she couldn't help but think that maybe it was better this way. There was some form of mercy in the fact that the majority of people didn't have any idea what was coming.

Virginia Ward no longer harbored any fantasies of a happy ending, not even for the nation she loved. Her work was not at all strategic but purely reactive and tactical in nature, clear-cut and eye-to-eye. She put a stop to things that were wrong; that's how she phrased it on those rare occasions when she was asked what she did for a living by someone who merited an honest answer. Desperate circumstances arose and she went out to meet them, and then she put things right and made that single problem go away.

This was how she wanted it; nothing ambiguous, no

soul-searching was required, and there was enough self-determination in her work to make it seem worthwhile. She retained the absolute right of refusal for these missions, and when she had the opportunity to choose an assignment for herself, she was free to take it on.

That bloody siege in Arizona had been one of her own choosing. The next, though, whatever it was, would no doubt be suggested for her by someone higher up, one of the many competing power brokers who worked their patient plots from behind the tinted glass.

The man she would soon be meeting was new to her. This made it even more important that her mind be clear. It was beyond unusual for her services to be requested—or even learned of—by anyone she didn't know personally.

As she was lost in her reading there soon came a quiet knock at the door frame. She signed out of her tablet, looked up, and motioned the visitor inside.

"Is this a good time?" the man asked, smiling.

"Good as any. Please, come on in."

He did, removing his jacket and laying it over his arm as he walked up near the bed. "Do people call you Ginny?"

"Not often."

"Virginia, then." He seemed to make note of her more visible injuries. "You took some damage out there tonight."

"You should see the other guy," she said without humor, and with hopes that the niceties would soon be coming to a close.

"I'll bet." He reached out and she shook his hand. "I've heard a lot about you, Virginia. My name is Warren Landers."

This guy was very well connected; that was the first impression he'd obviously sought to give her. His boss was a man named Arthur Gardner; he was the one who'd reached out to Virginia's people a few days before. Landers had been sent to Arizona to observe her previous mission, and after apparently finding her work to be adequate for his needs, he'd followed her here.

As usual in these cases, once his credentials were established she hadn't expected him to provide many other details of the organization behind him, and none were offered.

Mr. Landers sat and waited while she went through the backgrounder he'd brought.

At first blush the man whom Landers and his group were targeting seemed hardly more than a cold-blooded murderer. There'd been scattered sightings of him across the country and other seemingly random shootings along the eastern seaboard seemed to bear his signature as well.

He'd once been a military man with a sterling record, but upon returning home he'd apparently suffered some sort of a gradual post-traumatic breakdown. According to one supposedly reliable source, he'd later fallen in with a group of homegrown extremists. For almost two decades this organization had managed to stay under the law enforcement radar before suddenly popping up late last year.

"Thom Hollis," she said.

"Thom or Thomas; he seems to go by both."

She flipped through the upper corners of the remaining paperwork. "By the dates on these documents this has all been put together rather quickly. And recently."

He nodded. "That's true. This Hollis guy and the group behind him just made the President's kill-list. The White House is about to green-light a signature strike on them, so there was a bit of a scramble to get up to speed."

This "kill-list" to which Mr. Landers referred was a

relatively new development, at least among governments that still tipped their hats to the rule of law. Together with a small contingent of advisors the President would regularly meet to nominate and then pass judgment on foreign (and now domestic) "militant" individuals deemed eligible for termination without the benefit of due process.

"So tell me about this group."

"As you just read, Thom Hollis has been running with one of those right-wing domestic militias. Real throwbacks, Constitutionalists, religious fanatics, Sovereign Citizens, I'm sure you know the profile. They call themselves the Founders' Keepers, and I guess they want to drag us all back to 1789, slaves and all. You're familiar with George Pierce and the United Aryan Nations?"

"Of course."

"They're branches on the same tree, and apparently they're all in the process of joining forces. There was a showdown a few days ago up in Wyoming; the good guys finally had these people pinned, and they hit back with the kind of weaponry and tactics and numbers that tells us they're at a whole new level now. Most of them got away, and this Hollis guy split off from there."

"And the woman who's with him?"

"Her name is Molly Ross. Her mother was Beverly Ross, you might have heard of her, she was some kind of a libertarian activist dating back to the 1970s. She started this group and they seemed mostly harmless while she was alive, a lot of crazy talk but very little action. Mom put herself out of our misery last fall, killed herself, after the daughter and some of Pierce's men perpetrated that incident north of Las Vegas."

"That incident?"

"That *nuclear* incident."

Though Virginia knew exactly what he was talking about, it had seemed more judicious to pretend as though she didn't. This Landers guy didn't need to know how plugged in she really was.

Much like that recent and surprising launch of a Chinese-made ballistic missile from a submarine off the coast of Southern California, the cover stories about the Nevada explosion had flown in so thick and fast that the whole event had passed immediately into the wacky realm of the conspiracy theorists. It was a meteorite, it was a plane crash, it was a botched underground test—only a handful of people really knew what had happened, and their hard knowledge concerned only the fact of the unplanned nuclear detonation, and not the full story behind it. This was the first that even Virginia had heard of a specific terrorist connection.

"Honestly, Mr. Landers, this sounds like a job for the FBI, and the police."

"I would agree with you," Landers said, "but it's not so much what Hollis has done so far that's concerning us. He killed one of his own the other day, a guy named Ben Church, just a harmless old man from the group who was probably trying to talk some sense into him. Shot him in the head. You'll see it in the psych profile, they're calling that a 'triggering incident.' Anyway, they pulled some DNA and fingerprints from some handmade cartridges around that murder scene. Both belong to Hollis. And those other shootings you saw in the brief? The prints and the other evidence at those sites point straight to him, too. We've got some fairly good pictures from surveillance videos; he's traveling with a young female companion, and they're obviously disguising themselves but she looks an awful lot like Molly Ross."

"As I said—"

"With all due respect," Landers cut in, "I think this is a job for you. These killings are only a drum roll. They're laying the groundwork for a major terrorist attack, and as soon as the press gets hold of it these two are going to start getting their names in the paper, and that's just what they want. They want people to know who they are so everyone will know who's responsible when they do what we think they're planning to do."

"And what's that?"

"You and I both know there was a clear lead-up before 9/11. Small things that looked unrelated, and we only saw the connections after the attack. If we'd understood them before, we could have prevented a disaster and saved thousands of lives." He took a step closer. "Virginia, it's these people that were responsible for that near calamity last year. If they'd succeeded it would have made September 11th look like a garden party. Sure, the real facts never made it to the press, but you saw what happened. Even the nonspecific alert they caused was serious enough to move Congress to delay the fall elections; they still haven't happened yet. But they didn't stop after that. What these people have said very clearly to all of their underground followers is that something big is coming, something really spectacular, and they've promised that they're bringing it soon."

She closed the folder and thought for a moment. "All right. I'll take a thorough look and let you know what I think by morning."

"That's all I ask; just give us your thoughts. And one other thing. We've got an advantage here if we want it. We have a back channel to this Molly Ross that I think can help us find her and bring her in."

"What kind of a back channel?"

"It's why this situation has become personal for me and the men I work for. We've got a family member involved. He was duped into helping these people last year, and my hope is that he can provide you with some insights, and maybe even make contact. His name is Noah Gardner."

"I'd like to talk to him."

"Good. He's actually right down the hall."

"What a coincidence," Virginia said.

"I have to confess, it's my doing. Noah got caught in the cross fire in that firefight in Wyoming I mentioned. It's a long story, but when they told me earlier that you needed a checkup after your mission I suggested that they bring you here, just in the hopes that we all could get together and save some time."

"I understand."

"He's a good kid. They really got into his head, though"—Landers briefly twirled a finger by his ear— "Stockholm syndrome kind of stuff, especially with this girl. She slept with him, apparently, convinced him to help her with some corporate espionage, and it went downhill from there. He's probably still got feelings for her, despite the fact that she almost got him killed. And I'd expect him to sound a little paranoid after all he's been through."

"Okay, then. I'll go see him right now."

Landers checked his watch. "Now?"

"If he's awake. There's no time like the present. Do you want to come along? It sounds like you two are close."

"No, no, no, I'm a . . ." Landers seemed to struggle for a moment with exactly how to characterize himself. "I'm just a friend of the family. It's probably better if we keep this all between the two of you."

"Fine." She held out her hand and he shook it. "Now if you'll excuse me, I need to get dressed."

"He's in room 306, just a few doors down. And you've got my number," Landers said. With that he put on his jacket, subtly checked himself in the full-length mirror by the window, and left her with a plastic smile.

She met a lot of people in her line of work, and generally not by choice. Experience had taught her that the
worthiness of the mission often had very little to do with
any high moral virtues of the people requesting the job.

On his way out, this Landers person had said that
she had his number, and he was dead right about that.
In fact, she'd gotten that man's number pretty much the
minute he'd walked in her door.

CHAPTER 25

The leg that Virginia had worn to Arizona was a prototype and hadn't really been intended for the rigorous shakedown it received. And if anyone was back in the lab wondering, it clearly wasn't bulletproof, either.

She looked it over again, now nestled in its fitted recharging case against the wall, as she dressed herself in frayed denim cutoffs and a comfortable old T-shirt from her bag. They'd constructed this leg to be a photographic match of her natural limb, and as such it resembled the shapely and graceful lower-left appendage of a runway model. If David Beckham's real legs were insured for $70 million, this single artificial one probably beat them both in its replacement value—especially since it had been made under a government contract. When she returned it to Cambridge the bionics engineers there would learn a lot from the data it had collected, but they'd also have a few hundred hours of repair work ahead.

By contrast, the piece she now put on was much like her first prosthetic ever, the leg she'd worn when taking those first unsteady steps in the months after the combat injuries that had nearly killed her. As a prosthetic it was a portrait of utility, just carbon fiber and stainless steel and plastic with a wool-padded sleeve, a wide black Velcro harness, and an old Converse high-top laced up to its unisex foot. This was the only spare she'd brought along and it fit her very well, in more ways than one. There were no pretenses about it, no apologies, and yet in its very lack of adornments it held a certain kind of beauty that not everyone might pause to appreciate.

When Virginia checked the clock after her guest had departed she found it was later than she'd thought. If the subject of her upcoming interview was already asleep she'd just catch him in the morning. Meanwhile, the short stroll might do some good for her fresh aches and pains.

In the middle of the night the hallway was perfectly still, as were the Marine sentries stationed outside her own private suite and one other nearby. A few steps farther down she paused and looked past the guards into the room where the members of the Dell family were safely housed. Cots had been rolled in and the space well prepared so mother and children could stay together in comfort.

The boy was the only one awake when she peeked inside. Ronny was his name, she'd later learned. He sat up a bit when he saw her, she gave him a small wave, and with very little movement he waved back, though he didn't manage to smile. That was okay; we do these things one step at a time.

When she arrived at Noah Gardner's room she found him reading by a solitary light at the side of the bed. Before she could knock he'd put aside his book and motioned her inside.

"You're up," Virginia said.

"Yeah. They've had me knocked out for so long I don't know if I'll ever need to sleep again."

"I'm Virginia Ward."

He nodded. "They told me you'd be coming by."

"Do you feel like a chat now?"

"Sure," he said.

Rather than pulling up one of the low chairs, she came to the foot of his hospital bed, lowered the railing, and hopped up to sit and face him from near that end. "Do you know what I'm here to talk to you about?"

"Yes. You want to talk about Molly."

"Do you know why?"

"I was told there's a chance she can be brought in safely, and that you might give her that chance."

She nodded. "Where do you think we should start?"

"I think we should start with you telling me if that's a fact."

"If I get involved in this, Noah, I'm going to do what's right, for my country first and then for everyone else after that. That's what I do, and that's all I can promise you at this point."

"Fair enough, I guess."

"And I need to say, right now it doesn't look so good for her." She opened the background folder that Landers had given her. "She's gotten mixed up with some very bad guys, militant white supremacists—"

"Oh, get serious, now."

". . . and one man you might have come in contact with. A big guy named Thom Hollis."

"Hollis?" He laughed. "I never actually knew his first name, but you're saying Thom Hollis is one of these very bad guys she's mixed up with? The man's a teddy bear; he wouldn't hurt a fly."

"He had seventy-seven confirmed kills as a sniper in Iraq and Afghanistan."

"Really?"

"Really." She handed over a summary of the service record. "His longest shot was just over a mile."

For almost a minute Noah studied the papers and

looked through the old photos of the man. "So he was a soldier, and a good one. Surely you're not saying that makes him some kind of a lunatic."

"Of course not. It seemed like you were saying he was harmless, and I wanted to show you that maybe that was only an impression you'd been given. How long were you actually around these people?"

"A very short time. Just a few days."

"And would you say that while you were with them, they were honest and open with you about what they were doing?"

He thought for a while before he answered quietly. "No. No, they weren't."

"Let me tell you what it says here," Virginia began. "It says Molly Ross and her mother and these Founders' Keepers descended on New York City late last year, in part to recruit new members and to stir up some trouble in lower Manhattan. They had a rally and they sponsored some counterprotests on Wall Street and a similar scuffle at an international financial summit. Things got out of hand at the rally, shots were fired, and they got arrested. Then you pulled some strings and managed to get Molly and the rest of them out of jail, and then you slept with her that night.

"The next day you brought Molly Ross into your firm's corporate offices, gave illegal access to the place to her accomplices, and showed her how to retrieve some highly classified information concerning your father's government-connected clients. Meanwhile, another associate of Ms. Ross, a well-known agitator named Danny Bailey, met with a veteran FBI agent who secretly ran a radical white-power website on the side. Both Bailey and this agent were already under federal investigation.

"While you and Molly Ross were getting to know each other better, these two men flew to Nevada and hooked up with some close friends of George Lincoln Rockwell Pierce, leader of the United Aryan Nations, and all these men entered into a real-life conspiracy to destroy downtown Las Vegas and another target in California. They weren't just talking anymore, and they now had the means, the motive, and the opportunity to take action. Through this rogue FBI man and their own connections, Pierce's clan had come into possession of two previously hijacked nuclear devices, and they intended to use them.

"They spent some time at a strip club the night before the planned attacks. A last celebration, I guess. That night, and then again later on when they were starting their suicide run, Danny Bailey is known to have been exchanging text messages with Molly Ross. We have images of these men and their rigged truck from several security cameras along their route.

"These people kept an apartment in Manhattan that was raided. The agents found bizarre literature, radical tracts and survivalist stuff, anarchist's cookbooks, you name it. And there were traces of what appeared to be bomb-making materials there, too.

"That's about when you were helping Molly evade airport security at LaGuardia, after which the two of you caught a flight west toward a rendezvous with the bombers. You rented a vehicle for her, and you accompanied her at least part of the way to where she was going. Something must have gone wrong with the plan, though. One or both of the weapons they were transporting detonated prematurely, out in the old testing grounds in the Nevada desert." She closed the folder and looked up at him. "What do you have to say about all of that?"

"What do I have to say? Every word of it's accurate, but none of it's true."

"That's a little cryptic, Noah."

"More than just a little, Virginia."

"So none of this is true."

"Quick example for you. It says there that Molly and I slept together? And that's literally what happened. She was asleep, and I was asleep, and we were together in the same place at the same time. Look at the two of us here right now, you and me: we're in bed together. That's what I mean, this is what they do best, it's a lie with just enough truth in it."

"A lot of people would have to be deceived or complicit to put together a lie this elaborate."

"A lot of people *are* deceived and complicit. That's the name of the game."

"And whose game is that?"

"The people who run things. People like my father and the men he does his work for."

Warren Landers had said that young Mr. Gardner might sound a little paranoid, and whatever else she'd thought of Landers, at least that part of what he'd said was proving out.

"Let me ask you, then," Virginia said. "What do *you* think is happening here?"

"Do you really want to know?"

"Of course I do."

"I think the people at the top were trying to use terrorism as a tool to frighten the American people," Noah said. "Frighten them badly enough that they'd willingly give up all their power. And that power would then be used to fundamentally change this system of government, once and for all, to push it toward the one-world kind they can more easily control.

"I think they decided to entrap Molly and her mother and Danny Bailey and marginalize the people who believed in them. I think they wanted to paint them as the bad guys so that anyone who even talked about real freedom and the country's founding principles could be labeled as a racist nut or a dangerous extremist.

"I think all the fear-mongering from Washington, and the dismantling of the Bill of Rights, and the prosecution of whistle-blowers, and the gun-grabbing and the rampant surveillance and the police-state actions they're taking now, it's all clear evidence of that agenda. I think they did the same sort of thing after Oklahoma City and after 9/11 but they couldn't quite kill off the opposition from the liberty movement, so they tried to squash it once and for all last year. And you know what else I think?"

"No."

"I think they're about to try again."

Virginia made some notes and checked over her previous ones to see if there was anything she'd forgotten. "Okay, then," she said, "you've given me a lot to consider."

"Don't do that. Don't just wrap it up that way."

"What else do you want me to say, Noah?"

"I was honest with you, with the full knowledge that what I was telling you might sound completely off-the-wall. Now I'd like for you to tell me what you're going to do."

"Okay." She moved a little closer and looked at him directly. "I believe that you believe that what you've told me is true. You've been through a series of traumas, the kind that could cloud the mind of the strongest person I know. You're emotionally involved and that can add another layer that's very hard to see past.

"But trust me, I'm going to find the truth. Whatever their reasons were for bringing me into this, whatever their agenda was, I do my own thinking and I know right from wrong. And if I can bring Molly in alive, that's what I'm going to do."

"Thank you," Noah said. "You know, my father—whom I don't trust at all—he said that when I met you I'd know I could rely on you. I didn't have much faith in that, but now I do."

"I'm glad to hear it." Virginia gathered up her papers, returned them to the folder, and then edged to the side of the bed and lowered herself to a solid footing on the floor. "Now I'm going to need for you to reach out to Molly. Has she contacted you at all since you last saw her, or has she tried to?"

"I used to get notes from her, one of them had an e-mail address that I remember, but they always came through a third party."

"What sort of notes?"

"Mostly appeals for help with her work. There wasn't much I could do, just little breaches of security at the lockup where they were holding me before. Honestly, except for one or two of them in the beginning, I wasn't sure the messages were even coming from her at all. It might have been some underling of my dad's, testing my loyalty or whatever. Anyway, the notes stopped coming quite a while ago."

"Well, use your imagination. Try to reestablish a connection with her. Don't mention any of this, of course, and don't apply any pressure. Just make contact so you'll know for sure you can get a message to her when the time comes, okay?"

"Okay."

"Great." She shook his hand, a good solid clasp, and then she headed for the door.

"How are you and I going to stay in touch?"

"I'll be around," Virginia said. "In my briefing here it says they've arranged some light work for you during your rehab, is that right?"

"I hadn't heard."

"Someone will probably come by in the morning to tell you more about that. It should be good for you, though, to be around people. Anyway, I know where you'll be and you'll see me again soon. I'll let you know how things are going."

"Okay, but one last thing," Noah said.

"What's that?"

"Two things, really. First, I don't think you or anyone else can stop what these men are trying to do. Molly thought she could, and I thought so, too, for a while. That part of what you said about me is right, I got caught up in it and I was fooling myself, but I'm not anymore. It's too big, and the handful of people who actually know what's coming are too weak. So, even when you see it for yourself, I don't think you'll be able to stop it, and for your sake I hope you don't try. I don't care about myself or anything else anymore; I just don't want Molly to get hurt."

"I understand," Virginia said. "And what's the other thing?"

"Do you play chess?"

"I do. I'm pretty good."

"Then you know how this works. While you're thinking about your next move, the other guy's thinking, too. Against a superior opponent your moves are always enfolded in his."

"I'm not sure I know what you mean."

"If you're in this now, whether you believe it or not, you're already being manipulated. So am I. And if I'm right, then whatever move you're about to make they've already anticipated it and are three moves ahead of you. If you get into this game then you'd better win, and that means you've got to be ready to do something completely unexpected."

When she returned to her room the message light on her phone was flashing. She had thirteen new voice mails, all on the same subject and left in the order of ascending power and rank.

It seemed that Warren Landers hadn't been confident that he'd made the needed impression on her, so he'd kicked the matter upstairs as soon as he departed.

The undercurrent of these messages was all the same. The choice was still hers, naturally, but if she knew what was good for her, this Molly Ross business was a mission she should take on without delay.

Well, how about that.

These thirteen very important people had all taken the time to call Virginia Ward at 2 a.m. on a weeknight to express their strong support for what they put forth as a matter of unmatched importance. With oddly similar language they were calling for the immediate capture and incarceration of a blind girl who seemed to be nothing more than the last fading light in a patriot movement that had come too small and too late to make a difference.

Now you've got me interested, Virginia thought. *So let's see where this dark road leads.*

CHAPTER 26

M_ost killers get caught because they neglect the most important part of their job. You don't have to be a genius; the key to a clean getaway is long preparation before the fact. You plan to get out of there with all your bases covered, and then you do the deed, stow your weapon, grab your kit, and go.

It sure seemed like more, but until very recently Olin Simmons had committed murder only four other times. Two he'd gotten away with clean, but he'd been clipped for the third, and then one had been done from necessity in the ugly tile showers at Lewisburg.

Those acts were different than these current ones; they'd all been up close and personal. The first was hard only because it had been the first. The second was a robbery gone bad and that guy got what he deserved for trying to fight back. The next had been an ex-girlfriend; she'd made it so much easier just by being the malignant little bitch that she was, right up to the end. And the last had been a rite of passage in the joint, just some unlucky fish who got picked from the general population so a better man could earn his yard credentials. Everybody serves their role; that blood initiation had brought Olin Simmons into the brotherhood with George Pierce, and he couldn't remember feeling much of anything but pride when it was done.

Now he was killing with a purpose—two purposes, really. Warren Landers had said his first job was to "generate conflict," and that concept had taken some explaining before Simmons finally understood. The second job was pinning these soulless acts on someone else, and that was actually the only part of all this that was beginning to feel like a chore.

These weren't to be random killings, though they'd look that way until the cops pulled their heads out of their asses.

He'd started in D.C. with a young white mother who'd been filling up her hybrid SUV at the corner Gas 'n' Go. He waited from long-distance cover until she'd come out of the minimart with some chips and sodas for the kids in the back, and then he'd shot her through the heart as she opened up the side door.

She'd been chosen because of her many bumper stickers, all of which identified her as a proud supporter of the incumbent President and his many clever slogans. Her good looks and her gender would be a media bonus; she represented what they call a sympathetic demographic. This young blond mother of two, cut down in her prime by a deranged political extremist, would tug at America's heartstrings and be sure to make a splash on the nightly news.

He followed up as he'd been directed with a typewritten note to the newspapers. The text included threats of further violence, a blistering manifesto giving full credit to Molly Ross and the Founders' Keepers, and several ridiculous demands. One of these was a call for the President to withdraw his name from the upcoming ballot to clear the way to the Oval Office for an obscure candidate from the Libertarian Party.

The paper and the envelope carried another hidden message: partial fingerprints and a fleck of harvested DNA from the fall guy, Thom Hollis. For good measure Simmons had also tucked in an ounce of benign white powder to spread a little panic and ensure the ready involvement of even more government agencies.

There'd been a few other shootings that first day, meant to be linked only later to this same cold-blooded minuteman and his patriot accomplices. Near each location Simmons had hired a hooker of about the right size and shape to walk around with him for the benefit of the surveillance cameras on the street. Upon review of their footage the authorities would see a large bearded man in fatigues and a pretty young woman in dark glasses, apparently scoping out the area before their crimes.

Now on his path west he'd arrived in the windy city of Chicago.

This day's activity was more elaborate and had required a good deal of advance work and participation from other friendly local factions. Despite all the details, getting away with murder here should be a cakewalk compared to the previous day's work. A full-scale riot would make it so much easier to get lost and disappear toward the next assignment.

A protest march was scheduled for that morning. This was no small mob; it was part of a well-funded, centrally coordinated "grassroots" citizen uprising that was coincidentally popping up in many places nationwide. As times got worse their crowds had gotten bigger and bigger and the liberal press was continually showering these mobs with completely unbiased, universally positive coverage.

A lot of these people came out just because they were angry or scared. Many were hired or otherwise lured into involvement by promises of future favors in return. Those few marchers who actually understood why they were there were waving signs and calling for "direct democracy." *What a pack of pinko dumb-asses.* As Mr. Pierce might put it, a direct democracy was like asking a group of ten Nazis and two Jews to vote on their plans for Passover.

Well, if that's what they wanted, by God that's what they'd get.

The best thing that he'd learned from Warren Landers so far is that you don't have to aim at your foes to do them harm. Instead, if you shoot at the people you support while loudly endorsing your enemies, you can kill two birds with one stone. To make the heroes and villains real in the eyes of the public, sometimes you have to hurt the ones you love.

The protest organizers had published their route so that interested followers and new recruits could more easily join them. The police had also announced their crowd-control plans with lines of blue barricades put in place at vulnerable sites the night before. These sites included a financial landmark where a major confrontation was supposedly anticipated. And so Olin Simmons had known exactly where he needed to be.

He was crouched at the seventh-floor window of a vacant downtown office space near the mouth of the LaSalle Street canyon. He had the rifle by his side and was enjoying an unimpeded view of the riot line and the restless crowd beginning to swell to capacity in the street below the towering Chicago Board of Trade.

Everything was in place.

The police were out in force, with their commissioner and other higher-ups standing resolutely behind them. The rank and file were equipped for hand-to-hand violence, dressed in padded black, visors down, shields up, and weapons ready. The crowd was chanting louder—

they got bailed out, we got sold out—and a few planted among them would occasionally shout particularly fiery and profane epithets and threats right into the faces of the nearby lawmen. The area news teams were there, too, ready with mic and camera to capture any developments, no doubt with hopes to parlay any minor conflict into an on-scene report for the national network feed.

Because of its sheer size the throng of protesters periodically shifted and came into physical contact with the thin blue line. In response the police would push back against them, moving in solidarity at a bullhorned command. With each such cycle the anger was growing on both sides; the tension was becoming electric at the volatile border between opposing forces. This tinderbox was primed to ignite, and so it was time.

Simmons took out his flashlight, brought it up to the open window, and sent three quick high-intensity blinks down toward the street. Seconds later three flashes came back in answer to his signal. With that the action was under way, though there wasn't an agreed-upon instant when it all would come down. With just a little prompting the crowd itself would decide that moment.

He'd chosen several potential victims among the rabble. If you settle on only one, sure enough the lucky bastard'll get himself behind a street sign or a bystander and then you're stuck scrambling for a target of opportunity. With the exception of the cute female cop he'd singled out, all the ones he'd picked for that day were young blacks, clean-cut *Cosby Show* types whose yearbook pictures would look just great displayed below the tragic headlines.

The chants were growing louder and angrier, the individual confrontations at the line flaring higher. Olin Simmons picked up Thom Hollis's rifle and brought the preset scope up close to his eye.

A line of burly men in the back let out a bloodcurdling rebel yell and pushed hard against the crowd in front of them, driving like the Packers' defensive line against the training sled. At the same time a lit pack of firecrackers dropped to the pavement and the sharp reports sparked the beginnings of a panic among the pinned-in crowd. The surge of human pressure passed forward like a wave and the hapless protesters at the front were forced off balance and stumbling through the barricades.

As the police fell back a few of them were knocked from their feet and their partners responded with batons and fists and pepper spray. Some raised their guns, a spinning canister of tear gas was fired into the midst of the mob, and a regiment of more heavily armed reinforcements ran in to aid their brothers in uniform.

Olin Simmons took aim and shot the first young target in the side of the head, and then he took out a second victim before those around the first had even begun to react. He shifted immediately and found his woman cop, fired once, and then shot her again for good measure as she was going down.

At the unmistakable sound of gunfire most in the crowd would have run away if they could, but they couldn't. They were now caught up in a shared mentality of fear and rage and had ceased to be individuals at all anymore. Whatever their plans for this march had once been, all ideals were forgotten with that first scent of blood. A roar went up from the thousands in the mob, a stirring primal sound completely out of place on those formerly civilized midwestern streets.

Now the violence would play out on its own; no more was required of the man who'd started it. As new shooting erupted and the police line fell and the mob stormed across the fragile barrier between chaos and law and order, Olin Simmons was already gone.

CHAPTER 27

In the morning Noah found himself feeling well enough to get up and around. After checking his vitals and joining him in a light, bland, institutional breakfast, Dr. Ellen Davenport accompanied him outside for a chat and a breath of cool, fresh air.

Older and happier times were revisited as they walked together. The things that had happened since were left for another day. The grounds were quite tranquil and uniformly green, something like a golf course but without all the fun. When the edge of the property came into view, though, the sight stopped him dead in his tracks. You can gloss over a lot of things with tasteful landscaping but a high electric fence, manned watchtowers, and coils of concertina wire are features that speak louder than even the best-kept shrubberies.

Upon turning around for the journey back, Noah was treated to yet another sobering view. Their walk had taken them far enough away from the building they'd left to see it from higher ground and in the context of its surroundings. He'd awakened that morning with a lingering suspicion left behind by a bad dream, and this sight confirmed that it was true.

"What's wrong?" Ellen asked. She must have seen the look on his face.

"They brought me back. This is the same place where they held me before."

He'd seen it only once from the outside and that had been on his way out, months earlier. The complex had obviously expanded since then. New construction was under way here and there: one strange windowless building bristling with antennas and satellite dishes, a deceptively bright and inviting welcome center, a strip of sterile shops and generic eateries, and what looked like a set of his-and-hers, cookie-cutter dormitories that were a perfect match for several others in the line. The hospital wing where they'd emerged was only a small part of the overall development.

"I don't understand," Ellen said.

"Didn't anybody tell you anything about all this?"

"No. Your father said that you needed help, and that was all I needed to know. What kind of an operation is this?"

"It used to be called a fusion center. There are a lot of them around the country but this one's apparently becoming a whole new breed. You've been to Disney World, haven't you?"

"Sure."

"This place is like Epcot," Noah said. "You know, the Experimental Prototype Community Of Tomorrow? It's just like that, only from hell."

The walk back was considerably more introspective.

When they came to his room he closed the door and sat Ellen down in the corner as far from the ceiling camera as he could manage.

"I want you to go back to New York now," Noah said, "and then get on with your life as best you can."

"My life is fine, Gardner. I want to make sure you're okay—"

"Listen to what I'm saying. I'm not okay. I don't think I'm ever going to be okay again. I appreciate you coming here for me; you're the best friend I've got and that means more to me now than I can ever tell you, but this is a bad place and you need to get out of here as soon as possible."

His tone seemed to strike her even harder than the words themselves.

"All right," Ellen said. She looked hurt, and he was sorry for that. "They're redoing the floors in my apartment; I'd planned on being away for a while. I can't go home tonight or tomorrow, but I'll make all the arrangements to leave in a few days."

"Good. It's for the best."

"So you're saying I shouldn't even stop by and see you again before I go?"

He nodded. "I don't want you to be in danger, and I hope I get a chance to explain someday."

At precisely 7:50 a.m. a perky male junior executive dropped in to accompany him to his rehab work assignment. The man waited outside the room while Noah showered and shaved.

When he finally opened his door to the hall he was provided with one last fashion accessory. The young man who'd been waiting had been joined by a security guard, and together they fitted Noah's left ankle with an electronic tracking bracelet. It was formfitting enough so one's socks could be pulled up over it and was otherwise black and featureless, except for an intermittent green light and a yellow Talion logo on its side.

"This is just for your safety," the young man explained. He fiddled with his smartphone as the guard worked silently, and soon the small screen displayed a page full of data, an up-to-the-second status report on the new subject. "We can tell where you are and how you're getting along, twenty-four hours a day. Like they say, if you're not doing anything wrong there's nothing to be concerned about, right?"

"Absolutely," Noah said, as he finished replacing his shoe.

"We all have one here. You'll get used to it before you know it."

There were a number of moving color-coded lines and bars on the screen, and his escort cheerfully explained the purpose of several of them. Heart rate, stress level, oxygenation, psychogalvanic reflex—a rudimentary lie detector—and a blinking red dot on an overhead map that denoted his location to within a few feet.

"What's that one?" Noah asked, pointing it out.

"That's your blood alcohol level."

"Well. What will they think of next."

"It's not that a little drink or two isn't allowed. A reasonable amount of anything legal is okay. We just wouldn't want anyone to overdo it. No smoking, of course."

"Of course."

On the walk to the place where he'd been assigned to work, his escort gave Noah the guided tour, complete with an approved company line on the purpose and function of the complex. The weasel-worded language required continual mental translation, but this was the gist of it:

Despite the crumbling U.S. economy, money was no object for initiatives such as this. It was only right that the taxpayers should fund it; it was a big part of their future, after all. The place was evolving from the simple information-gathering site and detention center it had once been. It was now to embody the vision of an ideal community, a new approach to the concept of human society: peaceful, sustainable, tightly regulated, and when necessary, enforceable. It was designed to provide a perfectly level (and carbon-neutral) playing field for its residents in every approved aspect of their lives. All were taken care of, and all made their assigned contribution to the common good.

From each according to his abilities, in other words, and to each according to his needs.

The thousands of inhabitants already there were of two distinct types. The staff were only a small percentage of the total population. His guide stumbled a bit with his verbiage when describing the majority. They weren't prisoners—at least not by the strictest definition. They hadn't been arrested or charged with any crime and none were represented by counsel or awaiting trial. Still, this didn't change the fact that none of them could leave. But then again, why should they ever want to?

Of those two available residence classes, Noah's own new status was apparently yet to be determined.

Their destination was an old and stately five-story building that seemed out of place in its chillier surroundings. Skeletons of new structures were rising on either side but this one, it appeared, was being preserved as it originally stood.

Once inside they took an elevator to the top floor and then proceeded down a long hall with media and research rooms distributed along either side. These rooms were not unlike those in which he'd been forced to toil away when he was confined here before: dry rows and columns of identical desks and gray, half-walled cubicles arranged in a highly functional and completely impersonal workspace. The difference now was that these rooms were all unoccupied and they appeared to have lain empty for quite some time.

The door at the far end of the hall had a hand-lettered sign affixed above it that read simply THE FIRST CIRCLE.

When they reached the watercooler the man accompanying Noah pulled him aside and said, "I should warn you about this pair you'll be working around. *Warn* is too strong a word; just be aware that they're likely to seem a little eccentric. When the departments in this building became obsolete these two were the only ones we weren't able to reassign elsewhere. There are . . . special circumstances with both of them. And with you, too, I guess; that must be why they've assigned you here. In any case, if they get to be too much for you just let us know and we'll try to make other arrangements."

"Sure thing."

As they approached, the sounds of a heated conversation were clearly audible. His escort sighed and slid a keycard through a reader and as the lock clicked and he opened the door the bickering within stopped abruptly.

"Noah Gardner," the man beside him said, "this is Ms. Lana Somin, and that gentleman over at the typewriter is Ira Gershon." He pronounced the word *typewriter* as though the presence of such a quaint contraption was a bottomless source of amusement.

Both those names were vaguely familiar. The first thing that struck him about the girl was that she was obviously a minor; she couldn't have been a day older than fifteen. She was thin as a dime and pale like she'd never seen sunlight, dressed in faded black jeans and a fashionably ripped Wu Tang T-shirt.

The man was a grandfatherly senior citizen, but even at this first impression a boyish spirit seemed to shine through unaffected by his years. It took only a moment to realize how he recognized that face. Ira Gershon had been a longtime local anchor on the television news when Noah had first moved to Manhattan as a boy.

The girl didn't bother to acknowledge Noah's existence and she spoke instead to the man standing beside him. "I can't really handle another day of this old guy," she said. "I'm gonna do something desperate if you don't let me out of here."

"As we discussed," Noah's escort said, smoothly ignoring the girl completely, "let me know how it goes today. The front office will be interested to hear how you're getting along."

"Wait a minute, what is it I'm supposed to do here?"

"Just come on in and have a chair," Ira Gershon said. He still had the voice of a man born for broadcast. With the sweeping gesture of a gracious host he directed the new arrival to a nearby desk. "Sit down right here, son. I'm on a bit of a deadline but as soon as I finish up with this copy, we'll figure it out together."

CHAPTER 28

They'd set up a workstation for Noah, and while all office activities were no doubt closely monitored, his access to the Internet didn't seem to have any obvious restrictions. As the other two returned to their work he performed a few searches to try it out. The first subject was a young woman named Lana Somin.

The term *hacker* gets tossed around a lot in the media but this girl certainly fit both the original as well as the pop culture definition. Though she'd been given up for adoption at birth, she came from a family of certified geniuses, and her particular gift, as one of her lawyers had put it, was in the field of creative exploration. She was a whiz at breaking into places, digitally speaking, and she did so just to see if she could. After a bit of looking around, without stealing or even disturbing anything, she would promptly back out, cover her tracks, and leave the same way she came in. Her favorite places to go were those massively secure electronic fortresses that held themselves out to be impenetrable.

When she found a weakness in a security system she would venture in just far enough to record proof of the exploit and then inform the company involved that they had a problem. Many of them actually appreciated the service. If they disregarded her repeated notices or otherwise indicated that Lana should mind her own business, she shared her discoveries on a private blog for discussion among her anonymous online community.

Then someone had taken what they learned from her and done some serious crimes—a rash of identity thefts, wire fraud, targeted phishing scams, and the wholesale exposure of access codes and passwords to millions of user accounts. Some of these incidents got the attention of the Department of Homeland Security, and it wasn't long before Lana Somin was taken into custody.

Her otherwise clean record, her age, and the rules of evidence being what they were, she still might have avoided prosecution, but her foster parents had flipped out and cooperated fully with the authorities. She was tried as an adult and convicted, and the sentencing judge had really thrown the book at her. The whole process hadn't taken more than a few months, beginning to end.

The articles Noah scanned suggested that she'd been sent to some sort of a juvenile facility to serve out her punishment. Evidently there was more to the tale than that.

Ira Gershon's presence in this place remained more of a mystery.

It had been well over a decade since he'd last been on television and much longer since his heyday back in the golden age. That was centuries ago in Internet time. Though he'd once been a trusted nightly presence in millions of homes there simply wasn't much about him anywhere on the Web. There were a few pictures from his younger years, mostly with Gershon as the second face in a shot featuring someone else from the hall of fame of his profession: Paley, Murrow, Cronkite, Collingwood, Smith, Sevareid, Huntley, and Brinkley.

Some people have come to think that all information is waiting out there free and clear, that everything that's ever happened and everyone who's anyone is just a Google search away. But the universal library's being continually pruned and revised; more and more, knowledge is being systematically narrowed down, filtered, and sanitized, limited to only those things granted a permit to be properly remembered.

Noah's last search concerned *The First Circle,* the wording of that sign over the door outside.

He'd gotten the reference to Dante right away. In his *Divine Comedy* the First Circle of hell was on the borderlands of damnation, a place of mild despair without torment. Being sent there for eternity was considered a small measure of mercy, a lesser sentence granted to virtuous pagans while still denying them access to heaven. The sign here, though, was no doubt an even more subversive slap at authority, sent by way of Solzhenitsyn. In his book by that same title he'd written of Stalin's treatment of select, valuable prisoners rounded up in the purges. They were spared the more brutal conditions of the gulag provided they continued to obediently bow down to the will of the regime.

The old-fashioned clatter of the typewriter ceased with a last ding and a carriage return. There was a sharp ratcheting sound as a sheet of paper was pulled up and out.

"All right, new guy," Ira said, "how about if you proofread this piece for me? Let's see what you can do to pull your weight."

"Okay." Noah took the three pages and picked a red pencil from the assortment in his desk drawer. "You know, I used to watch you on the news every night," he said, as he began to read.

"Is that so?"

"Yeah. I was pretty young to be a newshound then,

but there was something very comforting about your delivery. I trusted everything you said."

"Back then I did, too." He indicated the story in Noah's hands. "I hope you know to be a little more discerning now."

As Noah began to read the piece he understood what Gershon had meant. This text was obviously nothing more than a load of talking-points propaganda for consumption by the wire services. Beyond the slanted content, though, there was another, more obvious problem.

```
Early yesterday in Chicago, what began
as a peaceful march for fiscal reform
and social justice erupted into a show
of violence and brutality unlike any-
thing seen in the city since the Days
of Rage in the late 1960s. When the
smoke had cleared four people lay dead,
including one police officer. Scores of
others were wounded, some critically,
in what organizers are calling a bloody
wake-up call and a rallying cry for
the many similar citizen groups arrayed
across a troubled nation.
```

"What's wrong with the lowercase *d* on your machine?" Noah asked.

"It's broken, that's what's wrong with it, and they've stopped making parts for the old girl." Ira had gotten up from his chair and he spoke from near the credenza by the wall. He was carefully slipping a vinyl LP onto the spindle of an ancient record player. "Do you notice how nobody fixes anything anymore?"

Lana spoke up. "Do you notice how I'm going to

stick my head in the oven and turn on the gas if I have to listen to Glenn Miller again today?"

"No, dear," Ira said, "no big bands today." The needle touched vinyl and soon a swell of smooth violins came drifting over the speakers, followed by the velvety tones of Nat King Cole. "Feast your jaded ears, young people. 'Stardust' is without any doubt the most beautiful song ever recorded by mortal man."

Noah continued to read and make his marks as the music played on, and the girl raised no further objections as she worked away at her keyboard. When he came to a part near the end of the text he stopped and looked over at its author.

"You're seriously going to submit this?" Noah asked.

"I can only write what I'm told these days," Ira replied. "My only job is to write it well enough. What, you don't believe what's there?"

The paragraph in question was near the end of the story. Unnamed sources in the Justice Department had confirmed that members of a right-wing domestic hate group were claiming responsibility for the shooting that set off the violence at a Chicago protest march. A string of other incidents established an escalating pattern of terrorist activity, moving west across the country. Evidence found at the scene also pointed to the direct involvement of their suddenly notorious leadership. This group called themselves the Founders' Keepers.

"No, I don't believe it."

"Oh, really?" Ira came back to his place and took a seat. "And why not?"

Noah didn't answer. Instead he looked around briefly for any obvious cameras or listening devices.

"They aren't watching us in here," Ira said. "There are other indignities we have to endure"—he patted his ankle, where his own house-arrest bracelet would be—

"but they've never bothered to spy on us in this room, not that way. Go on, you can speak freely."

"Okay. I don't believe the story because I know those people."

"Oh, I know that you know them," Ira said, "and I know more than that. I recognize you, too, Mr. Gardner."

He frowned. "I'm sure we haven't met before."

The older man nodded with the hint of a smile, holding eye contact for a little longer than was entirely comfortable, and then he abruptly changed his heading. "Are you finished marking up my copy?"

"Yeah."

"Then I'm finished with it, too. I don't need to see it again. Hand it over to my girl Friday there so she can type it up and send it out on the wires."

As Noah leaned toward her and held out his minor edits, Lana clipped the papers from his hand without looking over and with barely a pause in her typing.

"You must have some questions about what goes on here," Ira said.

"That's putting it mildly."

"Well, then, let me show you around a bit and I'll fill you in."

One wall was dominated by a huge flat-screen monitor. Noah's father had kept a nearly identical device running constantly in his private conference room. Its ever-changing display was a patchwork mosaic of running videos, pictographs on hot topics, graphs of market movements, headlines, and scrolling news items. All the little blocks were in constant motion, organizing and reorganizing themselves. Top to bottom, left to right, the order reflected the trending importance of each item. This visual gauge of popular interests would be of critical importance to the hive-mind of the press-and-PR juggernaut as it worked to shape the public discourse to its own ends.

The rest of the space seemed like a standard modern newsroom, though like the other rooms down the hall it looked virtually deserted. With the exception of their three places all the desks were unoccupied.

"Where is everybody?" Noah asked.

"All of this," Ira said as he gestured around them, "started as an experiment. The news would be created and supervised in places like this, managed from a central location, and then that approved content would be sent out for the people's consumption. What it took them a long time to realize, though, was that they were wasting a lot of effort. It turned out they didn't have to compel their messages by force. There was no need to trick the majority of today's pack of so-called journalists to do and say what they wanted. All they really had to do was ask."

Across the room but obviously within earshot, Lana Somin quietly put on a handmade tinfoil beret and continued her work without further comment.

Despite the girl's obvious skepticism this was a lesson Noah's father had taught him when he'd first begun to intern at Doyle & Merchant. A subservient press corps was one of the keys to power in the PR business. The same sickness had long ago infected politics: promises of access, reward, and advancement had become the primary driving forces for most reporters, especially the sharp and ambitious ones. Any pretense of truth-seeking was left by the wayside, stuck in the back of the briefcase with their diplomas, their pride, and their principles.

On the flip side, naturally, there was a swift punishment waiting for those who defied their industry's corruption. By way of example, Ira Gershon explained his present situation.

His last position in the mainstream media, granted as a favor from a retiring network CEO, had been as the executive producer of a weekly local investigative news segment. His contract included total control over staff and content; apparently no one upstairs had expected much controversy from an aging icon on the verge of being put out to pasture. He'd immediately landed in hot water over a segment on the widespread use of a cancer-linked growth hormone in the American milk supply. The manufactured hormone was the cash-cow product—no pun intended—of a multinational biotech giant. This company had its fingers in more than enough pies to get whatever it wanted, especially from the media. They killed Ira's story with nothing more than a threat to pull their advertising.

Needless to say, the problem wasn't that the story was false. It never ran, Ira sued his employer, and the only outcome of the protracted lawsuit had been a landmark decision in American media. The court ultimately determined, once and for all, that bald-faced lies in the news were perfectly okay. Journalists had neither the inherent right nor any legal obligation to go on TV and tell the truth.

The story that finished off his waning career, though, had been a multipart series about the sinister origins of the debt crisis that was currently rocking the world. It was his magnum opus, the treasure at the end of a trail he'd been following since the 1970s. The piece was well researched, carefully vetted, and it centered on a shadowy financier and economic plunderer named Aaron Doyle.

"Aaron Doyle," Noah said. "He was a principal at my father's company."

"Was?"

"Yeah, was. I met him a few times when I was a kid. He was old as dirt back then; he can't possibly still be around."

Ira Gershon sat thoughtfully for a moment.

"Noah," he said, "do you believe in God?"

"There he goes again," Lana sighed, from her desk several feet away.

"I don't know. Not really, I guess. Why?"

"Because I first met Aaron Doyle when I was a kid, too. He was old as dirt even then. And once you've seen the devil, son, trust me, it really helps if you believe in God."

CHAPTER 29

Noah felt worn to the nub by the end of his first workday, but though it was hard to admit, overall it hadn't been so bad.

This mix of feelings had been familiar in his old life in civilian PR. It was rewarding on some level to have spent eight solid hours on tasks he was very good at accomplishing, regardless of who he was doing it for or why they wanted it. A lot of people spend their days that way, he reminded himself, gritting their teeth at times to support someone else's agenda just so they can devote whatever free time they have left toward their own pursuits.

This new apartment, too, was a definite upgrade from the stark cell where he'd been housed during his previous sentence. His place was on the floor just under the penthouse levels and it seemed like any random executive suite at an extended-stay hotel. The furnishings, the art on the walls, the fabrics, paint, and carpeting were all of the sort that everyone could get used to and no one would particularly hate. It wasn't a home you were meant to make your own; it was simply an inoffensive and comfortable place to stay, and he'd stayed in much worse.

As Ira had explained it earlier, the lower floors and

some subterranean levels of the building comprised housing for the less privileged residents and a number of actual prisoners, political and otherwise. Their presence below you was meant as a reminder of the blessings you'd been granted, and the ease with which you could lose what you thought you were entitled to.

In the course of the day Ira had also told Noah how it was that he and Lana—two supposed rebels against the corrupt establishment—were seemingly helping the very forces they should hate. Some local activist attorney had gotten wind of Lana's age and situation, and before he could be bought off he'd come in and arranged for Ira Gershon to become her legal guardian. After that, as much as the men in charge would have loved to lock them both up and throw away the key, in exchange for their promise to cooperate they were granted a spot in limbo until the very minute she would turn seventeen.

As Noah approached the refrigerator, a screen set into the door lit up to inform him of the time and date, the weather, the indoor temperature, and his own full name. The appliance also informed him that Noah W Gardner, #078-05-1120, was almost out of nonfat milk. It further said that his dairy quota for the week had not yet been exceeded, and so if he touched YES a delivery order for a half gallon would be sent to the nearby market.

Creepy, but convenient.

He'd just picked out a meal tray from a stack in the freezer when, across the suite, a pretty woman in a bathrobe appeared at his bedroom door, drying her hair with a towel. He tried once to blink her away but she stayed right where she was, and then he recognized her. As much as the artificial nature of her left leg, it was that somewhat enigmatic smile that he remembered most clearly about Virginia Ward.

"Hi again," she said. "I didn't think you'd mind if I let myself in."

"No, not at all."

"My flight landed early and I needed to go over some things with you, and while I was waiting I thought I'd freshen up."

"Really, it's fine. I don't exactly feel like I'm alone in this place anyway, if you know what I mean." He held up the frozen-food tray in his hand. "Would you like some delicious low-sodium, gluten-free dinner?"

"That would actually be pretty good. I forgot to eat much today." She finished with her towel, ran her fingers through her hair a couple of times, and somehow ended up looking like she'd just spent half an hour in front of the mirror. "This is a nice place you've got."

"Do I have it, or does it have me?"

"You really shouldn't complain, if you think about it."

"I know. My father must have laid on the pressure, for the job and to land this place for me. I'm still not sure why he did that, but no, I'm not complaining."

"I'll tell you what," she said. "You put dinner in the microwave, I'll get dressed, and we'll get started on what we need to do, okay?"

"Good."

She returned just as the oven beeped to indicate their food was finished. He pulled out a chair for her but she chose another, one facing the door.

They talked as they ate, a little about Molly, but mostly about other things. As they reached their bland dessert Virginia asked him about his new job.

"It's strange," Noah said. "There are only three of us: me, an elderly man, and a young woman. Just a girl, really."

"What do you do, the three of you?"

"That's the strange part. It's busywork, mostly, although I did sharpen up some talking points for the White House press secretary in the afternoon. I feel sorry for this poor guy they've got in there now; it's like they're not even trying anymore."

"And what about the other two, your new colleagues?"

"The old fellow used to be on the news but it sounds like he didn't change with the industry, and so the industry pushed him out."

Virginia smiled. "Way out, by the look of it."

"Yeah, to hear him tell it he's made some powerful enemies, probably like everyone else here on our side of the bars. Whoever's running this show, they give him about one story a week to write, and that's probably just so they can keep an eye on him and make sure he's toeing the line. He spends the rest of his time writing fillers for syndication."

"Fillers?"

"Little blurbs to finish out a short column on the back pages of the paper. News people use them, too, and disc jockeys. Those random anecdotes you hear sometimes, 'did you know?'–type items, fascinating facts, stuff like that."

"What about the girl?"

"Lana doesn't say much but she's got some real talent. She mostly works at stirring up trouble on the blogs, starting comment wars on social news sites, that sort of thing."

"What's the value of that?"

"Are you kidding? These days it's enormously valuable. With everyone so connected it's the best place to mess with public opinion. Even though it's all anonymous, people seem to think they're just talking to a group of friends. Probably nine out of ten of the user comments you read on some of those sites are bought and paid for like that."

"Nine out of ten?"

"Sometimes ninety-nine out of a hundred, and I'm not even exaggerating."

"And all these fake opinions accomplish what?"

"Come on, you know better than I do. The CIA spends eighty-five percent of its budget on psychological manipulation."

"I've always managed to keep myself in the better fifteen percent."

"Here's the basic idea. You take an issue, present a strong and reasonable argument for both sides of the question, and then you proceed to belittle anyone who falls outside the two groups. Do that, and you've done a couple of things. First, you've divided a lot of the readers cleanly into two controllable factions, and implanted an easy-to-digest opinion that they'll repeat: liberal or conservative, Democrat or Republican, whatever. Second, you've made it seem to the undecided majority that there's really no right answer, no real choice. You make them feel like outsiders who don't belong, and that makes them more likely to shut up and stay at home drowning their sorrows on election day. You make thinking for yourself seem uncool and socially unacceptable, and nobody wants to be part of that."

"So that's all she does all day? She writes fake comments?"

"You make it sound easy but it really takes a lot of finesse to do it right. I looked over her shoulder once today and she was actually in a full-out argument with herself. Both sides had thousands of up-votes from the onlookers. Her real specialty is Trotskying, though."

"Trotskying? And what's that?"

"It's the visual form of content-scrubbing. She downloads photographs and videos from the archives, removes or changes things in Photoshop and other tools, and then she re-uploads the new material. It's what Lenin did to Trotsky after they had a falling-out; he tried to erase him from history, that's how the practice got its name. Only it's much faster now, and a lot more permanent."

"And that works?"

"She single-handedly helped the press squeeze a third-party presidential candidate out of the race over the last few months. He was actually getting popular for a while, raising some sticky issues for the front-runners, and now it's like he was never even there."

"There are so many channels available," Virginia said, "so many radio stations and newspapers and magazines. It just seems like it should be harder to control what we're seeing than you make it sound."

"It should be, but it's not. You've got to remember, only six corporations control almost all of the media outlets today. It was about ninety companies when I was born, now it's six. They don't have to corral three hundred million viewers, just three hundred executives, and they were all in my old Rolodex when I worked in New York. And it's not getting any better. Rumor has it, up at the very top the ownership's being consolidated down to only one."

As the meal continued the conversation shifted, thankfully, to topics other than his work. The interaction seemed genuinely friendly; Noah never got the feeling that she was working him like an informant, though in her own charming way she obviously was. In any case he felt comfortable with her, and he needed that.

"Do I know you well enough now to ask you how you lost your leg?"

"In the war," she replied, not bothering to tell him which one. "I was on my seventh tour, we were on our way back from a major engagement in Sadr City, an incredible meat grinder. It was street fighting, no time to think or plan, both sides just going at it for days. When it was over my detachment got out with no casualties; it was like a miracle, no one had a scratch. Then the convoy got hit by a string of IEDs on the road back to the base. We lost five, and that's how I lost my leg."

"Seven tours," he said. "Was that by choice?"

She nodded.

"Why did you keep going back?"

"Because my brothers and sisters were there, and we all took the same oath, and I couldn't see leaving them until the job was done." She seemed to become more thoughtful, as though her answer had left something important unexplained. "War is a terrible thing, but once we've made the careful and honest decision to send our volunteers out into it, once we've committed the blood of the best of us, we need to give them a clear goal and the full permission to win. And then when they've done that, we need to bring them on home."

"It sounds like now you get to pick your own battles."

"That's right, I do."

They were quiet for a while. When he saw that she was finished with her meal he took their recyclable trays to the kitchen and poured them both some coffee.

"Does the name Merrick mean anything to you?" Virginia asked.

"Merrick? No, I don't think so."

"Molly never mentioned anyone by that name?"

"No, not that I remember. Why?"

"It's just a bit of a lead that I'm following up." Virginia made some notes on her pad. "Did you see the story in the news today about the rioting in Chicago?"

"Yeah, as a matter of fact, I helped write it."

"There've been other incidents around the country, shootings mostly, but also some fires and robberies, threats to politicians, threats against property, at least one actual bombing, and now this thing in Chicago. If you draw a line on a map between these incidents, it's clear they're heading this way, east to west. Molly and her group are claiming responsibility for all of it, and that's looking very credible."

He shook his head. "It's not them."

"I'm talking about what the evidence clearly indicates."

He placed her coffee in front of her and as he sat down she reached into her bag and slid some blurry photographs across the table.

"Do you recognize anyone there?" she asked.

The pictures were time-coded and pixelated stills from surveillance videos. They showed a tall man in a long dark coat on a city street with a petite woman walking beside him.

"No, but it's pretty obvious who they're *supposed* to be," Noah said.

"What makes you think these aren't photos of Thom Hollis and Molly Ross?"

"Look at her clothes, for one thing."

"So?"

"That woman's wearing a tight short skirt and high heels."

"And Molly wouldn't own anything like that?"

"For Halloween, maybe."

"What about the man?"

Noah thought about that for a few seconds. "I can't say. He's the right size, but thinner than I remember him. I told you I don't think he would do the things you say he's doing, but I can't back that up, not with anything solid."

"Do you know what the term *signature strike* means?"

"No."

"It's a new kind of attack order, the kind that's been issued now for Molly and Hollis, just today. These drone wars the administration's so fond of now, the idea came from those missions. It doesn't just mean that Molly is now eligible to be shot on sight. It means that everyone around her is also a valid target."

"Good God," Noah said. "I've told you these people are no threat. They've got no power and no hope to get any. They're being scapegoated, you can see that, can't you?"

She rose gracefully above that question. "I asked you to reach out to her. Have you had a chance to do that yet?"

"No."

"Come on, then." She got up and walked to the laptop computer on the corner desk. "I don't know if it'll make any difference, but let's start trying now."

CHAPTER 30

By their second cup of coffee he'd composed and deleted several messages; none of them felt quite right. Though she was an ace at deception herself, Molly Ross was also a very difficult person to lie to.

"Clear out your mind for a minute," Virginia said. "Just talk to her. Like I said, just relax and communicate. Think about your relationship."

"I wish I had more to think about. We didn't have much of a chance to get to know one another. There wasn't a lot of time involved, not in the way you'd normally think of a relationship."

"But you seem to have gotten so close."

"I got close. I don't know, maybe she did, too."

"What did you talk about while you were together?"

"I spent most of my time saying stupid things, if I remember correctly. And I guess a lot of the things she told me weren't true."

"And yet you say that you trust her."

"I know, it doesn't seem to make sense. She tricked me, it was as simple as that in the beginning, but I don't blame her. Whatever I got from them I deserved; that's how I see it. What they were trying to do in those few days was better than anything I'd ever done with my whole life. Can you understand that?"

"I can." She sat back, considering. "Let's keep this simple." She leaned over him and clicked open a new message. "You're just trying to open a line of communication. We need to break through the clutter and establish that it's really you who's writing to her. Ideally it should be something that only the two of you would know about."

He thought for a moment, and nodded as he began typing. "I think I've got something like that."

The subject line he wrote was *As a fellow oenophilist, let me B Frank.*

"What's that word mean?" Virginia asked, pointing it out on the screen.

"Oenophilist. It's a wine word, and I only knew it because I was a spelling-bee geek. It was in a crossword puzzle we were doing in my apartment."

"And B Frank, as in . . ."

"As in Barney Frank. That's from a story I told her the night before."

"When you slept together."

"Right, when we literally slept together. She woke up at one point, and then she woke me up and asked me to help her get back to sleep. I asked her how I was supposed to do that, and she wanted me to tell her a story."

"That sounds like something she'd remember."

"She was very interested in anything about my father," Noah said, "so I told her one of his tall tales. It's the only kind of a bedtime story I ever got from him as a kid. No dragons or knights in shining armor, it was always about his work, and the one I told her involved Barney Frank."

"Did it work?"

"Like a charm." He cracked his knuckles. "Let me finish this up. You said to keep it simple, right?"

In the body of the message he typed a single line.

Molly, it's Noah. Write back to me. I promise you I can help.

After waiting for Virginia's approval he checked over the text once again and hit SEND.

With the message to Molly finally away, the fatigue of their separate days seemed to hit them both at once. Virginia asked if the couch was available for the night, and of course that was fine; he had the room and she wanted to stay close in case there was a reply. He brought out some sheets, a pillow, and a blanket as she changed in the bathroom, and then by the time he'd brushed his teeth and returned to say good night she'd made up the couch as tight as an army cot and had already tucked herself in.

Noah turned off the last lamp and there was just enough moonlight coming through the window so they could see one another clearly in the dark.

"I'm worried she won't answer," Noah said. He didn't say so, but he was also every bit as worried that she would.

"If she doesn't write back we'll just keep trying."

He nodded. "Last chance," Noah said. "You can take the bed if you want."

"No, this is better than I'm used to. I'll be fine. I'm feeling a little overstimulated, though; too much caffeine, I think."

"Yeah?"

"Yeah. I might have to hear that Barney Frank bedtime story."

"All right, if you think it'll help. It's going to sound kind of odd."

"That's the one thing I'm sure of right now. Just tell it to me exactly like you told it to her."

"Okay," Noah said, and when he spoke next he'd

taken on the soft and calming tones of a bedside storyteller. "Once upon a time, in a faraway land called Washington, in the United States House of Representatives, two powerful trolls named Lee Atwater and Newt Gingrich wrote a memo at the direction of their party's masters. With this memo they started a rumor that the new Speaker of the House, Mr. Tom Foley, was a homosexual, and possibly even a pedophile. Now, politics had always been a dirty business and always would be, but to many people on both sides of the aisle this was several giant steps over the line.

"And so a kindly elf named Barney Frank went to these two trolls, Lee and Newt, and he said, 'That's fine, you guys. You go ahead and keep on mudslinging. Knock yourselves out. But here's what I'm going to do. I'm going to go all scorched-earth on your hypocritical asses. Unless you take it back and apologize to my friend Mr. Foley immediately, I will march myself down to the floor of the House, and I'll huff and I'll puff and I'll blow six of your secretly gay Republican congressmen right out of the closet, live on C-SPAN.' And then all hell started to break loose in the back rooms of the castle where the real rulers lived."

"Oh, my goodness," Virginia said. Her eyes were closed and her voice was already drowsy.

"Yes, oh, my goodness indeed. And when King Arthur Gardner heard about this, he flew to Washington in the middle of the night and was so monumentally pissed that he almost didn't even need an airplane. When he was finished restoring peace and putting things right, the two trolls had publicly apologized, the President himself had denounced their actions, and more than a few heads had rolled.

"And the moral of the story is," Noah concluded, "in a government that's been systematically weakened by lies and corruption, secrets are the most valuable currency. They're the fuel that runs the machine and the leverage that keeps the greedy ruling class in power and under control, and my father wasn't going to stand by and see all those secrets wasted."

With the story finished, the room was still for a little while. By all appearances Virginia Ward had fallen asleep already, but as he moved to get to his feet she spoke to him quietly.

"Noah?"

"Yes."

"Do you think Molly would do that, if she could?"

"Do what?"

"That scorched-earth idea," Virginia said. "I'm just trying to understand her mind-set. Do you think she'd try something like that if she had the chance? Just tell all the secrets to the people at once, to wake them up so they could have a last chance to see the truth and try to take their country back."

He thought for a moment. "Yeah, that sounds just like Molly."

Noah sat there for a few moments longer but she didn't say anything more. Soon it was clear that Virginia was out for the night, this time for sure.

CHAPTER 31

Anger was only one of several toxic emotions that his doctors had long since forbidden him to feel. When Aaron Doyle read and absorbed his latest morning dispatch, however, he had become so enraged that it took a private EMS team with a crash cart to rush to his aid and bring his fragile physical systems back under control.

Down a rarely traveled hallway a communications room was maintained for those unusual times when he was unable to take an urgent meeting face-to-face. With the doctors still hovering he ordered himself wheeled there. He needed answers, and he needed them immediately.

An assistant adjusted harsh white lights and brought the banks of televideo equipment out of standby. A test pattern lit up to fill the white wall, and soon the lines and bars flickered away and the face of Warren Landers appeared in their place. The man looked startled and disoriented, as though he'd been awakened from a sound sleep only moments before.

"What can I do for you, Mr. Doyle?" Landers said. The image pixelated and stuttered as the technicians sought to stabilize the secure connection, and the sound of the remote voice was slightly out of sync with the picture.

"Let me ask you," Doyle said. "Do you understand my goals?" With a sharp motion of his hand he banished everyone from the room on his side of the conference call. As he continued, despite the oxygen flowing under his nose, his overtaxed lungs labored to deliver his words with the gravity he intended. "Do you understand what I've asked you to do for me, and why?"

"I believe so—"

"*If you understand*," Doyle hissed, enunciating each word with as much acid as he could muster, "then tell me why the last torchbearer of the sad ideals of the American spirit, this Molly Ross, is now being contacted by a former co-conspirator who nearly spoiled all of my plans only last year, and who also happens to be the son of my right-hand man?"

Landers appeared to be confused by the question. "Mr. Gardner said that was what you wanted, to let them make contact so we could—"

"Did Mr. Gardner also say that I wanted an investigator on the case, a woman who's apparently accountable to no one, who was trained as a peerless hunter-killer by the Central Intelligence Agency, whose zeal for seeking the truth is exceeded only by her nearly flawless record of actually finding it? Did he say I wanted that?"

"He did say that," Landers said, "but it's obvious now we've both been deceived. I take full responsibility. I'll fix this."

"No. I'll fix it myself." In all his years in this great endeavor, only twice before had Aaron Doyle come down from the mountain to take matters into his own able hands. This would be the third time, and hopefully the last. "I'm coming to New York immediately. I'll be there by nightfall tomorrow."

"What should I do before then?" Landers asked.

"Let your man George Pierce know we may need

him for something major soon, but not yet. Let things proceed. And if my old friend Arthur wants to lay his own son's head upon the altar as well, then all the better." He leaned forward and spoke his final words clearly so his intent could not be missed. "And to that end, it's time now to bid a permanent good-bye to Arthur Gardner."

"Yes, sir," Landers said, and he broke the connection.

With the call thus ended, Aaron Doyle rose from his chair and stood. His pains notwithstanding, he felt a new energy burning within him at the prospect of the days just ahead.

He walked to his study and sat down in his tall leather chair near the waiting chessboard, and then he addressed the identical but empty seat—William Merchant's seat—on the other side.

"I see what you've tried to do, William," Doyle said. "You're trying to use my own pieces against me. But patience was never your strength, and I'm afraid you've acted rashly now and shown your hand a bit too soon. Truth, and love, and virtue, those were always your favorite weapons in this old war of ours."

He leaned forward and could almost see his old opponent seated in the opposite chair.

"But as you'll remember, William, revenge is mine."

CHAPTER 32

Arthur Gardner had never been one to take much pleasure in simple things.

Food and drink were occasional necessities, friends a seductive risk with only superficial benefits. And sleep—sleep was a thief of precious time and the persistent bringer of unwanted dreams.

As he sat, long past midnight at the head of the empty table in his private conference room, he reflected on these and other things, and in the quiet, he wondered. These halls were filled with a visual record of his accomplishments. Doyle & Merchant, the company he'd helped build from modest beginnings, would live on and speak its own memorial, carved as it was into the very skyline of Manhattan. Yes, with it all nearly over he found he knew very clearly what he had done with his life. It was all the things he'd missed along the way that now consumed him.

The media wall before him flashed its ever-changing torrent of images and messages. From where he sat, he could shift its content as he chose, just by gesturing, and he did so.

A solid wall of marketing communications was the first category to come up on the display. Advertising was a dark art somewhat related to his own. From what he saw, the primary challenge these days seemed to be how best to portray young people—supposedly living exciting and enviable lives—while they did nothing but stare nonstop into the little glowing screens in their hands. Ads for reality shows, ads for helpful chronic pharmaceuticals, ads for luxury vehicles, ads for bankruptcy advisors, ads for credit cards: in every stage of decline there were still desires to be stoked and needs to be created, and a last bit of money in the public's pocket to be fought over and won.

His own business model was not centered in luring the gullible into wanting things they didn't need. Instead, he made them know things, and love and hate things, and fear things, and thereby he made them *do* things, and the profit in that had proven nearly limitless. Despite the exorbitant fees he charged, the process was actually pretty simple: make the people learn and remember lies while burying the very truths that could save them.

And if those frightening, liberating truths should ever come to light, what then? Would it make any difference? Now, with mankind facing the final precipice, could any revelation be powerful enough to open their eyes and turn the tide?

We would see. He'd done what he could, as his wife had asked. He'd set a last, far-fetched opportunity into motion, put the intrepid players in position, and then stood aside. It was out of his hands now; the rest was destiny.

"Sir?"

Warren Landers stood at the open door.

"Yes?"

"I know it's late but I'm glad I found you here. There's a problem in the London office and I'm afraid they need your thoughts."

Arthur Gardner sighed, and nodded. "We can do a conference call from here, I believe."

"No, our links are down and we don't have any techs on the night shift to make it happen. I've arranged for a video call at a vendor on Sixth Avenue. Come on, I'll drive you there."

Gardner met the gaze of the other man and waited, let a grim understanding pass between them, then he nodded once again, closed his book, and stood. Everything was in order, after all; he'd seen to that. There was no need for fighting it, then. He already knew his end was near, and he supposed this was as good a time as any to let it come.

"Let's get going, then," he said. "We mustn't keep our colleagues waiting."

They went together in silence to his corner office. Once there, he took a last long look around at all his treasured things, then walked to his private elevator and pushed the button, going down.

"It's been a real experience working with you, Warren," he said.

There was no response from the man waiting just behind him.

A pleasant *ding* issued forth from the elevator. The doors opened to a deep black emptiness.

Arthur Gardner's thoughts were already far away as he felt a firm shove at his back. And save for the grim prospect of a possible coming judgment from on high, there was almost no fear in him at all as he fell forward into the yawning darkness.

CHAPTER 33

Noah opened his eyes from a deep, troubled sleep to see the first light of the morning. Whatever he'd been dreaming had left him with a sense that there was danger all around him.

The first thing he did was check his e-mail for a reply from Molly. There was none, and so he wrote a variation of the previous night's message and sent it off, hopefully to find her. On his way to the kitchen, then, he saw that the couch was empty with the bedclothes folded at one end. A precisely handwritten note was placed atop the linens:

Was called away, but I'll see you soon.

V

Noah took the long way on his route to the office. As he walked he saw the same things he'd seen the previous day when he was out with Ellen Davenport, only now the sights seemed to mean something more.

The high fence and the watchtowers would indeed serve to hold people inside, but a sudden societal collapse would require an equally effective means of keeping other people out as well.

The new housing going up, the stores of nonperishable food and drinking water, the generators and stand-alone communication systems: it was all designed to make this a huddling place in the aftermath of a planned disaster. In that event this would be a command center as well, one of several meant to support a new form of government that he'd once heard his father describe—one that was poised and ready to replace the nation described in the quaint and obsoleted U.S. Constitution.

Even before he'd turned the last corner to the hallway near the office he could already hear his two colleagues in a heated discussion through the heavy door.

As Noah keyed himself in, there was no pause in the argument. Their contention at the moment seemed to be over the ins and outs of immigration policy.

"Do you want to know why," Ira Gershon said, "I don't believe we should just open up the borders to anyone who can manage to sneak across the line?"

"Because old Jews are racists and hate Mexicans?" Lana Somin replied.

"No, dear. It's the same reason we don't let everyone into medical school who says they want to be a doctor, and we don't let everybody into the NFL who's ever touched a football. We don't do that for the same reason that we can't just suddenly say that everyone who comes here is automatically an American. Because all those things are difficult, you have to work very hard to do them properly, and not everybody will have what it takes to make the grade."

The girl turned to her computer, where she quickly performed a search and brought an image up to full screen. It was the front page of some comedy blog based in France, one seemingly devoted to celebrating the laughable characteristics of the typical ugly American.

That day's selection showed a grotesquely overweight woman in a red-white-and-blue Snuggie cruising the mall in her three-wheeled scooter with the stars-and-stripes flapping from the handlebars.

"See that?" she asked. "This lazy tub of lard that looks like the Fourth of July threw up on her? What's so damned difficult about that?"

Noah edged his way to the counter for a cup of coffee, hoping to stay out of the fray.

"This is what you always do," Ira said. "You hold up some extreme example and then act like you've won the argument. As if that's what everyone who loves this country is like."

"Plenty of them are."

"What about the Constitution?" Ira asked. "Don't you think that makes us special in some way?"

"Words on a page."

"Really."

"Yeah. Just more empty words, written by old dead white guys with wooden teeth who owned slaves and got rich growing tobacco."

"Uh huh." Ira leaned back in his chair, thoughtfully. "You're a big fan of the Internet, aren't you?"

Lana seemed thrown off for a moment by what seemed like a drastic change of the subject. "Yeah. So?"

"And remind me, what's the government of the Internet like?"

"There isn't one," Lana said. "Not much of one, anyway."

"Is that so?"

"Yeah. There's a basic, scalable structure that's so simple it's brilliant, and then a few little groups that watch over protocols and standards to protect it and keep things stable, and that's it."

"Wow," Ira mused. "So those are the people that thought of Amazon.com?"

"No."

"Google? Facebook? Netflix? Reddit?"

"No—"

"How about eBay? YouTube? WordPress? Surely they thought of Wikipedia?"

"No, listen," Lana said. "The real stuff, the content, that's not their damned job. Regular people invented all those things, mostly individuals and little start-ups. What you're asking about is not some big government, there's no need for that. All that's needed is just the bare, boring essentials of a structure underneath."

"Oh," Ira said. "Kind of like a foundation."

"Right."

"So then, what's the job of the government of the Internet?"

"Like I said, it isn't much. Their job is mostly to stay out of our way. They protect and maintain the foundation, and just let things flow."

"They just let things flow."

"Now you've got it," Lana said.

"Gosh. That's worked out pretty well."

"It just totally changed the world within a few years. No big deal."

"Yes, I see," Ira said. "You realize, I hope, that you've just described the genius behind the U.S. Constitution, and the magic of capitalism and the free-market system."

Lana laughed out loud. "I think you forgot to take your meds this morning."

"There are how many millions of people on the Internet? Billions now, and somehow it's succeeded without tens of thousands of regulations. Sure, some of its citizens are only sitting by and watching, but a lot of them are using that unlimited freedom to build places, start businesses, create whole careers out of their imaginations. It's a perfect environment for invention. And somehow with just those few simple rules and a hand-ful of managers, it not only works, but like you said, it's changing the world."

Ira leaned to her, and continued. "That's what this country was meant to be. Hundreds of millions of imagi-nations, free to invent and reinvent and adjust to the changing times, succeeding and failing and succeeding again without a big, meddling government to leech off their treasure and get in the way. That's why it should be wonderful to live here, and why there's a lot to learn before someone's prepared to become a part of it.

"You just described the America those Founders envisioned, and they thought of it a quarter of a century before Babbage even designed his first steam-powered computer. So you see, kid? You might not like what our greedy, bloated government's made of America today. But just like me, whether you realized it or not, with all your heart you love what it was once meant to be."

A few seconds passed in a quiet stare-down, and then Lana responded matter-of-factly. "I hate you so much I can taste it."

"Just say it, you'll feel better. I won."

She got up abruptly and headed for the hall with the snack machines.

Ira leaned back in his chair again, seeming quite satisfied with himself, and he looked over at Noah. "I think I'm finally starting to get through to her."

"I really don't think so."

"And what about you, Mr. Gardner?" Ira asked. As had happened before between the two of them, the look on the older man's face suggested that there was more in his question than the words alone might suggest. "What do you think the future holds for the troubled land of your birth?"

"I agree with you. I think this country was a great

idea, maybe the best idea ever. Maybe it had a chance once, but now it's over; the other side's just too well organized. Now it's too far gone to save."

After a moment Ira looked quickly to the door and the windows as though to check that the coast was clear. He opened his bottom desk drawer and withdrew a small device, rolled his chair closer, and then handed the thing across.

"What's this?" Noah asked. It looked like nothing but a coil of wire and some clips and bits of junk mounted to a small block of wood, with an earpiece dangling from one side.

"*Shh*. Hide it, and take it home with you tonight. It's a radio."

"I've already got a radio—"

"Not like this one. Don't let anyone see it, and don't try to tune it; it's already set to the right frequency. Listen to it tonight before you turn in. We'll talk again tomorrow."

When the day was done, upon returning to his apartment, Noah immediately went to the desk and checked his e-mail. There was nothing but spam and some bureaucratic notices from the complex; again, he found no reply to his earlier messages to Molly. He wrote to her one more time, fixed a quick bite to eat, and reclined on the couch for some quiet thinking. The next thing he knew, he awakened suddenly, near midnight.

After a glass of water and a last check of his inbox he readied himself for bed, and that odd radio he'd been given came to mind. At least Ira had *said* it was a radio; when Noah retrieved it from his coat it still looked like some rejected craft project from a below-average Cub Scout.

As he lay down, he put in the earphone, expecting

nothing at all, but there was a faint, intermittent sound, windy and barely there. A short chain of copper-plated paper clips was hung from a connector labeled "Antenna," and when he held this in various positions the signal changed and gradually grew stronger. And then a man's voice came through, thin but clear and steady behind the static, and Noah cupped a hand over his ear and closed his eyes and listened.

"*. . . so nobly advanced. It is rather for us to be here dedicated to the great task remaining before us—that from these honored dead we take increased devotion to that cause for which they gave the last full measure of devotion—that we here highly resolve that these dead shall not have died in vain—that this nation, under God, shall have a new birth of freedom—and that government of the people, by the people, for the people, shall not perish from the earth.*"

There was more at the very end, delivered as though it was a common sign-off for these nightly underground broadcasts. It was only seven little words, but they left Noah troubled and sleepless for a good long while after they'd come in.

We are Americans, the anonymous man had said. *God bless Molly Ross.*

CHAPTER 34

Arthur Gardner hadn't died immediately from the effects of his tragic accident at the elevator.

In fact, it was several hours later, and still he hadn't yet managed to give up the ghost. As bad luck would have it he'd fallen only about fifteen feet into the empty shaft before striking a maintenance platform and coming to rest unconscious on its narrow steel ledge.

Well, when life hands you a lemon, Warren Landers thought.

His former boss's stubborn lingering-on might be made into a small blessing in disguise. As was so often the case in this job, one must roll with the changes, and thus he'd immediately set about making the best of this unexpected development.

Mr. Gardner was in that rare class of people who don't go to the hospital; the hospital comes to them. One urgent call to the multibillionaire's version of 911 and the quick and discreet process had been set in motion.

The victim was collected and brought to his own bedroom, which in the interim had been rearranged and fully equipped to support intensive care. His ragged wounds and fractures were stitched and daubed and splinted to the extent required to stabilize him, and the proper drugs were administered to make his final hours comfortable and quiet.

Quiet, in particular.

Sadly, he wasn't expected to pull through. This wasn't a medical opinion so much as a direct order, delivered by Warren Landers to the company physician in charge. After the proper inducements had been paid, the rest of the staff concurred and proceeded accordingly with Arthur Gardner's terminal treatment plan.

Another thing was made clear: not a word of this affair would leave the room until the time was right. Naturally, neither the press nor the authorities had been informed of the accident. The story would require some finesse. That, and a key witness still lived who might cast doubt on the official version once it had been conjured up. Everyone else who knew anything was bound by an ironclad nondisclosure agreement that would promptly ruin their lives and end their cushy careers should they ever rediscover their principles and go public.

It might seem to a layman that such a threat couldn't carry enough weight to engage a diverse group in the obvious cover-up of a first-degree murder. But Landers knew from long experience that it would be more than sufficient. Getting otherwise honest people to look the other way, that was the most common transaction in the world of public relations. The perpetrators of much grander crimes—institutionalized child abuse, stock market manipulation, the looting of whole economies, entire wars, in fact—had gotten away clean with far less leverage than this.

When the others had left the room, from near the archway to the bedroom he observed the broken man lying still among the tubes and wires and hanging bags of fluid. Save for his breathing he hadn't moved, but he wasn't sleeping, either. Without expression, as Landers looked at him, he was simply looking back.

An assistant came to whisper that a special guest had entered the lobby downstairs. Several others had begun flitting around the sprawling apartment, tidying and misting disinfectants and turning up the HEPA filters to their maximum settings. The reclusive VIP who was now on his way up was known to be sensitive to the many invisible hazards that might lurk about in a sickroom. Whether the germs were real or imagined he would want to know that his concerns had been respected in advance of his arrival.

A minute later everyone had disappeared, shooed into side rooms to clear the path for this visitor. Landers went to the front door and opened it, and there, wearing simple clothes and a demeanor of humble majesty—and not looking a day older than 110—stood the old gentleman himself, Aaron Doyle.

Mr. Doyle's entourage maintained a respectful distance as the two men had refreshments and walked together to the balcony, talking in low tones along the way.

Only the briefest matters of business were discussed: updates and statuses, confirmations and forecasts. Mostly it was a tour through the luxurious spaces of Arthur Gardner's apartment—it was a true Manhattan palace, and a reward soon to be passed to Warren Landers in recognition of his upcoming accomplishments.

In their larger objective, the final countdown had begun. If all was well, as it seemed to be, there would be little more to do than watch to see which variation of their coming victory would unfold.

Mr. Doyle could have supervised all this from the comforts of his home, of course, but it seemed only fitting that he personally attend to see his long-standing colleague off to his permanent retirement. As such it had been a pleasant surprise to learn that Arthur Gardner had indeed lived to see him one last time. With some overmodest reluctance Landers accepted full credit for having engineered this happy accident.

With the tour complete, the time had come to say their good-byes to the patient. The two men dismissed their escorts and made their way to the quiet bedroom.

Gardner couldn't be said to be unresponsive; his eyes showed recognition as the two approached, but there was no more to it than that. Aaron Doyle came close to his old and formerly trusted friend, and he reached out, turned back the sheet, and warmly patted the arm that wasn't broken.

"I'm so hurt that it came to this, Arthur," he said. "More than you'll ever know. But I'm here now because I wanted to tell you something in person.

"This was my will, what you're suffering now, this pain you're feeling and your death that's fast approaching; this is all by my hand. You've been like a son to me, and I wanted to come here and show you that I still have a strength that you seem to have abandoned. I have the strength to discipline my own."

From his bed Arthur Gardner was staring into the eyes of his employer. There was little emotion in his face and he said nothing at all. It wasn't even entirely clear, considering his injuries, whether he retained the faculties of speech.

"Your last wife . . ." Mr. Doyle paused as he tried to remember. "What was her name, Warren?"

"Jaime," Landers said.

"Yes, Jaime." Doyle *tsked*, and shook his head. "She wasn't as pretty as the others, not to your old standards, in any case. And a *waitress*, Arthur, and a noble citizen activist, a person so beneath the station of a man like you. A mismatch like that could never have ended well. You do recall, don't you? Though I rue the day, I was the one who sent you out to meet with her. And it was a simple thing that I'd asked, the same kind of errand that our Mr. Landers here somehow manages to perform time after time without falling in love and siring an heir with the object of his negotiations."

Still, there was no response.

"Those were critical times," Doyle continued. "We had a chance then, in the creeping malaise of the Carter years, to revive an uprising among the commoners and organize them into a force for our kind of change. She could have used her former notoriety, she'd been one of the only strong and principled voices among that 1960s rabble, but because of those very principles she wouldn't step forward and lead for us. She refused every gift we offered and wouldn't do what we needed her to do. Instead she bewitched you, and she very nearly turned you against me.

"But I recovered then, and I'll recover now. Despite the many hurdles put in my way by William Merchant our agenda is succeeding beyond my wildest hopes. We're molding the deluded young into an army of dependent ciphers. With your help we've conditioned them from birth to happily sign away their rights and vote as they're told, staring slack-jawed into one electronic screen or another and obediently parroting our every crafted word.

"The loudest radicals from the sixties and seventies are now firmly installed in the establishment, from the universities to the media to the White House, the courts, and the Cabinet Room. We didn't need your wife at all, do you see? Both she and her high-minded principles are long forgotten.

"I had her killed, you know." Doyle waited, as though

to see if his words were truly connecting with the shattered man before him; there seemed to be no change. "At first I did my best to keep you busy so that work might separate the two of you. But I could see you weakening and perhaps even planning to leave me one day, and so for your own good I did what I needed to do.

"Mr. Landers here arranged it. She had tried to steal from me, so I wanted it to be slow and painful and hopeless, and a particularly nasty carcinoma filled that bill quite nicely, I thought.

"And you came back to me when it was over, fully recovered from a handful of lost and lovesick years, and you were soon as hard and strong as ever—more so, if that's possible. I saved you then from throwing your future away. I saved your life, in a sense, Arthur. And now I've come to take it back again."

It might have been a trick of the light, but at this moment there seemed to be a glimmer of something stirring behind Arthur Gardner's eyes.

"Your son, too, will be joining you and his useless whore of a mother very soon. I know you were trying something, Arthur. Maybe you were only trying to save him. Maybe you've fallen into collusion with Mr. Merchant. Now I may never know. Why you chose to involve your boy again I'll also never know, but believe me, he won't go unpunished. It will all be over soon, for you and your bloodline, and with that knowledge you can rest in peace."

"So long, boss," Warren Landers added. "I'll see you at the funeral."

The room was quiet for a few seconds after. And then as the two men began to turn to leave, without warning the still hand on the bed arose and clutched outward and took Aaron Doyle firmly above his delicate wrist.

It was as though Arthur Gardner had saved his last

ounce of energy to allow himself a chance to respond, to speak with the strength he wished to show in this final confrontation.

"I do have something to tell you, Aaron," he began. His voice was strained and weak but steady as stone. "All this time I've helped you in your battle of wills against your old partner. At first the stakes were small, and then your goals grew larger along with their toll, and now it seems that your ambitions have reached a practical limit. Now, if you have your way, the whole world hangs in the balance. And I think that's finally too much. I think that won't be allowed.

"I've watched this war rage for most of my life. You move, your opponent counters, on and on I've watched the games unfold by your side. But I'm afraid there's something you don't know. You made a confession to me just now, and I have one of my own for you. There's something I've kept from you, something I learned myself only a few months ago."

"What is it?" Doyle asked softly.

"Bill Merchant . . . died . . . in 1979."

Gardner pulled Aaron Doyle even closer, his voice fading, his nails cutting into the papery skin at the forearm, and his eyes burned with the very last of his departing spirit.

"You now have to wonder, don't you, Aaron? If Merchant is dead, then who in heaven's name has been up there fighting against us for these past thirty years?"

CHAPTER 35

Noah's second day at work began much like the first, and he was getting the feeling that sameness and a dry routine were all he could look forward to for the rest of his life here. Ira Gershon was the only one who didn't seem to have given in to the structured monotony.

"Can either of you tell me," Ira chirped, as they were finishing their lunch break in the office, "just approximately now, how many possible different ways that a deck of cards can be arranged when you shuffle them?" He'd been fiddling with some cards, riffling them and then studying them, as he ate his cold turkey sandwich from its clamshell tray.

"I don't know." Noah thought about it for a few seconds; no branch of arithmetic had ever been his strong suit. "What's fifty-two times fifty-two?"

"Twenty-seven hundred and four," Lana Somin said, only half listening, and without even breaking her stride at the keyboard.

"I'll go with that."

"You're a little low, my young friends," Ira said, and he picked up a pencil from the desk. "There are about one hundred and fifty sextillion atoms in this little yellow stub, including the eraser, but that number isn't even close to the answer. The fact is, there are as many ways to rearrange this deck of cards as there are atoms in our entire galaxy."

"No way," Noah said.

"Yes way." He put down the pencil and then shuffled again. "And that means that of all the games and all the decks that have ever existed in all of history, it's almost impossible that these fifty-two cards right here have ever been stacked in precisely this way before, or that they ever will be again."

Lana slowly removed her headphones, frowning and looking very thoughtful. "I totally hate to say it, but he's right."

"Wonders seem so hard to come by these days," Ira said. "I take them wherever I can find them." He got up and walked to the phonograph. "What'll it be today? Old Blue Eyes? Duke Ellington?"

Noah shrugged. "I'm sure whatever you play will be fine."

"Then I guess you've never heard the Harmonicats," Lana said.

They'd just gotten down to work again when a red light flashed over the doorway and out in the hall a harsh buzzer began to sound. The other two stopped what they were doing, rolled back their chairs, and placed their hands in their laps, and at an urging from Ira, Noah did the same.

"What's this?" he asked.

"You'll see."

Two people wearing security uniforms came into the room, and one by one they visited the three occupied desks, examined the computers, opened the drawers, swept an electronic wand here and there over each of the workers and their belongings, performed cursory pat-downs, made some notes on their handheld screens, and then without saying a word left again and closed the door behind them.

"Where are we, at the iPhone factory? Does that happen a lot?"

"I told you there were no cameras in here," Ira said. "Spot inspections are one of the trade-offs for that." He picked up his cards again, and shuffled. "They're not supposed to keep a schedule but they've gotten very predictable. We won't see them again for a week or so."

This was Ira Gershon's day to write his newspaper fillers, and all through the morning he'd stopped occasionally to share a particularly interesting factoid with his coworkers.

"Did you know," Ira said, "that sea otters hold hands with their mates while they're sleeping so they won't drift apart in the night?"

"Some of us are trying to concentrate here," Lana snapped. "I swear I can't take much more of this. 'Did you know that ninety percent of all pumpkins come from Peoria, Illinois? Did you know that there are nine thousand metric tons of ants on earth? Did you know that Flipper's real name was Kathy, and when the TV show was canceled she committed suicide?' I know exactly how that fish felt, Grandpa."

"Dolphins are mammals."

The girl got up abruptly. "I'm going to the bathroom, and we're going to start this day all over, my way, when I get back."

The two men were alone, then, and Ira came closer and sat down by Noah's side. When he spoke his previously jaunty mood had darkened a bit and turned quite serious.

"Did you listen last night, like I told you," he asked, "to the radio that I gave to you?"

"Yes, I did."

"And what did you hear?"

"I got a late start, so I only heard the very last part of the Gettysburg Address. And at the end, the guy said, 'We are Americans. God bless Molly Ross.' "

Ira nodded. "I want to ask you about what you said yesterday, about it being too late to save this country. Is that how you really feel?"

Noah paused before he answered. "I don't want to believe that, but—"

"Then don't believe it. That's the first step. Noah, I know they're trying to get you to help them bring her in. Never mind how I know, I know. I'm here to tell you, that's not what you were meant to do."

"What do you mean? What *was* I meant to do?"

"Take this." Ira quickly looked both ways and then handed over a small memory stick on a neck-chain. There was also a sheet of paper, folded and sealed, tucked into its pocket clip.

"Is it from her?"

"No, smart guy, it's from me. Now, we don't have much time. You look at what I gave you there later tonight, listen some more to that little radio, and then after that, read what I wrote to you in that note. I hope it all may change your mind about things."

"Okay, but—"

"And promise me this: whatever happens, the three of us, you and I and Lana, we'll stay together. We've all made the same enemy, and I hope you can see that he's only keeping us around temporarily. We're only still here because they haven't figured out what to do with us exactly, but that won't last forever. I don't care about myself, but just like you, that girl was meant for bigger things than to wither away in this place. One way or another, whether it's fast or slow, that's what's in store for all of us. So if you get a chance to leave here you'll take us with you, understand?"

"Of course I will, if I can," Noah said. "That's a promise."

CHAPTER 36

Noah returned to his room that evening and after a quick walk-through to ensure he had the place to himself, he went directly to the computer.

There wasn't a doubt in his mind that everything he did on this PC was being monitored, right down to the keystroke. The only question was how closely. Was someone watching in real time or was the spying more passive? Ultimately he decided that it didn't matter; he was going to do what he was going to do.

The sealed note attached to the storage device that Ira had given him said "READ ME LAST" on its outer surface and so he put the paper aside for the moment. Then he found an open USB port on the machine, slipped in the memory stick, and watched as the screen responded.

A menu of videos appeared along with a listing of their archived locations on the Internet. The addresses were strange and unconventional, as though they referred to remote and secret places hidden safely outside the reach of the day-to-day corporate search engines. These files would be exceedingly hard to find if you didn't know where to look, and so they'd also be difficult to scrub away if those in charge should ever feel inclined to order them removed.

He clicked on the first one, not really knowing what to expect. Maybe it would be yet another stirring but toothless speech from a fringe-libertarian rally, maybe some clip of Molly or one of her faithful, firing up the fresh recruits back in the days before they'd all been made into outcasts and targets of terrorism investigations.

The video began to play then, and if he'd been given a thousand tries to guess what it would show, what he saw next still would have surprised him.

It was a transfer of a grainy old analog videotape. A reporter was introducing a story from the location of a large, loud Washington protest march that had taken place at the height of the Vietnam War, while Nixon was still riding high. The camera turned to the subject of the reporter's interview, and there stood a young Jaime Wilson—Noah's mother.

Though his mom did pop up for a few embarrassing seconds in that Woodstock movie, other than that Noah had only photographs to remember her by. Those pictures were from later on, when she'd become a wife and a mother. Here she seemed barely older than Lana Somin but as fearless and confident in front of the camera as any seasoned spokesperson could be.

In the various videos it became clear that she'd been at the heart of a number of grassroots organizations, all dedicated to fighting and exposing the corruption that even then was dragging her troubled country toward disaster. But, one by one, she'd left the groups she'd helped create as they'd gradually been taken over by provocateurs and radicals. These agents—people like Warren Landers—had either come to weaken her work from within or to push these once-peaceful movements toward the violent paths of the Black Panthers and the Weathermen.

He watched each clip in utter fascination, lost in the sound of her voice and the strength of a message even more relevant today than it was back then. This was a part of his own history that he'd never known before, and as she spoke it was as though her words were for him alone. When he'd gone through all the files he came back to that first one to watch it again. At the end the reporter had asked her to sum up her message to the young people of America.

"My message," Jaime Wilson said, "is that if you want things to change, first you've got to commit. Don't look to me or anyone else, look inside. Educate yourself, learn from history, this has all happened before and it'll happen again. And you can't just grab a sign and find a march and think you've made a difference. You've got to wise up before you rise up.

"Every generation thinks it's all going to be different when they finally get into power. They think a better world is coming just as soon as the old folks die off. Not true.

"This country only works if good people get involved. That better world you want won't come on its own, and if you think watching from the sidelines and making clever comments and sniping and whining is doing something, you'd better think again. Don't go to sleep at night until you've made this a better place than it was that morning. That's my message: you're the key. Without you we'll all be dead and gone before we ever see peace and prosperity again."

Noah got up from the computer in a daze, walked into the other room, and then saw Ira's little radio on his bedside table. He sat down, put in the earpiece, and listened to the faint signal coming through. It sounded like an old recording of a speech that was playing, though he didn't recognize the voice.

We are at war with the most dangerous enemy that has ever faced mankind in his long climb from the swamp to the stars, and it has been said if we lose that war, and in so doing lose this way of freedom of ours, history will record with the greatest astonishment that those who had the most to lose did the least to prevent its happening. Well, I think it is time we ask ourselves if we still know the freedoms that were intended for us by the Founding Fathers.

You and I have a rendezvous with destiny.

We will preserve for our children this, the last best hope of man on earth, or we will sentence them to take the last step into a thousand years of darkness.

With that the broadcast ended, concluding with the same sign-off as the previous night.

Noah was tired and troubled and it was getting late, but he remembered the folded note that Ira had given him. When he found it on the desk where he'd left it, he unfolded it and began to read.

Noah,

There's a reason you were born in these times, and yes, to the father and the mother you were born to. There's a reason you met Molly Ross when you did, if only you'll believe what I know to be true.

I see something in you, Noah, and Molly did, too. I always look for signs, messages of guidance

from above, and one was sent to me late last
night as I sat at my old, broken typewriter,
shuffling my cards and for whatever reason,
looking for a sign in the letters of your name.
And that sign was sent down to me then, in such
a way that only I could receive it. That's how I
know that it's real. I give it to you here.

    Believe it, Noah, and then go and be the man
you were born to be.

This previous section was handwritten; the final part was
only two short typed lines. The first of these was Noah's
own last name, though with that uniquely imperfect *d*
on Ira's typewriter it appeared to be misspelled:

`g a r d n e r`

He felt a knot in his stomach the size of a softball as he
read the line just below. There, the letters of his name had
been reshuffled and arranged into a new order.

`r   r e d g a n`

Oh, come on now.

He laughed aloud, sitting all alone in his room, and
he wished that Ellen or any other sane and rational
person could be there to help him counteract the crazi-
ness. No, it was beyond just crazy. Talk about grabbing
at straws—

Noah's thoughts were interrupted by a quiet knock
at the door. He walked over and opened it to find Ellen
Davenport standing there.

"Ellen," he said. "I was just thinking about you. I
thought you'd have gone home by now. Come in, you've
got to see this."

She stepped inside and hugged him for a long while, and there were tears in her eyes as she looked up into his. "I'm so sorry, Noah."

"Sorry about what?"

She frowned. "Hasn't anyone told you?"

He shook his head, having no idea of her meaning.

"Noah," Ellen said, taking his hands in hers. "This afternoon, your father passed away."

CHAPTER 37

In a frigid side room of the Douglas County Morgue, Virginia Ward sat with her notes in the midst of eight bagged-and-tagged bodies and a mounting collection of conflicting and unexplained evidence.

Since their first meeting she'd had no further interaction with Warren Landers, the man who'd originally engaged her in the matter of Molly Ross. He'd neither called for status updates nor replied to her routine contacts; ultimately she'd stopped trying. It was as though he'd changed his mind about involving her; perhaps he and his higher-ups had decided it would be safer to simply decide the outcome on their own and then turn over their verdict directly to the media.

That was already happening, in fact. The alleged details of Molly's agenda, her network of accomplices, and her criminal activities were becoming more and more public each day. Now it seemed that every reporter knew her name, and the obedient press was already drawing comparisons to Timothy McVeigh and the lead-up to the destruction of the Murrah Federal Building in Oklahoma City. The anniversary of that attack was fast approaching—on the same day that also marked the disastrous end of the Waco siege—and so speculation ran high that a copycat operation might be in the works.

These mounting fears were due to much more than just talk. A wave of violent hate crimes, random shootings, and bomb scares continued to spread across the country. These were all quickly linked and labeled as acts of domestic terrorism, and the heightening alert level had led many cities and towns to take severe measures that ranged from enforced curfews, roadside checkpoints, and house-to-house searches to airport-level screenings at malls, workplaces, schools, and any arena events that hadn't already been canceled for safety reasons.

Since she could no longer expect any help from the elusive Mr. Landers, some of Virginia's other powerful contacts had arranged for the highly unusual assembly of physical evidence that was currently on display at the morgue. She'd had no time to travel to each separate location, so it was all flown in from the other jurisdictions to meet her in Nebraska. An Omaha medical examiner had taken her through his own findings and answered her questions on some subtleties that lay beyond her own expertise.

The group of bodies in the room comprised six men and two women, each from a different scene along the terror route. All the males had been killed in the act of committing one of the aforementioned crimes—or right-wing terrorist attacks, as the news was characterizing them. Though DNA and fingerprint results were still pending, Virginia was satisfied that none of these dead people was Thom Hollis or Molly Ross. She was sure they were still at large, but that's where her certainty ended.

One of these dead men was suspected to have started a number of wildfires out west, a few of which were still spreading out of control. The local cops had determined that he must have misjudged the wind in committing his arson; the blaze he set had turned and overtaken him as he'd tried to run away. Beneath the scorched body they'd found a plastic pouch of literature with some of the pieces preserved undamaged. The surviving pamphlets and flyers were a mix of materials, most from the Founders' Keepers, and some assorted racist and seditious screeds from the United Aryan Nations. More like these had been found blowing around near the origin points of the other fires.

Fingerprints had been lifted from these materials and they all matched the index finger of Thom Hollis. "Matched" was an understatement, however; not only were they identical to the print from his military records, they were also virtually indistinguishable from one another. No other prints or partials were found, just those perfect copies from a single finger. It was as though they'd been lab-produced and then hand-applied, but too carefully, for the sole purpose of ensuring they'd be found. Such technology existed, of course, but it required facilities beyond the reach of all but the most well-equipped intelligence agencies.

After the recent murders committed by a high-powered rifle, ballistics evidence indicated that nearly every fatal shot had been fired from the same weapon. That weapon was now on the table beside Virginia, having been left behind in a sniper's nest in downtown Chicago. There again, Thom Hollis's single pristine fingerprint was found on the rifle and the bullet casings and elsewhere around the scene. Upon disassembling the weapon, though, a more diverse set of his other prints and even a dried fleck or two of his blood had been recovered from the interior parts.

The two young women here, both street prostitutes according to the authorities, had died in separate cities.

Each had been shot from behind, execution-style, and then hastily buried near the locations of a pair of seemingly random sniper killings.

The clothes worn by one of them appeared to be the same as those in the surveillance still that Virginia had shown to Noah Gardner. He'd said then that the woman in the picture wasn't Molly, and it seems he'd been right about that. But there was a passing resemblance to her in the mug shots of both of the dead women, and it seemed likely that they'd been chosen to create a reasonable facsimile for eyewitnesses to recall after the fact.

No doubt there were more like these two still out there waiting to be found.

Another of the dead men had drawn a pistol in the Chicago riot and wounded a policeman before being killed himself by responding officers. Like the others he hadn't yet been identified, but he did have a peculiar distinguishing mark on the inside of his left wrist: a line of five small yellow diamonds, faint enough against his lifeless skin that they'd been left out of the coroner's inventory.

There were a lot of tattoos on these guys and this one hadn't really stood out until she found similar ink on one of the other male bodies, and then another, and then on all the rest. A quick image search on her tablet found many matches to the pattern, but as she narrowed the results she happened upon something rather obscure that provided the first real break in the case.

This exact array of diamond shapes appeared in the coat of arms of the British House of Percy. The black sheep of this old, renowned clan, Thomas Percy, had helped plan the Gunpowder Plot with Guy Fawkes in the early 1600s. Despite the clueless use today of his grinning image on a mask as a symbol of freewheeling anarchy, Guy Fawkes had in fact been a violent advocate for the return of hard-line Catholic theocracy to the throne of England. In any case, when the plot failed Fawkes was hanged and quartered and Thomas Percy's liberated head ended up on display outside Parliament.

The Percy name was altered by some of its members when they later emigrated to America. Percy had been changed to Pierce.

Sure enough, there on his many ugly websites, George Lincoln Rockwell Pierce proudly traced his family tree back to those treasonous roots overseas, and the Percy coat of arms was displayed at the corner of every page.

In all the available writings and videos of Molly Ross and her deceased mother before her, Virginia Ward had found nothing that would indicate she would ever fall in with a man such as George Pierce, and much less would she sanction the kind of violence now being attributed to her.

She would have a great deal of explaining to do upon her capture, to be sure, but as of that moment Virginia had no reason to believe that Ms. Ross was anything more than an outspoken patriot and the focus of an elaborate setup.

But why, and by whom?

Thom Hollis, on the other hand, was still an unknown quantity. For now, she would consider him armed and dangerous until he proved himself otherwise, if he ever got that chance.

That last name, Merrick, had begun to come up again and again in the fringe-media coverage of the building threats and their alleged sources. Though it hadn't been specified publicly, Virginia had discovered the location of the particular Merrick family to which these rumors most likely referred. Several members of this family were politically active and the nature of their past support seemed compatible with the libertarian views of Molly

Ross and her people. By all reports they seemed to be model citizens, the salt of the earth, but that too would remain to be seen.

Now it seemed that Virginia Ward was officially running off the leash. But if the men who'd brought her in thought their sudden withdrawal would stop her search for the truth, they were dead wrong.

The Merrick ranch in Wyoming, then, would be the very next waypoint in Virginia's journey toward the truth. It was a lot to hope for, but perhaps the answers to all her questions were there.

CHAPTER 38

By and large, the men George Pierce had lost already were of very little concern to him.

Nor did he fret about the fate of those who would surely die in the bloody weeks ahead. This terror and turmoil he was helping create would soon transition to the war that he'd always wanted—a bloody battle against the tyranny of the elitists, their heathen puppets, and the one-worlders. At last the day of reckoning was coming, and all those who would give their lives in this final showdown, civilians and soldiers alike, could not have dreamed of a higher endeavor in which to make that sacrifice.

There would be a bleak period of adjustment, no doubt, a time of cleansing, reconstruction, and reeducation. Sadly, there were some so-called Americans who simply wouldn't be a part of this future. Twenty-five million or so was the conservative estimate his strategists had given him. But so be it; many more had been lost in the name of far less noble goals.

The end was near, and only a few tasks remained in the menial part he was currently playing. He'd gone along and done as he was told, biding his time and preparing to return to his own agenda when the time was right. And there was still one burning need in him, admittedly a personal vendetta, and he would have it satisfied before the night was done.

He didn't consider himself to be a man whose wrath was easily kindled, but if George Pierce had a flaw it was this: once he was wronged and his sense of justice was awakened, it wouldn't rest again until the books had been brought back into balance.

Warren Landers had recently made contact and ordered him to be ready if the need arose to move against Molly Ross and her people, wherever they were hiding. It might not be necessary at all, he'd said. The Founders' Keepers were to be implicated in the planning of a massive domestic attack of some sort, as if such high-and-mighty weaklings would ever be capable of doing such a thing. But that story wouldn't play if they continued to cower somewhere in a safe house, so Pierce's role would be to flush them out of hiding if they wouldn't come out on their own.

Landers was not a trusting man. He'd still insisted on keeping her location a secret. In the course of this conversation, though, he'd inadvertently said too much and let slip some important information.

Wherever she was hiding, Molly Ross was within a two-hour drive from the spot where George Pierce was currently standing in his war room. Two hours away over land: that was the time frame he'd been given in which to execute his role if called upon. With that knowledge he'd measured and drawn a small, scaled circle on the terrain map, with his compound at its center point.

Other scattered details further narrowed the possible locations. The place was rural and remote, far from the nearest town, he'd been told, and its two dozen or so able-bodied residents might be well prepared to mount an armed defense. Their large dwelling was in the midst of a great deal of private land, and that meant that if they managed to call for help it would be a long time in arriving. They were under surveillance from eyes in the sky, so it was known that Molly Ross and her people were still hunkered down in the same place they'd run to when they'd made their escape two weeks before.

Now the other puzzle pieces could be laid aside. Their unexpected nearness and the fact that a drone was orbiting above them: those two bits of information would be her undoing.

Pierce had used some of the money he'd been paid to buy an assortment of black-market radio gear and a set of classified schematics that had been on his wish list for a long time. With these items his technical men had built a home-brewed transceiver. This rig had actually first been invented by al-Qaeda engineers almost ten years before, back when American drones had first begun to play an increasingly publicized role in finding and killing their leadership. Later versions of this setup were rumored to be capable of disrupting or even taking control of the aircraft, but those weren't the capabilities he needed right now. All George Pierce required was to hack in and see what those airborne cameras were seeing, and to be able to ask that drone exactly where it was.

The men had brought in a folding table, set up the rig, and run the proper line to an antenna array outside. His most skilled communications specialists sat before the snowy display screen, tuning and tweaking the dials with a safecracker's touch, searching along the narrow spectrum for a faint encrypted signal somewhere out there, just within range.

Those Talion people Landers had hired to do his bidding were very well trained and equipped. Their gear, however, wasn't the latest tech available to the legitimate U.S. military. They had weaponry, helicopters, tanks,

APCs, and even jets, but it was all years old, the type of equipment often sold to second-rate allies overseas.

Their drones were yesterday's news as well, and the secrets of this particular class of craft had been studied and ultimately cracked by the very terrorist forces they'd been deployed to watch and harass along the Afghan–Pakistan border. A UAV maintains a constant data link with its controllers, and that signal can be captured if a man knows where to find it.

At last the picture swam and hissed and then stabilized. An image appeared, the same one he'd seen for only a second when Landers had shown it before: a large house, outbuildings and corrals, and sprawling open land surrounding it all. With a tapping on the keyboard an electronic inquiry was sent and back streamed a screen full of telemetry data, including the coordinates of the target residence.

The men let out a triumphant yell, one of them turned up the lights, and another called out the key data to be copied down. George Pierce bent over the large map on his table, traced the coordinates with his fingers, and quickly found the place.

"Feed those numbers into a GPS," he said, "then get all the men together, get everybody, but do it quiet." He was thinking of the skeleton crew of Talion mercenaries that Landers had left with him, camped in the field outside. Without any doubt part of their job was to keep watch over their hosts and report any hints of revolt.

But a time comes when every leader must face the Rubicon and make his choice to cross it or deny his destiny. This was a turning point, and although it had come sooner than he'd expected, he would not shy away.

"No," Pierce said. "We're not going to slink off our own land and sneak away to do what's right. Now listen up. Keep the man out there in the radio tent alive, and we'll persuade him to keep his boss informed that we're all still doing what we're told. As for the others, I want you boys to go now and kill everyone outside that ain't one of us. Take them all at once, and I don't want to hear any alarms go off, you understand? Make it quick and quiet and clean."

The men nodded, and a few of them smiled.

Then Pierce thumped the X he'd drawn on the map in front of him.

"And then you go there," he said, "all of you. Drive down to that ranch and murder everything moving. Man, woman, or child, it makes no difference to me. Kill them all and we'll let God sort 'em out. Burn the place to the ground, but you save one thing for me." He raised his voice so all could hear. "I'll give ten thousand in gold to the man who brings that Molly Ross back here alive to face the music."

CHAPTER 39

The Wyoming sky had become overcast and Hollis knew that sundown was only a couple of hours away. It had already been another hard day of preparations for the trip north to safety and there would be a long night of final tasks ahead.

A waist-high table was lined with a dozen open grab-and-go kits that he'd been putting together with the aid of his young helper. This job had mostly consisted of him telling Tyler Merrick what to fetch. Now the boy was late in coming back, and with just a few vital provisions still needed to fill up the survival bags, Hollis, after a few more minutes of waiting, got up to go and get what he needed himself.

As he set out for the distant pantry, along the way he confirmed something that Tyler had told him earlier: the local sheriff's squad car was in the driveway in front. To avoid being seen Hollis made his way toward the garage through paths outside and back halls that eventually took him past his own suite.

He paused at Molly's room and looked inside through the half-open door. It seemed she hadn't moved since the last time he'd checked in. The curtains were drawn and her dinner tray was on the side table, still untouched. She appeared to be sleeping, but then for the most part she'd appeared that same way for several days.

Together the two of them had soldiered through a lot of difficult times, but it had never been like this; he'd never seen her adrift this long with all the wind taken out of her sails. They say that time heals all wounds. He could only hope that would begin to prove out once they'd left this latest losing battle far behind.

Hollis considered stopping in to give her some recent news and then he thought better of it. He'd received an e-mail message, supposedly from Noah Gardner, via one of her older private addresses. The message offered Molly his help, whatever that might mean. Most likely it was some attempt at subterfuge, and whoever knew enough about their relationship to fake that note also knew enough to be a real threat. Even if it was actually Gardner who'd written it, though, it could be just as dangerous. Real or not, encouragement from a message like that was the last thing Molly needed to receive at the moment.

Since their last ill-fated meeting, the other members of his party had also been keeping to themselves and he'd seen very little of them. Meanwhile, the Merricks were all occupied with serious concerns of their own. It was becoming clear that they were the targets of a dedicated smear campaign, and the regional press had begun to relay some of these stories without even questioning their truth. There'd been three visits so far from the law, including this one from the sheriff that very afternoon. The first two were official but this time he'd evidently come calling off-duty, apparently to offer some unauthorized legal counsel to his old friends.

Along his route Hollis paused in the shadows near enough to the front door so he could overhear a bit of the conversation. As unbelievable as it sounded, the sheriff had come with his deputies to let this family know that they were soon to be the subjects of a federal terrorism investigation.

At length Hollis moved on, and before long he came to the small outbuilding that contained the supplies he needed. He opened up the metal door, but before he could step inside, the boy Tyler came running up to him, breathless.

"Oh man, I'm glad I found you," Tyler said. "Come on, my great-grandmother wants to see you."

Hollis frowned. "Well, I sure as hell don't want to see her."

"No, you don't understand. When she asks for you, you go. Believe me, you don't want her coming after you."

"Did she say what she wanted with me?"

"She never does. You'll find out when you get there." The boy reclosed the cooler door and locked down the handle. "Come on, seriously."

"I ain't ready for this," Hollis said.

"You don't know how true that is. Now let's go," Tyler said, and they started off. "I'll take you as far as the last hallway and then you're on your own."

CHAPTER 40

Her name was Esther, he'd been told, but under no circumstances was he to call her that to her face—not if he knew what was good for him.

After the boy had abandoned him at the corner, Hollis had kept his apprehension under control for the first few steps, but by the time he'd reached the entrance to the antiquated original section of the Merrick house, the long walk down the darkening, lamplit hall had begun to feel like the last mile to the gallows.

It was a trip back in time as well, those last twenty yards. The wood in the walls and the floor seemed to age and weather with every step onward. The clean, rustic look of the rest of the ranch was mirrored here but it had gradually changed its character, transforming from a quaint designer's choice in country décor to the old-fashioned real McCoy.

Hollis took a deep breath and rapped three times on the heavy varnished door.

The voice that came from inside wasn't at all what he'd anticipated. It was neither the screech of a winged harpy nor the weakened wheeze one might expect of a typical centenarian. It sounded spirited and sure and gracefully feminine, all that conveyed in only five little words.

"You come on in, now."

He opened the door and stepped softly into the front room.

She was seated in a cane rocking chair near her stone hearth, warmly outlined in the amber glow before the low, crackling flames. A round Dutch oven hung from a hook in the top of the firebox, and whatever concoction of beef and herbed gravy and root vegetables was cooking in there, it smelled so good it nearly weakened his knees.

The place was like a lovingly preserved museum exhibit, the very essence of the American West at the turn of the twentieth century. Beneath the rafters to a vaulted ceiling the rough log walls were painstakingly planed and shaped with every joint hand-fitted. The frame and structure looked as though it had been built with little more than a hatchet, a wedge, and a great deal of love and care.

The wide mantel was lined and hung with an array of archaic things: bear traps, powder flasks, articulated metal toys, nutcrackers, and cook's helpers. There were implements of various shapes and sorts made of wrought iron, bronze, hammered copper, hardwoods, and thick tanned leather. These relics recalled the essential technologies of a time gone by, things on which life itself had once depended but whose practical functions were now mostly long forgotten.

She sat there, rocking gently with her sewing in her lap, a cup of hot tea by her side, and the handle of a fireplace poker in the grip of one bony hand.

"Well, my stars," Esther said quietly, "if it ain't Lucifer's servant himself, Thom Hollis."

"Ma'am, with all respect, I'm nobody's servant, least of all—"

"Don't you say one word to me, not until I give you

my leave. The devil uses good people, too, once he sees they've lost their salt. Now find you a seat and pull it up here close. I need to see you good and clear and these eyes of mine aren't all they used to be."

There was an ottoman near the couch and he brought it over in front of her chair, and sat.

"The Good Lord has ways of herding lost sheep back into the fold," Esther said. "You do need to listen, though, otherwise He'll only speak His wisdom again, but louder and stronger the next time, in a voice that makes it harder to ignore. Do you understand me?"

"Yes, ma'am."

"No, you don't understand," she snapped, and it looked for a moment like she was about to swing the hook of that poker at the broad side of his skull. "You're either about Satan's work or you ain't got the sense that God gave geese, and we don't have much time to sit and ponder which it is." She leaned forward with the tractor-beam glare that he'd seen before only from a safer distance. "Best that I can figure, you're afraid, Thom Hollis, and fear in a man like you saps the will out of every blessed soul around you."

"I'm not afraid. I'm only trying to protect Molly—"

"She's protected already."

"She's not the woman she used to be, she's blind—"

"We walk by faith, not by sight," Esther said. "That girl's got a calling, and she needs you next to her for one thing and one thing only: to help her do what she's been called up to do. And some which way or t'other you've got the idea into your thick head that you know destiny better than He who shapes it, that you alone know what is and isn't possible. You tell her and her people to surrender His fight when the battle's hardly begun. And then you've got the crust to strut around here in high feather, like a tall dog in a meat house, like you think you're still on the side of right. You come into my home, talking back and prideful while you sit there given in to cowardice and sloth, makin' eyes at my granddaughter all the while. I saw you myself the other night in the billiard room, feet up in an easy chair like there wasn't a worry in the world, and drunk as a peach-orchard boar. If my husband was alive today he'd haul you out back on general principles and beat you like a rented mule."

"Ma'am, we've been through hell enough already—"

"Hell's empty, Thom Hollis," Esther said, "and all the devils are here. Even now their master sends them forth, at this moment they move against you, and even now the Lord whispers His will and gathers a fellowship set to come to your aid. But you don't see His miracles. You're afraid to be tested, you're afraid to stand up and believe—you fear to walk out onto the threshing floor. You're afraid if you try and are found wanting, you'll fail her. But in that very act of choosing not to try she's lost already. Do you see?"

He nodded slowly, and he really did see, though he didn't want to.

"Take my hand," Esther said.

He did. Her touch was electric, an immediate cleansing shock that passed through him head to toe and left him feeling thunderstruck and sober as a judge.

"The spirit has always dwelt among us," she said, "since long before it had a name and a nation for its home. It's burned in the hearts of millions in other lands who dreamed of its promise but never lived to reach these hallowed shores. It survived slavery and Civil War, depression, organized crime in the very halls of its government, and time and again it's weathered the looting and corruption and schemes of a ruling class that pledges no allegiance to anything but its own dark designs.

"Now that spirit lies dormant and shunned and forgotten in all but a precious few of even our own sons and
daughters. Its light dims but still it burns, it waits to be
awakened so this one nation and the love of true liberty
at its heart can be restored to her old glory. It demands
much of those that hear the call, and the first hard thing
it asks is courage.

"Now, then," Esther said. "Are we dust, or diamonds?
Will you be a slave to the creeping tyranny that's stalked
every try at moral government since time began? Or
will you be a free man who stands beneath the shield of
nature's God, clad in His armor, sworn to protect and
defend the founding bedrock of this wounded, blessed
land? Are you only human after all, Thom Hollis? Or are
you an American?"

After he'd left her, he stood outside under the darkened,
cloudy sky, near enough to a lamppost to see the keep-
sake in his hand, the gift that Esther Merrick had passed
to him as they parted. She'd given something of hers to
all of them, she'd said, something they might have lost
along the way.

*"So am I to understand that you're the trail cook for
this lot?" she'd asked as she walked him to the door.*

*"Among other things," he'd answered, "and in better
times than these."*

What she'd given him then was a saltbox; that's what
the old-timers would have called this little round, hinged
wooden case. Though it appeared to be solid when closed
against the elements, there were many small compartments accessible with a twist or a press along its sides.
These held within them a surprisingly wide variety of dried
herbs, ground spices, aromatics, and cracked peppercorns.
The deepest of the enclosures was reserved to keep an
ample supply of fine white salt pure and dry and protected.

Such a thing might not seem essential to survival, if one's goal were simply to live out one bland and tasteless day to the next. But that isn't really living at all—while the flesh may be sustained by little more than shelter, dry bread, and lukewarm water, the soul needs more.

There was a small handwritten note tucked into that last compartment, and this is what it said:

> Let us raise a standard to which the wise and honest can repair; the event is in the hands of God.

He began to walk again, and then to run, and when he reached Molly's room he knocked on the door but didn't wait outside for her to answer. Her dog alerted and stood at the foot of the bed as Hollis burst into the room, but he didn't bark or threaten, and Molly turned her face toward the noise.

"Who's there?" she asked.

"It's me, Molly."

"What's wrong?"

"That plan you were talking about the other day, the one I said was impossible and desperate and nothing but an elaborate attempt at suicide?"

She sat up. "Yes."

"I was wrong," Hollis said. "I'm in. By God, let's do it."

CHAPTER 41

The first urgent order of business would be the fabrication of a do-it-yourself anti-aircraft bunker in the barn east of the house.

Watching from cover, after only a few minutes with a pair of proper binoculars, Hollis confirmed that what he'd feared was true: a surveillance drone had been orbiting the ranch and it was still up there, circling. Under the prevailing conditions he might not have been able to spot it had the craft not descended under the overcast to maintain its view. Even at that lower altitude its distinctive outline was only barely visible against the backdrop of featureless gray clouds.

He kept it in sight as it followed an unvarying and apparently automated oval pattern at only a few thousand feet over the land. Not as big or as fast as the latest deployed versions, he noted, it was likely an older, unarmed model, maybe a Gnat, capable only of carrying various cameras and telemetry gear. It slowed drastically as it bucked the breeze on its inbound, upwind leg and was also flying much too low for its own good. Whoever was remotely piloting this thing didn't seem too concerned that his robotic spy might be discovered—much less that it could be vulnerable to a well-placed shot from the ground.

Night would have already fallen by the time they were ready to flee, but if they managed to bring that thing down then the darkness could be turned to their advantage.

While there was still a bit of daylight Hollis summoned the most skilled rifleman among the Merrick clan and asked him to come to the second-floor loft of the barn. He was to bring one of the family's Barrett .50 calibers, a tripod mount, and as many magazines of incendiary tracer rounds as they had in the stockroom.

Meanwhile the livestock were discreetly moved out of the barn and then a pickup truck pulled the second weapon into position through the back double doors: an eight-foot carbon-arc searchlight on a four-wheeled trailer, complete with its own diesel generator for power.

This light was of the same type as those used to sweep the night skies at movie premieres and grand openings, a distant cousin of those billion-plus-candlepower units that shone upward from atop the Luxor in Las Vegas. In the past the Merrick family had used this big thing and another like it to add some flash and pageantry to nighttime public gatherings and charity events at the ranch. Though it was not quite of military power, if their luck held out it would be more than bright enough for this job.

With a stopwatch they tracked the drone's flight path over three circuits and it proved to be regular as clockwork. As it approached the barn straight-on and against the wind there would be a narrow window of time in which that small, moving airborne target would become a sitting duck, appearing almost stationary in the crosshairs.

The tripod for the Barrett M82 was soon bolted down to the floor of the loft with the rifle aimed toward the oncoming leg of the drone's flight path. The searchlight was rolled into place down below. Both manned positions would be hidden from aerial view by the closed barn doors, at least until the time came to fully commit.

When that aspect of the operation seemed as ready as it would ever be, Hollis returned to the house to go over the rest.

When she laid it out for him again Molly's brainstorm was just as brash and hazardous a plan as he'd remembered it. The details looked different only in light of the fact that this was no longer just a spine-tingling topic of conversation. Now it was an actual, step-by-step layout of the events in their very near future.

As she spoke he watched a transformation taking place: Molly gradually became her former self again. By the time she'd finished with the overview she'd snapped completely out of her despair and reappeared as the same resolute and determined young woman he'd known for many years. His previous lapse in faith in her went unspoken; he'd let her down but only briefly and no further energy was wasted on apologies or explanations. They had much to do in preparing to leave, and he could also see that she shared his own overwhelming sense that there was very little time in which to do it.

With the plan now officially under way, Molly asked him to call two of the ladies to help her dress and get ready for their departure. While she was busy with that, Hollis gathered the other members of the group and told them what was next.

The meeting was brief and it began with the determination of who would and would not be taking an active part in the coming adventure. With the exception of Molly and himself, he told them, all the remaining Founders' Keepers were to pack up and make their way to the group's sanctuary to the north, just as previously planned.

Their trip would be no carefree walk in the park; the way home was difficult and some were still nursing injuries. It would be a brave and necessary contribution that they would make, to go on ahead and prepare a place for the remaining travelers should they somehow manage to return victorious. Since it was clear that the Merrick family had also become targets, any of their number who wished to make the journey upstate were welcomed to go that way as well.

As he returned to his own room and thought through what was coming, a major barrier to success became evident almost immediately: this mission required technical capabilities that none of the core group possessed, and there was no time to begin recruiting any outsiders.

As he considered his options, Hollis recalled that Tyler's mother might at least have the skills needed for one key phase. After he approached her with the idea, Cathy Merrick went to her dad and her son and they talked it out for a while. Ultimately she volunteered to go along, but with the further complication that Tyler had insisted on accompanying her.

While the young man had some facility with computers and an amateur's knowledge of Internet technologies, he certainly lacked the level of expertise they'd need if they actually made it to where they were planning to go. Still, Hollis agreed to take them both, with the full understanding that if things began to get too dangerous they were free to leave at any time.

The Founders' Keepers had always attracted a great army of passive followers and secret admirers, but relatively few active participants. More recently it seemed they had far more backbiting critics and outright bloodthirsty enemies than anything else. But as Hollis sat at the computer putting out urgent feelers for help in this endeavor he was surprised to find a number of people who were ready and willing to offer their service for precisely the things he'd needed.

In less than half an hour he'd booked charter flights and arranged a few levels of backup transport, acquired anonymous funding and lined up supply drops, ordered up a very special overnight parcel to be prepared and anonymously sent to the mission's final destination, and—most important—he'd scheduled a critical appointment for an upcoming afternoon of final preparations at a large, big-box home-and-hardware store on the outskirts of Butler, Pennsylvania.

He saw another e-mail, then, from an inside man in a detention center near Denver, Colorado. This elderly fellow—Hollis knew him only as Ira—was the source of the information he'd been passed all along about Noah Gardner.

There was news in this note that he had to share immediately with Molly. When he hurried to her room he found her all packed and ready to go.

"You know how you said you wished we could have Noah along on this thing," Hollis said, "but you knew it wasn't possible?"

"Yes," Molly said. "What is it?"

"I got word just now. His father's died."

She sat back, and he could see her thinking. There was obviously no love lost for old man Gardner, but his passing might well create just the opportunity they needed. Noah's help would be invaluable in what they were about to do, and now there was a way that they could find him.

"Where's Noah right now?" she asked.

"I don't where he is right now," Hollis said, "but at this time tomorrow night I know exactly where he'll be."

She nodded. "Change of plans?"

"Change of plans." He checked his watch. "Get ready to go, now. I'll go see if the coast is clear."

As he headed out of her room he had to pause at the corner of the hallway to the great room and wait. The sheriff and a deputy were visible on the porch outside the front door, but they were finally bidding good night to the Merricks and were on their way out.

And then as he watched, both of the uniformed men slumped and staggered forward almost at once. The distant sounds of the shots that had hit them arrived, and as they crumpled to the ground the full-on clatter of automatic gunfire erupted from beyond the yard outside.

Hollis wheeled and ran back to Molly's room. As he came through the door he saw the shadow of a dark figure just outside her window. He grabbed her and turned with her held close so that his body was shielding her. A close-range *boom* suddenly shattered the glass and a searing impact hit him in the shoulder and knocked them both out into the hallway.

As he turned his head to look behind them, pain subsiding and shock already setting in, he saw Molly's dog rise up and leap through the blown-out window frame and onto the man who'd shot at them. An intruder alarm was blaring, there were shouts and screams coming from everywhere, and then, all at once, the lights went out.

CHAPTER 42

Lieutenant Kyle Brassell leaned forward in his swivel chair, set down his coffee mug, and studied the escalating developments on the wraparound screen in front of him.

In the black status banner up at the top, the video display said MERRICK.

"Lieutenant" was a misnomer, actually—that's what he used to be, but there were no such ranks in the management structure of the Talion Corporation. He was an STS, a senior tactical supervisor. And as his soon-to-be ex-wife was so very fond of reminding him, he had been one of those for a very long damn time.

But at the moment he was his own boss, if only by default. His many superiors had traveled to other installations where plans were being finalized for some large-scale civil-disturbance deployment that was soon to roll out across the country. It wasn't clear whether this was just another training exercise or a live operation; sometimes one could become the other without much notice. Lately not a lot of information was trickling down to his level and he didn't want to seem pushy—or worse, insubordinate—by asking too many questions. He took it as a vote of confidence that he was left in charge of the facility and gladly accepted this opportunity to show them all what he was made of.

His standing orders were simply to monitor what was happening at this place on the screen—a Wyoming ranch a hundred miles away, thought to be harboring persons of interest in a suspected cell of domestic terrorists—and to follow established protocol should anything unusual develop.

In his experience, warfare was generally nothing but crushing monotony right up until the moment when everything explodes. This assignment had been no different, and now it looked like that moment of explosion had suddenly arrived.

Earlier in the day, Brassell had ordered his spotter drone to drop down below the cloud base. The view improved slightly at that level, but the picture it provided still wasn't adequate. On his own initiative he'd then vectored in two MQ-1 Predators from their positions on another nearby assignment, one displayed on an adjacent screen labeled PIERCE. Both aircraft were company-owned and at full combat readiness. Their more advanced sensors would improve Brassell's strategic picture even from their higher altitudes.

This move had felt a bit like an overreaction but the people minding the budget actually encouraged such overuse of resources and equipment. The Talion contract was practically open-ended and everything designated "anti-terrorism" was being handed a fat blank check from the taxpayers, so there was really no downside. In fact, a cynical saying had developed among some Talion employees with regard to using drones: "When in doubt, send three out."

But his order didn't seem like a waste at all—not anymore. In fact, the decision to send in more surveillance and muscle began to look like a stroke of George S. Patton genius once the shooting started.

A local law enforcement vehicle had been parked in the Merrick driveway for a couple of hours, and as the officers were leaving the house it appeared that two of them were suddenly gunned down in the doorway. Brassell had been reclining in his chair at the time and this sight was startling enough that he spilled his double espresso down his front and completely missed any clue as to where the hostile fire had come from.

The infrared cameras immediately picked out a number of distinctive flashes: armed positions responding from outside. No Talion forces had been ordered to attack the place—those must be other officers, he thought, possibly state and local police. That had to be it; they would have been placed out there to cover those who'd been sent into the house, perhaps in a now-failed attempt to negotiate a surrender.

A full-on gun battle was soon under way. Intelligence had obviously been correct about what this remote compound housed. Judging from the firepower now responding from inside, these Merrick people must have a substantial arsenal and enough trained men to defend themselves against all but the most heavily armored ground troops.

At first the assault seemed evenly matched but gradually the aggressors in the house and the outbuildings had begun to gain the upper hand. As he watched, the surrounding land became littered with motionless casualties and clearly the tide had turned. These Merricks and their terrorist accomplices appeared to be winning.

Brassell grabbed his tablet and called up the field action authorization for this engagement. Surveillance was all that was explicitly authorized, but people were dying out there—he had to do something.

The intel was rock-solid and all required signatures were in place, right from the top; he had every reason

to act. Law enforcement officers were already down, the
target personnel were high-value, their liberty-spouting
survivalist ideology fit the far-right-wing-militia profile
to a tee, and from what he could see on the screen, their
actions were clearly murderous and unprovoked. The
fugitives thought to be hiding there were preapproved
for a signature strike, and what he saw unfolding was a
clear enough indication that the ringleaders were indeed
inside, just as suspected. It all added up.

He knew it was time for a command decision but
still he hesitated.

Brassell thought back to a domestic-action seminar he'd
taken in his early training as a contract commander here.
The subject had been the Waco siege. The lesson from that
day had been clear-cut: *Don't let this happen on your watch.*
A prolonged and public debacle like the one that happened
down in East Texas was never to be allowed again.

It had taken a PR miracle to spin that fifty-one-day
siege and the subsequent killing of seventy-five American men, women, and children into a righteous government raid on a bunch of suicidal religious nuts who
got what they deserved. But from that day forward, we
were to err on the side of rapid and decisive action, far
away from the attention of the press. Act with authority
and the results could then be announced—or rewritten,
or hidden, as the case may be—once the outcome was
known and everything was back under control.

"Scramble the A-10," Brassell said, and a nearby run-
ner set off to make it so.

By the time the bird was in the air the gunfire on the
screen had long since died down and there was no movement at all from outside. Next he saw that a number of
trucks were leaving the area, traveling off-road and then
splitting up into a larger and a smaller convoy going in
two different directions.

At the moment all he had were cameras in the strike zone. "Where are my armed drones?" Brassell barked.

"Still inbound, sir, maybe twenty minutes out."

"Damn it," he spat, and he'd begun to pace. "What about the Thunderbolt?"

"About the same, twenty minutes."

"Okay." He hurried to the drone pilots' station and pointed out the fleeing vehicles. "Drop autopilot. I want you to shadow those trucks—"

"Which trucks? The ones going north or west?"

Before Brassell could answer he was stopped by what he saw on the screen.

A dazzling shaft of light was searching the sky in the video frame, and then the screen went nearly white as the swiveling beam found his drone. Immediately a dashed stream of bright yellow tracers shot up from one of the outbuildings toward the defenseless craft, which was hovering practically motionless as it labored against the strong headwind.

"Evade, evade, get out of there!" Brassell shouted, and the pilot pegged his throttle and slammed the joystick hard to the side. But the General Atomics Gnat wasn't really built for speed. As the craft gently banked into its turn the picture shook and flashed and pixelated. Various alerts and critical warnings crowded the display as bullets tore through the airframe; the tilt of the view increased and then inverted and began to spiral downward. They all watched the sickening spin tighten and the ground rushing up until the screen flashed to static.

Brassell composed himself. "Redirect the Predators. I want them after those trucks—"

"You've got a fuel problem, Kyle," one of the pilots answered. "Both those birds are going to have to turn back just about the time they get there."

This was information that might have been useful an

hour earlier, Brassell thought. But he was determined to make the best of the decaying situation and rise above the mental limits of his staff. When this was over nobody would be able to say that Kyle Brassell took a major terrorist incident lying down.

Without any eyes-in-the-sky those fleeing trucks would soon be long gone. He'd have to decide later how to deal with their escape in his report, but it certainly seemed wisest at the moment to avoid mentioning them at all. There was still a victory to be had, of course. That house and its outbuildings were standing tall and vulnerable, right where they'd always been.

"What's the load-out on that A-10?" he asked.

"It's an air-to-surface package; he's got six CBU-87s, cluster bombs."

"Good deal. Tell the pilot he's weapons-free on that whole property. Let's have a tight overlapping spread on those '87s, blacktop the place, and if anything's left he should take care of it with a cannon pass or two. Now what about your Predators?"

"They've got four Hellfires between them—"

"Okay. As soon as you get to five miles out, lock targets and let fly and then turn back to base for refueling." Brassell walked up to the screen and pointed to the main structures on an aerial photograph that had been shot days before. "That's your objective. Now let's light them up."

When the gun battle was done and all was quiet again, Esther Merrick had gathered her family, called the roll, and made her last wishes known.

Over their strong objections all her surviving kin had been sent on north toward safety as Molly Ross headed to the west toward California to pick up the last member of her team—or to kidnap him, if necessary.

After that she would go east to take this fight back to the enemy.

All of them had gone, then, except her eldest son. Despite the best appeal she could muster he would hear nothing of running away, being every ounce as stubborn and headstrong as the woman who'd raised him. She wouldn't leave the land that had been her family's home and heritage since her own grandmother was a child, and her son wouldn't leave her to stand this ground alone.

He was tall beside her as she sat on their front porch in her rocking chair, her mother's Bible in her hands, an old shotgun resting across her lap. It wasn't the first time blood had been spilled in defense of this spread, though perhaps it would be the last.

In any case, the trespassers who'd come to slaughter her family and friends were now all gone to judgment. Before too long she would be bound for glory herself, and while Christian charity forbade her to hate, if asked at the pearly gates to testify for these men she'd have a very difficult time conjuring up a forgiving word. Evil is evil, and no good comes of calling it by any other name.

From the direction of a low rumble off in the distance, five dim and moving points of illumination, like traveling stars, appeared in the darkened sky.

And so the end was on its way.

Esther Merrick had always saved a particular Psalm for those rare times when courage threatened to fail her. She raised her small hand and her son took it gently into his own.

"The Lord is my light and my salvation," she whispered; "whom shall I fear?"

"The Lord is the stronghold of my life," her son answered; "of whom shall I be afraid?"

The missiles came then, a second ahead of their terrible sound, and by the time the next and finishing wave of airborne destruction arrived to send everything physical back to ashes and dust, all souls once present at the Merrick ranch had already flown far beyond.

CHAPTER 43

Virginia Ward had seen the glow of a distant, raging fire from several miles away, but it wasn't until she'd driven up to the military-style roadblock that she finally let herself believe what was burning out there.

The Department of Homeland Security had blanketed the entire region with yet another nonspecific elevated terror alert, letting citizens know only that they should stay at home under curfew and await further announcements. Uniformed men at the checkpoint ahead were turning back the sparse traffic and pulling aside selected vehicles for searches and questioning of the drivers and passengers.

As she reached the front of the line she saw that these men were armed and organized but only a few were actually state or local police. The rest were contractors, all sporting the Talion insignia and behaving as if they had every legal right to do what they were doing.

After showing her identification she waited in her rental car as they huddled to discuss how to deal with such an unexpected visitor. After a number of tense calls up the food chain, at last an okay was handed back down.

She was given a coded site pass to hang around her neck and a few of the men directed her around the barrier and waved her onward toward the ranch. An escort van pulled out behind her, the nonofficial yellow strobes on its rooftop flashing all the way.

On her flight into the area Virginia had reviewed a backgrounder that included many photographs of the Merrick property. What she saw when she pulled up at the outer fence line bore no resemblance to those pictures at all.

The area was lit with portable banks of lights, smaller versions of the arrays one might see at an outdoor sporting event. All she could see under the glare was a cratered, blackened wasteland. To her right a few structures were still in flames, including what was left of the main barn and the shells of other smaller buildings. The fire trucks and EMS vehicles that had responded were being held away at the far perimeter. Evidently it had been determined that nothing and no one here would be worth the risk of saving.

A large number of corpses were scattered around the grounds, apparently lying right where they'd fallen, most with weapons still in their hands or by their sides. Next to each of them someone had placed a body bag topped with a weighted paper form and a Ziploc container for evidence or personal effects. As yet, however, it seemed that nobody had made a priority of tending any further to the dead.

Virginia got no special attention, either; these workers looked past her like she wasn't even there. Instead nearly all the suited-up personnel were sifting through the smoldering wreckage where the family house had once been.

She walked slowly into the scene, picking out details, trying to roll back time in her mind's eye to let the ruins tell their tale.

A sheriff's vehicle had been here for a while before

the shooting started—it was parked close to the residence, where a welcome visitor might stop. A deputy was dead at the wheel, clearly shot through the window as he sat waiting. The shotgun beside him was still in its mount, his sidearm was holstered, the radio mike was in its clip. He hadn't been expecting any trouble until it crept up and hit him from behind.

It occurred to her that the vehicle's always-on dashcam would be perfectly positioned to show a replay of much of the incident. As she bent by the broken window she saw that the camera had been ripped out by the wires and the car's black-box video recorder was gone along with it.

Virginia stood again and took a long look around.

As before, it seemed that no one was paying her any mind, though without any doubt she felt eyes on her from behind the darkened glass of the van that had followed her in. She walked on again, feeling more alone than ever and distinctly aware of the comforting weight of the pistol at her hip.

Three bodies were outside the house near the frame of a shattered window. One of them was shot but the other two had their throats ripped out; it looked like they'd lost a fight with either a large guard dog or a small bear. In all likelihood this spot was where it started, with the family inside their home, a company of bad guys creeping up to surround them from cover, and these three amateur assassins coming in close to a ground-floor window, maybe with a specific target in mind.

These men had come here for a massacre.

Whatever vehicles had transported them, all had been parked somewhere out of sight, though there had also been two massively armed pickup trucks on their side. One of these vehicles lay overturned, the other had crashed headlong into a ditch, and both looked like they'd driven here straight from the set of *Mad Max*. Each had a belt-fed machine gun mounted in its bed.

Virginia headed back out toward the edge of the yard and knelt down beside one of the dead men there. He'd been shot in the face, and by his posture and the placement of his rifle he'd apparently been killed while firing toward the house from a prone position. Like some of the others he had a U.S.-made light rocket-launcher slung across his back, though he'd never had a chance to fire it.

It all seemed to fit. These marauders had come prepared for a coordinated surprise attack on those inside. They obviously got far more of a fight than they'd bargained for once the shooting had begun.

There'd been a prolonged gun battle then, and it appeared that the Merrick family had won. Whatever had totally destroyed the house and the grounds, though, had happened after the fight was over.

She checked several of the bodies for those distinctive markings she'd seen on the skin of the perpetrators from other regions—that line of tattooed diamonds denoting members of George Pierce's organization. Some had them and others didn't, many were burned too badly to tell, but there was more than enough jailhouse white-power ink among them to convince her that they'd all come from the same wicked source.

A man was walking her way and she spoke to him but he took no notice, being so thoroughly absorbed in his iPad that she had to stop him physically to get his attention.

"Are you in charge of this scene?" she asked.

"Nope."

"Who is?"

"Over there." With a flick of his thumb he indicated a man standing nearer to the remains of the house.

Virginia turned and started that way without wasting another word. As she walked she crossed paths with several soot-covered workers leaving the rubble with salvage in their hands: computer components, hard drives, printers, laptops, and desktop units.

The man who'd been pointed out as the site manager looked up as she approached.

"Who the hell are you?" he asked.

She showed her ID. "Tell me what happened here."

He scanned her credentials under his flashlight. "Figuring that out is not my job. Who let you through the roadblock—"

"One more time," Virginia said. "What happened here?"

The man frowned for a few moments, as though he were performing a block of long division in his head. "Air strike," he said at length, "on some terrorism suspects."

"Who ordered it?"

"Who *ordered* it? Nobody ordered it; it's procedure. The rules of engagement ordered it. And why the hell are you asking me? I saw your ID, I know where you're from. You people probably wrote the training manual for all this, and you're asking me what happened here?"

She felt like putting her fist through something but it wasn't anyone or anything within her reach right then. "Who was in the house when the strike came down?" she asked.

"We haven't been through it all yet. Just two people as far as we can tell."

"Let me see them."

"I will," he said, "but there's not much left to see."

The bodies he showed her were burned and torn up far beyond any hope of a field identification. She snapped on a pair of thin gloves from her kit and knelt down with the remains to discover what she could.

One thing became absolutely clear after only a few minutes of the grim work. These two bodies by the house were not those of Molly Ross and Thom Hollis. Though in life they'd indeed been a large man and a small woman, both of these people had been much older.

"Where's everyone else?" Virginia asked. "I'm told over twenty people might have lived here, and somebody defended this place against an army of white-supremacist goons just a little while ago."

"Don't know anything about that," the man replied. "Wasn't part of my briefing."

But they must have been here, she thought. They must have escaped after the initial attack but before the air strike had come, and someone had decided that fact was to be kept quiet.

She stayed where she was, pretending to be performing a further examination though there was little more she could learn from those remains. She needed time to think.

Several years earlier, Virginia Ward had decided that the Big Picture was something she simply wouldn't acknowledge anymore. She believed she'd earned the right to retreat in this way. In fact, she'd paid for that right with her own flesh and blood. *Haven't I done enough for my country?* That's how she'd rationalized her withdrawal from the larger issues.

On the ground was where she'd chosen to live, face-to-face with good and evil, where a limited form of justice could always be done and she could see it done with her own two eyes. There was a perfect clarity in such small-scale engagements. No matter who she was working for or what their ultimate objectives might be, at least she could always know and do what was right in that moment of truth.

It had worked just fine for her that way, but always

with one nagging flaw: all the while a war had been under way, right here on her home soil, and she'd been involved only in its smallest details. The question that she'd somehow managed to keep at bay now loomed large.

Whose side was she on?

From everything credible Virginia had seen and all the data she'd collected, it seemed clear that Molly Ross and her people had never done anything but fight for their country by seeking the truth, albeit at times with tactics that bordered on the unlawful. In a way she'd taken up the role that the traditional press had long since sold out and forsaken. She'd made some very powerful enemies as a result, all the way to the top.

And the family that had lived in this place, the Merricks, they'd been known as pillars of their community until the recent smears against them had begun. Their only crime had apparently been material support of a legitimately patriotic cause that was dangerous and unpopular in the current climate.

And Noah Gardner was a good young man who'd never had a direction—he'd been a fellow bystander—and had finally found himself only when he'd gotten caught in the middle of a battle he was only now beginning to understand.

Those people were on one side of the war. And then there was the other.

George Pierce and his men obviously needed no further condemnation; their heinous vision of the future was crystal clear. But despite his FBI nickname, Pierce was no real general. He was only a puppet at best, one of many, and someone else was up there above him, funding, supporting, and pulling the strings. It was obvious to her now that Warren Landers must be a player behind the recently orchestrated turmoil, but he wasn't at the top, either.

Arthur Gardner, Landers's employer, had actually been Virginia's original contact in this matter. If Gardner was the ringmaster of this whole thing then why would he bring her in? He must have known that, given her reputation, she might uncover the truth. Was that what he'd wanted? Could it be that he'd come face-to-face with the same decision she was now facing, and that he'd made a bold choice of his own?

Thom Hollis was still the only wild card in her mind. With so much deception at work she still wasn't sure of who or what he really was.

And that was that; she made her decision right then. For better or worse, Virginia Ward had finally acknowledged the war and chosen her side.

She motioned for the fellow in charge to come nearer.

"What have you got?" he asked.

"Those two fugitives," she said, "Molly Ross and Thom Hollis?"

"Yeah."

Virginia did her best to never tell a lie, but in her line of work, sometimes there was simply no sound alternative.

"In my opinion this is them, right here," she said, handing him her card. "Congratulations, your air strike killed them both. The next time you report in you'd better tell that to your boss, on my authority."

Virginia hadn't been completely clear on her next steps, but when she returned to her car and checked her mail there was some shocking news that told her exactly where she needed to go.

Arthur Gardner was dead.

A private memorial gathering had been scheduled on the grounds of a highly exclusive club on the West Coast. It was set for the following day. The late

Mr. Gardner's son would of course be in attendance, as might other players as yet unseen. And if Molly Ross was still alive and on the run again—and if she was planning something like what Virginia was beginning to believe she was—then she might see this development as an opportunity to get in touch with Noah, and maybe to pull him into her service once again.

Virginia opened up a browser on her tablet and quickly made reservations for the next available flight to Sonoma County Airport, just a few miles east of the funeral's strange location.

CHAPTER 44

Noah had pledged to Ira Gershon that if he ever got a chance to leave that Denver compound he'd take his two coworkers along with him. At that time he hadn't believed there would ever be such an opportunity, and yet here they were—a promise is a promise. So when he'd been granted a travel pass to attend his father's memorial service, Noah had insisted that both Ira and Lana be allowed to accompany him, for moral support from his only friends in captivity.

Apparently even the most callous of deskbound bureaucrats has a hard time ignoring the wishes of the bereaved, especially when the request is delivered through the renowned attorney of a powerful family.

Formerly powerful, that is; the death of Arthur Gardner marked the end of the line for his brief dynasty, and with all due respect, Noah thought, good riddance to it all.

And so the flight to northern California found the four of them seated in the executive cabin of a small private jet—Noah, Ira Gershon, Lana Somin, and old friend Ellen Davenport—with four security guards buckled in behind them. Except for the crew, the rest of the plane was empty and so it had been a very quiet ride.

Toward the end, as the fasten-seat-belt light came on, Ira leaned to him and spoke in a hushed voice.

"Thank you for this, again," Ira said. "Not so much for me, but for her." He looked toward young Lana as he said this. She was in the far window seat, earbuds in her ears and her music playing loud enough that its muffled beats could be heard across the aisle. Her hand was to the glass and her gaze was intent and distant and directed outside. She looked as though perhaps she'd never seen her home planet from this altitude before.

"It might seem like a little temporary freedom but let's not get carried away," Noah said. "It's just a few hours, and then we're turning around and going right back to the grind again."

"You never know what's in store." Ira looked at him. "And I realize your upbringing couldn't have been ideal, I do. But still, you've lost your father, and I'm sorry about that."

"Thanks." That was one way to put it, that his up-bringing hadn't been ideal. In similar terms the last voyage of the *Hindenburg* hadn't been without its hic-cups. But though Noah was surprised to admit it, there was a trace of sorrow in him. His father did have his moments, and despite everything else those moments are what you remember when you finally realize there'll never be another.

Even before he'd stumbled into his star-crossed in-volvement with Molly Ross last year, Noah was certain that he'd been a disappointment in many ways. The biggest of these had probably been his complete lack of ambition in the field his father had once hoped he'd pursue. It wasn't public relations, it was politics that Dad had pushed him toward, and Noah had never felt any interest in that hard life whatsoever.

This thought brought to mind that wacky note that

Ira had given him the night before, the one that had contained that bizarre *r reagan* nonsense. He'd destroyed the note, of course; its contents could be incriminating for both of them. He hadn't forgotten it, though.

"You know, Reagan was far from a perfect man," Ira said, as if he'd been sitting there reading Noah's mind like an in-flight magazine. "Even his admirers admit to that. He didn't have the background most men in government have, he wasted a lot of years in what some would call a frivolous profession, he was a liberal Democrat for a while, he was a big fan of FDR and the New Deal even when he was old enough to know better.

"But flaws and all, he had a gift that his country needed, and he was brave enough to use it. He was good with people, he had those skills just like his father, but he got his heart and his vision from his mother. And it was a simple thing that he did, really. It didn't take a genius, just the right ideas and the right man at the right time. When a lot of us had lost our faith in America, he found a way to lead us to see the dream again."

"But that isn't me," Noah said.

"And how do you know that?"

"I'm not a politician—"

"Neither was he, at your age. You've got time. Hell, when he was twelve years older than you he was still best known as the star of *Bedtime for Bonzo.*"

"Look, thank you for those videos of my mom, that meant a lot to me. And I see what you're saying, I do, even though it's more than a little crazy. But believe me, you're trying to pin your hopes on the wrong guy. That business in your note, with the letters in my name? I'm sorry, but it's meaningless. You know that guy Reince Priebus, the front man for the Republican National Committee? If you take all the vowels out of his name it spells out 'RNC PR BS.' Get it? I know it would be fun to believe that's some hidden message, but it's just a coincidence."

"Think what you like," Ira said. "As I said, you've got time. All I hope is that if you ever get another chance to make a real difference, you'll find the courage to take it."

From the point where the limo let them off there was still quite a walk through the wilderness to reach the site where Arthur Gardner's memorial service was to be held. The rocky path wound through thickets of brush and stands of soaring redwoods to a timber-beam bridge that seemed to mark the end of the journey toward a place called Gaia Point. These were the secluded meeting grounds of the only club his dad had ever joined, the Ordo Seclorum.

That name they'd chosen means *the order of the ages*, so yeah, the membership had quite a high opinion of themselves.

Noah had been there once before at some father-son retreat back in his early teens, and he hadn't enjoyed the experience. It wasn't a funeral then, but a sort of after-party to the club's regular annual summer meeting. Once a year they all traveled here for a secretive gathering of the supposed cream of the crop from the intertwined worlds of politics, media, entertainment, commerce, old money, and the military-industrial complex.

The motto of the club was "Weaving Spiders Come Not Here." This was a warning that crass networking and shop talk were strictly prohibited lest the violators spoil everyone's fun. These titans were here to relax among their own, to smoke fine pre-embargo Cubans, to get roaring drunk and carouse, to occasionally run around buck naked, and to take a leak at the base of a two-thousand-year-old tree if they felt the urge. They came here to be themselves, in other words, with no fear of judgment from the lower classes.

Despite the posted ban on talking business this was nevertheless one of the places where the really big deals got done. The Manhattan Project had been planned in the central clubhouse, as had the wholesale cooperative thievery that led to the current worldwide financial crisis. Presidents were groomed and anointed here, scams hatched, cartels and monopolies formed, allies and enemies chosen, and wars approved. Once those decisions were made it often fell to men like Arthur Gardner to go forth to beat the drums and make the magic happen. That's why his memorial was being held in this place; it was one of the few environments on earth where his greatest accomplishments could be openly discussed and appreciated.

As they walked they passed into a clearing, into full view of a crystal lake with the four-story, moss-covered statue of a giant watchful owl enshrined behind a stone altar on the other shore.

"I always thought this place was just a myth," Ellen said.

"I really wish it was," Noah replied.

CHAPTER 45

With the exception of some perky young servers and the top-shelf call girls brought in by the busload to service these old reprobates, women were strictly forbidden from the main property. As a result the female members of Noah's group were escorted to one of the more remote and comfortable cabins to wait.

Ira chose to stay behind with the women and their guards as Noah left unescorted for the gathering by the lakeside.

There were world leaders in the crowd, past, present, and future, and many faces known from their regular presence in the news. There were also men familiar to Noah only because of his past work on their behalf. They didn't wish to be known but many of them were far more influential than those who craved the limelight. Though much of their scheming was focused on the United States, the majority of them lived elsewhere, being citizens only to the extent that such status could benefit their portfolio.

His father's body wasn't present, just a gilded vessel containing his ashes. These were to be scattered later in accordance with a provision in his will. The urn had been placed center stage on a pedestal beside an amplified speaker's podium, and a number of distinguished-looking gentlemen were assembled on the dais to deliver a final send-off. The mood seemed to be light, even jovial, like the prelude to a roast at the Friars Club.

An usher took Noah to a row near the front and pointed toward a seat that had a place card bearing his name. In the chair next to this one sat an elderly man he vaguely recognized. Their eyes met and after a moment's thought he remembered that face, though it had been a number of years since he'd seen it. Noah walked over to where this man was cheerfully tapping the cushion of the empty chair by his side.

Unlike the others nearby, who were dressed to the nines, this old fellow wore plain, loose, pale clothing more suited to a backyard barbecue than the funeral of a friend. And *old* was hardly an adequate word; he looked absolutely ancient, thin-skinned and dry as parchment, as if his fragile substance might begin to flake off and blow away in the slightest breeze.

"You can't be," Noah said.

"But I am," replied Aaron Doyle. "The one and only."

The speeches proceeded, with the crowd engaged and enjoying every one. Noah had heard all the various tall tales and anecdotes many times before, but he listened to them again as they were told with the new perspective of a last tribute. During a refreshment break before the concluding speaker, Mr. Doyle turned to him again.

"They'd asked me to stand up last and close things with a final word," he said, "but I told them it would be more fitting if that honor was passed to you."

"I'd rather not," Noah said. "I haven't prepared anything."

"I know you'll be fine. You've never been shy in front of a crowd, have you?"

"This isn't just any crowd."

"No, no it isn't, but I think your father would have wanted it this way. Just remember that you're among friends. *My* friends." Doyle sat back in his chair and patted Noah on the knee. There were skintight and nearly transparent gloves on those old hands, like something a clean-freak might wear to fend off the germs. "I've watched you for many years, Noah, as many years as you've been alive. We all had such high hopes."

"Well. Sorry if I let you all down."

"Oh, don't think of it that way. You've served a purpose, and you may yet live to serve another." Aaron Doyle considered him for a while, and then he spoke again. "Do you know why your father died, Noah?"

He was caught off guard by the question, and thought at first that the man had misspoken. "I was told that he had a fall."

"That's *how* he died, yes. I was referring to why."

For a few seconds Noah tried hard to reject the meaning of what he seemed to be hearing, but he didn't quite succeed.

"It was the same reason that your mother died," Doyle continued. "Even to the most insignificant degree in your mother's case, and in your father's only at the very end, they both had dared to try to stand in my way." The old man leaned in close. "And these trailer-trash rebels you became involved with last year? We'd hoped to push them into another futile act of desperation so we could permanently put their sad little patriotic cause into the dustbin of history. But I'm told their young leader, this special friend of yours, Molly Ross, she's now dead as well. No matter; terror isn't so difficult to create, and she'll still take the blame. We'll find another way."

Noah felt no fear and hardly any anger as all this sank in. The only thing he felt was a rising level of strength that seemed like it might be finding a permanent home in him where there'd been only emptiness before.

"Who do you think you are?" Noah said.

"Ask anyone here," Doyle replied. "For all intents and purposes, young man, I'm the king of the world."

The event had reconvened and the man standing at the podium had already introduced Noah by name a few seconds earlier. But he didn't move. He continued to sit, eyes locked with Aaron Doyle. A scattering of applause and clinking glasses began to urge the last speaker to the stage.

"If I learned one thing from Molly," Noah said, "it's that this is one country that doesn't need a king."

"Oh, it will," Doyle replied, "soon enough."

There was only a tepid ovation as Noah stepped up to the speaker's platform. His situation would be well-known to most of them, and these were people who had no great love or respect for the disowned and disinherited.

"My father was a great planner," Noah said into the microphone, "but I don't believe he ever planned to die. And yet here we are.

"He appreciated all kinds of poetry, and if you'd all join me in a toast I'd like to share a bit of verse that he liked, from Guiterman. Dear old Dad once said this should be etched onto his tombstone and that may tell you something about him that you didn't know. It's called 'On the Vanity of Earthly Greatness.' "

Going from memory, he recited the short poem.

> *The tusks which clashed in mighty brawls*
> *of mastodons, are billiard balls.*
> *The sword of Charlemagne the Just*
> *is ferric oxide, known as rust.*
> *The grizzly bear, whose potent hug*

> *was feared by all, is now a rug.*
> *Great Caesar's bust is on the shelf,*
> *and I don't feel so well myself.*

There was some good-natured laughter from the audience at this, and Noah picked up and then tipped his water glass toward the urn beside him. "Here's to my father, Arthur Isaiah Gardner, the man who elevated the art of lying into a weapon of mass destruction."

As to whether this had been an insult or a compliment, from the looks on their faces the crowd seemed almost evenly divided. When they'd all taken their seats again, he went on.

"I had very little time to prepare these remarks, but I think you'll all appreciate this story because I'm sure you haven't heard it before. I'd like to tell you about the only time that my father ever hit me. Now understand, he paid others to hit me a number of times, and not so long ago, but this was a blow from his own hand, and that makes it special.

"When I was a child, after my mother's death, my father and I lived alone. At the dinner table Dad would often present me with questions that he knew a kid my age couldn't answer, which is to say, I couldn't answer them to his satisfaction. This was what passed for light conversation between the two of us. I suppose if you want to be kind about it you could say it was his way of mentoring.

"These questions were hypotheticals mostly, on all sorts of subjects that were far beyond the grasp of an average middle schooler, and I failed miserably every time. It wasn't fair but I tried my best. And then one night, after he'd had a particularly hard day at the office"— Noah glanced briefly over at Aaron Doyle—"probably due to some trouble with the boss, he posed one of these questions to me and for once it seemed like its answer was totally obvious.

" 'If you had a time machine,' he'd asked, 'and you could take a gun and go back to 1930, would you track down and kill Adolf Hitler?' Now, the answer to that is clear, isn't it? Of course you would. If you could somehow stop his evil before it ever got started, who wouldn't? So that was my quick answer, yes I would, and when I said that he smacked me across the face good and hard. He wanted me to remember why I was wrong, I guess because he thought it might be important to me someday."

Through the tall speakers on either side his voice was reaching them all, and by then all attending had grown somber and very still.

"Sure, Hitler murdered millions and he caused un-imaginable suffering. If he'd had his way he would have reshaped the whole world into a living hell straight out of his sick and twisted imagination. But we have to take care not to give that one man all the credit for bringing the world to the brink. It was all planned out, you see; the crisis in that country was years in the making—not unlike the one we find ourselves in right now—and that's what opened the door for him. The times themselves finally demanded the rise of someone like him.

"The next world war was already inevitable, the Third Reich was coming regardless, and if it hadn't been Adolf Hitler at the helm on the side of evil it would have been someone else. Maybe someone more accomplished at hiding and executing his final solution, maybe a far superior general, maybe a more cunning diplomat who could have strung the Allies along until his scientists had won the race to split the atom. Maybe a craftier politician who would have listened to his advisors and allied with the Soviet Union instead of invading them.

If it hadn't been Hitler, it very likely would have been someone even worse.

"So, no, you don't go back and kill him, that was my father's strong opinion." Noah looked over at Aaron Doyle again. This time the old man didn't meet his eyes. "Hitler was weak, and flawed, he wasn't sane, and he also wasn't nearly as smart as he thought he was. So, as much as you'd like to wrap your hands around his throat and squeeze the life out of him, you have to let him live. Because Hitler, we could beat."

The audience was absolutely quiet, with the only things audible being the gentle movements of the lake and the sounds of the surrounding forest.

"I'll close on a personal note. I'm fairly sure our paths will never cross again. In fact after this performance and a conversation I just had, I've got a feeling I'm not too long for this life myself. That knowledge seems to have infused me with some freedom of speech that I'd forgotten I had, so I do hope you'll indulge me for just another minute.

"I was a part of your alternate universe for a long time, though granted, only a small cog in the machine. While I was among you I learned where all the bodies are buried, and a lot of them are buried all around us, right here. I know almost everything my father knew, and that's probably enough to send most of you to Leavenworth for the rest of your lives, assuming, of course, that justice really is blind. But let's face it, we all know that's never going to happen.

"There were a lot of rewards for keeping your secrets, and I enjoyed every one of them. And then last year I spent just a bit of time in another world—the real one, I now believe—and after that, as comfortable as I'd been before, I didn't ever want to come back.

"My father and I then found ourselves on opposite

sides of a very important battle, but I was no match for him at the time. I was late to that fight and I may be out of it completely now, but despite what I've just been told by Mr. Doyle over there, I don't believe it's over.

"I may no longer matter, but if this is to be my last appeal before such an august and influential audience, let me leave you with this: You don't belong here. This isn't the country for you. Go find a place where the people welcome the idea of a permanent ruling class; there must be plenty of them out there, but it's not here. Take your secret meetings, and your backroom politics, and your toadies in the press. Take your paranoid surveillance state, and your drones over the cities, and your warrant-less wiretaps, and your kill-lists, all your socialist pipe dreams and your fascist puppeteering. Take your self-serving transhumanist vision of one borderless world, united under your thumb. That might be fine for others, I don't know, but it's not for us. Get out and take all your damned lies with you, including the ones I helped you tell, and go loot somebody else if they'll have you. There's no place for your kind here. And now, gentlemen, good night, and God bless America."

He left the stage and walked up the aisle toward the path to the cabin, carried along by a swelling chorus of boos and hisses from the crowd that somehow felt better to him than any standing ovation ever could.

CHAPTER 46

Virginia Ward caught sight of Noah as he was coming back up the trail from the memorial gathering.

She'd arrived much later than expected, but having finally found this strange place, she'd been watching and listening to the distant proceedings for the last few minutes. She waved as he got closer and he picked up his pace when he saw her and began to jog the rest of the way.

The after-funeral fireworks show had begun just a minute or so after Noah had finished his bold little speech. Judging by the upswing in the revelry among the high-born assembly down there, any impact of his parting words had been short-lived at best.

For what it was worth, though, even at this distance she could tell that he'd succeeded in convincing at least one person down there: he'd convinced himself. There wasn't a doubt in her mind that Noah Gardner believed every word that he'd just spoken.

"Hi," he said, as he came near. "I didn't expect to see you until I got back to Colorado. What is it, do you have some news?"

"Nothing solid, I'm afraid. I found the place where I think Molly and her group were hiding out—"

"So did you bring her in?"

"No. Somebody else found her first. I got there after the fighting was done and there wasn't much of anything left."

"After the fighting." He swallowed hard. "So I guess it's true, then."

"What's true?"

"A man down there told me she was dead."

"By any chance was that man Warren Landers?"

"No. It was an old scoundrel named Aaron Doyle. Same DNA as Landers, only several rungs higher up the ladder of the damned."

"Aaron Doyle," she said, frowning. "Kind of a recluse, and he's big in finance, am I right?"

"Finance, currency manipulation, warmongering, genocide—turns out he's big in a lot of things."

"And he talked to you about Molly? Why would someone like that even know her name?"

"Because like any other cockroach, he's scared of the light."

"Interesting." They stood at a crossroads and she pointed toward the uphill trail. "Are you staying up this way?"

"Yeah."

"Walk with me." As they started off she briefly scanned their surroundings; there was a vague feeling that they weren't alone. In the late dusk she could see nothing of any concern, but the occasional booming flashes of the pyrotechnics overhead made her eyes reluctant to adjust to the dark. "You know, I've got a clearance that can get me into any room in the Pentagon, but these uppity bastards wouldn't even let me go beyond that corner back there."

He only nodded, and appeared to be engrossed in concerns of his own.

"I don't think it's true, Noah," Virginia said quietly. "I think Molly got away."

He stopped. "What?"

"Keep walking. I said I think—"

"You think she got away, or you know?"

"I don't know anything yet, but I wouldn't bring it up if I wasn't fairly sure."

He sighed, and showed a little relief as they moved along. "That's good to hear."

"When the news reported that your father had passed away I even thought there was a slim chance that she might learn of your furlough and be coming here to find you. But you still haven't gotten any messages from her, have you?"

"No, and I hope I don't. Why would she risk coming here?"

"I've got a theory about what she could be planning to do. It was something you said the other night, and if I'm right she might even try to get your help."

"Well, I hope she stays away. Whatever's about to happen to me I don't want her to get anywhere close to it."

"What do you mean by that?"

They were almost at the cabin steps, and he stopped and turned to her.

"Mr. Doyle made it pretty clear just now that my number's up. I think it was only my father's influence that kept me around this long, for whatever his reasons were. And what's left of my father's influence is sitting down there in an oversized pepper shaker right now. So I hope Molly doesn't come near me, and it's about time you walked away from all this, too."

She studied him for a few seconds. "That's not like me."

"It's for the best."

"Okay, that's your idea," Virginia said. "Now here's mine. I've been in touch with your family attorney, Mr. Nelan. Since you're the only remaining member of the family you've become his top priority, and he seems sure that he can get you freed very quickly."

"Really."

"Really. So for tonight, I'll call up some old friends. These are four guys stationed downstate at Coronado, and they're not just badasses, Noah, they *train* badasses. I'll watch your back until they arrive, and then we'll deal with your escorts and walk you out of here."

He didn't take long to think about his alternatives. "I like your idea better than mine."

"Good."

"And we're taking the people I've got with me, too."

"Of course we are."

"It's that easy?"

"I doubt it will be." She flicked the retaining strap of the holster at her side and made sure the weapon there was ready beneath the cover of her light jacket. "But cross your fingers."

They walked up the steps and he opened the door to the cabin. Despite all her experience, Virginia was frozen for a fateful instant by what she saw inside.

Two young women and an elderly man were huddled in the far corner. Four men in uniform were bound and gagged on the floor against the opposite wall. And there, in the middle of the room, with his pistol leveled at her chest, stood Thom Hollis.

"Down!" Hollis yelled, shifting his aim beyond and charging forward. She'd barely begun to react when gunfire erupted and she was struck from behind by the blunt burning impacts on her way down to the floor. She felt herself being dragged inside, saw Thom Hollis returning fire as he knelt between her and the door, protecting her, and then she watched him charge outside in pursuit of the attackers.

As consciousness drained from her she managed to clear her .45 from its holster, and with the very last of her strength, she grabbed Noah's arm and put her gun firmly into his hand.

CHAPTER 47

When Hollis came back through the door he had blood on his clothes and two more firearms than he'd left with. Some of the blood was his; he'd clearly been wounded at least once, though how seriously Noah couldn't tell.

If they were lucky there might be time for explanations later on but this wasn't the moment. Virginia was shot and still lying immobile and Ellen Davenport had begun to tend to her with the barest of medicine-cabinet resources at hand. But they had to move, and quickly. The gunfire might have been lost in the sound of the fireworks but that was no guarantee that a general alarm hadn't already been raised. The two failed assassins Hollis had run down and taken out wouldn't be the end of their troubles if they stayed where they were much longer.

"Wait," Noah said. He sat and pulled up the cuff of his slacks to show his house-arrest bracelet. "Three of us are wearing these damned things. We have to get them off or they'll find us before we get a mile away."

Hollis left his vigil at the window, pulled a Bowie knife from its sheath on his belt, and cut the strap off the device with a quick outward stroke of the blade. A small, bright blue dye pack spat against Noah's leg as the bracelet fell free. As it lay on the floor the pattern of its status lights changed to a flashing red warning signal.

The other two hurried over when summoned and Hollis removed Lana's anklet in the same fashion, but Ira stepped back when his own turn came.

"Leave mine on," he said. "I'll take the ones you cut off, and whichever way you run I'll go the other direction. That might buy you a little more time."

"You don't have to do that," Lana said. These were practically the first words she'd spoken on the trip, and they were said with a depth of emotion that Noah hadn't heard from her before. "You don't. We can—"

"Listen to me," Ira said. "You all know it's better this way." He looked to Lana. "I'll be fine whatever happens, kid, and you'll have a better chance. Now come on, we're wasting time."

Hollis handed over the other two devices, shook Ira's hand with a grim nod and a quiet word of thanks, and then said, "Let's go."

"We shouldn't move her," Ellen said, still down at Virginia's side. "She's hit her head, and none of these wounds seem life-threatening but that could change fast if she gets bounced around too much. I need to keep her quiet and get her to a proper emergency room right away, so I'll stay here with her—"

"No," Noah said. "I'm not leaving either of you here. Whoever's coming now isn't coming to help. We've got to get going." He bent and gathered up the unconscious woman in his arms, lifting her as carefully as he could. "It's what she'd want us to do, believe me."

Once outside, Hollis gave Lana Somin his compass and then set them on a path pushing east through the dark of the dense forest. He would follow, far enough behind to guard their flank. Noah looked back only once in the beginning and he saw Ira Gershon disappearing into the distance, moving as quickly as his age and fitness would allow, heading off the other way into the night.

It felt as though they'd traveled for miles before Noah felt himself giving out and he finally had to stop and call a rest.

Under the clouds and the canopy of the tall redwoods there were no stars or other points of reference—not that he would have known how to read them if they'd been there. Since a light rain had begun, all other sounds were drowned out by a steady pattering among the leaves. They could have been walking in circles for all he could tell, but according to Lana the compass assured her otherwise.

Virginia Ward was no better and still drifting in and out of consciousness. Ellen was tending to her, though, and at least she didn't seem any worse. As they were about to get going again Hollis caught up and let them know that their destination wasn't much farther on. Despite his own injuries, the big man then picked up Virginia himself, so effortlessly that it seemed he probably could have carried her all the way to the hospital if need be.

It wasn't long until they broke through into a natural clearing, just a strip of grassland nestled between a wooded hillside and a slow-running stream. There was a campfire with three people seated around it, two of whom Noah didn't recognize—a teenage boy and a woman who might be his mother, judging by their resemblance. But the third person he knew without any doubt.

There was that lovely face, the one that had stayed faithfully in his thoughts through every trial since they'd last been together. He hadn't yet allowed himself to imagine he'd ever see her again, but there she was, alive and well.

"Molly," he whispered.

The others proceeded on past him. Hollis brought Virginia Ward near to the warmth in the center of the camp and laid her down on a dry blanket. Ellen enlisted the others to help as she resumed her caregiving. Noah had begun to feel the burden of the miles they'd traveled but his fatigue seemed to vanish as he walked those last few yards toward the young woman waiting for him by the fire.

When he spoke her name again Molly heard his voice and looked toward him—toward him, but not at him. As he sat near she reached out with her hands and lightly touched his face, and she smiled, going over his features in that way, as though she were recalling him by feel alone. She pulled him close and kissed him and then wrapped her arms around his neck and held him tight for a long while.

"What's happened to you?" Noah asked.

"Didn't they tell you?"

"No," he said. "Nobody ever tells me anything."

It wasn't long before Ellen Davenport put her foot down and announced that her patients needed much better medicine than could be provided in these conditions, and they needed it soon. She had a friend from medical school who ran a private outpatient clinic a little over an hour's drive away, in San Francisco. They'd find a phone and she'd make the calls during the trip and arrange for a surgeon and the necessary personnel and facilities to be waiting when they pulled in. There was no room for argument this time; that's the way it was going to be.

Hollis had already lined up ground transport to meet them all at a rendezvous point just ahead.

The group would be splitting up now. There was a good deal of prep work to be done in western Pennsylvania and Hollis wanted to be certain that the coast was clear out there before Molly came to join them. To that end, Noah and Molly would stay the night at the San Francisco clinic as Ellen cared for Virginia there, while the advance team continued on. Then, when the signal was received that the mission was a go, they'd all be reunited out east.

The group left the campsite with no trace that anyone had ever been there. It was only a short downhill hike to the edge of a nearly deserted highway. Their timing was good; a moving glow soon appeared in the fog and a van arrived shortly thereafter. It pulled to a stop, flashed a signal with its headlights, and they were off.

CHAPTER 48

In this place where the world's super-elite liked to playact at rugged living, there was one large cabin that was always reserved and kept spotless and ready for a single, infrequent visitor. No one but his servants, his invited guests, and his closest associates had ever set foot inside since it had been built for Aaron Doyle in the early 1930s.

There he sat before the roaring fire, considering the status of the game that had been playing out for most of his long life.

Some moves had taken years to formulate—the ebbs and flows of political power, the debasement of a key currency, the patient process of swindling on a global scale— but in response to every move he made there always came an answer. These countermoves were so clear one could almost see William Merchant's hand behind them.

But the game had taken on a frightening new aspect following the dying words of Arthur Gardner. What he'd said had scarcely left Doyle's mind since, and now those words returned to him again.

If Merchant is dead, then who in heaven's name has been up there fighting against us for these past thirty years?

Who, indeed.

The die was cast, in any case. Whatever or whomever it was that he was playing against, whether flesh or spirit, the game must proceed. Deep in these thoughts, Doyle flinched then at the sound of a voice just beside him.

"I'm afraid I've got bad news," Warren Landers said.

"Tell me."

Landers bent and spoke into his ear, and as he did so he made a motion toward the door. Two guards entered with a small and bloodied man dragged between them.

They forced the prisoner to his knees in the center of the room. One of them held him where he knelt, slapped him hard across the face, and wrenched his arm behind him with a smart twist to bring him alert for the questioning.

"What's your name?" Landers asked.

The kneeling man was looking only at Aaron Doyle. His voice was winded and broken when he spoke, but the words were quite clear. "I thought you people knew everything," he said. "Don't you already know who I am?"

He was struck again, and Landers repeated his demand.

"Tell us your name."

"I'm Ira Gershon."

The other guard had left the room but now he returned and began to methodically spread wide, thin plastic sheeting in overlapping layers behind and around the prisoner, a precaution to keep any of the fine furnishings from being soiled.

"And your friends, Mr. Gershon, where are they?"

"I don't know." This denial was met with another blow and a twist of the arm hard enough to dislocate the joint. The kneeling man drew in his breath sharply, but he didn't cry out. His eyes were still fixed on Aaron Doyle.

"We have other avenues to find them," Landers said. "There's nowhere they can hide—"

"But they're not hiding anymore."

Doyle turned to the prisoner for the first time, and leaned closer. "What is it that she's going to do?" he asked.

"That, I can tell you," Gershon said. "Someday soon, she's going to win."

Landers sighed and gave a nod to the man behind, who'd now finished his preparations. He came around, drew his pistol, and stood ready.

Ira Gershon straightened himself up as best he could. "Would you let me pray a last time?" he asked.

"Go right ahead," Landers said. "Why not waste your last few seconds on earth with a plea to the empty sky?"

As the kneeling man set about his foolish ritual, Landers bent again to the ear of Aaron Doyle, lowered his voice, and spoke with assurance. "I have good people working on the forensics from their last hideout. They tell me to expect definitive information within a few hours, a day at the most. With some luck we'll know everything we need to. Whatever they do, you've planned for it, sir. We'll turn it against them and make the best of it."

Doyle nodded slowly, but he didn't seem so sure.

Landers stood, checked his watch, and turned back to the man on his knees. "All right, then. Have you finished?"

The pious silence dragged on for a few seconds longer and at last Ira Gershon unclasped his hands and looked up. "Yes, I'm finished."

Landers motioned to the executioner, who checked his silenced weapon for readiness, pressed the muzzle to the prisoner's forehead, pulled back the hammer, and waited for the final order.

"Hell of a lot of good all that praying did you," Landers said.

The man on his knees smiled at this, having made his peace with what was coming, and then he quietly spoke his final words.

"What makes you think I was praying for me?"

PART THREE

CHAPTER 49

Most American citizens wouldn't believe how difficult it had become to travel freely—untracked, unrecorded, and unidentified—within the borders of their own home country. What was once the norm had become all but impossible, and that had made Hollis's transcontinental trip to Pennsylvania not only dangerous but also very expensive.

He'd caught barely an hour of troubled sleep and felt achy and light-headed as he awoke. He was hurting, and it wasn't getting better. First he'd taken a glancing blast from a sawed-off shotgun at the start of that vicious gunfight at the Merrick ranch, then he'd been hit twice again as they made their escape from California.

These latest wounds had bled a lot but the bullets had passed right through without hitting anything vital. Noah's doctor friend had stitched him up and dug some day-old birdshot from his shoulder and the side of his neck. She'd strongly advised him to go to the hospital—sound advice that he'd obviously ignored—and then she'd given him a course of strong antibiotics, which he'd promptly left behind as he and the advance team left in a rush the night before.

He was still determined to grit his way through these

injuries, but he could tell he was weakening. The fever was real now, he could almost feel an aggressive infection spreading under his skin, and his left arm was growing more swollen and inflamed as time went on.

Hollis was semi-reclined in the passenger seat of an eighteen-wheeler that had picked them up for the final leg of their overnight journey. Lana Somin and Cathy and Tyler Merrick were in the sleeper compartment behind him. When he turned to check on them, mother and son were resting peacefully, but the young lady was not. Her gaze was far away and serene, but there were traces of tears on her cheeks that she hadn't bothered to wipe away.

They'd just passed through a commercial area of the town and soon their driver slowed and made his wide turn onto a rough service road.

The orange-and-black signage along this private thoroughfare carried the distinctive logo of HomeWorx, as did the tractor-trailer they were riding in. This company was a family-owned, mid-Atlantic chain of big-box home improvement stores, and up ahead stood one of its original locations, now converted to a regional distribution center. In recent years they'd had to close a number of locations and move their base of operations farther east, rendering this particular warehouse nearly obsolete for its original purpose.

"Take us around back, if you would," Hollis said.

He alerted young Lana and she woke the others. As the truck pulled to a stop at a loading bay in the rear of the warehouse, Hollis said his thanks to the driver and went inside to meet their contact. When he was assured that all was well he waved the all-clear to the other three.

The head of this chain had been a longtime supporter of Molly's mother and he'd been happy to help when he'd gotten the call. Ask anything, he'd said, and Hollis had asked for a lot.

So they could blend in as much as possible, the four of them were issued light-orange coveralls like those worn by the staff. After they'd changed, Hollis called them together in a cavernous vehicle bay, along with a small group of carefully screened employees who'd been put at his disposal for the day.

"Let me make something clear," Hollis said. "If this goes bad today, if we get cornered by the cops—I mean *actual* law enforcement—we won't put up a fight. We don't fire a shot or raise a hand to the police. If it comes down to that I'll go out and give myself up, alone, and all of you will swear on a Bible that I forced you here at gunpoint. They'll believe that right off, things being as they are. We'll send word to Molly beforehand so they won't get her, too, and then I'll take the fall for all this. Everybody understand?"

No one looked happy at the prospect, but they all agreed.

"Now," Hollis continued, "the clock's running, and I'd say we've got a good morning's work ahead of us. I've radioed the others that we're all clear so far but we don't know exactly when they're coming, so we've got to be ready ASAP. First, we need security. You"—he pointed to the heftiest of the local men and read his nameplate—"Hector, you pick your own partner, and then you two boys keep watch for anyone who doesn't belong here. Don't confront anybody." He slid a pair of in-store handheld radios across the table. "Just call me and tell me what you see. Keep that walkie-talkie on channel 14. Okay?"

"Okay," Hector said, and he nodded to the fellow next to him. "Him and me, we'll keep watch."

"Good. Check in with me every quarter hour." The two men left for their stations, and Hollis turned back to the other employees. "This place has got just about everything we could need but we'd waste a lot of time trying to find it all ourselves. Whatever these two ladies here ask you for, if you could jump on it and fetch their supplies, that'll be a great help. They may need some extra hands, too, so please, just be at their service. Now, Ms. Somin, Noah Gardner told me you're good with computers."

"I am," she said.

"We'll need some IDs. I'll show you examples when you're ready to start on them. They just need to be good enough to flash; no one's going to have time to look at them too close. And then there's this." He handed across a thick spiral-bound book that had been left for him in a locker there. "That's the system layout and the network administrator's manual from the place we're going after today. Take good care of that; it took a lot of doing to get it copied and slipped out of there for us. Now if you could get a head start on looking into the guts of what we'll be up against—"

She'd had a chance to read only the cover before she interrupted him. "I can tell you right now, there's no fricking way. A facility like this? It's not like in the movies. There's no way I could break into this system in one day, not in a month, nobody could, not from outside."

"Well, that's okay," Hollis said, "because we're going to be inside. If we all do our jobs right we're going to drive up to the front gate, big as life, and they're going to open up the doors and let us in."

With that bit of news delivered, Hollis saw the first shade of a smile forming.

"Cool," Lana said.

"Now, I want you all to assume that this is going to go off without a hitch. You don't have time for worries along with everything else. But Tyler and I will be making preparations in case things should go awry."

"I thought you said if we got caught we were going to give up," Tyler said.

"I said if we got caught by law enforcement. But if I see the kind of scum roll up here like those that came for you and your folks on the ranch, son, there's going to be some hell to pay."

"And what am I supposed to do?" Cathy Merrick asked.

"You're my graphic artist."

"I don't understand. What kind of art do you need?"

"Well, ma'am, near as you can manage, we need for that thing over there"—he pointed to a sun-faded and road-worn HomeWorx rental truck parked across the bay—"to look just like this right here."

Hollis opened a folder and passed it across the table to her. On top of the papers inside was a series of detailed color photos showing every angle of a hazmat emergency vehicle from the Pennsylvania Department of Public Safety.

CHAPTER 50

At the clinic outside San Francisco, Ellen Davenport had tended to her patient through the night. As the morning came, Ellen reviewed the chart once again and, satisfied that she was stable and comfortable, left to check in on her old friend Noah.

The sleep lab in this clinic had a one-bedroom suite designed and decorated like a space that might be found in a nice, normal home. It was made that way so that the slumber patterns of visiting subjects could be evaluated in a more calming environment than a cold and sterile hospital room. This suite was where Noah and Molly had been put up together for the night.

When Ellen looked in the door she found them sleeping in each other's arms, dressed in borrowed clothes they'd been provided with for their upcoming journey. It seemed as though they'd awakened earlier, bathed and gotten ready to depart, and then drifted off again in the midst of an intimate conversation.

Ellen had known this young man for a long time and he'd always been blissfully superficial in his relations with the opposite sex. This was a different picture; she'd never seen him like this, not with any other woman. The two of them looked like they belonged together, like they'd always been together, and like they didn't intend to ever be apart again.

Ellen left the sleep lab and took a long, hot shower. When she returned to Virginia's room she found her patient awake and as alert as the medication would allow.

"Where are we?" Virginia asked.

"We're in San Francisco. You're doing much better—"

"And where are the others?"

"Noah and Molly are in the next room. Everyone else headed off for Pennsylvania last night." Ellen checked her watch. "We've got a flight to catch soon ourselves, and I have to get them up in a few minutes. My colleagues here are going to take good care of you—"

"They shouldn't leave," Virginia interrupted. She made a move to rise but Ellen stopped her with a gentle hand. "None of you should leave. Let me talk to them."

"They're very determined—"

"Please, let me talk to them."

"Okay, shh. Just rest now. I'll send them in before we go."

Later, as Noah and Ellen and Molly buckled into their seats on the small private jet, he recalled their parting conversation with Virginia Ward.

She'd tried by every means to persuade them that the safest course was to put themselves under her protection, and she was probably right, but wisdom and reason had no effect on Molly. She was not going to be stopped this time and Noah wouldn't be leaving her side, and so the decision was made.

Once they'd left, Noah had insisted on one thing, however, and he'd gotten no argument. As soon as they landed for their connection in Illinois, Ellen Davenport would part ways with them, catch a cab to O'Hare, and travel on to New York alone. There she'd meet with

Charlie Nelan to figure out how to deal with the events of the last several days and begin to get her life back on track again.

The jet had been fueled and waiting for them at Hayward Executive Airport, near the bay. These arrangements were made by a well-to-do secret friend of Molly's group, the CEO of a chain of hardware stores in the East, and his gift had allowed them to sidestep the heightened security that surely would have snared them instantly if they'd tried to go anywhere near San Francisco International.

As the jet taxied out onto its assigned runway, Molly felt for his hand and squeezed it tight when she found it. Then she told him where they were ultimately bound.

Her objective was a maximum-security storage facility in rural Pennsylvania. It was the crown jewel of a group of fortresses operated by a company called Garrison Archives. Naturally, Noah knew this place well. They stored many rare treasures there, irreplaceable collections and priceless works of art, all preserved and protected in a controlled underground environment built to withstand even a nearby nuclear war.

But another, larger level of Garrison had a different purpose. It housed a vast chamber of secrets through which the highest levels of classified information flowed. This was the place where the world's most powerful entities—including many clients of Noah's late father—kept all the electronic records of their dealings, records that the world outside was never meant to see.

Molly planned a controlled release of the darkest of these secrets onto the open Internet, just as Virginia Ward had come to suspect. If the truth really could set us free, this one act should provide more than enough of it to do the job.

Assuming they actually made it inside, there wouldn't

be much time. She needed Noah—and his years of experience with such information at Doyle & Merchant—to help her navigate the sea of files and documents, separate the wheat from the chaff, and then package the best of it to be leaked for mass consumption.

He hadn't told her this, but even in the unlikely event that they were successful he had his own strong doubts about the lasting effect that such a release would have. It takes a lot of courage to see the truth even when it's right there in front of you. Denial is so much easier, and these days most people wouldn't know what to do with the truth if they saw it.

Regardless of his doubts, though, he was committed. Molly had said that she wouldn't blame him if he chose to back out and go his own way. But this was his own way, he'd told her, and his choice, for better or worse.

Soon the engines whined up to full power, and the small jet began to roll and then to rocket down the runway. There was no turning back now; a few seconds later they were in the air.

CHAPTER 51

The eastern region headquarters of the Talion Corporation, their showcase facility, was located just outside Philadelphia.

This ultratech command center in which Warren Landers now sat was the equal of anything the traditional U.S. military had to offer. It was the war room where potential Talion clients—including governmental and UN decision-makers—were shown the many expanded options offered by a covert army of mercenaries. Contract soldiers were clearly the wave of the future and Talion was at the forefront of that trend. This was evidenced by the river of public wealth that had already been flowing in their direction for more than a decade.

The company's founders and their insider cronies had gotten their corporate foot in the door with sweetheart contracts for wildly overpriced support services and limited security functions in Iraq and Afghanistan. These clever men were now poised to ramp up their operations into a nearly full-fledged branch of the armed forces—one with no oath or pledge to protect and defend anything but their sacred bottom line.

For the most part Talion had long since achieved this quasi-official status in various conflicts overseas, but that was only second prize. A success on this day could open a new and highly profitable front: a widespread domestic deployment, a standing army on U.S. soil that would dwarf the power and reach of the bumbling DHS and TSA.

Talion would soon be stationed on every corner, patrolling every street, acting as the unified enforcer of the coming surveillance state. All that was missing was a well-timed nudge over the finish line, another reawakening of fear, uncertainty, and doubt in the American people of the type that had been so effectively leveraged since September 2001.

Now there wasn't much left to block the way.

It had been Warren Landers's job to identify those remaining barriers and then remove them with extreme prejudice. The last of these had proven quite elusive—it wasn't a particular person or an organization, but rather a quaint, patriotic ethos that had so far stubbornly refused to die. Molly Ross—just a common person—had for many become its unlikely torchbearer. Now, finally, as those outdated American ideals and their pitiful spokesperson were barely clinging to life, he would have the singular pleasure of pulling the plug and burying their remains forever.

The computer equipment salvaged from what was left of the Merrick ranch hadn't yielded much of value at all. These days, though, it's not really what's kept on your computer that can reveal all your secrets; it's the little trail of breadcrumbs you've left behind you out in the cloud.

Anonymity is an illusion in the digital age and all attempts to hide behind it are only further acts of self-incrimination. All day long people obsessively write their own confessions: every search, every click, every comment, every poll, every Like, every chat, every status update, every friend, every call, every e-mail, every photo, every purchase, every connection—everything everyone does on their computer, phone, or tablet is in some way captured and filed and cross-referenced, to be sold or shared however its true owners desire.

Each fragment may reveal only a tiny glimpse of their most private selves, but these tech-blinded people never stop to think that someone could be out there reassembling their full, explicit picture in every revealing detail.

In this case, that someone was Warren Landers, and when the full picture was assembled, it revealed a very interesting new lead.

A man named Lawrence Cole, often mocked as "Liberty Larry" by the many clever quipsters on the left, had long shown support for a wide range of causes in the so-called freedom movement. This Mr. Cole was quite a character: a sportsman, a collector, an aviator, an inventor, a philanthropist, an entrepreneur—and an outspoken blowhard for the founding principles of an America that had only ever existed in his cockeyed dreams. He was also the chief executive officer of a regional chain of home improvement stores.

And there it was: a single message sent from one of Cole's poorly disguised private e-mail accounts was the only relevant thing so far that had been retrieved from fire-damaged hard drives brought in from the Merrick raid.

The retrieved message simply said:

> *Everything is set. The entire shop will be at your disposal. Godspeed, LC*

No physical address had yet been found for this "shop"; details must have been transmitted through another message or another medium, but this was more than enough to get the ball rolling.

Whether the fugitives were caught in transit, cornered in this new hideout, or trapped in the midst of whatever ridiculous act of valor they were planning, the outcome would be the same.

There would soon be a brave intervention by the U.S. government's new security partners, a daring shoot-out with those flag-waving, violent domestic terrorists, the homeland would be made temporarily safe again, and a new kind of hero would step forward to receive the thanks of a grateful, trembling nation.

Landers made two calls. The first was to deploy a pair of security men to each retail location owned and operated by Lawrence Cole. His home and his other residences were also to be put under total surveillance—the full monty, warrant-free wiretaps and all. Based on his outspoken and nearly seditious public profile it was a major oversight that he wasn't being watched this closely already.

His second call was to a friendly link in the command chain of the Department of Homeland Security.

The course of action that Landers recommended to this useful idiot had been ordered only once before. But there was credible information from a high-level unnamed source—or so he claimed—that a hostile group called the Founders' Keepers, known to have recently been in possession of a weapon of mass destruction, could now be in the execution phase of a major operation.

Their plot was not yet clear, he told her, but it could very well involve an airborne attack against a high-value target in a major metropolitan area on the East Coast of the United States.

CHAPTER 52

A little over an hour into their flight, in what might later qualify as the understatement of the year, the pilot had informed his three passengers that there could be some rough weather up ahead.

For his next announcement minutes later, though, he didn't use the intercom. Instead he leaned around in his seat and motioned for Noah to come forward for a talk, all by himself.

The cabin wasn't quite tall enough to allow him to walk upright in the aisle and he had to duck to squeeze his way through the narrow cockpit door and into the vacant second seat up front.

"What is it?" he asked.

"The NTAS has issued an alert. I just got the text. It says there's an imminent threat from a domestic terrorist cell, and that these people may be headed for the East Coast."

"What?"

"Yeah, this is bad. The FAA's grounding all flights, just like after 9/11, but so far they're being a little more methodical about it. I've been directed to reroute immediately and land at Denver."

"Denver? Denver International?"

"Yeah—"

"We can't land there. We're probably at the top of the watch list, you understand that, don't you? We'd never make it halfway through the terminal without being identified."

"I've got no alternative, and I didn't call you up here to discuss our options. To order a thing like this, these people aren't fooling around. If we don't land where they tell us they'll send up the jets to put us on the ground another way. I've already set the course. I just wanted to let you know so you could tell your folks back there on your own."

Noah broke the news to Molly and Ellen as gently as he could and then, over the next half hour, the three of them discussed it all and decided what to do.

Assuming they didn't immediately walk into a dragnet upon landing, Ellen would slip away from the other two as quickly as possible and then lose herself in what was sure to be a sea of stranded passengers from other diverted flights. She'd then hire a car if she could and make her way to New York by any means available.

As for Noah and Molly, they would try to do the same, only their destination would be any nearby safe house they could contact after landing. The mission was over; escape was the best they could hope for at this point. It wasn't much of a plan, but it seemed to be the only alternative.

As the flight wore on they sat and considered their situation; the sullen mood was broken only by occasional bouts of turbulence from the storms that had been promised all morning. Ellen was quiet but obviously frightened, and Molly had spent most of her time in silent prayer. Noah, however, felt surprisingly calm, having long since written off any extended visions of his own future. If this was the end of the line he was satisfied just to be next to her again, even if it was only for a little while longer.

The flight soon descended through a deep and dark gray layer of clouds to emerge in the midst of a heavy rain. There were a few steep banks and bumps and jostles, and before long Noah heard the gear descending and felt the craft settling onto its final approach. By the view out the window visibility was near zero; he could barely see past the tips of their wings.

A minute later the touchdown came with an unexpected jolt and they rolled out to near the end of the long runway.

Just as the pilot had slowed sufficiently for his turn toward the gate, Molly cried out "Stop!" so forcefully that the man up front applied the brakes and brought the craft to a screeching halt.

"What happened?" the pilot called back. "Did we hit something?"

"Just stay here for a second," Noah said, and he turned to Molly. "What's wrong?"

"I've got a terrible feeling," Molly whispered. "I think they're waiting for us."

"How could you be so sure of that?"

"I don't know, but I am. Please, just believe me."

"I can't just sit here on an active runway," the pilot said, and the jet began to roll again as the engines wound up.

Molly gripped his hand tight. "Noah, please. We've got to get out, right now."

Mere intuition isn't much to bet your life on but at that moment he found it was good enough for him. Noah went forward and spoke to the pilot, who soon made a reluctant adjustment and slowed their advance toward the distant gate to only a few miles per hour.

"Are you two serious?" Ellen asked. "You're getting out of a moving airplane? What about me?"

"You have to come with us," Molly said.

"I *have* to? What do you mean by that—"

The rain and wind whipped in as Noah swung up the door and the sound of the engines drowned out the rest of that conversation. He knelt and lowered the steps to their locking point about a foot above the scrolling pavement.

"We've got to move, Ellen; you're just going to have to trust me," he said, holding out his hand. "Now let's go."

With that Ellen picked up Molly's duffel bag and helped her manage the last few feet across the aisle. The door of the rolling plane was on the side of the fuselage opposite the terminal; in these conditions, if they made it to cover quickly enough there was actually a chance their exit from the aircraft might go unseen.

"You two first!" Noah shouted over the noise. "Hit the ground running and stay low; you've got to get clear fast so the wings don't knock you down. Head for those markers at the end of the runway and get down behind them. I'll be right along."

"Oh my God, look!" Ellen said, pointing across the cabin.

Through the line of round windows, far away through the driving rain they could see a large number of bright yellow strobes suddenly appearing and then beginning to fan out and accelerate in their direction.

"Go now!" Noah said. The two women descended the two steps and then on their own count of three they jumped to the pavement hand in hand. They nearly fell but soon regained their footing and took off toward the cover of the tall grass.

Noah followed, running beside the jet to lift and fasten the stairs before he closed the door to lock the exit behind him. As the jet rolled on he crouched down low and dashed toward the spot where he'd last seen his two friends running.

CHAPTER 53

When Hollis returned to the major-appliances area of the warehouse he found young Tyler completing his assigned work on the last of six fifty-gallon water heaters.

The tall white cylinders had been arranged at strategic points around the huge floor space. Each was tipped forward at a shallow angle and aimed toward the glass atrium at the front of the place and the parking lot out beyond. They were supported in place by many stacked bags of dry quick-set cement to the side and behind.

From where he stood it all looked something like a complement of field artillery, and so it should.

"How're they doing in the back?" Tyler asked.

"They're doing fine. Right on schedule."

The two of them went down the checklist on each of the prepared tanks in turn. They'd been filled with water to the level directed, relief valves disabled, feed pipes permanently sealed, and thermostats recalibrated to allow for extremely hazardous but precisely controllable settings.

Tyler had done the math again and again and Hollis rechecked it himself; eighty-five thousand pounds of pressure would not forgive much of an error. There were variables and unknowns aplenty, but these improvised weapons seemed as ready as they would ever be. All the calculations said they should perform as expected if called upon. His hope, of course, was that they'd never have to find out.

"Time to give these bad boys the smoke test," Hollis said.

"What does that mean?"

"Let's crank 'em up."

These were premium commercial water heaters with digital readouts for internal temperature and stress. All were hooked to backup generators in case the power failed, just like the equipment being used by the team in the back.

As the tanks began to heat up Hollis adjusted each of the units identically and he and Tyler worked to reinforce the surrounding sandbag supports while periodically watching the numbers climb.

When the PSI gauges neared 250—far above the manufacturer's rated safety zone but still within worst-case specifications—the controls were reset to hold that high-pressure condition perfectly stable. Out of caution, though, he would leave some of their helpers stationed with instructions to watch those readouts and call out immediately if the pressure on any of the heaters should suddenly start to climb.

The survival bags they'd brought with them had included pay-as-you-go cell phones, to be used sparingly and for emergencies only. The phone in his pocket had begun to vibrate and he took it out and read the screen. The unsigned message there said: check the news.

"What now?" Tyler asked.

"Come with me."

On the way to the back they stopped into an unoccupied office where a series of monitors were set up

and ready for viewing. There was an old TV and a DVR
with basic cable channels and a number of flat-screens
showing insets of the various security cameras around
the warehouse. A ham radio transceiver was also up and
running for code and voice transmissions, and a laptop
with an Internet connection sat right beside.

When Hollis saw what was dominating the news he
raised the volume and they both watched and listened
for a while.

"Oh man," Tyler said.

The country had been shaken in recent days by a
wave of shootings and other violence, all of which were
being attributed to a single domestic militia group. Now
the evolving reports were hinting that this group had ties
to practically every prominent person and organization
right of center. On one of the more obedient channels,
Molly Ross and her people were actually being named
as key players behind these terrorist acts.

And there was something new: a specific, imminent
threat had reportedly been uncovered. Within the last
half hour the entire country was put on high alert, with
all flights grounded, mass transit halted, and citizens
directed to stay in their homes as the authorities and
their armed security partners combed the streets to try
to find and eliminate the danger.

There was more. Even if the DHS and the FAA hadn't
shut down air traffic, the worsening weather probably
would have. By all reports, conditions were fast developing that could usher in a line of major storms across
the Midwest of a severity seen only once in a century.

His phone rang, a voice call this time. Hollis checked
the caller ID and then motioned for Tyler to come near.

"I have to take this alone. Go and see how your mom
and the others are getting along," he said. "There's no
need to mention what we saw there on the news. Not yet."

When the boy had left, Hollis answered the call, and it brought only more bad tidings.

All the stores in the HomeWorx chain had been visited by agents from a private security firm, a big one with deep government connections. The various stores were many miles apart, some entire states away, and these teams had descended on them all almost simultaneously. Uniformed, armed men were in the process of searching the places and questioning employees, and they weren't leaving when they were done. While there was no sign of them yet in this area, it was surely only a matter of time.

Hollis ended the call and sat down, feeling another wave of dizziness and fatigue. Despite the aspirin he'd been swallowing by the handful, he felt worn down to a shadow; his fever and its underlying cause were still worsening. His eyes took a while to focus on the television screen. He watched with only half his attention as he tried to work his clouded thoughts through the dire situation at hand.

Facts were facts; there seemed to be no way that Molly could get there now, much less arrive before they were all found and apprehended. Judging by when they got started, she and the others would be grounded somewhere out west, lucky if they'd avoided capture, but with no hope of getting any farther.

Along with his withering fatigue, reality was settling into him now. He sat there for some time, feeling only weakness and defeat and the weight of the losses already suffered and a gathering dread of those yet to come.

Could they all really have come this far only to have it end this way?

As if in answer to this question, what came upon him then was neither sound, nor touch, nor any other humble sense of the physical world.

But without any doubt it was an answer, one so clear

and certain that its truth would not tolerate denial. It was a sudden *knowing* from some source so sure and supreme that to even ask for further evidence would be an insult to its majesty.

Hollis looked again to the television screen, and a single, quiet word materialized and voiced itself in the center of his mind.

behold

The station's chief meteorologist stood before a moving satellite image of the continental United States. The man seemed quite astonished by what was happening—he'd actually called it a miracle—and he was working hard to maintain a scientist's demeanor as he spoke. Using the map projected behind him, he explained the three unlikely and converging elements of what he'd begun to term the perfect storm.

A powerful cold front driven by something called the Colorado Low had rapidly developed in the mid-latitudes. This alone was very unusual for that time of year; an unprecedented late-April snow was already being forecast in Dallas. The second element was a strong jet stream that had suddenly begun to dip far southward, its track shifting from a nearly straight path across the country into a rolling curve that resembled a turbulent sine wave spanning many hundreds of miles. And last, pushing in from the west, the effects of a strong El Niño were jamming all these forces together, smashing the descending cold air masses against the rising warmth at the front. The result, the man said, could soon be an impenetrable line of violent thunderstorms stretching two-thirds of the way across the country.

The enormous natural forces he'd described were replaying over and over in animated graphics on the map. The weatherman had said the individual principles at work were well understood, of course, but it was the sudden appearance of these three phenomena together that practically defied explanation.

Hollis reached out and gently touched the weather map on the screen, tracing the movements there, and as he did this, right down to his soul, he understood.

"What are you doing?"

The lights clicked on, and it was Tyler's voice he'd heard from the doorway behind him. Hollis turned that way but didn't answer.

"You look pale, man. You'd better take a rest."

"I don't need to rest," Hollis said.

"So, what are we going to do?" the boy asked. "Nobody's asking me, but it looks like we'd better call this whole thing off while we still can, right?"

"No," Hollis said. "Molly's on her way here now."

"How's that even possible? Aren't you watching? There's not a plane in the air across the country and the weather's getting so bad they couldn't get here even if they *were* allowed to fly."

"She's on her way, under God's protection."

"Look, this is the fever talking. How the hell could you even know that?"

"I know it." Hollis stood, and though the flesh was weakening there was also a new strength in him that he hadn't felt before. "I don't know when, or how, but I know she'll be here. So let's you and me pull up our socks and get ready for hell and high water, son, because until she arrives, this is where we're going to stand."

CHAPTER 54

For what seemed like an eternity the three of them could only wait as Noah watched the now-vacant jet taxi very slowly toward the main terminal. The pilot was apparently doing what he could to buy them time as he was escorted all the way, hemmed in on every side by a small fleet of security vehicles.

The only cover they had was a low runway marker they were huddled behind; that, and the driving rain and midday gloom the lingering storm had brought in with it.

When it seemed safe enough, he and Molly and Ellen left their hiding spot and ran. They had no destination in mind and no goal but to work their way farther and farther from the lights of the airport, sprinting and stopping again from one bit of cover to the next. They crawled down a series of shallow ditches and then through a buried drainage duct with churning water rising up to their chins. They stumbled across a runway through the swirling wake turbulence of a landing jumbo jet. They ran into the open when they had no other choice, certain as they did so that they must be standing out starkly against the flat and deserted terrain toward the outskirts of the huge property.

After scaling a chain-link fence at the end of what

seemed like an hour of muddy, grueling struggles, they managed to reach the shoulder of a multilane road that was packed bumper-to-bumper with slow-moving traffic. Noah held out his thumb in the universal sign that they needed a ride. A number of drivers went out of their way to ignore them but at last a man in an SUV stopped and motioned for the three to walk over and get aboard.

As they climbed into the rear seats and closed the door, the driver smiled and said, "Having some trouble?"

"Don't get me started," Noah replied.

Their driver had a few fresh towels in a gym bag and he cranked the heater to such a level that it must have been uncomfortably toasty for him. While nothing was going to dry them completely, the steady blast of warm air began to beat down the chill.

Talk radio was playing as they settled in; the driver was intent on the broadcast discussion, so there was only a little light conversation with his new riders. Thankfully he didn't ask any probing questions, though early on he did inquire as to where they were bound. Noah simply answered that they'd been stranded on their trip across the country and were trying to reach a friend to stay the night. This did nothing to explain the condition in which he'd found them on the side of the road, but their rescuer only nodded and left it at that.

Traffic continued to be stop-and-go until it finally eased to the point that they could begin to make some real headway. They'd hardly traveled thirty miles, though, when everything ground to a halt again. The cause of the snarl was just barely visible far ahead. At first Noah thought it was an accident, but no; there appeared to be a highway patrol roadblock extending across all lanes in both directions.

"Could you take this exit right here?" he asked, keeping his tone as casual and unconcerned as he could.

"Here? Nobody's going to be flying tonight—"

"I know, it's okay, this is where you can leave us. You've been very kind but we don't want to wear out our welcome."

The driver flipped on his signal and eased his way across two jammed lanes of unhappy motorists to take the off-ramp for Centennial Airport.

As they rode Noah leaned down to Molly's ear and described what he was seeing. Centennial was a major hub in its own right, high security and all, so walking into the main terminal was out. They drove on down the access road with Noah reading her the signs as he looked for any promising place where they could just hole up for a while and take a breath so they could plan.

"That's the one," Molly said. "Let's go there."

From near the bottom of a list of far-flung airport facilities on the very last sign, he'd just read her the name of Blue Sky Air Charters. It seemed as good a choice as any and Noah let the driver know.

Down the side road the whole area appeared to be under construction or major renovation. When they'd been let out, the three of them took shelter under the awning of an unmanned security booth outside the long, wide Blue Sky hangar. The lit interior of this giant enclosure seemed like a semi-organized flea market of aircraft parts with a single, partially disassembled vintage plane being worked on at its center.

Soon they noticed that an elderly man in coveralls was gesturing for them to come in out of the rain. There was no other nearby option; as they approached the man he wiped his oil-smudged hands with a rag and then held out his right for Noah to shake, which he did.

"I'm Bill McCord," the man said. "Goodness, you three look like you've been rode hard and put away wet. Are you lost?"

"A little bit," Noah said, smoothly bypassing his own introduction. "We need ground transportation. If we could make a call from here it would be an enormous help."

Mr. McCord nodded thoughtfully, and then he gave all three of them the once-over, first Noah, and then Ellen Davenport, and then Molly.

"I think I know that pretty face," he said.

CHAPTER 55

$\mathbf{M}$r. William McCord was not really the aged grease monkey that his first impression had suggested. He was a war veteran of distinguished service, in fact, though he spoke of this humbly. He was also a man so full of stories that he seemed to have a very hard time containing them all.

The plane under restoration was being prepared for the air-show circuit and he'd been brought in to oversee the final detail work. It was an old Lockheed Lodestar C-60, a relatively rare item, and once finished it would duplicate the very craft that Mr. McCord had flown as a command transport pilot through the end of World War II. The first official flight was coming up soon; it was to be a ceremonial trip to ferry a few of the most decorated surviving American aces to the war memorial in Washington, D.C.

Though long retired, he was one of a fast-dying breed and the last of his kind who'd actually served aboard this particular plane while it was active in the U.S. fleet. He was at Blue Sky only as a consultant, he'd said—some worsening health problems had ended his barnstorming career—but the owners of the C-60 were kindly allowing him to putter around the old girl on his own time as the real work proceeded by day.

It was a beauty all right, though one had to look past the missing engine housings, the half-finished paint job, and the many leaning ladders and gaping access panels to really get a feel for what the final result might be.

They'd been scheduled to run up the rebuilt engines that afternoon but the bad weather had put a stop to that. When everyone else had gone home and called it a day, Mr. McCord had stayed behind, leaving the hangar open in front so he could watch the advance of the oncoming storm.

This chatty old gentleman had managed to cover all these and other subjects on the short walk as he brought them inside. When they'd nearly reached the twin tail of the parked aircraft, Molly stopped and held out her hand for him.

"Mr. McCord?" she said.

"Yes, dear."

"You'd said you know who I am, is that right?"

"I do, Ms. Ross."

"Then I think it's important that we sit down for a few minutes and have a serious talk."

"Why, that would be my great pleasure. And hey, later on let me show you all around my baby here." He patted the side of the plane. "We finished the inside first; out here it still doesn't look like much to write home about, but she's gonna be a peach. You know, I flew MacArthur all over Japan in a bird just like this one. That was 1946, when I was just barely old enough to buy myself a beer."

"Before we get the tour," Noah said, "is there a telephone we can use? A landline?"

Bill McCord pointed toward a small cluttered room in the far corner. "Be my guest, the phone's right in the office on the corner table. There might be a box of sweatshirts in there, too, so you all can shed some of those wet clothes." He took Molly's arm then so he could help her up the couple of stairs into the passenger cabin of the C-60. "Now, young lady, you come along right this way."

Ellen went straight for the phone as soon as they reached the little cubicle in back. She hadn't spoken in a while, and all things considered, Noah couldn't blame her for what she must be feeling.

"I'm sorry I got you into this," he said.

"That makes two of us."

"Ellen, look—"

"Look?" she snapped. "Look at what? I just ran a damned triathlon across Denver International Airport, I'm apparently a fugitive from justice, and I've got men chasing after me with *guns,* Gardner. I've treated more bullet wounds in the last two days than I'll see in the rest of my career; it's like a traveling emergency room with you people. I really don't know what you've gotten yourself into, and I'd do anything for you, you know that. But this isn't my fight."

"That's what I used to think, that it wasn't my fight," Noah said. "And if you want to know exactly how we all got to where we are today, that pretty much sums it up."

With the air transit shutdown in full effect it took more than a few calls and a price that was several times the market value, but at last Ellen had managed to line up a pair of cars from a local service. Once that was done she'd apologized to Noah in her way, and of course he'd understood. Right and wrong aside, in matters of life and death we'd all at least prefer to make our own decisions.

Noah found a box of company sweatshirts and after the two of them had changed he took an extra and they headed back toward the front of the hangar to wait.

When they stopped at the plane they found Molly and her new friend sitting across from each other in the passenger cabin. McCord had wrapped her in a plush blanket and brought her a cup of hot coffee from the small galley near the back. The two were deep in a conversation about the Founders' Keepers and the state of the world in general.

It turned out that their host was more than a little familiar with Molly's group and their goals and had been so for many years. By his enthusiasm he seemed to be completely unfazed by the more recent smears against her character and reputation. As she spoke he was looking at Molly as though he were in the presence of a visiting dignitary.

The interior of the aircraft had been lovingly restored with all the style and luxury of a far more romantic era in civil aviation. Wood, fine leather, and polished metals adorned every crafted surface where plastics and polyesters were the norm in the assembly-line products of today. Along with all the classy touches it had also been fully appointed with more modern features—including onboard medical equipment stored close at hand—to ensure the comfort and safety of the aging heroes who were to be ferried to Washington on the refurbished plane's first flight of the present century.

Ellen took a seat as Noah walked up the inclined center aisle. From a spot near the cockpit he saw the first of the cars his friend had ordered. The long black sedan pulled up and then came to a stop outside.

"That was quick," he said.

He picked up Molly's duffel bag, told the others to relax where they were for the moment, and then exited the plane and began to walk toward the parked car to let the driver know they'd be along soon.

When he was halfway there a second car appeared, moving more slowly, and soon it made the turn onto the inbound straightaway.

The rear passenger door swung open on the unmarked vehicle parked in front of him, and Noah froze where he stood.

Everything looked right, but something was wrong.

After another moment he thumped his forehead as though he'd forgotten something, made a polite gesture toward the car that said *wait just another minute, please,* and then turned and walked back into the hangar. When he was nearly to the plane he stole a glance over his shoulder and saw the driver and another man standing by the side of their sedan; just standing there in the rain, watching. A third man had emerged from the other vehicle, which had by then pulled up to park near the first. That guy was also watching, and though it was hard to tell for sure at this distance, he appeared to be speaking into his lapel.

Noah stepped up into the cabin with the others. "We've got trouble," he said.

He went up the aisle so he could get a hidden view out the windshield and Bill McCord followed him forward.

"Those guys in the cars, you think they're the ones who're after you?"

"Looks that way." Noah could feel the seconds passing too quickly to stop and think. Other vehicles were arriving, headlights off, and were easing around either side of the hangar as if on their way to cover any exits to the rear.

The two men hurried back to the set of seats where Molly and Ellen were waiting and Noah told them what he'd seen.

"How can that be?" Ellen asked. "We used somebody else's phone and I made the calls. They're not even looking for me."

"They're looking for Molly," Noah said, "and she knows me, and I know you. That's all it takes; it's not that hard to make the watch list anymore. They don't need a warrant and it's all done by machine. They can monitor every single call that's made and listen for keywords, listen for voiceprints—I guess I just didn't realize they'd reached the point where they could do it in real time."

"So what now?" Ellen asked.

"I don't know."

"We're not giving up," Molly said. "We can't."

"Molly," Noah said as he knelt down next to her, "we're surrounded in here. If we don't come out now they're just going to come in after us. I don't think we've got a choice."

"And I don't think they're here to take us alive, Noah."

They all let that prospect sink in as more precious seconds ticked by.

"Well, if they're not going to let you walk out," Bill McCord said, "what do you say we fly?"

Half a minute later the two women were securely buckled in and Noah was sitting in the right-hand seat up front.

He wasn't to do anything he wasn't told to do by the man in the captain's chair, not that he would have known where to even begin. With the exception of the add-on GPS, what looked like a radar screen, and a small computer display, there was nothing remotely recognizable in the wall of dials, levers, and lights arrayed in front of him.

"If you've got any doubts, say so now," McCord said.

"No doubts here," Noah replied, though his heart felt like it was trying to pound its way out of his chest.

"Okay, then. Hang on to your hat."

McCord put on his headset and motioned for Noah to do the same. Then he flipped a toggle and with a shrill mechanical groan the tri-blade propeller to the left began to turn over. Almost immediately a sharp thud put a hole through the Plexiglas windshield on the pilot's side as the sound of a gunshot echoed through the hangar. McCord ducked and hit the switch labeled PRIME and then he cracked one of the throttles barely ahead. The left radial engine coughed and spewed a billowing cloud of dirty white smoke but after a few more pops and revolutions it thundered to life.

"Keep your heads down!" Noah yelled to the rear, and new shooting erupted from two positions up ahead.

Ladders and racks of tools clattered to the floor outside as the plane jerked forward and began to roll. The right-side engine was balking and McCord fought the rudder and the brakes to straighten out his taxi and compensate for the one-sided thrust. As the men out front were advancing and firing at will, another hail of gunfire broke out from behind. The plane shook and veered as the wing impacted and overturned a bank of work lights. Just then the other engine belched fire and started up with a roar.

Noah was shoved back into his seat as Bill McCord jammed the throttles forward and the plane surged ahead. The rear passenger door had still been hanging open but it slammed closed from the sudden forward momentum. Between where they were and freedom there were fifty cluttered yards inside the hangar, two men who were now retreating but still firing their automatic rifles, and an open gap between the tall outer doors that looked like it might almost, but not quite, be wide enough to clear.

"Those cars outside," Noah shouted over the noise, "are the wings going to make it over those cars?"

"That's among my concerns!" McCord shouted back.

As their forward speed reached the first milestone the tail lifted and the cabin leveled with the pilot working hard to hold his straight line and thread the needle that was fast approaching. The gunmen dove aside and an instant later the view ahead and above opened up as they cleared the confines of the hangar without an inch to spare at the wingtips. Noah held his breath and braced himself as they rocketed through the parked cars with the wheels and the arcs of the spinning propellers passing just between them.

McCord wasn't celebrating this astounding exit, and he wasn't stopping, either. He didn't call the tower for clearance and there wasn't going to be any stately roll-out toward a distant assigned runway. The plane tore through the long, deserted parking lot, picking up speed all the way, and when they'd bumped across the access road only flat grass and concrete lay before them.

As the pilot pulled back on the yoke the wings caught a gust and the ancient plane leaped into the air at a perilously steep angle. Their speed dropped off and for an endless moment it felt like the craft would give out and spin into the ground, but the wings somehow leveled and seized the lift again, and against all the laws of man and nature, it seemed, they were flying.

CHAPTER 56

Though the aircraft was shot full of holes and whistling like a sieve, no one inside had been struck by any of the bullets that had passed through the outer skin. And, as the Rocky Mountains were behind them and theirs was now the only plane aloft in the entirety of U.S. airspace, the odds of a midair collision seemed nil. These were the only two bits of reassuring news that Noah Gardner could come up with at the moment.

The instant they'd broken ground they'd been picked up on radar and the tower had ordered them to land immediately. Bill McCord was known to the controllers at Centennial and at first he'd responded with a vague tale of a medical emergency on board the plane. That dodge didn't hold up for very long; the familiar, concerned voices in their headsets were soon replaced by others. As the climb-out continued toward cruising altitude the firm orders coming over the radio escalated rapidly to warnings, and then to threats. The commander at Buckley Air Force Base, having earlier brought his forces to their highest level of alert, was already in the process of sending up four fighters to intercept them, and if necessary, to bring them down.

"We've got three choices now," McCord said, "and none of them are great." He punched a button and the urgent chatter on the radio went quiet. "We can land now and get arrested, we can keep doing what we're doing and get shot down, or we can try to evade the pursuit and run."

"Run? How can we outrun an F-16?"

"We can't, but we can go where they'd have a hell of a hard time trying to follow us."

Noah looked his pilot over. The man was gray as a ghost and already breathing hard from even the initial ordeal he'd already been through; who could tell how he might fare against what could lay ahead?

"Are you all right, Bill?"

"I've been better. Now go and see what your friends want to do."

"Okay. I'll be right back."

"And I'll be right here."

Before he even asked them he'd already known what Molly's answer would be. She was bound for Pennsylvania, come what may. Ellen didn't put up a fight; she seemed stoically resigned at this point to whatever gruesome death the fates might bring. But Noah also had another concern to share with her.

He bent to her ear and said, "Doctor, I think after this next part you need to come up and have a look at Mr. McCord."

"Why not right now?"

"Because if we take his mind off his business right now we might not get to the next part at all."

As Noah strapped himself into his seat again he told Bill McCord that they'd decided not to surrender, but to press on. The man nodded, and then he pointed out the altimeter on the control panel and carefully explained how to read it.

"We're going down to the deck pretty soon and I'm going to have my hands full and my eyes straight ahead. When that needle starts to drop I want you to call out every thousand feet and then do the same in hundreds toward the end. Got it?"

"Got it. So we're at almost ten thousand feet right now, and I'll call out every thousand on the way down."

"And then hundreds, below two thousand. That's what I need."

With that understood the pilot put the plane into a shallow bank to the right. When he leveled off again the compass read due east and there was a solid wall of churning black clouds dead ahead, a massive curtain drawn across the sky that towered from the surface up higher into the heavens than the eye could see.

"We're not going that way," Noah said.

"Pennsylvania's that way."

"We're going *into* the storm?"

"That weather will blot us out on the radar, and if they actually follow us in, with any luck those jets'll be looking for us up high while we're running down low."

"What do you mean, *if* they follow us?"

"You've gotta be real smart to be a fighter pilot"—McCord nodded ahead—"and a man would have to be dumb as a bag of hammers to fly into that."

The plane shook violently as a pair of shock waves pounded against the outer hull. Two jets had come from behind and streaked past on either side, so fast that it looked like the old C-60 was standing still. Before they reached the approaching storm front the fighters peeled off in opposite directions, heading around in wide arcs that would ultimately bring them into position for another warning pass, or for an easy kill.

Bill McCord hit more switches. The navigation lights

and strobes outside went dark, as did all interior lights except for the dim glow from the dials in the control panel.

"Cinch up your seat belts!" McCord shouted behind. "This is going to get pretty rough!"

Seconds later the windshield went completely gray as they breached the wall of the storm. The craft lurched suddenly upward; it felt like an elevator shooting to the top floor ten times too fast, only to be dropped again into a plummeting dive to a level far below where they'd started. Noah had his eyes glued to the altimeter and he watched as the needles fought to keep up with the rapid, random changes.

"Grab on to the yoke," McCord said. There was a duplicate set of controls in front of the right-hand seat. "Don't add or take away from what you feel me trying to do. I just want you to be ready to give me a little more strength if I need it."

"Okay." As he took his grip Noah could feel the violence of the weather tearing at the control surfaces outside, but also there, in answer, were the sure and steady responses from the man right beside him.

"Here we go," McCord said.

The yoke pushed slightly forward. With no horizon or any other visual reference out the windows, there was only a gradually building press of acceleration and the counterclockwise wheeling of the altimeter to tell them they were now descending.

"Eight thousand feet," Noah said.

The plane was buffeted by a rapid series of powerful forces, some rocking them to the side, others lifting, others punching down from above. Three of the bullet holes in the front windshield suddenly joined as a whitened crack snapped between them.

"Seven thousand," Noah said, and only seconds later he had to call out again. "Six!"

He felt the forward pressure on the yoke begin to ease and then pull back. "Five thousand." Their rate of descent was barely slowing at all.

"Give me a hand!" McCord shouted.

Together they pulled back as one, and Noah watched as the altimeter responded, but only sluggishly. A sudden burst of hailstones hit them all at once and then was gone.

"Four thousand feet." A blinding flash of light illuminated the clouds outside as a crack of nearby thunder reverberated through the interior. The yoke was fighting them both and it seemed the storm was intent on pushing its foolish intruders all the way to the ground.

"Twenty-five hundred!" Noah shouted, having missed the previous mark by a second or two. "Two thousand!"

There was another bright flash outside and for the first time since they'd taken off he could see the earth down below. He'd begun by then to call out the altitude in hundred-foot increments.

"Thirteen hundred. Twelve hundred. Eleven hundred . . . one thousand . . ." The descent was slowing at last, and Noah could feel the press of the Gs shifting as the plane finally passed through the bottom of a leveling curve. "Nine hundred," he said, and after a few seconds more added, "and holding steady there."

CHAPTER 57

The small radar screen in the front panel showed only a solid sea of pulsating multicolored blotches ahead and behind. Similar displays at ground stations or aboard any aircraft still in pursuit would show much the same. With no transponder, and hidden in the depths of all those angry clouds, their plane's tiny signature would be all but invisible, just as their pilot had predicted.

When the radio was tuned to an automated weather station the report said there was an end-to-end string of severe thunderstorms forming up in a line across the region and far beyond, with worsening conditions likely to spawn the same kind of weather precisely along their route toward the East Coast. That meant this journey wouldn't be getting any easier.

After a little over a hundred arduous, ground-hugging miles Bill McCord announced that he felt it was safe enough to ascend to an altitude where the turbulence might be less punishing. If they'd really slipped their pursuers then higher was better; it had been a brutal ride so far and more than once a sudden downdraft had nearly ended the trip.

They were tossed around repeatedly on their way back upstairs, and then without any warning the ride smoothed out and leveled off. There was a sort of kick and then a strong push from behind, and while watching his instruments the pilot explained that they must have happened onto an unusually low-traveling jet stream and were being temporarily borne along on the rapids of this powerful river of air.

For the first time there were a few moments to assess the situation and think.

All the shooting had done some damage and not all of it would be visible. A small section of the control panel was cracked and dark. There was a faint smell of sour smoke in the air, with no obvious clue to its source. Some gauges indicated warning conditions, none immediately serious but a few that seemed to be gradually worsening.

"Get a load of this," Bill McCord said, pointing to an area of the panel near the controls for the landing gear. There were two lights to indicate that the wheels had retracted safely into their wells. Only one of them was lit green.

"What does that mean?" Noah asked.

"I hope it means that bulb's burnt out. If not, I guess we'll find out what it means when we go to put her down."

It was nearly as noisy as it had been before but the unusual steadiness of the flight gradually induced a calming effect that was almost eerie. Outside of the occasional bumpy air there was no sensation of movement. McCord had informed Noah that due to the added thrust of the tailwind they were traveling quite a bit faster than this particular plane could normally go, at least under its own power.

"I'm going to go back and check on the others," Noah said.

"That's okay, but don't stay unsecured any longer than you have to. This is nice and smooth right now but it'll get ugly again without any warning."

As Noah unbuckled his seat belt Ellen Davenport popped her head into the cockpit. Despite the stress of the situation she was now in physician mode and appeared calm and in perfect control.

"Mr. McCord," she said, "I understand you've had quite a workout up here. Noah told me you might not mind if I came up and checked you out."

"She's a doctor," Noah said.

"Aw, don't spoil it for me," McCord said, and he gave Ellen a friendly wink. "Here I was thinking that was the most flattering thing I'd heard from a lady in twenty-five years."

Noah left the two of them alone and walked down the aisle to sit next to Molly.

"Are you holding up okay?" he asked.

She nodded. "Are we alone?"

"Yes."

"Can I tell you a secret?"

"Sure."

She touched his face, again as though remembering the details of the sight of him with only the tips of her fingers, and then she pulled him close and held on tight.

"I'm scared," she said softly.

At that moment there were any number of perfectly reasonable things to be afraid of, but he could tell by the way she'd spoken that she didn't mean any of those.

Molly said no more and neither did he. They only held one another, and in that quiet togetherness there was an understanding that had no real use for words. She was afraid, and so was he. She was worried that maybe they weren't doing the right thing after all, and so was he. But they both knew they were on the right side, without any doubt, and knowing that, maybe together they could find the strength to put their fears behind them.

After a time there was a gentle tap on his shoulder and he looked up.

"I need you up front," Ellen said.

When they'd gone forward she stopped him after the last row of seats, near the array of medical equipment they'd seen earlier.

"What is it?" he asked.

"Now don't panic."

"I'll do my best. What is it?"

"I think he may have had a heart attack," Ellen said. "Come on, help me with this."

She pulled a high-tech-looking electronic case from its clips on the cabin wall and handed it to him before searching out and gathering some other items from the cabinet beneath.

"What is this thing?" Noah asked.

"Among other things it's an emergency defibrillator, but it can also show me what's going on with his heart, and that's the part I need. Come on."

Bill McCord was still flying just as he'd been before, though Ellen had hooked him up with under-the-nose tubing fed from an oxygen tank she'd secured with duct tape to the armrest of his seat. There was no room for three in the cockpit, so Noah stood just outside, holding the now-activated device in his hands where the doctor could see its screen and reach its controls.

Ellen prepared two adhesive pads and applied one to the upper-right side of McCord's chest and the other lower down and toward the left. She then connected the long thin wires and plugged them in, made some adjustments, and touched a button on the front of the unit.

She watched the display as the machine began to read and analyze the inputs and report its findings. As she looked up at Noah he could see there was bad news but when Ellen spoke her voice was calm.

"Bill, your heart is beating a little too slowly and I think we need to give it some help. You know what a pacemaker does, don't you?"

"Sure."

"That's what we need to do; we're going to regulate your heartbeat. One of the functions of this machine is something called external pacing. Most pacemakers are implanted under the skin, but we're going to accomplish that very same thing from the outside."

"Okay."

Ellen made her final checks and adjustments. "This can get very uncomfortable. I know you can handle it. Normally I'd give you a sedative and something for the pain but I can't do that in this situation. Understand?"

"I understand. Let's do it."

She patted his shoulder, checked the attached pads again, and touched a switch on the machine.

"Do you feel that?" she asked.

"Yeah, that's just a little tickle, doesn't hurt a bit."

"That's because it's not doing its job quite yet." Her eyes were on the display screen as she slowly turned a knob on the front panel. "I'm going to increase the current now until I find your capture threshold—that's the point where your heart responds to the signal we're sending. As I do that what you feel is going to get more intense."

Bill McCord was as engrossed in his piloting as ever but his expression hardened bit by bit as the current advanced. At last the machine gave a tone and then began to beep softly at an even, steady rhythm and Ellen left the setting where it was. Without disturbing his grip on the yoke she took his pulse at the wrist as she counted off the necessary seconds on her watch.

"That's good," she said. "You're doing great. Other than the jolts this machine's giving out, you should be feeling better. Do you?"

McCord didn't speak, but he glanced up at her and nodded. Despite the sharp and repeating irritation he must have been enduring, he did look much better already, from the strength of his posture to the color returning in his face.

"I'm going to stay up here with you and make sure you're all right. What we need to do next is find the nearest place to land so we can get you to a hospital."

Noah started to speak up but she shut him down with one sharp glance.

"Doctor," Bill McCord said, "could I see you alone for one minute?" His voice was stressed by the treatment he was receiving, but there was also a good deal more vitality behind it than there'd been before.

"Of course," Ellen said, and she took the device from Noah and excused him to the passenger compartment.

It was quite a while later when Ellen Davenport emerged from the cockpit and motioned for Noah to join her up there again, which he did.

"Mr. McCord feels very strongly," she said, "that he can persevere with this flight all the way to the end. I did everything I could to convince him otherwise, but he wouldn't be persuaded. So I made a deal with him. I'm going to stay up there with him, and if I see any change, anything in his condition that I don't like, we're going to find an airport and call ahead and be met by an ambulance for him."

"Right behind that ambulance there'll be more of the same kind of men we saw back in that hangar."

"I know that." She took a step into the narrow doorway, keeping half her attention on the monitor and lowering her voice so her patient wouldn't hear. "This man's got third-degree AV block, probably brought on by a heart attack. I don't even know how he stayed conscious through all this, and without that little battery-powered machine I've got plugged into a cigarette lighter? We'd all very likely be dead by now. I'm making the only choices I've got in a bad situation, Noah. This is just life support, and there's no guarantee it'll last very long. My obligation is to do what's best for him, and if I make the call, that's what we're going to do."

"You're right," Noah said, "of course you are. That's the way it should be."

"I'm glad you feel that way." A moment or two passed, her expression softened a bit, and she went on. "He's doing what he's doing now because of Molly, you know," Ellen said. "While I was up there rendering my clinical opinion all he was talking about were the things he'd heard from her and her mother over the years. He thinks we're at some big turning point right now; he told me he was up here serving his country again, flying this one last mission, and that it was a lot more than the three of us he'd be letting down if he failed. I'd say it was the morphine talking, but I haven't given him any."

They flew through a brief patch of turbulence and when it evened out Ellen reached over to make a tiny adjustment to the defibrillator. When she seemed satisfied that things were stable again she turned back to Noah.

"Those people who're after you and Molly—at least I see now why they're so desperate to get rid of you," she said.

"Why is that?"

"This vision she's got for the country, it seems to be contagious."

Later, as the flight proceeded, Noah and Molly sat close together and spoke about a subject they'd never had much time to cover before. They talked about their future, on the wild assumption that such a time would ever come.

CHAPTER 58

After hours of waiting to receive any encouraging news from the field, Warren Landers had finally begun to pace the floor.

He was learning that the position of leadership he'd so long coveted came with its own set of challenges, some of which he'd been unprepared to meet on such short notice.

At the moment his chief concern was this: while it's easy enough to push a band of idealists toward an act of desperation, it's much harder to predict precisely when and how they'll make their move. He'd called in many valuable favors to prompt the current nationwide terror alert and was now feeling the significant personal and professional exposure of what he'd done. Having essentially promised an imminent attack, he so far had no such thing to deliver.

Earlier in the day his chosen patsies had been found through technological means and were quickly cornered at an airport in Colorado. So far, so good; to have killed them there would have been an outstanding win. Any number of frightening stories of their thwarted plans could have been constructed and fed to the waiting press, thereby stoking the climate of fear and putting everything right back on track for the desired declaration of a national emergency.

But no, they'd somehow escaped and the circumstances now demanded a media blackout until more was known. By the apparent condition of the old puddle-jumper they'd left in, they would be lucky to have limped fifty miles. Judging by the weather they'd flown into, that estimate might be high by half. The last reliable radar returns showed the fugitives falling from the sky like a stone but no crash site had yet been found.

If this all ended in a whimper, with the dangerous domestic terrorists Landers had himself reported being found tomorrow, stranded harmless and unarmed in a muddy cow pasture, the consequences would be dire. He'd promised a clear and present danger and now it must be found, or at least faked from some credible evidence. For his business partners, for his own standing and career, for the backroom political machines that were already poised to trumpet the long-awaited appearance of the mythical violent libertarian revolutionary—for many reasons he now needed a headline-worthy event.

A young man appeared at his door.

"Yes, what is it?" Landers asked.

"I think I know where these people are headed."

"Show me."

He'd brought a folding map with him and he spread it across the desk. It had a number of locations circled in black in the Northeast and mid-Atlantic and only one in red, farther west. "This hardware chain, you'd told us to send a team to all the stores and they didn't find anything—"

"I know that."

"Okay. But we missed something. They've shuttered a bunch of stores in the past ten years and we didn't look at those, of course, but they'd taken one of them and turned it into a sort of clearinghouse for old inventory. They give all the merchandise there to the needy, disaster relief, and such." He pointed to the red circle. "And that place is right here."

Landers put on his reading glasses and bent close to the map.

Butler, Pennsylvania.

Of course.

"Do we have anyone in this area?"

"Only a few assets and they're not that close. We moved almost everyone farther east. Should I reroute the units we've got nearby to this place?"

"No," Landers said. "Now listen to me. Send whoever's available to the front gate of location number seven of Garrison Archives. It's outside of Butler. They can't miss it: it looks like the entrance to Fort Knox built into the mouth of an old limestone mine. Tell them they're to immediately lock that gate down tight."

The young man was writing down these orders in detail. "We could get some help from local law enforcement and the DHS—"

"Absolutely not. This is all ours. It's going to be a feather in Talion's cap and we don't need to muddy the waters with eyewitnesses. We'll announce what's happened when it's over."

"And what about that warehouse?"

"I'll handle that myself."

"It's a six-hour trip from here by car, maybe more with the terror alert—"

"We're not going to drive," Landers said, "we're going to fly. I want you to go and see that a helicopter gets prepped for combat if there's not one ready in the arsenal now, and tap four good men to come with me. How long will that take?"

"I don't know, maybe an hour."

"You've got fifteen minutes."

"Yes, sir."

Landers enjoyed a cup of coffee while he waited, made a few necessary calls, wrote a note to update Aaron Doyle, and then brought up a recent satellite image of his objective. It was a big, open building, relatively isolated from any commercial or residential development, and it looked like there was only one road in or out.

Like shooting fish in a barrel.

"You're ready to go, Mr. Landers."

The young man who'd proven so valuable had returned to the doorway, far ahead of schedule and having done exactly as he was told. As Landers stood and put on his coat he looked the fellow over. "What's your name?" he asked.

"Rutherford, sir."

"See me when I get back, Mr. Rutherford. This is good work you did, and I'm going to have a lot more for you in the future."

"Thank you, sir."

As he strapped himself in and went about starting the engines, Landers rechecked the route and thought it all through. There was bad weather coming in but with any luck they'd beat it, get the job done, and be home in time for a late dinner and a modest celebration.

He would have been more comfortable going in with greater force, but Talion was spread quite thin across the country. Most of the men and resources had been deployed to make a public show of strength for the company, making appearances at the many smaller incidents he'd spawned with the help of George Pierce. After today's heroic crescendo there would be more to work with, and great new opportunities on the horizon.

And George Pierce was another matter. He'd been

useful enough but he would no doubt be cooking up a mutiny before very long, and that would have to be dealt with swiftly. Putting him down would be a great pleasure, though this and many other rewarding deeds would have to wait for a less eventful afternoon.

That old saw was true: there really is no rest for the wicked.

Warren Landers confirmed his final clearance with the tower. Shortly thereafter the last of the men boarded and stowed another long case of ammo for the M134 minigun mounted behind him. An assortment of gas canisters and satchel charges were already loaded.

Without further ado he lifted off into a high, rock-steady hover, and then he pitched the craft sharply forward and set them off with all available speed on his course toward western Pennsylvania.

CHAPTER 59

Hollis awoke with a start, sweaty and tense and even more weary than he'd been before he closed his eyes. His swollen arm had been killing him and he'd put his head in his hands for only a moment, he'd thought, but the clock on the wall said he'd been out for almost two hours.

"What's happening?" he asked.

Young Tyler was at the table across the office, still monitoring the radio.

"No change," he said. "They're working in the back; the manager guy sent the rest of the employees home, like you said, and left us with the keys. I'm waiting to hear any news that comes in, but there's nothing so far. I would have woken you up if there was any reason to. It seemed like you needed to sleep. Man, are you seriously okay? Because you look like a crap sandwich."

"I'm fine," Hollis said, though his voice didn't sound it. "Who's watching those water heaters?"

Tyler pointed to a nearby TV that showed six inset close-ups of the temperature readouts on the tanks. "Wireless home security system," he said, "from aisle seventeen. Lana and I set it up over an hour ago. This place has got everything."

Hollis stood and waited for his balance to settle. "That was good thinking," he said. "You stay, I'm going to go and check on the others."

When he rounded the last corner into the vehicle bay he could hardly believe his eyes.

The extra hours of unexpected waiting had been put to very good use by Cathy Merrick and her helpers. For the first time he saw the finished product stripped of all the masking tape and drop cloths.

The old road-beaten company truck she'd been given as a blank canvas had been steam-cleaned, repainted, and ingeniously augmented with repurposed items from the plentiful warehouse shelves. The truck was transformed from stem to stern into the glossy spitting image of a Pennsylvania hazmat emergency vehicle complete with realistic siren horns, diamond-plate running boards, rooftop strobes, and more.

If you got close enough, some of the lettering appeared to be of the press-on type one might use to put an address on a mailbox, but it was so well integrated that the overall look was near perfect. Most every other label, official seal, and logo was hand-painted, including the government-coded license plates. The only visual clue that these things weren't real was that the artist was still touching up her work here and there with a makeshift palette and a tiny brush.

"This is outstanding," Hollis said.

"Thanks." Cathy Merrick swept her bangs from her eyes with her wrist and looked up at him. "I think it'll pass, as long as no one gets too close. Let me show you where it's weak, though."

The overall shape and size wasn't correct and there was nothing that could be done about that; she'd accomplished what she could with deceptive shading and other airbrushed optical trickery. Still, it looked good enough to fool almost anyone unless they broke out a tape measure with a set of factory dimensions.

The other standout problems were the doors and windows in the back section. The HomeWorx truck had only a wide roll-up door in the rear. The vehicle it was meant to impersonate featured double doors that opened from the middle with tinted windows in several places. This glaring difference would be noticed by anyone who'd ever seen a medical show on TV, much less by a trained security detail.

The missing doors and windows had been painted on, so realistically that it seemed like you could just reach out and open them right up. Some chrome hardware, smoky Plexiglas, and black-rubber molding was spot-glued in place to add some 3-D realism to the art. But despite the almost uncanny illusion this was indeed the weakest link. It looked great at a glance and it all might withstand a quick viewing from several feet away, but it would not hold up to any extended inspection.

"I think it's going to be okay," Hollis said. "You've really outdone yourself here." He felt a little dizzy, and pulled over a folding chair to sit down.

"Are you all right? You look like you've just run a mile."

"I'll be okay."

Cathy put down her brush and paints and felt his forehead with the back of her fingers. "You're burning up."

"I know, I'll be okay. Why don't you show me what else we've got here. We might have to drop everything and take off any minute now."

Cathy took him around and went through the rest of the work. The laminated, pin-on ID tags Lana Somin had made at the computer station were picture-perfect, gilded replicas of the examples she'd downloaded from the Internet. They'd even crafted some actual badges from molded hot-melt glue, embedded safety pins, and gold metallic paint.

There were two cobbled-together uniforms, one for the driver and another for a front-seat passenger. These had been dyed and decorated from materials on hand, jailbreak style, using generic work shirts and pants.

Since it was possible that the driver's compartment of the truck might have to endure a brief viewing, it had been dressed up as well. Tool carriers disguised as medical bags and a number of 3M full-face respirators from the paint department were conspicuously placed. A hanging microphone on a coiled cord was clipped to the sun visor with its loose plug stuffed into the ashtray. A handheld radio scanner was mounted near the glove box and would be turned up loud and tuned to police frequencies to provide realistic background noise in the interior.

"One of those uniforms is for you and the other's for me," Cathy Merrick said. "In fact, we should get dressed now. I'll be driving, you'll sit up front, and everyone else will be riding in the back."

It was all good work, much better than he could have hoped for.

As she'd been showing him these things, Hollis was also thinking about what this woman had been through in recent days. The courage she and the others were displaying was something to admire considering all that had happened and the unknowns ahead. People often don't know what they can do until they're called upon to do it; he'd seen this sort of grit in wartime, of course, from civilians and soldiers alike.

None of it was mentioned, but the burden of what they'd lost was there as well, in each of them. The hurt was held in check only by the urgent needs of the moment and the acceptance that a proper memorial for the fallen would have to wait for another time.

Just as Hollis had finished changing his clothes, Tyler ran up and handed him a notepad.

"Molly and the others," the boy said. "I don't know how they did it but they're coming by plane, and they're on their way in." He pointed to a set of numbers he'd copied down. "Those are the coordinates of an old private airport outside of Boyers, about twenty miles up the road. I've already put the location into the GPS; that's where they're going to try to land."

"When?"

"Soon. Half an hour, maybe."

"Okay, then," Hollis said. "Let's get ready to move."

It had begun to rain and the high raftered ceiling was clattering softly and resonating with the occasional peal of thunder. But as he stopped and listened, he found another noise was growing there as well.

"Do you hear that?"

Tyler listened, and then he nodded, frowning.

"You all stay back here," Hollis said. The only firearms they'd kept were the handguns from the grab-and-go bags they'd taken as they fled the ranch. He took one of these pistols, tucked it into his belt in back, and then pointed to the bunker of cement bags the employees had helped them stack up earlier. "All three of you stay under cover until I come back. I'm going to go out and see what's what."

Though the sun was still up, the overcast sky appeared very dark through the tall glass windows at the front of the warehouse. By the time he'd reached the center section of the place the steady, airborne noise he'd heard had become unmistakable.

A searchlight from above began to sweep the length and breadth of the parking lot outside, and soon a black helicopter descended into view. Its insignias were those of the ruthless mercenaries who had laid waste to the trail behind him all these months. Its cargo bay was open and it was hovering close enough that he could clearly see the barrel of a mounted machine gun swing around and lock its aim in his direction.

CHAPTER 60

The last few seconds before the shooting started crept by slowly enough to let a flood of separate thoughts tear through Hollis's mind.

The defensive preparations he and Tyler had made earlier were meant only as a last-resort deterrence against ground forces. He hadn't factored in a threat like this, perhaps because once they were trapped from the air the rest of the plan would collapse and they'd have no chance to get away.

He could give himself up now, as he'd told the others he would do if the law rolled up and there was no escape. But these weren't lawmen, and the thought of turning his people over to a pack of murderous thugs was nearly as bad as the idea of leading them into a fatal last stand.

And Molly was still on her way into the area. If he could delay things here by even a little, it could make time for the others to send off a message so she at least might escape capture.

A quick decision was needed, and so he made it.

He would walk out to give himself up, confess that he'd forced the three in back into unwilling service, and then hope that his friends would use the short distraction of his surrender to get on the radio and try to warn the others away.

Hollis raised his empty hands above his head and stepped out into the open.

The men outside didn't hesitate. As he took the first step forward the gun flashed and the windows shattered and he dove back for cover as a furious volley of bullets tore a ragged furrow up the aisle where he'd stood only a moment before.

The helicopter eased forward and dropped lower as its pilot tried to give the gunner a better angle on his target. Hollis held himself flat to the floor as the torrent of gunfire cut another swath across the interior, shredding everything in its path to flying shards and splinters. And then the roar of the gun outside stopped abruptly; seconds passed, and the echoes faded.

If this lull in the destruction was due to a jam then the odds had shifted, even if only slightly. It was an opportunity to either retreat or advance and only one of those offered slim hope. Hollis stood and threw caution to the wind and drew his pistol, charging forward, firing toward the cockpit and the open cargo bay.

The sheer surprise of seeing this rash counterattack against an armored aircraft must have far outweighed its actual threat to its occupants. As the chopper banked and veered away, one of the men in back was either hit by a lucky shot or simply lost his footing and fell, arms flailing, sixty feet down into the pavement.

The helo had disappeared around the side of the building but it likely wouldn't be gone for long. Hollis ran outside to the fallen body, took the AR-15 strapped over the dead man's shoulder and a spare magazine from his pack, and then hurried the length of the warehouse back toward the vehicle bay.

There was a heavy thump from overhead as something hit the ceiling. He ducked behind cover and a second later an explosion shook the place and peeled back the metal roof high above the south side of the warehouse. Shiny canisters fell through the new opening, spewing sparks and yellowish gas as they bounced and skittered across the floor.

When he reached the others they were taking shelter within the igloo of stacked sandbags, just as he'd asked. He retrieved the respirators from the front seat of the truck and helped the three of them strap on the masks before he applied his own. As the stinging gas began to blow through the space he directed Lana and Cathy back into hiding and then turned to Tyler.

"It's not much of a chance we've got but I need your help!" Hollis shouted through the clear mask. "Follow me!"

The boy nodded without hesitation, and they set off running.

The two of them reached the nearest of the water heaters they'd prepared earlier and Tyler helped steady the heavy cylinder as Hollis put his shoulder to it and lifted it upright so it was standing as designed on its stubby legs. He twisted the thermostat control to its maximum setting, tapped the boy's arm, and they ran on to the next one.

Another explosion rocked the air from above and another jagged hole tore open in the roof. Rain poured in to mingle with the water already spraying from the overhead sprinkler system, which had been set off by the smoke and drifting gas.

They'd just managed to get the last of the heaters aimed upright and set on high when gunfire erupted from overhead and they were driven again to cover. It wasn't the big gun that was firing this time; maybe that beast really was out of commission. The helicopter was

fighting gusting winds and the three-round bursts coming from the remaining men in back made a lot of noise
but so far weren't proving accurate.

"I don't know how much time we've got before those
water heaters blow on their own," Hollis said, "but it's not
much. Get to the back and get your mom and the girl
ready to go. Tell them to stay down and cover their ears
tight, and you do the same. This is about to get loud."

Tyler looked reluctant to leave but he did what was
right and took off running for the rear of the warehouse.
The gunfire from above shifted to follow his sudden
movement, the bullets clanging in the rafters and rico-
cheting off the high shelves along his path. Whatever
they were using to track their targets, it wasn't only
visual; it seemed as though they could see through solid
walls.

As the helicopter appeared through one of the holes
in the ceiling, Hollis stepped out from cover and opened
fire on it with the AR-15. That seemed to do the trick of
drawing attention away from the others; a new barrage
of bullets rained down around his position as he ran for
the front and then on outside into the parking lot.

Hollis tore the respirator from his face as he crouched
behind the metal base of a tall light pole. The helicopter
was hovering above the battered warehouse, pivoting
around so the men in the cargo bay would have a clear
shot at him and the others from a safer range.

He reloaded and readied the rifle, brought the scope
near his eye, took aim at the base of the first distant
water heater—the one that was almost directly below
the aircraft—and then squeezed the trigger.

The cylinder exploded with the force of a healthy
stick of TNT, sending the bulk of its chassis rocketing
upward through the roof, trailing vapor and debris five
hundred feet into the air.

It was a clean miss, but the craft was buffeted by the shock wave and began an evasive sideways drift, left to right across the width of the warehouse. The men in the back were still firing at him, the impacts of their shots working closer to him by the second. He kept his patience, tracked the building speed and movement of the helicopter, and breathed the first real prayer he'd offered in twenty years. He then sighted down on his remaining targets and shot them in sequence, right to left:

1 . . . . 2 . . . . 3 . . . . 4 5

The pilot of the craft must have sensed what was in store, because the helicopter had jerked suddenly upward and pivoted toward safety, but his reaction came too late.

Each water heater blasted upward through the roof, one after the other, in a relentless line toward his oncoming flight path, until the last of them just barely clipped the chopper's aft end. It was just enough; the impact hadn't looked like much but the tail of the craft was destroyed.

With no force to counteract the torque of the main rotor the helicopter began an uncontrolled spin, whirling faster and faster as it descended toward the far side of the parking lot, where it crashed in a bright, fiery explosion of unspent fuel and armaments.

Hollis pushed himself to his feet and walked slowly toward the burning wreckage, scanning the area for danger as he went, his weapon at the ready. He reached the crash about the time Tyler and the others pulled up beside him in the truck.

In the back of the ruined chopper were the burned remains of three men.

The pilot's seat was empty.

CHAPTER 61

By the time the tiny airfield came into view Noah noticed that the plane's fuel gauges had dipped to near zero and one engine was running rough.

Though the old C-60 had clawed her way through battering turbulence and ice and lightning strikes and equipment failures, in the end its pilot had endured even more. Despite his brave front Bill McCord was clearly fading and it had become a continual struggle for Ellen Davenport to preserve the weakened function of his heart. The only saving grace was that one way or another, the flight was nearly over.

Ellen watched from the right-hand seat as the pilot eased down the throttle, set the flaps and trims, flicked on the nav lights, and pulled the lever that would hopefully lower the landing gear. There was a grinding and a deep mechanical rumble from behind and below them as the undercarriage descended. McCord took his eyes from the windshield for only a second when the sound had ceased; he checked the status lights of the gear and shook his head.

"Hold on tight," he said. His jaw was clenched, his voice only a harsh whisper spoken through the unrelenting torture of the shocks from the pacing. "I don't know if both the wheels are down, but either way, we're landing."

As the throttle was pulled back farther the right engine faltered and then coughed and died with a final wheeze. The plane slowed and yawed perilously and the pilot responded to correct his crumbling descent.

Every minute of his many decades of flying experience must have come to bear in those last few seconds. With utter concentration and some last measure of untapped strength he somehow straightened them out. He eased the craft into a gentle bank that would put the bulk of the weight on the only wheel they were sure was down and locked, and then he held all the battling forces steady under his hands as the ground rose up to meet them.

"There they are," Hollis said.

Through his passenger-side window he'd seen the faint lights of an approaching plane wink on against the backdrop of black thunderheads rolling in from the west. All the adrenaline from the battle at the warehouse had deserted him along the ride and the pain and weakness he'd felt before was returning, worse than ever.

Cathy Merrick pulled the truck to a stop as they reached the end of a long dirt road. Just ahead was a little country airfield with no tower, lights, or services, just a grass-lined runway probably used only by crop dusters and private pilots practicing their touch-and-go landings.

They both rolled down the windows and though the sound of the approaching aircraft was just barely audible it didn't sound right at all. The descent grew unsteady as they came on; they were way too high and moving too fast to land and the wings weren't fully level. Soon Hollis could see that only half the landing gear was down.

When it passed the far end of the runway the plane

settled in and flared, banking subtly as if to favor the side with the missing wheel. It flew down the length of the pavement, holding itself in the air and bleeding off speed, and then when it seemed the air could support it no longer it lost its lift and dropped the last few inches to the ground.

It rolled out and slowed on that single wheel, the tail came down, and then the unsupported wing tipped and fell into sudden contact with the pavement. The one spinning propeller shattered at impact and threw its blades, the plane skidded and veered, showering sparks and grinding along until at last it skidded into a sharp half turn and came to a silent, smoldering halt.

As they drove out onto the runway Hollis pulled a small fire extinguisher from its clips below his seat. He jumped out before the truck had fully stopped, fell, and got up and ran as best he could to the side at the rear of the fuselage. When he found the door he pulled it open and climbed inside.

Noah Gardner was already helping Molly out of her seat belt and together they brought her out and clear of the wreck. When she was safe the two men returned to the plane and walked up the tilted aisle to the cockpit.

There they found Ellen Davenport kneeling by the side of an elderly man who was slumped and motionless in the pilot's seat. As they approached, they saw that she was straightening the old man's disheveled clothes, smoothing a few bits of broken glass from his thin white hair, and gently easing his hands from their steadfast grip upon the wheel.

"When we stopped," she said, "I looked over, and he was gone."

The patter of a light freezing rain had just begun, quietly pecking at the metal skin of the aircraft. In the distance Hollis heard the unmistakable sound of sirens on the way.

"Ma'am," he said softly, "I'm afraid we need to go."

"I won't leave him like this."

"Ellen—"

"You two go on," she said. "I've got my phone. I'll wait until you're long gone, and if they haven't found us yet, I'll call it in."

Noah had known this woman long enough to recognize a final decision when he saw one, and he didn't argue.

"Thanks for everything you've done for us," he said.

Before he could stand to leave she stopped him with a touch.

"This man got us here so you could make a difference," Ellen said. "Don't you dare let him down."

Once all were safely assembled in the truck and they were back under way Hollis checked the time-to-destination on the GPS. When ten minutes remained he took out the last of their disposable cell phones, punched in a number, and listened. He waited until the phone on the other end picked up and then he pressed the button that ended the call.

Sixty seconds later his phone rang twice and then went silent again. That was the signal that all would be ready up ahead.

Cathy Merrick looked over briefly from the driver's seat, and he nodded to her.

"That's it," Hollis said. "From here on out it's do or die."

CHAPTER 62

Their insider at Garrison Archives was a young mail-room intern who'd been planted in her job months before.

Like most spies, much of her role up to then had involved simply blending in and waiting. Recently, however, she'd been given three important duties to perform for Molly Ross and the Founders' Keepers.

First, she'd smuggled out a copy of the internal network architecture documents—it was amazing what low-level employees have access to when they're put in charge of the shredder and the photocopy room. Next she copied down a few key PIN numbers from a security guard's crib sheet and ordered a duplicate access card for all the inside doors. Once these things had been gathered she'd addressed a padded envelope to Mr. Thom Hollis, care of HomeWorx, Inc., and forwarded it all to a UPS private mailbox in the nearby town of Butler.

Third, she'd intercepted a special-delivery package when it arrived by courier at Garrison—said package having been constructed and sent by some tech-savvy co-conspirators—and after business hours that same night she'd punched a pattern of holes through the outer cardboard of the box and placed it as directed, high on a shelf in a utility room near an open vent for the air-conditioning and environment control system.

And last, at some unspecified time in the very near future, she would be ready to put on a small performance for her coworkers.

Here's what she was supposed to do: once she'd gotten the go-ahead signal, and when her nose detected a very specific fragrance wafting through her workplace, she was to mention the smell to her colleagues, fake some vertigo and troubled breathing, and then faint dead away on the spot.

The first steps were already accomplished. When an announcement came over the PA system that a threat had been received of a possible chemical or biological weapons attack against the facility—and that this was not a drill—she knew that her final task would be required within minutes.

Anyone who's gotten a whiff of actual cyanide gas and lived to tell the tale would confirm that its odor of bitter almonds is quite different from the familiar nutty scent of the supermarket variety. The real thing would certainly bear little resemblance to the cloying, sweet almond scent that would soon begin to show itself in the cool filtered air throughout the Garrison underground facility.

Rooms away from where Molly's planted intern waited, the package she'd received and prepared came to life as a cell phone inside it received a call.

The ringer electronics of the phone activated a microcontroller-enabled circuit board and the salvaged heating element from a head-shop vaporizer warmed up to a bright orange glow. Servo motors whirred, pistons worked, gears and rollers turned, and at a rate of a drop per second, two ounces of Italian amaretto began to drip with a hiss onto the hot metal.

Moments later, pungent white smoke began to waft through the holes in the box, soon permeating the utility room before being sucked into the recirculating air of the HVAC system.

The minute the WMD threat had been announced all seventeen hundred employees stopped working and awaited further instructions at their posts and desks. Despite the nationwide alert that was currently in force, no immediate evacuation had been ordered. Garrison was a high-profile and somewhat controversial facility among some elements of society, and such threats were not that uncommon.

Often, after a few minutes of break time the all-clear would be sounded and everything would quickly return to normal. They were protected by many levels of security, after all, and safely ensconced more than two hundred feet beneath ground level in a rock mine hidden under a mountain.

The main Information Services room seated nearly two hundred workers, all arranged in an open grid of rows and columns of identical desks and computer workstations. The space was one of the original dug-out areas of the mine, and while the room was large it also felt somewhat claustrophobic due to a low suspended ceiling overhead.

As the employees waited out the alert period with solitaire games and chitchat, the only person still working seemed to be the mailroom girl. She rolled her cart up one row and down the next, dropping off letters and memos and making light conversation with those who bothered to acknowledge her.

Near the center of the room, the girl suddenly

stopped, looking troubled. She coughed a bit, put a hand to her chest, and leaned on her cart as though she might swoon.

"Does anybody smell that?" she called out, and suddenly the room got very quiet.

Some of those near her rose at their desks and acknowledged that yes, there was an unusual odor.

"It smells like—" Her knees seemed to weaken and her voice was strained as she tried to speak again. "It smells like . . ." And with a last guttural gasp she grabbed her throat and crumpled to the floor.

As some came to her aid the clear signs of physical distress began to spread rapidly to others. Another collapsed, and then another, and many covered their noses and mouths with handkerchiefs or shirtsleeves and hurried for the exit to escape the now visible, seeping gas. As fear took hold and threatened to spark a stampede toward the safety of the outdoors, someone with their wits still about them ran to the wall, broke a pane of protective glass, and pulled the big red lever that sounded the general alarm.

Even before the last of the many hundreds of employees, managers, technicians, and guards had evacuated, those near the back of the crowd saw the leading vehicle of the first-responders speeding up the private road toward the facility.

A series of security barriers that were set up earlier had been pulled aside as soon as the state of emergency within the complex had been announced. All the gates were still manned but they were now standing open so as not to impede the arrival of the rescue workers.

As the first hazmat truck arrived it slowed briefly at the farthest checkpoint and then was waved on through. The lights and sirens of many others were approaching in the distance; police, EMS, and fire departments from all over the surrounding region had been automatically summoned by the internal alarm.

The evacuated crowd parted to the sides of the road to clear the way and the first truck rumbled past them and through the fortified entrance of Garrison Archives.

Once the vehicle had disappeared inside, the remaining stragglers were quickly escorted out to safety and then, oddly enough, the massive double doors of the entrance swung closed.

CHAPTER 63

Noah stood off to the side as their now-empty truck was backed up and parked with its bumper jammed hard against the closed, inward-opening doors. It wasn't until he heard that solid crunch of metal on metal that he allowed himself to accept it:

They were in.

With the fearless exuberance of youth, Lana Somin had already set to work in the abandoned guards' booth by the front gate. A cloned keycard and PIN number of the night-shift supervisor were among the items they'd been passed by their insider. Using these, within a minute she'd reset all other access codes to random numbers and done what she could to lock out further changes.

Such measures obviously wouldn't hold forever. The entrance to this place was built like a giant bank vault and was probably strong enough to withstand the assault of a small tactical nuke. All that strength wasn't much comfort, though. Somewhere in an engineer's notebook there was a contingency plan for this very scenario and that engineer's phone would be ringing very soon. Once the people outside fully realized they'd been scammed they would bring whatever it took to force their way back in.

There was no time to waste and the clock was already running.

A number of low-slung electric people-movers were parked near the entrance. All six members of the group piled into one and set off down the main two-lane corridor with Cathy Merrick at the wheel. Despite the ordeal of their journey, all were in good shape, with the exception of Hollis. He was clearly weakening, his neglected fever was spiking, and those were only symptoms of something underneath that was probably growing worse by the minute.

The look of the place was an odd visual hybrid, part cave and part corporate. Twelve feet above the smooth pavement of the indoor road there were heavy cables, conduit, air and water ducts, and periodic amber lighting running along the rocky ceiling. The offices and workrooms they passed were like those you might find in any upscale high-rise, but the pitted walls of the tunnels leading between them appeared to have been carved out with tools no more subtle than dynamite and jackhammers.

After a half mile of dim, descending straightaways they began to realize that their hand-drawn map was far from perfect. Its errors and omissions led to some maddening backtracking and wrong turns. Valid routes looked the same as dark unfinished passages dwindling off toward dead ends. There was a great deal of new construction and very little signage to guide them. Apparently, if anyone got this far into the place without an escort it was assumed that they should know exactly where they were going.

Just as it seemed they were hopelessly lost, they rounded a bend and happened onto the very room they were looking for. It was a huge space filled end to end with identical desks and computer stations. The label

INFORMATION SERVICES: CLOUD 79 was displayed above the entrance.

As they pulled over and parked they were met by a young woman with a Garrison ID pinned to her shirt. She introduced herself as Claire; she was the mailroom intern who'd helped them get this far. Once the rush for the exit had begun she'd slipped away in the confusion and hidden herself until the rest of the employees were gone. Now that they had a knowledgeable guide with a key to nearly every door, the real work could begin.

Molly's aim seemed simple enough: to find the most frightening truths buried here in these vast archives of above-top-secret data, and then to release it all into the sunlight. It was her feeling that if the people finally saw the authentic documentation, if they could follow the actual tracks of the conspirators who were bent on destroying her country, then the good citizens of the United States of America would wake up all at once and be moved to act to save their nation.

It was a noble idea but Noah's doubts were still lingering. Many, many damning truths had already been told in the past and most were soon forgotten. Often in those cases it was only the whistle-blowers themselves who'd been punished for the crime of speaking out.

Still, it was Molly's hope that this time would be different. If the facts could be brought out in this definitive way—with all the evidence, all the connections, all the answers to that key question, *who benefits?*—then the resulting shock to the system might finally be too powerful to ignore.

The seven of them split up onto three tasks. Molly and Noah would prioritize a list of evidence they wished to find hidden within these nearly limitless memory banks. Lana Somin would worm her way into the front end of the master database with Tyler Merrick standing by to assist as he could. Lastly, Hollis, Cathy Merrick, and the new girl, Claire, would take a set of site blueprints and try to find an alternate way out of the place for when the time came to cut and run.

Faced with such little time, but free access to all the answers she'd ever wanted, Molly seemed to struggle at first to narrow her scope to the most important things. Just as a starting point the two of them came up with a list of keywords to be searched once Lana had gained access to the computer system. These topics came to them in no particular order of validity or priority as Noah wrote them down:

> *Frederic Whitehurst, Sibel Edmonds, and the*
>   *FBI*
> *Gary Webb and Nicaragua*
> *Kathryn Bolkovac and DynCorp*
> *Katharine Gun, Karen Kwiatkowski, and Iraq*
> *Julia Davis and DHS: Google, Facebook, NSA,*
>   *CIA*
> *Trapwire, Abraxas, Stingray, RIOT, and TIA*
> *Trailblazer, NSA, Stellar Wind, Wiebe, Roark,*
>   *Binney, and Loomis*
> *AT&T, Mark Klein, and Room 641A*
> *LIBOR, rate-fixing, derivatives, the Tower of*
>   *Basel, BIS, and worldwide central banks*
> *Anything to do with the shadowy foundations,*
>   *conglomerates, investments, and under-*
>   *the-table political funding linked to a man*
>   *named Aaron Doyle*

Molly stopped and asked him to read back this partial list. As Noah did so he saw in her face that she was feeling exactly as he did.

They'd just scratched the surface and it was way too

much already. And at the same time, it wasn't going to be nearly enough.

The truth behind nearly all these individual revelations—the secret partnerships, the hidden influence, the lies and corruptions and scandals, the high crimes against the American people perpetrated by their supposed leaders—it was already out there on the open Internet for anyone to uncover for themselves.

The problem wasn't a lack of evidence but a basic human bias: we see only what we're prepared to believe. After all, Molly and her mother and Danny Bailey had each spoken out on most of these things in the past, and where had it gotten them? Nowhere, except that two of them were dead and the other was about to play her last remaining card.

"It's no good," Molly said, and the expression on her face was desolate. "It's not going to work."

"We're here," he replied. "There's no use giving up now. Come on, let's do what we came to do."

Tyler Merrick walked up then and said, "Lana's ready for you now."

The three of them hurried over to where the young woman was immersed in the database system. Several employees had left themselves logged in when they'd fled their desks and that had saved her some work cracking passwords.

As requested, she and Tyler had also set up for the video portion of the project.

A large TV monitor was mounted above the desk where Lana sat. Other monitors like this were all over the place. Its screen displayed insets of live feeds from several security cameras around the facility, including views from the front entrance and various rooms and key intersections. In the center there was a larger rectangular picture that currently showed an empty chair next to the desk.

"Molly should sit there," Lana said.

Noah helped Molly to the seat as Tyler adjusted the Webcam to center her image. He repositioned some floor lamps to perfect the lighting until the picture looked as good as it ever would, given the circumstances.

"Where's this video going?" Noah asked.

"No place yet. We're all set to feed it to her website and to some other video hosts when she says go. I've got a backup stream running through a modem that's older than I am and a dial-up connection on one of their secure phone lines. Even if they cut the Internet fiber optics, they probably won't think to also cut those phones. The quality may be pretty bad but it should stay live. When I flip the switch this feed will take over all the security monitors in the place, so everybody here will see the broadcast, too."

"And you're into the data system already?"

"I am. You should know, that layout I got is just a part of what's here. The old part."

"But all the dirt we're looking for, it's still in there?"

"Oh yeah, it's in here." She leaned and glanced at Molly's list, chose the LIBOR rate-fixing heist, and keyed in some entries. Her screen filled with lists of private correspondence, phone records and transcripts, names and places and minutes from illegal meetings that had planned the recent theft of tens of trillions—enough hard evidence to convict a hundred insanely powerful people if it should ever be exposed.

Throughout all this Noah stayed at Molly's ear, describing everything he saw. "What you've got on the screen there," he said to Lana, "what can you do with that?"

"This little piece? I can print it, I can save it locally, I can zip it up and send it to a place on the Net where we can pick it up later and do whatever we want with it. If you really want to spread it around I can make a torrent and put it up on the Pirate Bay. But if we're going to do anything online we need to do it soon."

"Why?"

"They could catch on to what we're doing any minute and when they do they'll shut off our high-bandwidth access to the outside—like I said, everything but this old modem carrying the video over the red-phone line."

"Why didn't they shut it down immediately?"

"It's a last resort," Lana said, "going dark is like doomsday for a place like this. They've got a ton of redundant high-speed connections, massive pipes for all the data flowing in and out, and it's all automated so their clients can have access 24/7. These people live and die by their service record. If they take themselves down, they'll have a lot of explaining to do. My guess is that they'd prefer to keep this little incident a secret as long as they can. We know they're pretty good at keeping secrets.

"But once they really realize we're in here with our hands in the cookie jar? Yeah, they can kill all those links from the edge-routers upstream. I'm working on some half-assed solutions for that—like the dial-up connection for the video—but what I come up with will be slow as hell by comparison, like 1990s slow. Anything big that you want to send from here, we'd better get on with it."

"Why don't we just send it all?" Tyler asked. "To hell with it, just do a mass release, while we still can."

"No," Molly said. "We don't have any idea what's in there. The corporate and diplomatic and financial and military intelligence secrets—the way the world works now, they're all entwined. We could help our enemies and murder our allies. We could expose every American undercover agent everywhere. We could get a lot of people killed and start a few wars in the process. Letting it all loose without a filter is not an option."

"So what do we do?" Lana asked.

Molly didn't answer, so Noah handed over their handwritten list. "Start with those things while we're thinking this through. Do what you said, find everything related, package it up, and burn what you can to a DVD or something. If the high-speed lines stay up, hide it outside somewhere so we can get it and use it later on."

"Okay." As Lana spoke this word the lights overhead flickered briefly. She frowned, did a quick diagnostic on her machine, and then looked over at Noah again. "That's it," she said. "We're already screwed. They've done it; we're cut off." She typed and clicked to verify this, and then quickly checked the modem line for a carrier. The distinctive screech was still there on the speakerphone. "Yep. Every outgoing connection except the one for the video is down."

That news was bad, but the picture on the security monitor brought even worse tidings.

Outside, many hundreds of evacuated employees were being pushed back far away from the entrance. A convoy of black SUVs rolled up; the familiar Talion yellow crest adorned their side doors. In the distance, a long line of heavy equipment and weaponry was pulling into a ready position.

The work had barely begun and their grand plot was already uncovered. Now they were trapped in the vault they'd risked everything to get into, with no way to get back out.

"So you're sure that dial-up video link is still streaming out," Noah said.

"Yeah," Lana replied, "but it's not going to be anything like a hi-res broadcast. The stream's just hooked up to one obscure old node in Michigan—"

"Okay, then. Molly, it's your decision. In the time we've got left we can sit right here in front of that camera and you can say what you want, and I'll read off some of these things we've found so far, and we'll keep going until those guys break in here and do whatever they're going to do to us. Nobody may ever see it, but at least it's something after all this. Or, I can go now and find Hollis and the others and see if they've found an escape route, and if they have then we can still try to run. Either way, I'm with you."

He could see her thinking for long seconds, and at last she seemed to come to a very hard and final decision.

"Go and find Hollis," Molly said. "I guess we've got to run."

CHAPTER 64

That was it, then. If Hollis and the others had discovered an alternate route to the outside, the time had come to take it.

They'd gone off on their search a while ago and Noah and Tyler set out to find them, leaving Molly and Lana in the computer room with a promise to hurry back soon. Escape was the only priority that remained, and time was short.

Noah could feel it now as well as hear it: a harsh vibration had begun to rattle the walls. It had been soft and isolated at first, but soon it was everywhere, as if the entire mountain above them was trembling under the bit of a giant drill press.

Tyler was the first to spot his mother and Claire and Hollis. The three of them were on their way back, coming up one of the dark side-corridors. As Noah and the boy ran to meet them they saw that the big man barely seemed able to stand on his own.

"Did you find a way out?" Noah asked.

"I think we did," Cathy Merrick replied. "It's an air shaft from the oldest part of the mine. It's steep and it's pretty tight and we didn't make it all the way up but it may be the best chance we've got."

A shuddering *boom* resonated through the corridor as a layer of dust and a loose tile or two fell from the ceiling.

"Where is she?" Hollis breathed. "We have to get Molly." His eyes were bleary, his voice barely audible.

"How bad is he?" Noah asked.

"He's not good at all." Cathy Merrick was supporting him with Claire on his other side.

"Tyler, you stay here with them," Noah said. "I'll go back for Molly and Lana. We're getting out of here."

As he ran he was careful to memorize the twists and turns of the path back to the computer room. When he came to a particularly confusing crossroads he had to stop for a moment to regain his bearings.

Another of the many wide-screen video security monitors was mounted near the ceiling at this corner. Lana had obviously flipped that switch she'd mentioned; the picture showed multiple views from all over the facility and in the center stood the empty chair from which Molly had hoped to deliver her broadcast exposé over the Web.

On the outside view he could see technicians and laborers working hard on the front gate. Judging by the ever-increasing sounds of digging machines and the occasional detonations they were also trying to come in via other avenues.

A familiar discoloration along the wall reminded him which way to go and he ran full out the rest of the way. When he got to them Lana was still working at her place and Molly was off to the side, praying. He went to the desk first.

"Come on, let's pack it in," Noah said. "We're leaving."

"There's something here you need to see," Lana said.

"Not now, we don't have the time."

"We've got time for this. She wants you to see it, and you may never get another chance."

Just one more minute, he told himself. That would give Molly a little space to finish her prayers—heaven knows they needed all the help they could get—and then they would go. "Okay, make it quick."

"One of the items you wrote down, 'Trapwire, Abraxas, Stingray, RIOT, and TIA,' do you even know what those things are?"

"It was just something I remembered from my father's work in New York, from last year. No, I don't know what it is, but it seemed important and awfully secretive."

"Well, this is what it is," Lana said. "TIA stands for total information awareness. It was a post-9/11 program that supposedly got killed because it was too scary, even for those times. But it's still alive, and it's right here, linked directly to that giant intelligence complex they've built out in Utah. I'm going to use it now to do a search on you. Take a look at what comes up."

She typed in his name and hit ENTER, selected his specific record from the resulting list of other Noah Gardners, and moments later a flicker of cascading documents, forms, and profiles flooded onto the screen.

"That's not a surprise," Noah said. "Of course they're keeping tabs on me. What would you expect after all this—"

"Wait. Now give me any name at all, someone from high school; pick the most boring, harmless person you can think of."

"Howard Pankin from Great Neck, New York," Noah said. "I don't see the point of this."

Lana entered the name and again the screen filled with an elaborate profile. It was every bit as extensive as Noah's had been. There were hundreds, maybe thousands of pages of detail: locations and driving routes, purchase histories, private accounts and memberships, political leanings, medical records, school records, financial statements, friends and associates, phone records and transcripts, Internet tracks—and photographs.

These weren't just the pictures this ordinary man had taken and put up on Facebook; they were pictures *of* him from every angle and life situation. They were from traffic cameras, street cameras, store cameras, work cameras, restroom cameras, phone cameras, bus and subway cameras; even his gaming console and his Webcam on his own home computer had supplied a folder of embarrassing images in which he clearly didn't know he was being monitored.

Noah leaned closer, trying to understand. "What does this mean?" he asked.

"It means they're watching every last one of us," Lana said. "They're linking all their electronic eyes and ears together, storing everything about us, cradle to grave. They're building a case against each of us so nobody can ever step out of line without getting punished for it. Don't you see, it's the individuals they're afraid of. They can use this to predict who's going to cause them trouble and then stop them before they ever get started."

"Good God."

"Yeah. Take a look." She called up a master listing of all records in this massive table. The number of entries flagged *USA* was 347,168,099.

As he watched, that number incremented by one.

"And that means . . ."

"Another serf was just born, in St. Louis," Lana said. She brought up that new record. There was a first photo, with tiny hand- and footprints right beside. The data form started out empty but it didn't stay that way for long. Soon the first few fields filled in. It was a boy, he was Caucasian, he was born to a single mother in the fifth generation of a family supported solely by the State, and even before he had a name, he had a number.

"How are we still seeing this?" Noah asked. "I thought the Internet was down."

"Not this," Lana said. "I don't think this thing ever goes down."

Another blast shook the room, this one nearer still, and it snapped him back to the situation at hand. "Let's move," he said, and as Lana gathered her things he went over to Molly and knelt beside her.

"Honey, we really have to go now."

She shook her head. "I changed my mind," she said. "Lana told me what she found. I have to show them—"

"It's too late, Molly. We're too late to show them anything. We have to try to get out of here, and then we can think of what to do next once you're safe."

She didn't answer, but at his gentle urging she let herself be lifted up and led along. He held on to Molly's hand as the three of them ran back along the path to where the others were waiting.

Hollis was visibly worse by then and fading fast. Noah and Tyler shared some of his weight as they all set off on the winding path toward an exit they weren't even sure was there.

The rough corridor gradually narrowed until up ahead they saw the last door between the modern construction and the older passages of the mine. They'd just dragged themselves through this portal when another explosion rocked the place. This time the tremors seemed to spread and multiply as though a deep fault in the mountain had been disturbed. The earth heaved and everyone was thrown from their feet.

When it was quiet again, Noah reached out to find her hand again, but Molly was gone.

The door behind them slammed shut and he heard the bolt on the other side slide home.

"No," he whispered.

Noah clawed his way to the door and threw his fists against it, calling out to her. Through the small glass window he could see her in there feeling her way back along the route they'd come. He grabbed the handle and strained against it with everything he had but it held fast. Desperate, he took the flashlight and ran ahead to look for another way around, but the tunnel only constricted further. From that point on there was no other way back.

His companions cleared the path as he returned to the sealed door. Through its cloudy window he could just see the security monitor mounted high on the other side. The wide screen still showed the multi-inset view that Lana had wired together before.

And soon there she was, in the middle of the screen. Molly had found the chair they'd set up for her in the computer room and was seated there. She leaned forward and felt for the microphone, touched the button on its base that would activate it, faced the nearby camera, and began to speak.

On the upper corner of the monitor he saw the fortified entrance at the front of the place being pushed inward and the truck they'd left to block the way skidding aside like a toy. The gigantic blade of a bulldozer pulled back through the opening and then a squad of men rushed in.

Noah pounded again on the door, harder and harder until he felt the bones in his hands nearly break against the unyielding metal. When there was no more will in him he pressed his ear to the thick glass. He could just barely hear what she was saying over the intercom speakers inside.

"I came here to tell you the whole truth," Molly said, "and then I got here and realized that's been tried before. These people who want to run the world, all their secret knowledge is here, but you don't really need those secrets to see what they're about. All you have to do is look around you, and really listen. They've already told you exactly what they've got in mind for you.

"It's not their own secrets they're so interested in keeping anymore. It's your secrets they want. They're building this vast, all-seeing eye, I'm sitting here in the midst of it, and I know you've heard about pieces of what they're doing, but do you realize why they're doing it? They're trying to see into your heart, people, into every corner of your mind, and believe me, it isn't so they can answer your prayers. It's a power they want because it belongs to God. Most of us have only sat by and watched as they stole everything that's ours. Now they're trying to take what's His, as well.

"It won't be me that continues this fight to restore what's been lost; it's got to be you. All of you, anyone who hears this, it's up to you now. I'm not asking you to all be the same, to all think the same; it's your precious differences that once made this country great, and can still make it great again. All I'm asking you to do is remember what it means to be an American.

"I've talked enough; I'm not going to say any more. No more talk about the past. I'm going to let your enemies show you who they are, and the evil that you good people are up against in this battle that never ends. Let them show you what's always at the end of this one-way, progressive road they're building toward your future. And then it's up to you to choose whose side you're on."

There was a clatter in the background and Molly raised her empty hands in surrender. There were tears in her pretty eyes, not because she was afraid, he imagined, but rather because there was so much she'd left undone.

A man in full body armor walked up beside her, put the muzzle of his pistol against her temple, turned briefly to share this moment of triumph with his gathered colleagues, and then shot Molly Ross in the head.

CHAPTER 65

His mind was struck numb with shock and sorrow, and Noah was still moving only for the sake of the others.

Had he been alone he would have waited to be found and then gladly died fighting them with his raw and bleeding hands, just so he could feel in some small way that he was beside her again. But he wasn't alone, and so they ran.

The tunnel shrank to barely shoulder-width as the path continued to ascend. They were exhausted, arms and legs worn out from the long climb, dragging their wounded and barely able to keep their footing on the slick stone. The climb only got harder but still they pressed on.

Noah was in the lead when he smelled fresh air and soon after he saw the metal grate at the end of the line. He braced himself against the drag of the slope and kicked hard into this final barrier, and again, and again until it began to weaken at the rusty frame and finally gave way.

He pulled himself from the tunnel and emerged into a small clearing; there wasn't any visible sign of civilization on this side of the mountain. Tyler Merrick was next. The two of them together helped the others out and onto the cold, wet ground and when that was done there was no strength left to stand.

No one arose from where they lay. Whether it was fatigue alone, or that plus all the sadness and defeat of what they'd just endured, they all stayed right where they were, motionless but finally breathing freedom.

"All of you, hold it right there."

The firm, cold voice had come from a shadow near the trees.

Hollis was lying motionless beside him and Noah reached over for the gun in his belt, but before he could touch it a boot came down hard on his injured hand and pressed it to the turf. The blinding glare of a flashlight hit his face.

"Who are you?" the man asked.

If this was to be the end, Noah thought, then he should answer as Molly might have done.

He was worn out and winded, his chest still ached from the strain of the run and from the loss of her, but he brought himself up to an elbow and looked the man above him in the eyes. Noah formed his words carefully, giving a breath to each of them so at least one by one they'd be as strong as she would have wanted them to be.

"We . . . are . . . Americans."

He fully expected to be shot in the next moment and he would have taken that bullet with no regrets.

But it didn't happen.

Instead the man picked up the pistol Noah had dropped and then took a step back. He then made a motion toward the trees and another of them came near.

"There were only four places you could have come out, Mr. Gardner"—the man was helping Noah to his feet as he spoke—"and we covered them all. If we'd gotten here sooner maybe we could've—"

"I don't understand. Who are you?"

"Virginia Ward sent us," the man said. "We're here to take you home."

CHAPTER 66

That word *home* meant something different to all six of the survivors, but for each one it was also just another treasured thing from a past to which they could never return. The nearest they could come was a place they'd only heard about from Molly Ross, but never seen. That was their destination.

Over the first fourteen hundred miles they traveled in short, guarded segments from one safe house to the next. In these caring hands, after several days of good food and rest and medical care it wasn't too long before all were on the road to a full recovery.

Virginia Ward's men had left them near Cheyenne, then. From that point on, Thom Hollis knew the way.

They rode northwest as far as the main roads would carry them, divided up and hidden among the sleeper compartments of a convoy of long-haul truckers sympathetic to the cause. The final leg of the journey was taken on horseback and later on foot from the last place of friendly sanctuary just south of the Bighorn Mountains.

Though the weather was mild, the terrain was as harsh as it was unspoiled, and without a savvy woodsman for a guide Noah and the others would have never made it through the rugged wilderness. Even experienced hikers, hunters, and adventurers stayed away from this part of the high country. Many who'd wandered into the region in the past had been lost, never to be seen again.

Of course, that's why the settlement was founded where it was; why Molly and her mother had chosen this patch of remote, forbidding land as their place of last refuge for the Founders' Keepers. Though the route to get there was hazardous, in a place like this her people might be safe from the worst of the world outside.

Noah hadn't known what to expect upon his arrival, and at first glance there wasn't much to see.

From a hill overlooking the valley ahead he was able to count only a handful of simple dwellings and a broken dirt path that wound between them. At this distance the man-made additions to the woods were nearly invisible among the tall aspen and evergreen trees. Hollis came up to his side and pointed out nine more structures, for a total of thirteen.

At the end of this last long day of travel, now with only a final half mile to go, Noah sat to rest and think for a while, and Hollis sat beside him while the others went on ahead.

"I'm sorry," Noah said, after a time.

"You're sorry for what?"

"I should have kept her from going back into that place. I should've protected her."

Hollis smiled at that. "One thing I learned about Molly a long time ago. Once she set her mind to something, wild horses couldn't drag her off it. You couldn't have stopped her. Hell, I tried and I couldn't stop her, either. Just put yourself at ease about that, at least. She did what she felt she had to do, like always. The Lord moves in mysterious ways."

Noah looked over at him. "That God business, that's new for you, isn't it?"

"Yeah, it is."

"And what brought this on?"

"Had my eyes opened up, I guess, in the course of those last few days. I finally heard His voice."

"You heard a voice."

Hollis nodded.

"And this was when you were running a fever of what, a hundred and five?"

"Nevertheless."

"But we lost this one, Hollis. Molly's dead, and so are a lot of other good people. We accomplished nothing at all in Pennsylvania. Everyone who was chasing us before, as far as we know they're all still after us. I don't really see any answered prayers here. If this is God's will, I don't understand it. That voice you heard might as well have been coming from hell."

"A month ago I might've said the same thing," Hollis said. "Come tomorrow, you might feel different."

It was nearly sundown and, after a few more minutes of quiet reflection, they got to their feet again and continued on. At the border of the clearing the path became gradually wider, graded even, and cleared of a late-season snow.

First they passed a small log cabin with firelight warming its interior in the dusk, a wispy curl of wood smoke from its chimney dispersing in the light breeze. Next came what appeared to be the beginnings of a general store, and a closer look through its picture windows confirmed it was exactly that. The shelves inside were filled with provisions: canned foods, fuel and lamp oils, medicines, dried meats, burlap bags of seed and grain, soaps and other essentials, batteries, and a cache of ammunition and some hunting and trapping needs.

At the midpoint of the main thoroughfare stood a longer, taller building, solidly and artfully constructed, with wide doors and a heavy brass bell hung beneath its awning. It could have been a meeting hall, a school, a storm shelter, a church, or a fortress, depending on the needs of the day.

Some of the small, simple homes appeared to be occupied; others were dark. As he walked along he saw a checkered curtain pull aside behind a front window. The face of a child came close to the glass. She smiled and gave a little wave, and as he returned the greeting Noah was touched by the honest, innocent nature of the exchange. This little girl had greeted a stranger with no concern at all for his intentions; if he was here, he was a friend. Surrounded as she was by her family and her neighbors, within these protected borders there wasn't much for her to fear.

Noah stopped walking then, and Hollis soon came up beside him.

He was looking at a small, handsome cottage near the end of the path just ahead. Snow had settled in highlights on the shingles, the railings, and the windowsills, like the frosting that puts the final touches on a gingerbread house. There were in-ground doors to a root cellar by the stairs to the porch, a lean-to in back for tools to tend the grounds, and facing east, a sunroom with a wooden bench swing. A low split-rail fence enclosed a small plot to the side where a flower garden might be planted in the spring.

As Noah looked closer he saw that there was a large dog lying by the steps to the front door. The animal sat up abruptly as it noticed the two men, and then after a moment it reclined again. It seemed as though it had been there for a long while, patiently waiting for someone to return.

"Here we are," Hollis said. "This is your place now. That's what she would have wanted."

Noah had seen this fine little home and its grounds before, of course, in a pencil sketch pinned up on Molly's bedroom wall in that loft long ago in New York City. An artist's rendering will sometimes endow a beloved thing with such an abundance of romance that its subject, once seen in person, can't help but disappoint. But this place was every bit as beautiful as the dream of it she'd once drawn, sight unseen.

He awoke alone in her bed to the sounds of conversation and the smells of fresh coffee and frying bacon in the next room.

When he paused at the doorway he had to blink a time or two to be certain of what he saw. Hollis was by the fireplace tending the meal, and at the table nearby sat Virginia Ward.

"Hi," Noah said.

"Hi." She slid a stack of envelopes toward him. "I brought you some mail."

"How the hell did you find us here?"

"It wasn't nearly as hard as it should have been," Virginia said. "That's one of the things we need to talk about right away."

Over breakfast the three of them discussed many things. Chief among these was the unexpected aftermath of their mission to Pennsylvania. Noah had said that they'd lost this one, that nothing had been accomplished there, and at first that had seemed to be true.

Though the evil powers-that-be had been poised to make the most of any threat that might have materialized, when it was all over the nationwide terror alert had been quietly rescinded and no hint of the incident at Garrison Archives had yet appeared in the traditional press.

Nothing had happened—that was their story and they were sticking with it. All evidence to the contrary was being mocked and shouted down as usual. The blackout seemed complete. And it would have stayed that way, except for one small thing.

Despite every attempt to stop it—including a government-ordered shutdown of the entire domestic Internet for several hours that fateful night—Molly's final video had found its way out of Garrison via the modem that Lana had set up, trickling out over a single analog phone line. That one copy reached the public download section of an old-school dial-up bulletin-board system in Michigan, and from there it began to multiply and spread.

For every copy that was scrubbed away ten more soon reappeared. Home-brewed DVDs of it began to turn up on store shelves, inserted into the cases of popular movies. News of it passed from inbox to inbox, whole websites sprang up devoted to it, and finally, the top alternative news site on the Internet linked to it, and then it was everywhere. Now, weeks later, the impact was not only hitting, it was growing stronger every day.

Meanwhile, the so-called mainstream press was following their usual script. Hired experts were marched before the cameras to debunk the grainy video as a fake. Molly and her cause were once again being vilified, laughed at, and denounced. For a short time the video itself was actually blamed for inciting the recent wave of violence—even by the President himself—but that blatant lie was soon withdrawn when it became clear that the people weren't going to buy it. The old script didn't seem to be working as well this time around.

Calls had begun to flood the switchboards of elected representatives and the demands to know the truth were rapidly becoming too numerous for the politicians to ignore. After witnessing the brutal murder of Molly Ross at the hands of a government-sponsored killer, a growing audience of people from across the political spectrum were digging deeper, learning the facts behind her simple message of liberty, and hearing in it all an urgent call to action.

There was suddenly great power in this nonviolent uprising that had been begun by the Founders' Keepers. And with Molly now gone, it was beginning to seem that this power was falling into the hands of Noah Gardner.

"I don't think so," Noah said. "I'm just not the right man for the job."

"Read your mail," Virginia replied, passing the stack across.

The first letter was from his attorney, Charlie Nelan. He'd met with Ellen Davenport and quickly freed her from any fallout of her involvement over the recent weeks. She'd like to come for a visit—in fact, Charlie added, they both would, as soon as things settled down a bit.

After sharing his condolences he also noted that Noah's father's estate might take a while to settle but there was a minor sum of money that could be made available immediately if it was needed. This interim fund amounted to a little less than $90 million.

All the other letters were from politicians and the power brokers behind them.

Some were household names from both major parties, two were outspoken libertarians of long-standing influence, others were up-and-coming voices in the very beginning of their careers. They weren't exactly asking for endorsements, or offering them; it was still too soon to judge what the benefit of that would be. But the elections were coming, and it couldn't hurt to talk. They just wanted to let him know that they were on his side—tentatively, and privately, of course—and to open a line of direct communication for the future.

As he was finishing his reading Hollis retrieved the coffeepot and brought it to the table. "We're going to need to do some new construction," he said. "We've got a lot of new people, and I hear there's more on the way."

"What about this dog?" Noah asked. "I'm not really a pet person."

Having eaten his breakfast earlier, the animal had found a comfortable perch near the back window. He was a handsome beast, looking more like a well-groomed wolf than any domesticated species. To say he was aloof would be a serious understatement, though. Unlike most dogs in Noah's experience, he didn't seem to crave much contact with anyone.

"His name's Cody, but don't expect him to answer to it. He was Molly's through and through. He'll likely come to tolerate you after a spell, though," Hollis said, refilling their cups as he spoke. "In my case, it took six months or so. Just keep your hands away from his mouth and don't ever look him in the eye, and you should be fine."

"I know a family that I'd like to see settle here, if it's what they want," Virginia said. "A mother and three kids. They've just lost their dad."

"Right now I don't know how we're going to buy the materials for all these homes," Hollis said, "but we're not going to turn anyone away. God'll provide, I'm sure."

"We can afford it," Noah said. "Go and buy whatever you need."

"These folks give a lot of charity, but they're very reluctant to take it."

"It's not charity, then. Tell them they can pay me back down the road."

The front door had been left wide open to let in the early morning air. The dog had begun to growl and they turned to see that a large man had quietly walked up onto the porch. He stopped at the doormat, removed his hat, and nodded a greeting.

"What can I do for you?" Noah asked.

"Are you Mr. Gardner, then?"

"Yes."

"George Pierce sent me," the man said.

In a flash both Hollis and Virginia had stood and drawn their pistols, sending their chairs clattering to the floor behind them.

"Please," the man said, showing himself unarmed. "I've just come here with a message, nothin' more."

"I'm going to count to ten," Hollis said, "and mister, it's gonna go quicker than you think."

"Mr. Pierce, he says he calls a truce," the man said, rushing his words. "He says there won't be any trouble, long as you don't make none for him. He says if you want, he can even send up some protection. Hell, if I could track you down, somebody else sure can, too."

Hollis thumbed back the hammer on his pistol, but Noah raised his hand.

"Hold on."

"Hold on?" Hollis said.

"That's what I said. Let's let him finish."

"Thank you, sir. Now, Mr. Pierce says he's going to do you a service, and he don't expect nothin' in return. You've got one big problem left out there lurking, and him and me, we're going to make it go away. When you see what we've done for you, you'll know, it's a show of good faith. After that he'd like to meet you in person, sometime in the future, wherever and whenever you say. That's all in the world that he asks."

The room stayed silent for a while. Through his excessively humble manner, this man seemed to be making an effort to appear less threatening than his physical presence might otherwise suggest. Several rough, black letters were tattooed across the backs of his fingers. Taken together, they spelled out "Y O U R   N E X T."

Noah took a deep breath, and then said, "Okay."

Pierce's man nodded and smiled, backed up a few steps with his eyes on the guns, gave Virginia Ward a good long look, up and down, and then turned and walked away toward the tree line.

The three of them went to the door to watch this stranger until he'd disappeared into the woods. During this time the dog came up next to them and sat there, close to Noah's side.

"What did you just do?" Hollis asked.

Virginia answered for him. "He did what he had to."

"There might be a hundred more of his men out there right now," Noah said. "As of today the only defense we've got is you two, and anybody else here that can handle a gun."

"That's just about everybody," Hollis said. He'd stepped to the side window to scan the rest of their surroundings. "These aren't city people here, and they're ready to fight for what's theirs—"

"Well, I'm not quite ready for another war today," Noah said. "Tomorrow, maybe, but not today. You heard him, it's a truce, not an alliance. It's never going to be that, but I'm not going to get us all killed before we even get started. Now come on, let's sit down. I need some help to think this through."

They all took their seats, with Hollis and Virginia across from him at the table.

Of course, he knew what Molly would have done. She would have stood her ground no matter the cost rather than make any sort of a deal with the devil. But Molly was gone, and if seeing things only in purest black-and-white had killed her, then purity be damned. And as he thought about it, he'd realized what he owed her. For a lot of his life he'd had no direction, but now he found he wanted more than anything to see her work and her vision for the country survive. If getting there meant getting his hands a little dirty for the greater good, maybe he'd just have to accept that.

Virginia Ward reached across the table and patted his arm.

"Welcome to politics," she said.

Noah called a meeting of all the residents, including the brand-new ones and the surviving Founders' Keepers, to be held that evening at the central hall. He'd asked Lana and Tyler to find a way to stream a live video of the proceedings; there was apparently quite a growing audience out there, in this nation and in others around the world, waiting to see and hear what would be next.

That night, when the fireplaces were lit to warm the place and they'd all been gathered together, he stood up and assured them that he didn't plan to speak for very long. There was much work and planning to be done, but that evening wasn't the time.

On the upcoming Sunday there would be a memorial service, he told them, for Molly and the other loved ones who'd been lost. Soon a monument would be erected on these grounds for a more permanent remembrance of their sacrifice, a place where all could visit and honor those who'd fought and died to keep them free.

As for the future, his message was simple: the battle would go on, but there was going to be a change.

"There'll be no more time wasted," Noah said, "in trying to convince people who refuse to get the message. That's over now; I'm pulling up the gangplanks. We've lost too much already trying to wake people up who won't even be bothered to think for themselves. From this point on it's not going to be about what we say, but what we do.

"So, to all of you out there who can see me or hear my voice, this is what we're going to do. We're going to found this country again, starting right here. This place is where the future begins, and if you're really up to the challenge, you're welcome to come here and roll up your sleeves and be a part of it. We're small now, like a pebble dropped into calm water, but what we build and what we become will spread out from here, and grow.

"And to our enemies, I've only got this to say. You can do your worst, and I'm sure that you will, but mark my words: Liberty is not going to end here—not in my generation.

"This piece of ground is where we stand. We're going to give everyone here and everyone out there something to work for, and fight for, and hope for. We're going to give these children a free land to inherit and pass on. And I know that in these times, with all the damage that's been done, that may sound like a grand ambition. But when it comes to aiming high, believe me, I learned from the best.

"Moving forward, we'll each do what we can. For my part, I'm not much of a hand with tools or farming or any other practical skill, but I'm not completely useless. To protect you and represent you, I might someday have to go and run for office, maybe to serve in the capitol down in Cheyenne. Someday after that I might even have to hold my nose and travel to Washington, D.C., if any shred of a constitutional government is still standing there by then.

"But all that's in the future. For now, we have some new resources that will help sustain us through these early days, and we also have new friends who'll do the same.

"I want to welcome all of you. It's not going to be easy, but I doubt any one of you would really expect it to be. You know, as I do, that our rewards will only come from the trials of the struggle ahead."

Noah looked around at all the faces before him and it occurred to him then that he should stop now, and take his own good advice. There'd been more than enough said already; it was time to begin to do. With a few closing words the meeting was over and he bid them all good night.

Despite what Hollis had said about him, that dog seemed to have taken an immediate shine to his new roommate. On Noah's walk home the animal emerged silently from some hunting expedition in the nearby woods and sauntered up beside him, and then stayed with him all along the way.

When he was almost to the cabin, Noah paused at a great granite stone that had been hauled up and placed to the side of the main trail. The dog sat beside him, and waited.

This was the stone that would serve as the basis of the monument he'd mentioned to the crowd. It was still quite rough from the quarry and would take a great deal of work and polish before it was done. But when it was completed, it would no doubt still be standing with its message for a thousand years to come.

A stencil had been perfectly hand-lettered and taped in place to serve as a guide for the stonecutter's chisel. Noah read over the closing words there, and when he was finished he read them once again, aloud.

What we obtain too cheap, we esteem too lightly:
'tis dearness only that gives everything its value.
Heaven knows how to put a proper price upon its

goods; and it would be strange indeed
if so celestial an article as freedom
should not be highly rated.

There weren't going to be any names carved on this memorial stone. There would be far too many, and too many more were still to come. This fight had been going on since the dawn of man and it certainly showed no signs of ending anytime soon.

He took it slow along the path as he walked the rest of the way, and when he reached the cabin he found his friend there, already tending to some minor maintenance around the hearth.

"Nice speech," Hollis said.

"Thanks. Hey, I need your help with something. Probably you and Lana and Tyler."

"Just name it."

"Back in Colorado, Ira Gershon gave me a little radio to listen to, something Molly's people—" He stopped himself. "Something *our* people used to stay in touch in that prison. It was just some wires and a few pieces cobbled together; it didn't even need a battery. I wish I could show it to you but I had to leave it behind."

"Sounds like an old foxhole radio. Hell, I just need a coil, a razor blade, a pencil lead, and a safety pin, and I can toss together one of those before lunch tomorrow. If I can dig up a crystal and a cat's whisker it'll be even better, just like uptown."

"No, I don't need a receiver," Noah said. "I'm going to need a transmitter."

Hollis thought about that for a moment, and then he smiled and stood to leave. "Okay, then. I'll see you in the morning."

When he'd gone Noah found that though he was tired he wasn't quite ready for sleep. He went to the front window, where the dog, Cody, was again sitting and watching the landscape, as though a loved one might still be out there, trying to find her way home.

Noah had little idea of what the coming day would bring. He wasn't certain of very much, in fact, but he knew one thing for sure. Now he had what he'd lacked for so many wasted years. Now he had a mission.

Aaron Doyle and his minions, Warren Landers, if he was still out there alive and scheming—they would all soon be wishing for the days when they had only Molly Ross to worry about.

EPILOGUE

As morning came to his desert paradise, as the dawn's first light touched the very pinnacle of his crystal palace in Dubai, Aaron Doyle stood at the tall, wide windows and listened to the rain begin to fall.

This time it wasn't any mere man-made shower that he'd summoned for his own brief amusement. As uncanny as it was in this arid climate, these angry clouds had formed completely of their own accord. As he'd watched, they spread and filled and darkened, they flashed and rumbled, moving slowly inland from the roiling sea at the bidding of the hand of another.

The storm worsened, the overcast advanced to hide the eastern sun. He felt something arising within him, something that had been rare indeed through the many triumphs and defeats in his long, storied life.

For just one terrible moment, he was afraid.

The doubt lingered only briefly and then it was gone, and then a comforting fury rushed in to fill the awful vacuum in his heart. On an impulse he pushed open the sliding door and the violent wind and rain lashed in and nearly struck him down. But he kept his feet beneath him, fought back into the face of the tempest, reached out blind, and staggered to the rail.

"Here I stand!" Doyle shouted. "And here I'll stand against you, to the end!"

He raised his spindly arm and shook his fist to the heavens, bellowing his rage over the rising thunder, and as he swore damnation on anyone or anything that would ever dare to challenge him again, he felt more alive than he had in many years.

When they'd searched for their frail master and spotted him through the windows, the servants were so overcome with worry that a brave few finally risked his wrath to venture out onto the narrow balcony and bring him back inside.

They'd walked him to his study, and there he sat before the fire, wrapped in thick blankets and surrounded by fussing caretakers. There was no need for all this concern; he was strong again, so strong it was far beyond their understanding. He sat up when he could endure no more coddling and dismissed them with a motion of his hand.

He had wasted several precious days in the doldrums, but that was over now. Embraced in the solace of all his relics and his priceless material things, he collected his thoughts and considered his options in the light of the recent events.

These latest developments had been quite unexpected, but how invigorating it was to have the gauntlet thrown down before him once again. It was a new beginning; the game was now reset to its starting positions. Though he harbored no real doubt of his ultimate victory, he felt eager as a child for this final, deciding contest to commence.

Aaron Doyle looked across the ancient chessboard, and gave a sly old smile to the empty chair on the other side.

"Very well, then, Mr. Gardner," he said. "Your move."

AFTERWORD

As readers of *The Overton Window* already know, I love "faction"—fictional novels that are rooted in fact. *The Eye of Moloch* fits that genre well, and I hope you'll spend some time searching online for any of the words or events included in the story that you suspect might have some truth to them.

I don't want to ruin *all* of the surprises, but here are a few things to get your hunt started.

In Chapter 1 we see the impressive strength of the country's domestic weapons arsenal. The following information gives a look into some of the known capabilities of the Department of Homeland Security.

"Modernizing the Department of Homeland Security's Aerial Fleets," *Lexington Institute,* Daniel Goure, February 29, 2012, http://bit.ly/10381jR.

"Why Is the Department of Homeland Security Buying So Many Bullets?" *Fox News,* February 14, 2013, http://fxn.ws/YhfT2r.

"Homeland Security Is Serving Warrants Using Mine-Resistant Vehicles," *Business Insider,* March 4, 2012, http://read.bi/13sAGH3.

In Chapter 3 there is a reference to George Lincoln Rockwell. He was the founder of the American Nazi

Party and continues to be an influential figure for the Neo-Nazis and White Nationalists of today. He believed all blacks in America should be deported to Africa and every Jew dispossessed and sterilized. He was assassinated in 1967.

"1967: American Hitler Shot Dead," *BBC*, August 25, 2005, http://bbc.in/9OSe0w. http://news.bbc.co.uk/onthisday/hi/dates/stories/august/25/newsid_3031000/3031928.stm.

William H. Schmaltz, *Hate: George Lincoln Rockwell and the American Nazi Party*, (Brasseys, Inc., 2001), http://bit.ly/ZvXvFY.

More from Chapter 3:

America has its own history with the Nazi Party. In February of 1939, twenty thousand supporters attended a German-American Bund rally at Madison Square Garden. Among other things, the speakers condemned President "Franklin D. Rosenfeld" and his "Jew Deal."

"German-American Bund Rally Address by Its Leader Fritz Kuhn," *National Archives,* February 20, 1939, http://1.usa.gov/ZvXTUU.

Though George Pierce's character was created for the story, it is true that at least one American who had past associations with the Ku Klux Klan was voted into office. Former KKK Grand Wizard David Duke was elected into the Louisiana House of Representatives in 1989.

"Winner in Louisiana Vote Takes on G.O.P. Chairman," Frances Frank Marcus, *New York Times,* February 20, 1989, http://nyti.ms/17K7BGF.

In depicting radical white-supremacists as the muscle behind enemy actions, we were faced with the need to use some particularly ugly and objectionable words in dialogue. For the worst of it, then, it seemed best to use actual quotes from some prominent public figures who'd largely been given a pass for their language by the press. Some of the racist and bigoted phrases used by the George Pierce character are among these. For example, in 2007 Joe Biden described then-Senator Obama as "articulate, and bright, and clean." In a 2008 campaign interview, Obama outlined some negative characteristics of the "typical white person" and Senator Harry Reid reportedly said that Obama was a "light-skinned" African American "with no Negro dialect, unless he wanted to have one."

"Biden's Description of Obama Draws Scrutiny," *CNN*, February 9, 2007, http://bit.ly/17tRjyL.

"Barack Obama Tries to Explain That 'Good People' Still Hold Racial Stereotypes," Michael McAuliff & Michael Saul, *New York Daily News*, March 21, 2008, http://nydn.us/1778iZo.

"Reid Once Called Obama Light-skinned with 'No Negro Dialect,' Media Mostly Mum," Noel Sheppard, *NewsBusters*, January 9, 2010, http://bit.ly/6D08kt.

Some of the racist comments that George Pierce uttered to Molly Ross are references to actual quotes from President Harry Truman and the late Senator Robert Byrd. For example, in a 1911 letter to his wife, Truman wrote, "I think one man is just as good as another as long as he's honest and decent and not a nigger or a Chinaman."

"The Conversion of Harry Truman," William E. Leuchtenburg, *American Heritage*, November 1991, http://bit.ly/11aoAQL.

In 2001, former KKK recruiter turned Democratic senator, Robert Byrd, said, "My old mom told me, 'Robert, you can't go to heaven if you hate anybody.' We practice that. There are white niggers. I've seen a lot of white niggers in my time. I'm going to use that word. We just need to work together to make our country a better country, and I'd just as soon quit talking about it so much."

"Top Senate Democrat Apologizes for Slur," *CNN*, March 4, 2001, http://bit.ly/1038JxI.

When George Pierce says, "This is your army. We're ready to march. Now let's do what we have to do and take these sons of bitches out," he's repeating a quote from Teamsters president James Hoffa. Hoffa was appealing to President Obama in 2011, urging an open offensive against the Tea Party.

"'Let's Take These Son of a Bitches Out': Teamsters President Hoffa Calls for War on Tea Party at Obama Labor Day Event," *The Blaze*, September 5, 2011, http://bit.ly/1038LWj.

In Chapter 6 there is a reference to Silas Deane (1737–1789). Deane was the first diplomat to be sent abroad on behalf of the American colonies. He was sent to France as a secret agent to obtain financial and military assistance and to investigate the possibility of an alliance. But his reputation suffered when he was accused of making personal financial gains while working as a representative of the people. Letters also surfaced that put into question his loyalty toward the American colonies. Deane was recalled by Congress and eventually went bankrupt. He died under suspicious circumstances while on a boat traveling from France to America.

"Silas Deane" *Encyclopedia Britannica*, http://bit.ly/IRkyl6.

In Chapter 7 the characters use technology designed to gather tactical data and images through walls. This is real: researchers at MIT have developed a radar system that provides real-time video of what is going on behind solid walls. The question remains, however, what type of surveillance technology is already in use that has yet to be unveiled to the public?

"Seeing Through Walls," Emily Finn, *MIT News*, October 18, 2011, http://bit.ly/nVw40j.

In Chapter 8, Warren Landers says, "We're going to spit upon our hands, hoist the black flag, and begin slitting throats." This is lifted from controversial American journalist and critic H. L. Mencken (1880–1956). Though he routinely challenged representative democracy, despised organized business, and constantly criticized the American middle class, Mencken continues to be influential for the Libertarian movement. One quote of his that many people still find relevant today is: "The men the American people admire most extravagantly are the most daring liars; the men they detest the most violently are those who try to tell them the truth."

"The Libertarian Heritage," *Libertarianism,* http://bit.ly/IoFtvO.

The Oxford Dictionary of American Quotations, Margaret Miner and Hugh Rawson, (Oxford University Press: 2006), p. 27, http://bit.ly/11kuz20.

In Chapter 12 we read about the National Defense Authorization Act (NDAA). This is real, as is the timing of its passage. On December 31, 2011, while many Americans were on vacation and not paying attention to the news, President Obama signed the NDAA for fiscal year 2012. This is the first time in American history that a U.S. law allowed the military, per order from the president, to detain U.S. citizens indefinitely, without a trial. Despite signing the bill into law, Obama said in a statement, "I want to clarify that my administration will not authorize the indefinite military detention without trial of American citizens. Indeed, I believe that doing so would break with our most important traditions and values as a Nation."

"Statement by the President on H.R. 1540," *The White House,* December 31, 2011, http://1.usa.gov/uUNb0v.

In Chapter 14 Warren Landers threatens to turn against his ally George Pierce, a tactic that was used effectively by Adolf Hitler on June 30, 1934, when he ordered that hundreds from his own party be killed in an effort to eliminate potential threats from his rank and file. It has been dubbed the "Night of the Long Knives."

"Night of the Long Knives," *History.com,* http://bit .ly/9O5lkz.

More from Chapter 14:

Diocletian was a Roman Emperor who ruled as a dictator. His empire grew to have "more tax collectors than tax payers." He instituted failed price-fixing policies to combat inflation, and the sons of tradesmen were forced to replace their fathers in an effort to resolve labor dislocation. Diocletian justified these measures by uniting the country against an enemy; his biggest target became the Christians. Though it was never proven, he blamed Christians for fires that broke out at his palace and used it as an excuse to start the Great Persecution, a decadelong purge that killed about two thousand people.

"Diocletian: The Worst Persecutor of Them All," *Christian History Project,* http://bit.ly/ZBb4AO.

In another scene, Warren Landers tells George Pierce that more than forty people were killed in just one weekend in Chicago. This is true: forty-one people, mostly African-American, were shot and killed in Chicago in the span of just three days (March 16 to 19, 2012).

"'Race Wars' Part 1: The Shocking Data on Black-on-Black Crime," Tiffany Gabbay, *The Blaze,* April 9, 2012, http://bit.ly/XTGxhx.

Warren Landers also reminds George Pierce that abortion has been used as a genocidal weapon against the people he hates. Legalized abortion has killed more than 16 million African Americans.

"Black Abortions: Necessary Health Care Policy or Genocide?" Palash R. Ghosh, *International Business Times,* July 17, 2012, http://bit.ly/RUI7kx.

In Chapter 15 George Pierce goes on a rant about the JFK assassination. According to some conspiracy theories, Lucien Sarti was really the person who shot President Kennedy from the grassy knoll. The theory was presented by a British television program *The Men Who Killed Kennedy* in October 1988 and claimed that Sarti was a French gangster who was hired by U.S. organized crime to kill the president.

"French Accused of Killing JFK" *Observer-Reporter*, October 27, 1988, http://bit.ly/11mTjae.

Nearly sixteen years after the tragedy, the House Select Committee on Assassinations concluded that while Oswald was firing from the Book Depository, another shot was fired from the grassy knoll. Needless to say, some of the methods and conclusions of the HSCA continue to be controversial.

"JFK Assassination Records" *National Archives*, http://1.usa.gov/EIWIP.

In Chapter 16 the plethora of violations that have been levied against the Merricks is laid out. This intimidation tactic is becoming easier and easier for our government to use as it keeps adding new rules and regulations—many of which are either impossible to understand or comply with. From 2009 to 2011, 11,327 pages have been added to the Code of Federal Regulations.

"Under Obama, 11,327 Pages of Federal Regulations Added," Penny Starr, *CNS News*. 10 September 2012, http://bit.ly/TNVB00.

In Chapter 18 Aaron Doyle summons the rain that he later watches fall. This is not an exaggerated act of science that we included simply to show how powerful he is, it is a currently functioning technology. In 2010, Swiss scientists from Meteo Systems International were able to create fifty-two rainstorms in Abu Dhabi.

"Scientists Create 52 Artificial Rain Storms in Abu Dhabi Desert," Josh Sanburn, *Time,* January 3, 2011, http://ti.me/eztSo3.

"Secret Scientists Claim to Create Rain in Arab Desert," Matthew Hall, *AOL News,* January 10, 2011, http://aol.it/fclvhz.

In Chapter 22 Virginia Ward sees a sign along the road from the Bureau of Land Management advising people to refrain from traveling through the area due to a high rate of crime, especially drug and human smuggling. This sign is an exact copy of one found on Interstate 8, south of Casa Grande, Arizona.

"29 Gunmen Dead in Shootout 12 Miles from the Arizona Border," *Borderland Beat,* July 3, 2010, http://bit.ly/ZvZrOV.

More from Chapter 22:

Virginia talks about a confluence of events that lead to a number of guns, drugs, and money falling into the hands of a Mexican drug cartel. The ATF did, in fact, implement a gun-walking operation, called "Fast and Furious," that purposely put about two thousand guns into the hands of criminals. Many of these weapons are now either unaccounted for or have been used in serious crimes, including one that resulted in the murder of a U.S. border patrol agent.

In 2011, the media discovered that agents from the Drug Enforcement Agency had smuggled and laundered drug money. The agents said their intent was to bring money into Mexico to learn how criminals, primarily drug cartels, move their money around and where they keep their assets.

In 2009, Jesus Vicente Zambada Niebla, a high-ranking member of the Sinaloa cartel, was arrested in Mexico City for drug trafficking–related charges. After his arrest, he claimed that he should be allowed to go free due to an agreement between the U.S. and the Sinaloa cartel allowing them to traffic drugs into America in exchange for information on competing cartels. At the time of publication, Niebla is awaiting trial.

"Evidence Suggests Cover-Up in ATF Scandal, as More Guns Appear at Crime Scenes," William La Jeunesse, *Fox News,* September 2, 2011, http://fxn.ws/odCrp3.

"U.S. Agents Launder Mexican Profits of Drug Cartels," Ginger Thompson, *The New York Times,* December 3, 2011, http://nyti.ms/uFX7l4.

"High-Ranking Mexican Drug Cartel Member Makes Explosive Allegation: 'Fast and Furious' Is Not What You Think It Is," Jason Howerton, *TheBlaze.com,* August 9, 2012, http://bit.ly/XvDL2x.

Los Zetas is, of course, a real Mexican drug cartel. The group was started by former Mexican special forces troops (trained by the U.S.) and is now considered the largest and most dangerous drug cartel in Mexico. The United States has called the Zetas "the most technologically advanced, sophisticated, and dangerous cartel operating in Mexico."

"Los Zetas Called Mexico's Most Dangerous Drug Cartel," Michael Ware, *CNN,* August 6, 2009, http://bit.ly/10M7lN.

"The Cartels Behind Mexico's Drug War," Kazi Stastna, *CBC News,* August 28, 2011, http://bit.ly/qT-BADa.

One of the key leaders of the Zetas is really known as "the Executioner." His name was Heriberto Lazcano, and he joined the Zetas in 1998 after he deserted from the Mexican Army. In 2003, Lazcano took control of the Zetas and became widely known for his extraordinarily brutal tactics. (Some reports say that he fed his rivals to tigers and lions that he kept at his ranch.) Lazcano was killed in 2012 after a shootout with Mexican armed forces.

"Mexico Says 'The Executioner' Is Dead—But Where's the Body?" Tim Padgett and Ioan Grillo, *Time*, October 10, 2012, http://bit.ly/YzWWI6.

"Heriberto Lazcano Dead: Mexico Zetas Boss Killed by Accident, Navy Says," Olga R. Rodriguez, *Huffington Post*, October 10, 2012, http://huff.to/QVSlNU.

In Chapter 24 Warren Landers tells Virginia that Thom Hollis and the Founders' Keepers have been added to the president's kill list. Although it should sound outrageous that our president could be granted the power to unilaterally authorize the killing of American citizens on U.S. soil, this is now a reality.

The National Defense Authorization Act has a section that not only legalizes martial law in the United States, but also allows the military to detain people indefinitely without a trial. In addition, both the president and Attorney General Eric Holder have refused to rule out the possibility of a drone strike against an American citizen on U.S. soil if they believe that citizen is "engaged in combat."

"NDAA: What Obama Hoped You Wouldn't Notice About This Bill," Zack Fulkerson, *Policymic*, January 2013, http://bit.ly/W1HILe.

"Holder Does Not Rule Out Drone Strike Scenario in U.S," Terry Frieden, *CNN*, March 6, 2013, http://bit.ly/15w8y3t.

"Video: Ted Cruz Gets Eric Holder to Admit That Killing Americans with Drones on U.S. Soil Is Unconstitutional," Debra Heine, Breitbart.com, March 6, 2013, http://bit.ly/11vRiKo.

In Chapter 27 Noah explains to Ellen that the facility in which he is being kept is called a "fusion center."

Fusion centers, which are located around the country, are complexes used to collect, analyze, and share data concerning threats to the U.S. between all levels of government. That may sound great, but transparency is required. The public must understand what this data is, how it's obtained, and what the privacy implications are.

"State and Major Urban Area Fusion Centers," http://1.usa.gov/NqY4bk.

"Fusion Centers: Force Multiplier for Spying in Local Communities," http://bit.ly/ZCvsl5.

In Chapter 29 Noah goes to his fridge and sees a display that alerts him that he is almost out of milk and offers him the ability to immediately place another order. Smart appliances are becoming more and more prevalent, and while they can often be very convenient, they can also have some serious downsides.

In 2007, the California Energy Commission proposed new rules to allow utilities to override people's thermostats in their homes during "emergencies" in order to prevent widespread outages. Fortunately, these proposals were met with outrage and never came to fruition, but many still believe that California, and other states, will soon try again. If that happens, it's not hard to see that smart thermostats could be just the beginning of the government's intrusion into our homes. (Imagine what Mayor Bloomberg could do if he could see in real time what you're taking out of your refrigerator to eat!)

"California Seeks Thermostat Control," Felicity Barringer, *New York Times*. January 11, 2008, http://nyti.ms/104s0P6.

"The Thermostat Nanny," John Seiler, *Cal Watchdog*, January 18, 2010, http://bit.ly/fAG9N1.

More from Chapter 29:

Noah mentions a technique known as "Trotskying."

It is not an exaggeration. Take a look at these photos of Stalin from the Soviet Union:

"Falsification of History," http://bit.ly/13Mhew.

Noah tells Virginia that just six corporations control almost all of our media today. This is true. General Electric, News Corporation, Disney, Viacom, Time Warner, and CBS now control 90 percent of all media in the United States.

"These 6 Corporations Control 90% of the Media in America," Ashley Lutz, *Business Insider,* June 14, 2012, http://read.bi/KXHRyn.

In Chapter 30 the bedtime story that Noah tells Virginia is not fictitious. Lee Atwater really did spread a rumor that Thomas Foley was gay, and Barney Frank threatened to out six homosexual Republican senators on the floor of the House.

"Clinton's Sexual Scorched-Earth Plan," Jonathan Broder and Harry Jaffe, *Salon,* August 5, 1998, http://bit.ly/XVrLvM.

In Chapter 33 Noah walks into an argument between Ira and Lana regarding U.S. immigration policy. While the media seems to want to make people believe that the U.S. excludes far more people than it allows in, the fact is that the United States accepts more legal immigrants than the rest of the world combined.

"300 Million and Counting," Joel Garreau, *Smithsonian* magazine, October 2006, http://bit.ly/92IGo6.

In Chapter 36 the portion of a speech that Noah hears through his radio is from Ronald Reagan's 1964 speech "A Time for Choosing." Some credit this speech as the one that put Reagan on the map and resulted in his election as president sixteen years later. Here's another snippet from it, but it would be worth your time to read the whole thing.

You and I are told increasingly that we have to
choose between a left or right, but I would like
to suggest that there is no such thing as a left or
right. There is only an up or down—up to a man's
age-old dream, the ultimate in individual free-
dom consistent with law and order—or down to
the ant heap of totalitarianism, and regardless of
their sincerity, their humanitarian motives, those
who would trade our freedom for security have
embarked on this downward course.

"A Time for Choosing," Ronald Reagan, October 27, 1964, http://bit.ly/3XTwG9.

In Chapter 37 Virginia finds the same tattoo on many of the male victims that she examines. The markings point to the House of Percy, from which George Pierce is descendant. Thomas Percy was, in fact, of this line and was a co-conspirator in the Gunpowder Plot that attempted to kill King James I and blow up the House of Parliament. Fortunately, the plot was uncovered before any harm was done and the conspirators, including Thomas Percy, were executed.

Today the symbol of Guy Fawkes, the man who was discovered actually guarding the gunpowder, has been turned upside down to become one of resistance against a tyrannical government. His symbol has been adopted by different movements, including "Anonymous" and "Occupy Wall Street."

"Thomas Percy," *History Learning Site,* http://bit .ly/11LLiNp.

"The Gunpowder Plot: A Detailed Account," David Herber, *Britannia History,* http://bit.ly/12t1HHH.

"How Did Guy Fawkes Become a Symbol of Occupy Wall Street?" Edward Lovett, *ABC News,* November 5, 2011, http://abcn.ws/sWBXJC.

In Chapter 38 George Pierce fantasizes about the new United States that will come after the revolution. He also recognizes that there will initially be a tough period when those Americans (about 25 million) who cannot assimilate must be eliminated. In the late sixties and early seventies, an FBI agent infiltrated a radical group known as the Weather Underground. They too were preparing for a new United States and believed their top priority after the revolution would be to reeducate all Americans and eliminate those who would not accept the indoctrination. According to their estimates, that would be about 25 million people. Check out this clip from the 1982 documentary "No Place to Hide" for more.

"FBI Agent Larry Grathwohl–Bill Ayers' Weather Underground Plan to Kill 25 Million Americans," http://bit.ly/11sap51.

In Chapter 40 the quotes recited by Esther come from well-known sources. "We walk by faith, not by sight" is from 2 Corinthians 5:7 and "Hell is empty and all the devils are here" is from Shakespeare's *The Tempest*.

2 Corinthians 5:7, King James Version, http://bg4 .me/117WrX4.

William Shakespeare. *The Tempest*. Act 1 Scene 2. http://shakespeare.mit.edu/tempest/full.html.

In Chapter 44 Noah arrives at the Ordo Seclorum, where his father's funeral is being held. This place was inspired by the Bohemian Grove, a club north of San Francisco in the Redwood Forest, where the world's richest and most powerful men meet for two weeks every summer. The club's real motto is "Weaving Spiders Come Not Here," a slogan alluding to the idea that business discussions are to be left outside the gates. Unfortunately for members, that has not always been the case. The Manhattan Project was reportedly planned here, as were several other world-changing events.

The Grove also really does have a giant forty-foot stone statue of an owl on which one of their main rituals is centered: the Cremation of Care. In this ceremony, the men, dressed in robes, sacrifice the effigy of a child known as Care, who symbolizes the worldly cares of the men.

"Bohemian Grove: Where the Rich and Powerful Go to Misbehave," Elizabeth Frock, *The Washington Post,* June 15, 2011, http://wapo.st/jjvBHF.

"Masters of the Universe Go to Camp: Inside the Bohemian Grove," Phillip Weiss, *Spy Magazine,* November 1989, 59–76, http://bit.ly/L7XZK0.

In Chapter 51 we see Warren Landers in the Talion Corporation showcase facility. While Talion is not based on any single military contractor, the United States government has outsourced many combat and support functions to various powerful private companies, with Blackwater (now renamed Academi) being the most well known.

"The Blackwater Plot Deepens," Jeremy Scahill, *The Guardian,* November 11, 2009, http://bit.ly/11BHdv.

More from Chapter 51:

After collecting all the computers from the remains of the Merrick ranch, Warren Landers is able to get a clear understanding of who Lawrence Cole, the owner of the home improvement stores who aids Molly and Hollis, really is by sifting through his online records. This is not an exaggeration. The National Security Agency (NSA) gathers as much data every six hours as has ever been stored in the entire Library of Congress. And now the NSA is building a top-secret $2 billion facility in Utah to store and analyze the data it is collecting. This facility will reportedly be five times the size of the U.S. Capitol and, according to some published reports, it could hold 5 zettabytes of data—that's as much data as contained in 310 billion iPhones.

"Every Six Hours, the NSA Gathers as Much Data as Is Stored in the Entire Library of Congress," Dan Nosowitz, *Popsci.com*, May 10, 2011, http://bit.ly/lmRSwd.

"The NSA Is Building the Country's Biggest Spy Center (Watch What You Say)," James Bamford, *Wired*, March 15, 2012, http://bit.ly/FOPeok.

"NSA data center front and center in debate over liberty, security and privacy," Catherine Herridge, *FoxNews.com*, April 12, 2013, http://fxn.ws/11vmERo.

In Chapter 55 Noah alerts Ellen to how easily their movements can be monitored by government surveillance. While some liberties were taken for the sake of the story, there is a very real push for these kinds of capabilities in future law enforcement. In March 2013, the FBI's general counsel said it was a "top priority" to modernize surveillance laws so that it can keep up with the expanding technological communication abilities of Americans. The FBI has also proposed a law that would require Internet companies to make their customers' social networks and e-mail providers more "wiretap-friendly."

"FBI's Lawyer Says Modernizing Surveillance Law for Real-Time Online Snooping Is a 'Top Priority' in 2013," Gerry Smith, *The Huffington Post*, March 28, 2013, http://huff.to/YLLMQg.

In Chapter 62 we visit Garrison Archives. While this fortress of archived secrets and priceless treasures does not exist, it is based on some actual facilities, like Iron Mountain in Pennsylvania.

"22 Stories Underground: Iron Mountain's Experimental Room 48," Lucas Mearian, *ComputerWorld.com*, December 9, 2009, http://bit.ly/8yILhS.

In Chapter 64 we see the Total Information Awareness (TIA) program in action. TIA was developed by the Information Awareness Office (IAO) in 2002 in response to 9/11. The *New York Times* reported that the TIA program sought to "revolutionize the ability of the United States to detect, classify, and identify foreign terrorists by developing data-mining and profiling technologies that could analyze commercial transactions and private communications."

In 2003, Congress defunded the IAO after the public voiced privacy concerns, but various projects continued to be funded, including those dedicated to "processing, analysis, and collaboration tools for counterterrorism foreign intelligence."

In March 2012, reports surfaced that TIA was being fully resurrected by the National Security Agency with the construction of a state-of-the-art data center in Utah.

"Overview of the Information Awareness Office," Dr. John Poindexter, *Federation of American Scientists*, August 2, 2002, http://bit.ly/8rVjcZ.

"Total Information Awareness," Jeffrey Rosen, *New York Times*, December 15, 2002, http://nyti.ms/TewDa2.